ELUSIVE LINKS

A STORY *of* CONNECTION, COMPASSION *and* COMPETITION

DAN A ROSENBERG

ELUSIVE LINKS

A Story of Connection, Compassion and Competition

979-8-9865511-0-4 (ebook Kindle)
979-8-9865511-1-1 (Amazon paperback)
979-8-9865511-2-8 (Amazon hardback)
979-8-9865511-3-5 (IngramSpark hardback with dust jacket)
979-8-9865511-4-2 (IngramSpark paperback)

Cover Design by Marko Marković and Dan A Rosenberg.

For Abby

And our granddaughters
Penelope and Olivia

And their grandchildren

TABLE OF CONTENTS

PART II

PART III

PROLOGUE

Manhattan, New York, USA
Thursday, November 17, 2011

There was always much to gossip about following the first afternoon session at Sotheby's. Who was represented? Was there enough bidding? Were the sale prices high enough? What would the rare treasures fetch in the next session?

A faint bell sounded, barely audible among the clinking china intermixed with hundreds of conversations. Those who heard the prompt took a last sip of their beverage and drifted towards the auditorium. Should anyone approach the entrance with a plate or cup in hand, an immaculately groomed door attendant would ask, "May I take that for you?"

A screaming ambulance, southbound on York Avenue to New York Hospital, drowned out the second reminder. The ushers went into action, as unobtrusively as possible, whispering that the session was about to begin. A who's who of art dealers and agents filed into the room.

Bidders, agents, attorneys, and hangers-on settled in their seats. The auctioneer cleared her throat and began stiffly.

"We will commence this session with lot number one-one-two, a book printed in Spain in the second half of the fifteenth century. On the back cover of your sale catalogue, you'll find a photograph. The piece includes commentary on Leonardo da Vinci and Archimedes, as well as mathematical tables devised by Abraham Zacuto. Those tables were subsequently refined by Zacuto for use by the Portuguese explorer, Vasco de Gama, on his voyage to India in 1497. We will start the bidding at five hundred thousand U.S. dollars."

A placard was raised from the back row. The ever-vigilant auctioneer, looking over the rims of her glasses, raised her right arm, gavel in hand, and pointed towards the extended arm. She identified the person and amount, "Thirty-nine bids five hundred. Do we have five hundred and fifty thousand?"

An unknown female face, black, fronted with red framed glasses, hair gathered tightly in a bun, stood rather than raising her paddle. Somewhat stunned by the breach of protocol, the gallery silenced. The lithe figure calmly called out with authority, "Two million."

The crowd started rumbling. The auctioneer raised her voice, trying vainly to continue the bidding action. Finally, she yelled, "Fair warning." Two seconds later, her gavel banged with a loud thud. "Sold, two million dollars, to bidder ninety-three." A thunderous outburst of cheers and applause erupted as the attendees fully grasped what had occurred.

Three minutes later the winning bidder entered the cashiering room. She was received by a finely tailored middle-aged man. "Good afternoon, Ms. Wright."

"Tamara, please."

"I'm Martin Perez." He gestured towards a chair. "Please make yourself comfortable while I print the arrangements for one-one-two. May I get you something to drink?"

The courtesy was declined but the chair was taken. A hidden keyboard triggered a single page from a near-silent printer beneath a mahogany desk. After a cursory review, Perez rotated the document, presenting it on an elegant blotter with a Mont Blanc pen cradled to the side. "Please confirm the shipping address and insurance amount. We have already verified the banking instructions."

She felt as if she had extracted Excalibur, anointing the transaction, touching the pen's nib on the pertinent items. "Everything looks in order. Thank you." She signed at the bottom of the page.

"And we thank you."

"May I sit here for another minute and let the buyer know?"

"By all means. Enjoy the remainder of your day." Perez exited the room.

She retrieved the mobile phone from her purse then composed a text message. "San. It's done. Awesome. See you soon."

PART I

"All the great evils which men cause to each other because of certain intentions, desires, opinions, or religious principle, are likewise due to non-existence, because they originate in ignorance, which is absence of wisdom."

Moses Maimonides
(1138 - 1204)

1

MARBELLA, PROVINCE OF MÁLAGA, SPAIN

NINE YEARS EARLIER

TUESDAY, JULY 23, 2002

Manhattan to Madrid to Málaga to Marbella. *Figures*, thought Sandy Cole as she unpacked two miniature M&M bags, compliments of Iberia Airways. For a second, she considered opening one. No need for a sugar boost with her high energy level, despite flying coach and a six-hour time change.

Twenty-five and well-traveled, this was her first international business trip with her employer, Columbia University. Tomorrow she would attend a conference as a member of the research team studying government interaction with religious belief systems.

No time to waste today. Sandy rummaged in her suitcase for her bikini, wrap, and sandals. As a native of Maine and a diehard downhill skier, applying sunscreen was second nature. She removed her wristwatch and reset it to local time, 11:05 a.m. Sliding it into the top drawer on the nightstand, she noticed a Gideon Bible. She'd seen hundreds but never cracked one.

She changed quickly, applied SPF 45, and exited with the Bible. Before heading outside, she stopped at the concierge desk to confirm her ride at 4:00 p.m.

Following a short walk on the beach, Sandy settled into a chaise by the pool. She ordered a Coke Light from a roaming waiter. The drink was sitting on the small table next to her when she awoke twenty minutes later.

She leaned up, took a sip, and opened the Bible. A bookmark slipped out. In the middle of it, the name of a church was printed next to a crucifix. Underneath it, Sandy noticed some handwriting, "*Christo = amor, Sin*

Christo = infierno."

Sandy sunk back into the lounge chair to ponder the equations, Christ equals love and without Christ equals hell. Raised as a Jew, she couldn't help thinking about the pair in the context of her excursion later in the day.

····◆····

Skirting the center of town, the driver did his best to navigate the heavy traffic on the short trip to Temple Beth El, an Orthodox Jewish congregation, less than two miles east of Marbella town center.

Sandy joined the tour a few minutes late. The grounds and the buildings were immaculate. She was moved by the intimacy of the synagogue with room for a hundred congregants, not including two small opposing balconies for women, all framing a breathtaking pulpit and Torah Ark.

The guide claimed it was the first synagogue built in Andalusia sometime after 1492. He speculated that construction may have commenced as early as 1491. What wasn't discussed was the hell promulgated on the Jews between 1491 and the building's completion.

As Sandy slid into the cab for the ride back to the Hotel Dinamar, she fumbled for her phone, intending to call her mom. That would have to wait as jet lag enveloped her. She closed her eyes.

2

GIBRALTAR, KINGDOM OF CASTILE, SPAIN

FRIDAY, APRIL 6, 1492

Numbers fascinated Ben Solomon. Much to his mother's chagrin, the seventeen-year-old had little interest in the Numbers before Deuteronomy. Until the time of his Bar Mitzvah Ben had shown some interest in the Bible, but always with a bias for the arithmetic. He could recite the verse detailing the cubits of Noah's ark. He was intrigued with Moses' rulers of tens, hundreds, and thousands. Even seven days and seven nights entertained him at a young age.

His near obsession didn't bother the elder Benjamin Solomon. The demand for bookkeepers had burgeoned as Gibraltar prospered. However, in the last few years, as Ben's mind continued to develop, he became preoccupied with the numerals zero through nine and the endless possibilities for their combinations, permutations, and concatenations.

More concerning to Mother was Ben's attitude towards marriage. Under no circumstances would Ben allow his father to provide *mohar*, the gold and silver fee to in-laws, for women Ben had no desire to lay with. The women he did want, he could not have.

Ben pushed his straight black hair off his face, as he looked down to revere his most valued possession, a book on mathematics. It wasn't bound with fine stitching. The pages weren't slit with precision. It wasn't thousands of years old. However, for a printed book it was ancient. The date stamped on the first page was A.D. 1474. According to Father, Ben's book was printed on one of the first printing presses in Spain. Ben prized it as if it were the Torah.

He gazed upward, tilting his head slightly. His daydreaming was interrupted as a willowy figure darted past him, then postured near the front door of the modest row house.

"I think," paused Ben. "It is time to go outside."

"You do too much thinking is what I think," mocked his younger sister, Rebecca.

"Maybe."

Ben got on well with Becca. Although she teased him quite a bit, she believed he was a genius. With more than three years age difference, Ben had grown up as her protector rather than her rival.

Mid-afternoon on Fridays Mother performed her pre-ritual ritual of errands before Father appeared for the Sabbath, which commenced at sunset. Ben and Becca would spend at least two hours together every week during Mother's excursion. Until two years ago, Becca was Mother's dutiful assistant. With the onset of puberty, she didn't want to be the little helper anymore.

When Mother first delegated the Becca watch assignment to Ben, he was content to remain inside with one eye on his numbers and the other on his sister. Becca's constant stream of suggestions broke his every attempt to concentrate.

Eventually, Ben devised a simple game. Becca would draw a triangle with a ninety-degree corner. Next, she used her outstretched hand to measure the lengths of the two sides that formed the right angle. Ben would then estimate the long leg of the triangle using the Pythagorean equation, squaring each of the sides, adding them together and then taking the square root of the sum. It didn't take long for Ben to calculate the third side in his head, but he pretended to concentrate intently, taking minutes to deliver the result. He told Becca he was researching the answer in his book.

Ben knew Becca would tire of this, so he tried to keep the game interesting by tweaking it periodically. He allowed her to select any two sides. He also let her measure the lengths with any standard she wanted. Sometimes she used her baby finger, the edge of a utensil or a small piece of ribbon. This worked for a while.

Becca was perceptive enough to know that Ben was manipulating the situation. She didn't care. She was happy to engage with her brother. However, Becca provided the ultimate refinement to the game. After several months, she insisted they go outside so she could construct larger and larger triangles. Ben realized his sister had outmaneuvered him.

He followed Becca out the door. Most houses had narrow frontages with shared walls on both sides. The Solomon house was on the northern end of the *aljamas*, the Jewish quarter. Contrary to the walled shtetls of Eastern Europe, the *aljamas* did not have, nor need barriers. All Gibraltar residents knew where the line was drawn. On one side were those who ate cheese off the same plate as meat from animals without hooves. On the other side were Sephardim who spoke Ladino, a marriage of Castilian and Hebrew.

"I want to see how smart you are today," teased Becca.

"A little smarter than yesterday, I hope," replied Ben, half in jest.

"Then you will be up to the challenge."

"You have intrigued me sister."

Most Gibraltar streets were narrow and steep. The pair usually descended to the "flats" where large triangles could be paced off. Today was different. Becca changed tack and started up the slope. The early spring sun warmed the air. After a few minutes, both stopped at the same time.

"Are you thinking what I'm thinking?" queried Becca.

"Probably. I started to perspire more than a trifle."

"Me too. And Mother's nose is extra sensitive on Friday nights."

The siblings took the opportunity to scan the Mediterranean waters. It was serene and beautiful. Then Becca closed her big brown eyes and faced the sun. She also had straight hair, longer, but not as dark as her brother. She tied it in a simple knot to help keep cool.

Becca continued, "Perhaps we ought to ask the rabbi if he can combine some of the commandments."

"Now what thoughts are rumbling around in your head?"

"Something like, honor thy mother and thy father on the Sabbath and keep it holy by smelling good."

"Now I know why women can't be biblical scholars."

"Maybe I'll be one. Let's keep going."

In a hundred feet, they picked up the pace as the street leveled off temporarily. They rounded a corner and noticed two men approaching, still some distance away.

"Walk behind me," said Ben sternly, as he immediately shifted from Ladino to Spanish.

"I will not," replied Becca in Ladino, resisting her brother's command, but at the same time, sensing his concern.

Ben continued, "I do not know one of them. Just do as I say until they pass from view. Don't speak and keep your head down too."

"Alright, alright," acquiesced Becca.

The carefree afternoon quickly dissipated. Ben and Becca continued walking single file as the men approached side by side. These men were not laborers. Their conversation was animated.

Ben slowed his pace to get a better look at the oncoming duo, trying not to stare and doing his best to be nonchalant. He recognized Señor Méndez, a good family friend and loyal client of Father's.

Ben relaxed as the distance between the two pairs diminished rapidly. The men were now only ten feet away. Ben was about to say something but stifled his impulse to speak, shivering for some reason. He made eye contact with Señor Méndez.

In an instant, an unspoken conversation occurred. Keeping his head still, Méndez moved his eyes sharply to the right, glancing at his companion. He then re-established eye contact with Ben. His eye movements were repeated.

Becca followed Ben past them in silence.

The strange feelings from the awkward encounter with Señor Méndez dissipated as Becca located a tree at the top of a smooth rock slope. She then pointed to another, which jutted out near the slope's bottom where the terrain changed.

"I challenge you to predict how long it will take a ball to roll from one tree to the other."

Becca was confident that Ben could not address this solely with his magical triangles. When he told her this would take some time and effort, she wasn't surprised. When he told her he would need help to make the calculations and execute them, she was elated. She tried to mask her enthusiasm by looking downward as she smiled.

They needed to take several point-to-point measurements. Intending to use Ben's pace as the standard, they soon realized there would be too much variability when ascending, descending, or traversing the steep rock face. Becca's shorter pace would be more accurate.

Becca suggested the sash from her dress, which she estimated to be about one of her paces when laid flat. Ben thought about it and realized that it would take hours to place the sash end to end on the ground to accomplish the measurements. Then Ben was struck by an idea so simple yet so practical.

Becca removed her sash and handed it to Ben. They found a level area. Ben asked her to start walking, stopping her immediately as she placed her forward foot on the ground. While she held this position, he anchored the sash to her ankles with tension in between.

This configuration allowed Becca to use her normal step for pacing consistently. They made the measurements quickly with Ben recording the results in his head. He then unbound Becca and she re-tied the sash around her waist.

Ben smiled. "When I give you the answer, you'll be challenged to determine if it is correct."

····◆····

There were no further encounters on the trek home.

Ben and Becca entered the house and grinned immediately. Contrary to their earlier concerns about Sabbath hygiene, they had nothing to worry about. A mixture of appetizing smells from Mother's preparations permeated the house.

Mother heard the two enter and made her standard announcement, "Ben, Becca, we're just about ready to begin the Sabbath."

Becca scanned the room. "Why isn't Father home? The sun's almost down."

Mother explained, "When I saw your father midday, he told me that he has a meeting with Señor Méndez after work. He'll be home in time."

Ben and Becca turned to each other, but Mother continued firmly, "Children, please help me prepare the table."

An odd command as Mother had attended to every detail. The only thing missing from the table were their appetites. Ben and Becca took this as their cue to sit down.

Mother always prepared a treat for the Sabbath meal. The display tonight was above and beyond. It wasn't the quantity of food on this Friday night, it was the variety of offerings. Almost every square inch of the table was covered with one dish or another to the point that making room for anything else would require Ben to make some calculations.

In the center tray fresh apple slices were arranged in a pattern around a sectioned bowl, half filled with cinnamon and the other half with honey. The four place settings had a series of small dishes arranged around a main plate, as if they were planets orbiting the sun, as learned men knew.

Based on the smell-induced stomach rumblings, Ben and Becca anticipated that paella of seasoned chicken and vegetables would soon occupy the empty dishes. For the moment, they surveyed the smaller dishes filled with pomegranates, figs, and nuts.

Mother took her seat at the table and eyed her handiwork. After a few seconds, impatient to talk about the series of events disrupting the Friday afternoon pattern, Becca began to speak, "Mother..."

Mother abruptly placed her index finger to her lips, to maintain the silence. Respecting her mother, and the evening's solemnity, Becca complied.

Not more than a minute later, Benjamin Solomon entered the house, placed his papers on a chair by the door, and proceeded to wash his hands.

In another break with the Solomon Friday protocol, he walked behind Becca on the far side of the table, placed his hands on her shoulders, bent forward, kissed her on the top of her head, and whispered, "Shabbat Shalom." Slowly, he stood upright, soaking up this beautiful moment.

An identical greeting was bestowed upon Ben and then concluded with Mother. However, Mother received a kiss on her cheek rather than her head. Just as Father's hands retreated from Mother's shoulders, she began reciting the blessing over the Sabbath candles.

As he had since his Bar Mitzvah, Ben recited the blessing over the Sabbath wine. In turn, all four sipped from the wine goblet that belonged to Mother's grandfather. Mother drank last, which was the signal for Father to bless the bread, as he did every week.

Father turned to Becca, "Go ahead sweetheart, please finish with the blessing over the Challah."

Today seemed to be nothing but firsts, so Becca forged ahead. She tore four small pieces from the Challah, the Sabbath bread. She kept one and passed the tray. Raising her morsel just short of her mouth, she stopped to ensure all attention came to her. Becca recited the prayer, then in one swift motion, she jammed the bread into the corner of her mouth. Before anyone else could finish chewing, she let her frustrations flow forth in a staccato monologue delivered in a single breath.

Shifting from Hebrew, the language of prayer, to Ladino, "We saw Señor Méndez today. He acted strange. We came home. It's Sabbath. No Father. He was visiting with Señor Méndez. Mother prepares the best meal ever. Father kisses us on the head. I bless the Challah. What is going on?"

"Amen," said Ben quietly in support. He had to admire Becca for not only speaking her mind but echoing his concerns.

Picking up her knife and fork, Mother appealed to Ben and Becca, "Please, let's start eating and Father will explain. Seems like I am the only one that didn't see Señor Méndez today."

"Before I start talking," temporized Benjamin, "Let's enjoy the meal Mother has prepared. And please tell me about your day."

The next few minutes passed quietly as hunger prevailed. Then Father, Ben, and Becca took turns complimenting Mother on the feast she had prepared.

After the exaltations subsided, Ben tried to verbalize the eerie feeling, compounded by the non-verbal exchange, when passing Méndez and the stranger. Becca explained they started their walk in the opposite direction today, which is the only reason they encountered the men.

Father took a deep breath. "I asked Mother to make a special dinner. We should celebrate the end of an era and the new challenge that God has given us." He hesitated for a moment. "Children, you saw Señor Méndez with a minister from Seville. It seems that on the last of March Ferdinand

and Isabella issued an edict of expulsion. Ben, how many Jews are there in Spain?"

"About eighty-two thousand."

Father continued, "We all have to..."

Becca interrupted, "Leave? I don't want to leave."

"Perhaps Father was somewhat imprecise," countered Mother. "Spain will be free of Jews."

Becca frowned as she tried to comprehend, "I don't see a difference."

Fighting back her tears, Mother responded, "We can...Benjamin, I can't say it."

Father finished the sentence, "Leave or convert to Catholicism."

Becca retorted, "What kind of choice is that?"

Benjamin reminded Becca that for a long time there had been constant pressure to convert. "Many of our friends are now Catholic."

Ben picked up the cue when Benjamin looked his way, saying, "Father's right. A hundred years ago, there were about two hundred and ten thousand Jews in all the Spanish kingdoms."

Becca persisted, "We just became part of Spain a few months ago. What about my Muslim friends?"

Father truncated the discussion with positivity. "I don't know but you can see that Mother and I are not overreacting to the situation. We know it is not in our hearts to convert, even superficially. We are already making plans." That was an exaggeration, but he and Mother didn't want the children to panic. "Now, let's enjoy this special Sabbath together."

3

Marbella, Province of Málaga, Spain
Wednesday, July 24, 2002

A reddish tinge graced the horizon as the oppressive summer heat of southern Spain finally succumbed to a gentle, cooling breeze. Only one soul remained on the driving range as daylight dwindled rapidly. Rusty Stephens stole a few moments to savor the serenity and solitude.

As one of the top touring professional golfers in the world, Stephens had seen his share of beautiful scenery. To soak it up without a gallery of thousands, the omnipresent press, other players pounding balls, and even his trusted caddie, was special indeed.

Back to business. He used his club to pull a ball into position behind a divot that had grown symmetrically to over a foot in length. Now, his pre-shot routine. Every pro had a pattern of preparation that was used on the course. Unless Rusty was working on a special drill, he followed his routine religiously, even on the practice range.

Rusty stood two paces behind his ball, feet slightly apart. He gripped his pitching wedge, pointing it downrange at his target. A second later, he dropped his left hand from the club. He guided the clubhead to the turf, just outside his right foot. He extended his right arm, focused on his target, and drew a breath.

A few years ago, this part of his routine irritated his playing partners since it seemed lengthy, though it wasn't close to the forty-second limit before a player went on the so-called clock. And it was no quirkier than Sergio Garcia tightening and loosening his grip incessantly before starting his swing, or Larry Mize adjusting his right pant leg before his takeaway. Besides, the Brits loved it. Reminded them of a casually dressed replica of Patrick McNee posing during the closing theme of the classic BBC television show, *The Avengers*.

His routine moved more traditionally from this point. He placed both feet together then moved them shoulder-length apart, facing the ball. He made one practice swing then edged forward to address the ball.

The strength in his forearms was evident as he gripped the club tightly for only a second as a reminder not to strangle it during his swing. The back of Rusty's head, his shoulder blades, and hips created a perfect plane. He eased the club back as he had thousands of times before. A sizzle pierced the air as if a sheet of finely milled paper had been ripped in half. The clubface smacked the ball. The auditory feedback, lasting a fraction of a second, let Rusty know he had delivered another acceptable shot.

There was still enough daylight for another twenty to thirty balls. Rusty nudged another ball from what looked like a half-built pyramid. He began his pre-shot routine.

His caddie, O.T. Sills, approached, staying out of view. O.T. didn't fit any stereotype. He was heavy but not fat with a light brown skin tone, blue eyes and light, wavy hair. With years of lifting and carrying Rusty's forty-five-pound bag, O.T. was solid and dexterous. Now he looked comical, maintaining his stealth, moving in slow motion, hunched over, and tiptoeing.

About twenty feet away, he realized any further attempts to move closer might reveal his position. He stopped. Slowly lowering himself all the way to the ground, he quietly scanned the thicker turf behind the practice area. Careful not to ruin the silence, he bent forward using his forefingers and thumbs to tear a single blade of grass as its base. Maintaining his crouch, O.T. anchored the thick strand lengthwise between his thumbs fashioning a crude instrument. He wedged the tips of his thumbs under his nose and covered his mouth with it.

O.T. drew a big breath slowly. He exhaled rapidly making a warbling sound, lasting a few seconds. It could only be described as Donald Duck trying to muffle a sneeze. He vaulted to attention as if he had just trumpeted the arrival of royalty. Hands at his side, angling his head slightly skyward, O.T. announced, "Hear ye, hear ye. It is time for all twenty-six-year-old blond, WASP multi-millionaire golfers, to adjourn to Marbella for wine, women and song."

"Thought you split," Rusty responded quietly without looking up.

"I was going to."

"But..."

"You'd never forgive me if you got a hernia carrying that fat ass bag of yours. On second thought, maybe a hernia would do you some good.

You'd be forced off the links for a few weeks with a crew of hottie nurses lined up to give you sponge baths."

"You might miss a few paychecks with my thing in a sling," quipped Rusty.

"True," replied O.T., raising his eyebrows with his lips curled downward as if Rusty had made a good point. "But it'd sure be fun watching you turn various shades of red."

Silence. Pre-shot routine. Back swing. Smack. Sizzle. Golf ball vanishing from sight in a rising arc with just a slight draw back to the left.

O.T. continued, "How 'bout we get outta here and get some yang for your yin?"

Rusty had heard hundreds of variations on this theme, ever since O.T. started as his caddie at Georgia Tech. He smiled. He was ready this time. Mocking O.T. but in a perfect monotone without raising his voice, he said, "Hear ye, hear ye. It is time for all horny twenty-five-year-old mixed breed caddies to chill, as no self-respecting bachelor in Spain dines before 10:00 p.m."

O.T. grabbed Rusty's driver. He slid it from the bag while simultaneously yanking a white handkerchief from his right pocket. He jammed one corner of the cloth under the head cover. He then waved his makeshift flag in surrender.

The club was returned to the bag sans handkerchief. O.T. then changed the bag from its upright position, laying it on the ground. He did this carefully, not as much to protect the contents but to position it for seating. He would likely be there for another half-hour based on the ritual he and Rusty had established over the years.

During practice sessions, O.T. was dutiful but not intrusive. He always maintained a supply of balls, clean clubs, a good ear, and ready to makes notes as necessary. As each session ended, Rusty would insist that O.T. relax while he hit a few more. It was never a few more. More like a couple dozen more. But O.T. didn't mind. It was a chance for him to enjoy a few minutes with his friend rather than his employer.

O.T. wasn't quite sure why Rusty encouraged him to take the afternoon off. Perhaps because there was less pressure preparing for an exhibition. Perhaps Rusty didn't want to hold him back from a night on the town. Perhaps a million other reasons. But old habits die hard. O.T. lowered himself onto the bag and began his vigil.

Silence. Pre-shot routine. Smack. Sizzle.

Silence. Pre-shot routine. Rusty stopped.

He turned to O.T. and said calmly, "Let's pack and plow."

"Really?" somewhat in disbelief.

"Really!" responded Rusty bugging his eyes and pushing his head forward to squelch any doubt about the decision.

O.T. grinned and quickly stuffed balls, tees, and towels into the closest pocket on the bag. He looked like a panicky teenager tossing his clothes under the bed. O.T. knew he could organize the contents later, but he wanted to get moving before Rusty had a chance to waffle.

It only took a few seconds for O.T. to call out, "Ready."

"Really?" Rusty responded sarcastically.

"Really!" O.T. grinned back, mocking Rusty's bug-eyed expression.

Rusty laughed as they walked from the practice range.

····◆····

Victor's Beach Bar was packed with people of every color, shape, and size. Although mid-week, it was difficult distinguishing one night from another in summertime Marbella. Tonight, the decibel level was extremely high. However, the open-air structure helped dissipate the crowd noise enough so one could talk without screaming.

In the two minutes since they arrived, O.T. recognized a half dozen languages. He wasn't worried about communications as much as finding a good place to hang. Rusty was concerned about crazies recognizing him. O.T. sensed this and tried to put him at ease.

"Relax. You're a long way from home. You don't have a hat on. You don't have sunglasses on. You don't even have a golf shirt on. You're lookin' good, a bit too preppy, but good."

Stopped behind O.T., Rusty motioned his hands forward to get back on track. O.T. inched forward. Rusty drafted behind him as they worked their way around the bar's perimeter. True to his skills as a caddie, O.T. spotted the line. He aimed straight ahead for the left corner of the deck jutting towards the Mediterranean. Then he faded slightly to the right where there appeared to be some people leaving.

Many hazards had to be avoided. Lit cigarettes dangled waist high, searching for exposed skin. Various libations, supported by extended elbows, were poised for launch. O.T.'s progress was steady. They made their way to a small round table with several chairs bunched around it, and several empty glasses clustered in the center.

A twenty-something woman remained at the table. Rusty and O.T. waited patiently for her to follow her table mates. Two minutes seemed like ten. O.T. then noticed two couples approaching from the opposite direction, taking dead aim at the table. Not wanting to lose the table and overcoming his fears about doing something culturally inappropriate, O.T. leaned towards the woman's side, speaking slowly, and enunciating with his best monotone, "May…We…Sit?"

The woman turned, looking directly at O.T. and Rusty. Her face caught Rusty's attention. There was something intriguing about it. It may have been the combination of her dark auburn hair and big brown eyes. Or perhaps it was the proportions of her nose and her eyebrows, plucked to perfection but slightly asymmetrical. Maybe it was the stylish glasses resting on her head. She shrugged her shoulders.

O.T. tried to use some hand signals. He pointed at Rusty and then himself a few times in rapid succession. Next, he opened his hands and gestured towards the chairs. The unwritten dialog was complete with a similar motion from the woman and a simple, "Prego."

O.T. and Rusty seated themselves. With his position established, O.T. wanted to thank his benefactor. Without much of an accent, he smiled, nodded, and said, "Gracias."

Rusty wanted to laugh but maintained his composure, trying not to embarrass the woman. He leaned towards O.T., "I'm not a linguistics expert but I think she offered us the table in Italian, and you thanked her in Spanish."

O.T. retorted, "Well, we're in Spain. I think she got the idea, and we got the table, so all in all, I'd say we're doin' okay."

Rusty caught a glimpse of the right hand of the mysterious woman. She raised it to move her hair back behind her ear. A diamond stud graced her lobe. But it was her hand that caught his attention. It was beautiful, elegant yet strong, with slim but not bony fingers.

As he brought his eyes upward, Rusty imagined her hands were a manifestation of her entire body. His fantasy was interrupted in a split second when O.T. finally flagged a waiter, announcing, "Relief is on the way."

After stopping by a nearby table to deliver drinks, the young man maneuvered between Rusty and O.T. His earrings weren't as nice as the mystery woman's, but the small tattoo on his right shoulder worked nicely with his blue tank top and off-white linen pants.

"Buenas noches, bonsoir, good evening, beuna serata, guten abend, goedavond," was recited by the waiter, quickly, with the proper accents in each case.

O.T. couldn't discern whether this was part of the club's rehearsed patter or just a creative dude. He felt compelled to volley back, "Kanbanwa good buddy."

Without missing a beat, the waiter pointed to O.T. and smiled. Not to be outdone, he addressed the entire table in his best southeastern U.S. accent, "What may I bring y'all?"

Rusty rotated his right hand into a palm up position and deferred to the woman. She put up both hands and declined with a smile. Rusty then looked up at the waiter, "Heineken please."

O.T. piped up, "I'll have a Bombay sapphire martini. Cameron, try a martini. I'm paying."

"Thanks Brian, but I'll stick with beer."

Rusty and O.T. had an unwritten rule that they use their legal names when addressing each other in public away from golf. To some extent this helped reduce their profile. Even golf's casual followers recognized the name Rusty Stephens and often O.T. Sills.

The waiter returned relatively quickly given the congestion. He set down the two drinks and hustled off, obviously not concerned about payment. Cameron and Brian raised their glasses as they always did, and toasted in harmony, "To another great trip." This was their longstanding acknowledgment that whatever the golf gods brought them, it beat commuting to an office every day.

Brian sipped his martini, then stood and said, "You got the beer and I gotta pee. Be back in a few."

After thanking Brian for his public service announcement, Cameron tried not to stare at his remaining table mate as she sipped her drink while surveying the room.

Activity around them continued at an energetic pace. Everyone, well almost everyone, was engrossed in loud repartee. What seemed like an infinite silence to Rusty lasted about thirty seconds.

The woman turned to Cameron. "I couldn't help but eavesdrop. You both seem to get along well, which is great, especially if you're taking lots of trips together." She sounded as American as one could get.

"Uh...hello. You speak English," questioned Rusty rhetorically.

"You sound surprised. Why?"

"Not sure. Come to think of it, we just spoke at you, made an assumption, and a bad one at that. Hi, I'm Cameron Stephens. Nice to meet you."

"I was having some fun myself," said the woman with a smirk. "Sandra Cole. My friends call me Sandy. Can we have some more fun with your friend, Brian, right? How about massaging my shoulders when he comes back?"

"Here, now?"

"Take a look around this place. No one is going to think anything of it, except your friend."

Sandra turned around in her chair to get into position. Cameron placed his hands on her shoulders, reluctantly at first. When her supposition about the rowdy crowd proved correct, Rusty put more vigor in the rubbing. They both relaxed in silence for a minute.

Sandra kept a lookout for Brian. As soon as she spotted him, she began rolling her eyes, subtly licking her lips, all the while not moving her head so that Cameron wouldn't panic and stop. As Brian got within earshot Sandy started her soundtrack.

Mixing in low guttural moans every few seconds, Sandy began her slow monologue in a sexy French voice, "J'adore vos mains. Tu es très gentil. Incroyable. Quelle nuit. Superbe. Merci mon nouvel ami."

Brian pulled his chair back from the table and turned it around. He straddled it, propped his chin on his joined hands and rested them on the chair back, elbows extended. He grinned, "Holy shit. I'm going to soak this up for a few minutes, just to make sure I'm not dreaming."

4

GIBRALTAR, KINGDOM OF CASTILE, SPAIN

FRIDAY, APRIL 20, 1492

For the first few days after hearing all Jews would be vanquished from Spain by summertime, the tight-knit community shared the same emotion, disbelief. As traveling merchants and bureaucrats brought more news to Gibraltar over the next three weeks, reality set in. Each visitor seemed to inject more sand into the Gibraltar machine which had run so successfully for so long.

The Catholics talked about who would provide commercial financing. The Muslims were concerned that other children of Abraham, the descendants of Ishmael and Esau, would be banished in the future.

The Jews worried about their very existence. Could they stay in the place they loved as *Marranos*, secret Jews, practicing two religions, a hollow Catholicism to the public and a pious Judaism, confined to whispers in the home? Or could they find it in their hearts to abandon Judaism altogether as *Conversos*? If they emigrated, where would they go? When would they leave? What could they take? Who might help them? Would families be torn apart?

Change was hard to notice on a day-to-day basis. But after three weeks, there was a palpable difference. Animated conversations gave way to calculated and guarded language. Small talk was extinguished whenever it cropped up. Public debate morphed into private speculation. Familiar faces looked down and away.

But today, Gibraltar had a purpose, its purpose, trade. Three ships anchored in port within hours. Normal traffic averaged one ship per week. Two crafts, arriving several days apart, could be accommodated without too much duress in the summertime, when days were long.

However, rough seas forced one ship to idle in deeper waters for over a week. Another ship experienced delays at its prior port, so it too had to idle when it arrived. As fate would have it, the third ship was precisely on schedule. Working by lantern light was always dangerous. It would be particularly challenging with the captain of each ship jockeying for priority.

The volume of arrivals thrust the community into action. Goods had to be extracted from the vessels' holds and transported. Items to be shipped required staging on the docks. Taking inventory was a necessity before off-loading, then after off-loading and again after loading. Ben would count goods while Benjamin would handle accounting for the warehouses of Señor Méndez.

It would be a hot day for this time of year. The prior week's stiff winds were only kind enough to leave the slightest breeze behind.

Ben had been instructed to begin work on the last of the three vessels that had arrived. He wasn't sure why, but it didn't matter much to him. As he walked along the waterfront, he inhaled deeply in anticipation of spending days in ships' holds.

Upon locating his first assignment, he took position at the bottom of the gangplank. He raised his arm slightly to catch the attention of a deck hand. Ben called to him, "May I board as an agent for la Empresa de Señor Ricardo Méndez?"

This all sounded a bit stiff to Ben, but his father had lectured him on the importance of protocol in commercial transactions. He was put at ease when a man replied simply, "Come."

Ben climbed the wooden walkway. An encouraging hand was extended to him, helping him over the port gunwale. In fact, this fellow didn't look much like a sailor at all. His hands were relatively smooth, and his face not unduly weathered. His beard and mustache were neatly trimmed.

"Welcome on board the Niña."

"Thank you. I am here to itemize the ship's cargo before we off-load and on-load."

"I'll show you. This job should be easy for you. There isn't much in our hold now. This isn't a regular merchant vessel. If you must come back after we take on provisions, I suppose you will have a lot more work."

Ben had been told to limit his interactions to those necessary for completing his work as quickly as possible. So, he let the conversation drop and followed his guide below deck. Two sailors, slightly more typical of those Ben had seen on other crafts, looked up as Ben stepped off the ladder.

"This man is here to take inventory. His name is..."

This was far more conversation than Ben ever had with sailors, but he didn't want to lie and needed to maintain formality as he had been taught.

"Señor Solomon."

"Ah, a wise man," said his guide as he looked Ben over. "I'm sorry. I'm keeping you from doing your work. My name is Mino. Call for me if you need any assistance, Señor Solomon."

"I'm grateful for your offer," Feeling more at ease. "People call me Ben."

As he began his routine, Ben noticed immediately there were few items for exchange. The cargo consisted entirely of earthenware jugs and wooden casks for transporting food and water. To ensure accuracy he counted the containers twice.

About an hour later, Mino found him and invited him for a break, some fresh air, and a drink of water. This never happened before, but Ben wasn't surprised at this point.

"That's very kind of you, but I can't be seen taking a break."

Mino replied, "We considered that. Follow me."

Ben complied and they ascended above deck into an area where some sails had been hoisted about ten feet and draped on the deck to block the view from onlookers.

"See," said Mino. "We picked a convenient time to dry and furl our sails."

"I do see," said Ben suppressing a smile as a goblet of water was handed to him. There were two others in the makeshift enclosure, so Ben did not drink immediately. Somewhat unsure of the situation, he forced a "hello."

"Luke's the name, nice to meet you."

"And I'm Duncan."

The three sailors sat down on the deck and Ben followed suit. The new acquaintances wore traditional seaman garb, but like Mino, they seemed just a little too tidy. Luke's lamb chop style sideburns were groomed precisely, and Duncan didn't have any facial hair.

No one drank. The silence caused Ben to stare down into his mug. Mino winked at Luke and Duncan.

Luke piped up, "Ben, you must be busy with three ships in port. What time will you finish tonight?"

"I need to be home by sundown."

"Duncan chimed in, "It's Friday today, isn't it?"

As if rehearsed, Luke responded, "Indeed it is."

He and Duncan raised their goblets, as did Mino. Ben hoisted his to meet theirs.

"*L'chaim*," said Mino with perfect guttural inflection on the second syllable. He took a drink.

Good thing Ben didn't have a mouth full, or he would have sprayed his hosts. The three sailors had a long laugh at the startled expression on Ben's face.

Mino collected himself. "Sorry Ben, we'll do the introductions again. I'm Michael."

"I'm Luis."

"I'm David."

Ben relaxed, took a sip of the cool water, "Tastes good, thanks. *L'chaim*, here's to life."

The break did not help Ben's productivity after he returned below deck. He was fascinated with the information he had just received and the thoughts it provoked.

Likely due to their precarious situation as Jews, Ben felt an immediate bonding to Michael, Luis and David. They weren't much older than him.

The nineteen souls on the Niña would join two other ships on an exciting expedition engineered by Christoforo Colombo, an Italian, financed by the Spanish royal family.

Ben completed his work. He thanked Mino for the hospitality. As he prepared to disembark, Mino told Ben life would be difficult for the Jews in Spain. Ben walked down the pier to his next assignment, feeling fortunate his parents had forged a plan for his future.

···♦◆♦···

When Ben made his request to board the next ship, a crew member responded by waving his meaty arms twice, in rapid succession, as if to say, "get your ass up here pronto." Ben reacted appropriately, head down, and quickly climbed aboard. He passed several sailors on the way to the ship's holds. Despite his rapid pace, he could not help but smell their perspiration, sweat, and body odor.

For once he was happy to be below deck, challenged with a variety of materials and containers to count. He hunkered down for a long afternoon. To fight the boredom, he refined the calculation of each barrel's cylindrical volume by estimating the variance in circumference between its cover and bulging midsection.

An hour had passed when Ben heard some intermittent laughter. Each outburst abruptly ended, like a maestro bringing his orchestra to a crescendo and then commanding its silence. The pattern continued for several minutes, with each eruption increasing in volume.

He reasoned this would be a good time for a break. It wasn't.

As soon as Ben felt the sunshine on his face, he heard the snap of a whip punctuating the laughter. The crew had formed itself into a circle of sorts. Peering through the hodgepodge of halyards, stays, and shrouds, Ben could see a pair of exposed ankles near the center of the gathering.

Ben observed in silence as the whip was passed from one crewman to the next. The sailor studied his prey and then snapped the weapon. The crackling sound caused the jeers.

Apparently, each man in the circle would have an attempt to deliver his best blow to the fair-haired lad caught in their web. The young man hopped from foot to foot as if the deck's surface was littered with hot charcoal. It did no good as the next sailor reached his mark. The victim shouted, "*Verdommer*." Damn. A few drops of blood oozed from the newly embossed red line just above his right ankle.

Ben hesitated. He wanted to do something. At the same time, he didn't want to create problems for Señor Méndez and his father.

The whip was passed to the next perpetrator. He began to circle the whip overhead, taunting his victim. He was just about to strike at the dancing youth when Ben yelled instinctively, "Help!"

The dozen sailors, as well as their prey, froze momentarily.

"I need some of you to help down here. Now! Hurry!"

Four of them started towards Ben. In the confusion, the victim darted from his torture cell.

Ben scurried back into the ship's hold in a state of frenzy trying to justify the emergency he had just created. Adrenalin pumping, he quickly lifted four heavy jugs onto a flimsy wooden shelf that he wedged his shoulders to support. Then he maneuvered a fifth container onto the feeble platform, clearly exceeding its capacity.

The sailors entered the hold. They saw Ben's precarious position. They moved forward to secure the jugs and lower them to the floor. This would have worked had they removed them in reverse order from Ben's placement. Instead, as any competent sailor would recognize, the remaining jug, on the end of the shelf, was now without ballast. The man of math and angles lunged for it. But Ben was blocked by a large body.

The jug landed with a thud. Though no visible cracks or gushing liquid, the distinct smell of salty brine immediately permeated the confined space.

Another sailor, in neater, cleaner, and better fitting clothes, entered the hold. Ben surmised he was the captain or first mate.

He demanded, "What in the Lord's name is going on here?"

Three of the sailors looked towards the other, expecting him to speak. He was an unsavory looking sort, with a wide scar the length of his right jaw, visible as his gray beard no longer grew there. With his two remaining middle fingers on his right hand, he pushed his hair back and thought for a moment.

"This little shit was counting the goods and called for help."

"Why?"

"There'd be too many jugs on that there ledge," pointing to it with his index finger. He was tryin' to hold 'em up so as they wouldn't come crashin' down."

"Who put them up there in the first place?"

"I did sir," replied Ben.

"Boy, I've been moving cargo by sea for more years than you have been on this earth. We put it in its place to stay and I've never seen it moved by any clerk during a counting."

"I thought it would help sir."

"Did I speak to you boy?"

"No sir."

"You go tell the company I want money for that jug, its contents and twice that again for the aggravation and time to replace it."

"Yes sir."

Ben was certain now this man was the captain and would have his way. He consoled himself by thinking he had done the right thing regardless of any penalties imposed on Father or Señor Méndez. His relief was premature.

The captain had climbed halfway up the ten-step ladder to exit the hold when he looked back at the crew and said to the sailor who had done the talking, "Jaw, where were you and the other men when you heard the call for help?

"We were teachin' the Dutchman a lesson aft."

"Then how could you hear him if he was down in here holding up the shelf?"

"He put his head above deck to holler at us."

"Tell me then, Jaw, or any of you other bright men in my command," he said sarcastically, "How could he put the jugs on the shelf, run over here, climb the ladder, call for you, and then get back to hold it up so nothing would fall?"

No one answered.

The captain continued, "I suspect he was trying to distract all of you. What were you doing to the Dutchman?"

Jaw looked quickly at his compatriots and said, "Just shoving him around a bit."

The other men mumbled in agreement.

"Why?"

"He was sayin' there's nothin' wrong with the Jews and didn't see no reason for them to leave Spain. He's always thinkin' he's smarter than us and now he's smarter than the King and Queen. The crew didn't take well to that."

The captain stepped back down off the ladder. He turned to Ben, "Are the King and Queen right?"

Ben had to say something. He hedged while trying to be respectful, "I don't know sir."

"You don't know if our King and Queen are right?"

Jaw piped up, "Maybe he needs some teachin' too."

"Just don't bother me. I'm going back to my quarters."

The captain turned and climbed back out of the hold.

"But sir..."

Ben's voice was stifled as Jaw cupped his mouth and extended his two fingers across his face. If that didn't horrify Ben enough, one of the other sailors removed his grungy bandanna, bunched it, and stuffed it into his mouth. Ben tried to make a break for the ladder. He didn't have a chance. The sailors subdued him, tied his hands behind his back and forced him up the ladder.

His leggings were gathered up, exposing his calves. The crew circled around him to repeat the violent game he had witnessed earlier. Ben made up his mind to play the game by his rules. He would not dance. The first crack of the whip was a warning. He did not move. The second lashing wound its way around both calves but only drew blood on his right. Tears formed in the corners of his eyes. He did his best to fight them off.

Just as the whip was ceremoniously passed, the mainsail's boom came crashing down. Several sailors were injured, one fatally, his head dangling from his neck by a thread of tissue. Two men were trapped and screaming for relief as their legs were partially crushed and pinned under the huge wooden pole. Heavy ropes and pulleys also fell to the deck, making it more difficult to move.

Jaw was unharmed. He frantically tore at the mess, trying to help his mates. He turned and saw the Dutchman removing lines from their cleats. He yelled, "You whore. Everybody..." as another beam struck him on the head and silenced him.

Ben ducked to get out of the way of any further falling objects. The next thing he knew, the soiled material was removed from his mouth and his hands were freed.

"Please, you must follow me," was all the Dutchman said.

5

Marbella, Province of Málaga, Spain
Thursday Morning, July 25, 2002

O.T. opened his eyes a few minutes before his wake-up call. The sun was up, but thankfully the housekeeping staff had closed the curtains during turn-down service. With his cottonmouth, he stumbled toward the suite's kitchenette. O.T. opened the mini-fridge and rubbed his eyes, adjusting to the light. There were almost too many choices. He grabbed a small bottle of cranberry juice, twisted off the top, and guzzled it.

He opened the front door expecting to find a Spanish language paper, which would be of little use to him on the throne. Neatly arranged on a polished wooden tray was today's *Herald Tribune* and a single flower in a vase with an envelope leaned against it. The Marbella Club couldn't do enough for its guests, particularly the rich and famous. O.T. was neither, but he was Rusty's entire entourage on this trip.

He grabbed the tray, closed the door, and retreated towards the bathroom. He chuckled as he picked up the envelope. It was addressed to Mr. Brian. When they checked in, the concierge, bell captain, and front desk personnel, showered them with formal salutations. Most of these people were old enough to be their parents so both he and Cameron insisted on their first names. They didn't anticipate the outcome, but it was charming in a way, reminding Brian of watching *Bonanza* with his grandparents, hearing Hopsing call the Cartwright boys Mr. Adam, Mr. Hoss, and Mr. Joe.

O.T. opened the note. It was Rusty saying he would not weight train this morning and they should meet for breakfast at the original time. Hopefully, thought O.T., *Sandy Cole was behind this breakdown in discipline.* He would have to wait a little longer to get the details on what transpired after he left them at Victor's.

In the meantime, he took his time in the bathroom. However, he saved the skinny newspaper for his second bottle of juice on the balcony overlooking the Mediterranean.

A few minutes before 9:30, O.T. headed to the restaurant. The morning was beautiful and relatively cool. It was breakfast rush hour, so he was glad they had reserved a table on the patio.

"Señor Brian," greeted the hostess. "Señor Cameron is already waiting for you."

"Gracias, Señorita."

O.T. followed her to the table where he found Rusty focused on the sports page, literally one page, which was the entire *Tribune* sports section. As he sat down, Rusty looked up from the paper.

"Looks like the Braves are getting some good pitching again this year."

"Yep. Let's just hope they don't peak before October. Got your note. You probably needed extra shut-eye after last night."

"I just couldn't be inside a sweaty gym on a morning like this. I jogged a few miles on the beach and did some push-ups." Without hesitating and looking back at the paper, Rusty continued, "I'll save you the trouble of asking. We stayed up late...talking. I could have slept 'til noon."

"How was she?"

"Really great. Nice Jewish girl," said Rusty non-judgmentally.

"Now I'm really jealous. They're super-hot as long as you follow Hebrew. You gotta caress them from right to left."

Shaking his head, Rusty questioned rhetorically, "Where do you get this stuff?"

A waitress stopped by the table offering O.T. juice and coffee. He accepted the coffee, declining the juice. He turned to Rusty. "Did you order?"

"Yes but go for the buffet if you want."

Normally, O.T. would do two rounds at a breakfast buffet, but he didn't want to leave the conversation hanging. Before the waitress could retreat, he quickly ordered scrambled eggs and bacon then turned back to Rusty.

"So gimme the skinny. She looks like she's got a killer bod."

"Hate to disappoint you, but we just talked. I really like her. Smart. Going for her PhD. Research assistant to an anthropologist at Columbia. She's here for a conference and I'm hoping to catch up with her again."

"Does she know what we do, or did you give her the partial story?

It was true that among other things, Rusty and O.T. represented several sports apparel lines and equipment manufacturers.

"I felt like I could have told her anything, but it just didn't seem necessary. She's not particularly interested in professional sports. Her mother's a teacher. Dad's a doc. Hacks around on Wednesday afternoons and Sundays when the weather's nice. Older sister played high school soccer. Anyway, Sandy was more interested in why we seemed to hit if off…Was I religious growing up, what's my favorite food, did I like Atlanta, had I ever seen *The Shawshank Redemption…*"

"Did you find out where she grew up, where her folks live?"

"Near Augusta."

"Well, that's encouraging. At least you have one thing in common."

Rusty paused, sipped his orange juice, and smiled back at O.T. "Augusta, as in Maine, not Georgia."

O.T. let the clarification settle in. He contemplated the next few things he would say to Rusty. His job required he give his opinions. O.T. knew that a golfer's performance was as much mental as physical, so he felt compelled to relay his thoughts on anything that might help or hinder Rusty.

In the past, O.T. would likely say whatever popped into his head. His knee-jerk reactions were usually spot-on but sometimes created tension. Over time O.T. learned to relay facts patiently, letting Rusty process them, which worked out better. He slowly added more milk to his coffee even though it was already too light for his taste.

O.T. began speaking deliberately, "Sandy sounds like a real nice person, and fun too. Obviously, she has a good sense of humor. But damn. Northern girl, southern boy. Doctoral student, college athlete. Outspoken, reserved. Jewish, Episcopalian. Do you really think it's a fit?"

Rusty shifted his gaze directly at O.T. valuing his perspective, "Something clicked with her. But you're probably right. It looks like a low percentage shot, but...oh good, here comes our breakfast."

A waitress placed the tray on an expandable stand nearby. Another waitress walked over to join her co-worker. They served Señor Cameron and Señor Brian, simultaneously lifting the cloches from their plates.

As the twosome vanished, O.T. said, "I really wanted to say, 'Ta da' when they did that."

"Thanks for sparing me. Eat. I don't think we have much time before Seve, José-Maria and Sergio show up. And I need a few minutes to go back to the room before we head out."

Attempting to imitate the waitress, O.T. said, "No problem, Señor Cameron."

6

RANCHO MIRAGE, CALIFORNIA, USA
SAN DIEGO, CALIFORNIA, USA
THURSDAY MORNING, JULY 25, 2002

This would be a hot one thought Tommy Torres when he leaned out the apartment's front door to grab the Desert Sun, the valley's local paper. The mountains were particularly striking this morning, contrasting an azure blue sky. He stopped for a moment. No clouds and no haze from L.A. He closed the front door of his modest two-bedroom castle and retreated to the kitchen area.

As he did most every morning, he paused for a minute to view the refrigerator door before opening it for orange juice. Three pictures, cropped to three by five, were held in place by fruit magnets. Tommy always scanned them from left to right.

The only black and white photo pictured all four of his grandparents on his parents' date farm, located less than twenty miles away. Tommy had taken the photo with his Kodak Instamatic camera over thirty-five years ago. He could almost inhale the dusty farm smell.

As he remembered his grandparents, his gaze shifted to the right, which evoked a range of emotions. Extracted from his wedding album, his parents flanking his bride, Karen, all radiated big smiles. While his parents had aged, Karen had hardly changed. She didn't have time. She passed away a week before their daughter, Sonya, was to celebrate her fifth birthday.

Tommy's parents had grown up with Karen's parents. They knew her from the day she was born. Her death devastated them too.

He completed his daily roller coaster ride by focusing on a recent photo of Sonya, and her older brother of two years, Louis, taken the last time the three of them were together. Karen would have been a proud mother. Sonya had just earned a full scholarship to UC San Diego in pre-med. Louis made a ten-year commitment to fly with the Air Force. Tommy tried not to worry too much about Louie's deployment at the base adjacent to the Baghdad airport.

Some people needed to go to church every day, make confessions or take Holy Communion. While he was inclined to do so after Karen died, it wasn't practical with the children and his work. But he told his parents he prayed daily, which in fact he did, albeit genuflecting towards an appliance.

His cell phone vibrated on the kitchen table, abruptly ending his meditation. Rarely did he receive calls at this hour of the morning. He flipped open the phone to see his office number, the local real estate arm of Marriott.

"This is Tommy," rendering his upbeat salutation on auto pilot.

"You may want to get here ASAP. The daily office meeting was canceled so we can start the timeshare tours at 8:30. The concierges have been busy signing up people. Must be some contest going on or something."

"Thanks Zoe," said Tommy halfheartedly.

"Thought I'd give you the heads-up. I know it messes up your golf training."

"Another speed bump. Appreciate the call. See ya in a few."

Tommy quickly opened the fridge door, grabbed the quart carton of Minute Maid and unfolded its cootie-catcher top. He bypassed the glassware, tipping the carton upward. He gulped as he kicked a half dozen golf balls into the corner, so he wouldn't trip on them when he returned. Been there and done that, spraining his ankle. Thirty seconds later, he was out the door on his way to the timeshare office.

····◆····

The selling team didn't have a dress code, but most of Tommy Torres' male colleagues dressed in shirts and ties. That didn't bother him in the least. Depending on the weather, Tommy wore a long or short sleeve Ralph Lauren golf shirt with Khaki slacks. After all, he was selling timeshares on a golf course, so he wanted to look like a golfer, which he was.

He tried to keep his cap on as much as possible, always choosing one that might elicit a remark from his prospects. If the conversation turned to golf, Tommy casually offered a free lesson as an incentive to sign-up.

Today, he didn't have a chance, nor need to talk about golf. He sold three timeshare units to two different families. To boot, both transactions concluded in the early afternoon, so he headed to the driving range. He was enjoying a nice run of late. If it continued, he could scale back his hours in a few months and still generate the same income.

At age forty-five, he had five years until he could join the Senior PGA Tour, soon to be renamed the Champions Tour, a euphemism, at least for him, since he had never notched a victory on the PGA Tour.

He had a lot of work to do on his game, and not much time. He loved golf. If he could just get all his muscles to remember when on the course, he could have a nice career. Practice was the key to muscle memory and dealing with the pressure of competition, particularly with players who had been winning tournaments for decades.

This afternoon, Tommy focused on distances of 75 to 125 yards. A friend of his, on the maintenance staff at the resort, had crafted some wooden planks which Tommy could slide under an AstroTurf mat. Boards of different lengths could be stacked and offset to simulate various fairway terrain.

He felt good about his regimen and the workout. He packed up his car thinking *it sure would be helpful to have my caddie and best friend practice with me more often*. But Carlos had to put food on the table.

After strapping himself into the driver's seat, he retrieved his mobile phone. He refused to practice with it.

Three messages. The first two, from the office, confirmed clean credit reports for the morning's buyers. Those were the kind he liked, just listen, and delete. Sonya left the third message. She sounded agitated. She needed to talk with him as there was a problem with her scholarship award. He tapped the buttons to call her.

She answered, "Hello." Now he knew something was off since she didn't say, "Hi Papi."

"What's wrong?"

"There's been some government cutbacks and the general scholarship funds will be reduced."

"How much?"

"I was told twenty-five to fifty percent. Papi, I feel terrible."

"Don't worry about it. There's nothing you could've done about it. Now, go do what you're supposed to do. Get good grades."

"Thanks, Papi. Gotta run. Love you."

"You too." *So much for going part-time anytime soon.*

7

Marbella, Province of Málaga, Spain
Thursday Afternoon, July 25, 2002

Rusty enjoyed the company of two Spanish golf legends—Seve Ballesteros and José-Maria Olazábal, and the emerging phenom, Sergio Garcia. While all three spoke English, they reverted to Spanish occasionally to poke fun at Rusty.

The atmosphere on the fairways was competitive but friendly for golfers during an exhibition. The affluent gallery was more serious. Over the last half-hour the organized betting pool increased handsomely. The main beneficiary would be charity, but a few lucky spectators would end the day with fifty thousand more Euros in their pockets. So, there was a keen interest in each shot.

Official scorers tracked progress and prepared to deal with tie-breaking rules that made the American football playoff berthing look like child's play.

O.T. had never seen Rusty so relaxed on a golf course. He had to ask, "Hey, what's come over you this morning? Someone spike your coffee?"

"No pressure, I suppose. We should do these kinds of events more often."

"C'mon, it's me you're talking to. I've been with you for what, hundreds of rounds, and you're definitely weird today. It's Sandy, fess up."

"Well, I checked my email after breakfast. There was a message from her."

O.T. chided, "Glad this didn't happen the morning of The Open," referring to the British Open.

"Don't knock it, I'm playing well."

O.T. got serious, "Well enough but with no intensity."

Sergio overheard the conversation and felt compelled to needle Rusty, "O.T.'s right. I've also played a lot of rounds with you, and you seem, how do you say it in the States, *p.w. 'ed*." Pussy whipped.

Rusty countered with, "I think you've had enough English lessons."

Sergio didn't relent, "Hey Seve, José-Maria. Rusty's in love."

Seve's turn, "A woman?"

O.T. jumped in, "It's a she and she's hot."

"Perfect," said Seve with a smile. "The tabloids need something else since they gave up trying to prove that José-Maria and I hung out with The Village People."

"Let's play some golf," said Rusty, truncating the chatter as they approached his ball, some 260 meters downrange just right of the 11th fairway's center. The Spaniards respected Rusty's conservative choice of a 3-wood to put the ball into position. However, they chose driver and their shots rolled past the end of the fairway into the rough. With the length of this par-5 the Spaniards had to lay up then shoot for the green on their third shots.

From the fairway Rusty applied a little extra to his second swing, attempting to reach the putting surface, or the dance floor, as many commentators called it. The distance was perfect, but the shot leaked to the right leaving Rusty's ball three meters to the right of the green in thick and patchy rough, which looked like a dense scalp of spiked hair. The limited landing area on the green between Rusty's ball and the pin, left him short-sided, a difficult position.

Seve's competitive nature went into overdrive. "Better stop thinking about your lady."

Rusty couldn't help but smile as he let the comment pass.

The three Spaniards played back into the fairway then selected pitching wedges for their third shots. They all found the putting surface, coming to rest past the flag stick, leaving tricky downhill putts on an undulating surface. The closest to the pin was José-Maria at four meters. The gallery of mere mortals applauded vigorously, but these world-class competitors were disappointed.

The American studied his lie in the rough.

After a moment, O.T. simply said, "Rusty."

Without responding, Rusty yanked the lob wedge from his bag. Custom shaped to a sixty-three-degree angle, it was one of the loftiest in the business.

"One time," said Rusty.

Rusty opened his stance and the clubface, adding even more loft to the upcoming shot. Following his pre-shot routine, the lob wedge cut into the rough like a scythe. The ball emerged from its grass prison, landing not more than two centimeters on the green, then rolling, seemingly in slow motion, to less than a meter from the cup. It was a shot even Phil Mickelson, known for his lobs, would be proud to execute.

Rusty quickly touched the brim of his cap with thumb and forefinger to acknowledge the gallery's thunderous appreciation. Then he said to his playing partners, as the crowd settled, "Looks like you guys just p.w.'ed yourselves," ostensibly referring to their pitching wedge shots.

The banter continued with the good vibes spilling over to the fans as the round headed towards its conclusion. About four and half hours after taking the 1st tee, the customary post-match ceremonies commenced. Mother nature cooperated so nicely that the speeches, in Spanish, didn't bother O.T. who usually got antsy as soon as the last putt was drained.

Rusty's head was elsewhere. He nearly walked off the 18th green before he was awarded with a one by two-meter cardboard check payable to the Rusty Stephens Foundation."

O.T. nabbed Rusty as the formalities ended. "I spoke with the three amigos. We don't have to hang around. What time are you supposed to meet Sandy?"

"She made a dinner res at ten. Said I should stop by her room any time after eight."

"So, you'll be there at one minute before eight."

"Nope," said Rusty. "I'm going to play it cool, one minute after eight."

8

Waterville & Sidney, Maine, USA
Tuesday Afternoon, July 23, 2002

Herman Cole's surgery patients, at least the few he had this time of year, were stable. Mainers, with optional procedures, tended to avoid the scalpel during the long days of summer, preferring to spend as much time as possible outdoors, enjoying toasty days and cool nights.

He liked to end his rounds early at Thayer Hospital on warm and sunny days. It was about 3:30 as he walked towards his SUV. He had driven his last vehicle, a Jeep, for fourteen years. Finally, he took the plunge into the cockpit of a Pathfinder with automatic this, automatic that, and seat warmers, which he had to admit were handy in Maine.

About twenty feet away he pressed the button on his key fob to pop the door locks. Opening the front door, he stepped up, dropping his reading material on the passenger seat. His next stop, Starbucks. Waterville finally got one. It had a drive through, but only tourists used it.

At the counter, a woman in front of him fumbled through her purse to extricate loose change for a cup of chai tea. The barista recognized him.

"Hi Doctor Cole. Be with you in a sec."

Herman put up his hand in a half wave to acknowledge the greeting. He wrinkled his face as he realized he was spending over three dollars for a cup of coffee, ordering it using a lexicon created by a marketing genius in Seattle who had somehow decided tall meant small.

The other patron completed her transaction leaving Herman as the sole customer in the store.

"The usual, Dad?"

"No foam today sweetheart, just a large decaf with plenty of skim milk," emphasizing large in mock resistance to conceding a Venti to his daughter.

"Are you okay? I almost had your cappuccino going."

"Everything's good. You?"

"Fine."

She handed him the coffee.

Herman handed over several singles. "Thanks for adding the milk. Usually, I have to have a discussion about how much room I need for it. Sure is handy knowing the person that runs the place. What time are you done?"

"Four."

"Great. Why don't you meet me by the pond at Colby? I'll be hanging out there for at least an hour. If you're a few minutes late, no problem."

"Now I am really worried. Isn't this your private unwind time?"

"It is, but we don't talk enough, and this place is usually too busy to get a word in edgewise."

"You know Dad..." said Sally. She contemplated her next few words. As if the pause cued actors in the wings, four gabby teenage girls entered the store.

So much for that thought Herman. He waved to his daughter much the same way he greeted her. Returning to the Pathfinder, he backtracked past the hospital turning onto North Street then Campus Drive to Johnson Pond.

He parked the SUV, then eased his coffee from the cupholder. He opened the back door and tried to use his free hand to organize the week's accumulation of magazines, journals, and papers. Finally, he placed his coffee on the roof, gathered and balanced the stack on one arm, reclaimed the coffee, and used a foot to close the door.

He walked purposefully to balance the load, then dropped the pile on a park bench. Time to relax, enjoy a sip of coffee and the slight breeze. Just enough to keep cool, but not blow his reading material all over the place.

After he pulled off his shoes and socks, he began picking up each publication for triage— peruse and discard, read and save, or deal with it later. He then attacked the peruse and discard pile. For sure, he had to take a quick glance at The *Waterville Sentinel's* sports section. The other members of his Wednesday foursome would undoubtedly discuss the upcoming weekend's pro golf tournaments.

Twenty minutes was enough to get through the first stack. Herman dug into the next pile. He lost himself in a detailed article on technological advances in arthroscopic surgery. When he finally came up for air, he glanced at his watch. It was almost 4:30.

He started to collect his reading material when Sally walked over to him, left hand extended with an ice cream cone. "You can't leave yet. I already called Mom and told her to chill."

"Did you tell her you were going to fatten me up too?"

"Hey, it's Gifford's yogurt and one dip isn't going to kill you. You look great."

"Thanks, tastes just like ice cream."

Herman smiled, attacking it before it dripped. Sally tugged her long-sleeve work shirt from her jeans, pulling it over her head, even though it was a button-down. She wore a tank top underneath. She sat on the bench, bunched her shirt, wedged it between her shoulder blades, and leaned back.

"Nice out. Thanks for the invite." Sally continued, "I know you want to ask me how I'm doing but it always comes out that you're not happy about it."

She looked towards him, pushed her sunglasses into her auburn hair and spoke in a pleasant, truthful, manner. "You try to make people feel better every day and so do I. Just because you chose to make sacrifices to help them in your way, doesn't make my way less meaningful."

Herman pondered her words, then conceded, "I suppose you're right."

They agreed on something, which was rare these days. They let the feeling sink in. Neither one knew what to say next.

Herman finished the last morsels of his cone as they sat quietly.

Sally broke the silence, "I'm enjoying this Dad but I have to go soon."

"How much of a grace period do I have with your mother?"

"A couple hours, so you can read some more with impunity. By the way, I got an email."

"Don't you get a lot of emails?"

"I got one from Sandy with an interesting message."

Still playing along, Herman said, "Don't you get a lot of interesting emails from Sandy?"

Sally popped up, kissed her father on his forehead and trotted off. As she stepped into her car, she turned and said, "She might be in love." She closed the door and drove off before Herman could react.

He picked up a recent issue of *JAMA, the Journal of the American Medical Association,* and immediately tossed it back down. Sally's tease had totally distracted him. Herman collected his reading material and headed back to the SUV.

Since Sally had bought him a few extra minutes, he opted for Rice Rips Road, heading towards Oakland, avoiding I-95.

Beth picked up, "Hello."

"I'm on my way, should be there in about twenty give or take. Had a nice visit with Sally."

"That's great Herm. Did she..."

"Beth? Beth?"

This stretch of road had spotty cell coverage, so he didn't try her back. He'd be home shortly.

····◆····

Herman steered the Pathfinder off the road onto the gravel driveway towards the house. He slowed, not as much worried about vehicle damage from the crunchy volley of rocks, but more concerned about the fourth lady in his life, Katy. The golden retriever always roamed around late afternoon waiting for him.

Today was different. As he edged the car forward, Katy ran out of her dog door by the kitchen and started circling rapidly. Herman opened the car door, stepping down, "Girl, what's wrong?"

Katy barked once.

"Is it Mom?" Katy barked again.

As Herman ran towards the house, Katy retreated through her private access.

Beth was stretched out on the kitchen floor. By the look of her position, it didn't appear she had fallen. Herman knelt, placing his hand to her forehead. She was slightly warm to the touch. He gently lifted her head. He could smell Katy's saliva on her forehead. Beth opened her eyes and began to move her lips.

"Shh," said Herman, pushing aside a few strands of hair that had matted. "Just relax for now. I think 'ol Katy may have helped you stay cool. Turning to the dog, he commanded, "Good girl, go get my bag."

It wasn't surprising a retriever retrieved. That Sally and Sandy had trained Katy to do this was truly remarkable. After they first laid eyes on her in a small shop in Millinocket, on their way to Baxter State Park, they bugged Herman and Beth for an entire weekend. They literally bought the doggie in the window on their way home. During the transaction, Beth was concerned that they had adopted a third child. But sibling rivalry worked well, at least for Katy, as Sally and Sandy tried to out-cuddle each other with the young pup.

Keeping his left hand behind Beth's head, he reached upward towards the sink, felt around blindly, before his hand happened onto a fluffy dish towel. He grabbed it and fashioned a crude pillow. He arranged it underneath Beth's head and gently moved her into a more stable position.

Katy returned with Herman's medical bag and waited patiently, ready to release it from her jaws. Beth reached forward with her right hand, rubbing the dog behind her ears.

Calmly and methodically, Herman performed a routine exam, checking vital signs, heart, eyes, and ears. At 100° Fahrenheit, Beth's temperature did not overly concern him. Her reflex response on the left side wasn't as pronounced as it was on her right. In most cases, a sprint to the nearest hospital would be in order, but the difference was very slight, perhaps too subtle for most physicians to notice.

Herman gently placed his hands under her arms and lifted her. He felt some swelling on her left side as he guided Beth to a chair. He opened a cupboard, retrieved a drinking glass, filled it with tap water, and placed it on the kitchen table in front of her.

Herman squeezed Beth's hand as husband, not doctor, "Relax and drink a few sips at a time. I'll be back in a couple minutes. Just want to check a couple things on the computer."

He went into his study, fired up his computer, not even sitting down. Navigating to a physician's assistant site, he entered a few metrics, which supplemented his preliminary assessment.

Returning to the kitchen, "You seem fine, but I want to have some tests done."

"Okay," replied Beth. "By the way, Sandy says she met a guy in Spain."

"Sally said something about it this afternoon. Europe? Situation normal, I'm always the last to know. Jewish? Spaniard? Age?"

Beth answered nonchalantly, "Don't know, don't know and don't know? And besides what difference does it make? We wanted the girls to be independent."

Herman sighed, "Agreed. Sounds like you don't know too much about the mystery man either."

9

MARBELLA, PROVINCE OF MÁLAGA, SPAIN
THURSDAY EVENING, JULY 25, 2002

The door to Sandy's room was slightly ajar with the brass swing door guard extended to block its closure. With a bottle of wine in each hand, and another under his left arm, Cameron gently tapped the door with his right foot.

"Cameron, is that you?"

"It is."

"Come on in."

Across the room, with her back to the door, Sandy continued to focus on her computer screen.

"Sorry to be rude, but I just happened onto something interesting. Be with you in a minute."

"No problem. Can I bring you a glass of wine?"

"All I have is some hotel dessert wine."

"I brought some of the local vintages, a white, red and a rosé. You pick."

Sandy turned, removed her reading glasses, "Look at you. Here I am buried in my PC and you're so thoughtful. I should be kvelling."

Cameron laughed. "I'm not sure whether that's good or bad, but whatever it is, I'm happy to open some wine while you finish what you're doing. I know I'm early by Spanish standards."

"Rosé sounds good. I think there's a corkscrew in the mini-bar." She turned back to her PC.

Cameron placed two bottles on the counter and jostled the rosé into the bucket of ice by the minibar.

He found the wine glasses. Not a wine connoisseur by any means, he had learned enough to go through the proper motions when needed. Since all the glasses in the room were the same, he didn't have to worry about selecting the right one. He poured two glasses halfway and placed one on the desk next to Sandy.

Upon hearing the glass find its resting place, Sandy managed, "Thanks, another minute and I'm all yours."

Cameron sat in the cushioned loveseat placing his glass on the small coffee table designed to work with the couch. Reflecting on his pleasant but long day, he took the opportunity to relax, closing his eyes.

Whether a minute or an hour went by, Cameron didn't know at first. He opened his eyes to see Sandy with her wine glass raised, "Okay, let's start with a proper toast. To your health Mr. Stephens. Cheers."

"And to yours, Ms. Cole," lifting his glass to touch hers. "Cheers."

After sipping and lingering for a moment, they both said, "So" at the same time. Chuckling at the simultaneous silence breaker, Sandy took a second sip while motioning for Cameron to speak.

"What was so interesting on your PC?"

"Normally I'd be catching up on research for the guy I work for. But a couple months ago, I was really bored and did some searches on my family tree. One thing led to another and now I'm sorta fascinated by genealogy."

"Sounds like fun. Brian and I are always joking about his lineage."

"Obviously he doesn't mind. How did that happen"?

"What?"

"Always joking about it."

"Brian seems like a mixture of unique characteristics, all good ones, but I call him a mutt anyway."

"Maybe we can find something interesting about him."

"Really?"

"C'mon, let me show you. Bring your wine."

They got up from the couch. Sandy pulled the desk chair out, "Have a seat."

"I'm not a computer person."

Sandy smiled, "I know you can email which is more than enough."

Feigning a concert pianist, Cameron sat down slowly, pulled the chair up a few inches, elevated both hands, shook his fingers for a second and placed them on the keyboard.

After observing the little vignette, Sandy said, "And I thought Brian was the one with the shtick."

"What's stick?" mispronouncing it.

"It's shtick, not stick. I'll explain later. In the meantime, you'll need to use the mouse."

Sandy stood to Cameron's right, slid her glasses down her nose, glaring like an exam proctor. She guided Cameron to her drop-down list of favorite places. When the menu of choices appeared, Sandy suggested the name of a URL, an index to a site on the Internet, that she had found helpful when starting a new lineage investigation.

Whether it was the combination of wine, Sandy's instruction, or the ease of browsing, Cameron had little difficulty. A search box appeared. He typed in Brian's last name. As Sandy anticipated, many variations were returned for "Sills."

"Hmm" mumbled Cameron. "There's a bunch and then some."

Sandy explained, "This is the tedious part. There's a lot of sites. Did Brian ever say anything about his name?"

Cameron bent his head back and looked up to the ceiling to concentrate. He stayed in the posture for more than a few seconds, which prompted Sandy.

"You know...I owe you a massage, but it doesn't mean you have to stop browsing." Without waiting for a reaction, Sandy adjusted herself directly behind Cameron. In a therapeutic like manner, she lightly pressed down on his shoulders then applied a little more pressure with her thumbs extending them just below his shoulder blades.

As he relaxed from Sandy's kneading, Cameron recalled that Brian's family name may have been hyphenated at some point. Sandy said, "Good," although she knew this could be challenging as there were fewer names but more places to look for them.

Steadying her left hand on Cameron's shoulder, she leaned forward. With their cheeks almost touching, she extended her right hand on top of his, guiding the mouse to a link she wanted him to click.

"Okay," said Cameron, seemingly acknowledging her instruction, but enjoying her scent and her wonderful fingers.

As Cameron added a hyphen to Sills in the search criteria, Sandy returned to the massage. She could feel the definition in his back muscles as she increased her pressure. Her hands moved up towards his neck. The on-line response to Cameron's updated query was not forthcoming but neither seemed to care.

Sandy placed her hands along Cameron's jaw line. Her thumbs rubbed behind his ears. Cameron closed his eyes. Sandy eased his head back. She leaned over him, lowered her head, and found his lips with hers. He opened his mouth to receive her exploration. The chair seemed to edge back on its own as Sandy sat on Cameron's lap. His silk trousers did little to conceal his arousal.

As they continued to taste each other, Sandy lowered her hands to unbutton her blouse. Having done so, she returned them to Cameron's face, pulled back slightly and opened her eyes. She waited patiently for Cameron to raise his eyelids. When he did, she gazed into his eyes, just for a moment, then unabashedly guided him to her breasts.

Cameron elevated his hands under her shirt taking time to savor the curve of her back. No bra to disturb the contour. As he began caressing her nipples, Sandy quickly released his head, wrapped her arms tightly around his shoulders and pulled him to her. A moment later, a long and low moan, emanated from deep within her.

As the tension dissipated from her body, she relaxed and leaned back. Neither said a word. Slowly, she started to unbutton Cameron's shirt. Looking at him intently in the eyes, she coyly asked, "Can we can delay our dinner reservation?"

Replying in kind, Cameron said rhetorically, "I take it you're not hungry."

"Oh, I'm hungry... for more dessert."

10

Gibraltar, Kingdom of Castile, Spain
Tuesday, May 1, 1492

Roberto Méndez knocked on the Solomon's front door. Esther opened it.

"Señora Solomon."

"Señor Méndez," she exclaimed, somewhat startled. Only once had Méndez visited their house. Recovering, she forced a normal sounding, "Good evening."

She shifted her eyes briefly to the man next to him. He wore a similar coat and hat, but obviously ill-fitting and not tailored well. Méndez skipped the return salutation. With an urgency in his voice, "May we come in?"

"Welcome," replied Esther.

Méndez motioned to his companion to advance in front of him with a formal Dutch expression, "*Astublieft.*" After you.

Though Esther wasn't fluent in Dutch, hearing Méndez address the other man this way added to her concerns. She called out, "Benjamin, come. Señor Méndez is here with an associate."

Benjamin entered the room with Becca in tow. Méndez made the introduction. "This is Johan Witte from Amsterdam. His father's the director of an important trading company and a partner in commerce with me. Johan, please tell them what happened."

Johan fidgeted with his hands, looking down, then up at Méndez for reassurance. Méndez nodded.

The Dutchman began, "Your son saved my life."

Esther implored, "Is Ben okay, where..."

Méndez cut off Esther while placing his hand on her shoulder. "He's safe. Continue, Johan."

As the Dutchman began to recount the day's events, Méndez excused himself to attend to nature. He headed around the house, ostensibly to the outside for relief. However, he was focused on something else. Méndez quietly entered the back of the home. He looked around, quickly and intently, to ensure he was alone.

Leaning up against the wall was a chessboard. He located the sack containing the pieces. He reached into his pocket, grabbed a handful of coins, and carefully poured them into the sack. As he repeated with a second handful, he kept thinking *I wouldn't have a business without this man.*

Méndez returned as Johan reached the final portion of his monologue. Various emotions, from pride to anguish to hate to love, swept over Benjamin, Esther, and Becca.

Much as he began, Johan reiterated, "Ben saved me." Consumed by the aura in the room and blinking rapidly to fight off tears, he concluded, "He's my brother now, as if we share the same blood."

Méndez didn't let the moment linger more than a few seconds. In a matter-of-fact manner, he stated, "It will be dark soon. Johan, you know what to do. Don't bother with the garb. I'll dispose of that."

Johan stood up, awkwardly, nodded to Becca and Esther. He extended his right hand to Benjamin who responded immediately in kind. As if a major accord had been agreed upon, Méndez bonded his hand over their connected right hands. Méndez released his grasp, saying, "Go on now. It's time."

Johan exited purposefully.

"Benjamin, let's talk privately."

"Señor Méndez..."

Méndez stopped him by extending his arm and hand, "After all this time working together, you can certainly address me as Roberto, in your own home."

This lightened the atmosphere slightly before Benjamin continued.

"Then Roberto, if it is acceptable, I would like Esther and Rebecca to hear whatever you have to say."

"Very well then." He sat and faced the family.

Not surprisingly, Roberto stated that neither Ben nor Johan would be safe in Gibraltar. He talked about ways in which the situation might be managed under normal circumstances. But such was not the case now in Spain. Sadly, he reported on the evil spirit of vigilantism was sweeping over the countryside based on the recent decree. The depraved felt empowered to act without accountability.

Relying on his business acumen, Roberto dissected the situation. He told them Johan would depart that night traveling back to Amsterdam by land. Ben also had to leave immediately. However, a trip by land was too risky for him from Roberto's perspective. Searches were already underway. Crew members had blanketed the area and would be in the *aljamas* shortly. Sizable rewards were offered for his capture. While there were inherent dangers in sea voyages, Roberto was passionate that Ben could be smuggled out safely.

Roberto segued to the main topic, "I suppose you know that all of you should leave Spain."

Benjamin, with Esther on one side of him and Becca on the other, took hold of their hands, before replying, "We came to that conclusion once we heard conversion will not guarantee our physical safety. It's just a matter of time. We have been planning for a while."

Esther tried to contribute with some sense of optimism, "Lisbon seems right."

Becca stared despondently at the floor.

Roberto leaned forward for the last and most difficult part of the interaction. He sighed and spoke deliberately, "I'm afraid in this part of the world, we haven't learned enough from your brilliant scholar, Maimonides, on how to treat people. My sources to the West tell me Portugal will follow the way of Spain. You may be able to live there peacefully for a year or two, maybe five at the most."

Roberto moved his eyes from Esther to Becca, who continued to look at the floor. After a few silent moments, she looked up at Roberto. He continued, "Casablanca and Fez were once good cities but there will be such an exodus to the South, Benjamin will be relegated to menial labor. Amsterdam is a prosperous trading center and I suspect that someday it will be a major port. You should go North to Holland."

Benjamin extrapolated, "With Johan."

"Yes, with Johan," said Roberto quietly.

"When?" questioned Benjamin. But he knew the answer as he tightened his grips on his wife and daughter.

"As you said Benjamin, it is just a matter of time. I know this will be difficult for all of you, but you have to leave before dawn to rendezvous with Johan."

Becca returned her father's grip while barely adjusting her empty gaze at the floor. Esther buried her face in Benjamin's shoulder as her tears moistened his shirt. Becca spoke tentatively, as if afraid of more bad news, "What about Ben?"

Roberto closed with, "I will get a message to Ben to meet you in Amsterdam. I'm indeed sorry for you and hope that one day Spain will come to its senses."

Becca said resolutely, “I will gather my things.”

Her matter-of-fact reaction seemed to strengthen both Benjamin and Esther.

“Thank you for this, Roberto, Señor Méndez, my friend,” said Benjamin, resigned yet relieved. “Let’s have some sherry so you can give me the details.”

11

GIBRALTAR, KINGDOM OF CASTILE, SPAIN
WEDNESDAY, MAY 2, 1492

Ben had managed to fall asleep in Mino's berth, which was little more than the second highest hammock in a stack of four. When all four were occupied, the sag in the middle placed one's head higher than the arse of the man above him.

With three other similar configurations in the small quarters, sixteen men could rest when the tools and supplies in the room were stowed properly. The captain and his first mate had their own quarters.

At sea, there was always an empty hammock as night watch duty rotated among the crew. However, the Niña was in port.

Luke and Duncan fabricated a reason to go ashore for a few hours. Luke conducted some general reconnaissance. Meanwhile Duncan met clandestinely with Señor Méndez, who had arranged for Ben's sequestration on the Niña.

Both returned just after the captain's hourglass emptied for the first time. They let Ben sleep. When he awoke about two hours later, Luke and Duncan entered the sleeping quarters while Mino posted himself outside of the room's entryway.

Struggling to get upright in the hammock, Ben eagerly petitioned, "David, Luis. What did you learn?"

Luke placed his index finger over his lips then whispered, "First of all, you must always call us by our Christian names on ship. Sorry if we were too casual in our jest with you the other day while the skipper was ashore." Raising his voice slightly Luke continued, "I'm afraid it is not safe for you to exit the ship right now. There is a frenzy of activity in town. Sharks are smelling blood." Luke then detailed how Ben's good deeds had been misconstrued and exaggerated to suit the thirst for revenge.

Ben concluded, "Can't I just wait it out here?"

"I wish it were that simple," continued Luke. "The search would eventually lead to the ships. But, by a twist of fate, we are departing immediately. Captain Pinzon received word we must sail to Palo de la Frontera without delay." Now whispering, "So, my brother, in some strange way, you are in a good place, given the circumstances."

Ben leaned forward, about to speak. Luke anticipated and cut him off, "No doubt you are concerned about your family and the man who helped you. Duncan met with Señor Méndez and will explain."

Duncan repeated a brief, yet carefully constructed monologue Roberto Méndez had him memorize. It addressed the key facts in logical order. Méndez, with coaching from the elder Solomon, knew this would be necessary for Ben to embrace the plan.

Duncan spoke about antisemitism, the dangers for the Jews in Spain and Portugal, the limitations of Africa, and the opportunities to the North. He explained that the Dutchman could not remain with his ship. He would travel with Ben's parents and sister.

Ben listened intently. As Duncan began to conclude, "Amsterdam, will be your..."

Ben interrupted, "That journey will take at least seventy-two days."

Duncan looked at Luke. Luke returned the look. They both looked at Mino.

"What?" said Ben breaking silence.

Duncan looked back at Ben, "How did you know that?"

Ben wanted to hear more details, so he tried not to be sidetracked. "It's just something I can do with numbers and distances. Tell me more. We can talk about my calculations later."

"That we will indeed," said Mino. "Continue Duncan."

Duncan listed the major stopping points along the anticipated route for the family. Ben knew meeting them en route would be difficult but not impossible. Despite the anguish he felt for his family, he was comforted that a plan existed. He confessed, "Destiny has brought me to you. I am eager to meet the ship's captain and the rest of your mates."

Luke clasped his hands in front of his chest. Seemingly lost in thought, he rocked back and forth, as if davening in prayer. He stopped his motion, "The problem is that the captain and most of the crew do not know of you."

Duncan continued, "We're not sure of the proper approach. Unfortunately, that's the one part of the puzzle Señor Méndez left for us to solve."

Mino leaned in and contributed, "Please stay in here, and try to rest more, while we deliberate on this. Isn't there one more thing, Duncan?"

"Right Mino."

Duncan reached both hands behind his back under his shirt. His arms looked like flapping wings as he dislodged the object tucked into his leggings.

Duncan brought the object forward in his right hand. For protection, it was wrapped in some tattered cloth and bound with some thin remnants of rope. Having been told how important it was, Duncan joined his left hand to it and presented it to Ben as if it were a treasure they might find on their voyage.

Ben took the book and said, "My gratitude to all of you and for your commitment to my book.

12

NEAR SAN ROQUE, KINGDOM OF CASTILE, SPAIN
THURSDAY, MAY 3, 1492

In contrast to the reserved persona Johan exhibited at the Solomon house, he greeted Benjamin with a hearty handshake as they arrived at the rendezvous point in the early light. Johan then extended his hand to Esther. She reciprocated with a brief grasp, prompting Becca to reach out.

Although barely nineteen and not bulky in stature, Johan carried himself with authority. His blond beard had been neatly trimmed, lining his angled jaw. A few beads of perspiration glistened in the morning sun. Johan had been working hard to prepare for the journey. Becca couldn't help but notice the defined contour of his shoulders and arms.

"I have an honor to make a journey by you," said Johan in relatively good Spanish. He continued, "I will try to speak some Spanish on you, but it is important you learn the language of Amsterdam. She is an old city, of nearly four hundred years, and we have our own way to talk."

Benjamin appreciated Johan's reference to his city using the feminine gender and replied, "*Ik versta.*" I understand.

"You do know some Dutch. And your accent is good."

"I've worked with traders, so I've learned out of necessity. I have more to learn. My wife and daughter even more."

"We will have plenty of time, I'm afraid," said Johan, glancing down, dejected, as his life had also been upended. He continued, "I know you are all very tired, but we should prepare ourselves, then we can rest. We should depart tomorrow before dawn."

"Very well," said Benjamin. "Allow me a moment to get the women situated," realizing he had just referred to his daughter as an adult for the first time.

"Of course," replied Johan, oblivious to Benjamin's epiphany.

Johan showed Benjamin how to form a makeshift tent composed of two tarps secured between trees with stakes at the corners. This would provide them with privacy and protection from the elements.

Benjamin took a deep breath and exhaled rapidly, slumping his shoulders. *My new home, I should ask Esther if we should attach the mezuzah from the doorpost of our house onto a tent pole.*

Esther made her way to the shelter to lie down. Meanwhile, Becca fidgeted with the few Solomon possessions they were able to take with them. She would pick something up, view it for a moment and return it to its original place. It was almost as if she was examining and cataloging ancient artifacts.

Benjamin noticed and suggested she get some rest along with her mother. But Becca was too agitated. A rustling tree, with some low hanging branches outside the perimeter of their makeshift site, distracted her. She edged towards it.

Johan and Benjamin busied themselves with re-organizing for the trip. They unloaded the Solomon cart, placing the durable and perishable goods in separate areas. After completing that task, they began melding the provisions Johan delivered.

They worked methodically. The process was relatively simple. A hand motion here or there seemed to be all that was required. They placed the goods back in the cart, thoughtfully balancing the load for the oxen.

Johan sat down. Benjamin was about to join him but wandered over towards the tarps instead. Esther was sound asleep, and he half expected Becca to be napping.

"Have you seen Becca?" asked Benjamin of Johan.

"I didn't pay attention to her as we worked."

Benjamin called out her name several times, increasing each broadcast in volume and urgency.

"Please stay here with your wife," urged Johan. "I will find her."

Before Benjamin had a chance to react, Johan sprinted from the campsite. He reconnoitered the surrounding area which he had surveyed the prior evening when setting up for the Solomons. He had a good idea of Becca's general direction.

Johan made his way to the trail they would use later for their journey. After fifty or so paces, he moved into the brush to the East. He canvassed that area moving slightly southward repeating her name in a normal sounding tone. The area wasn't inviting for humans. As expected, he didn't find Becca. He repeated his search in a westerly direction.

Johan navigated a small stream, following it to a pond. Finally, as normal sounding as his solicitations, a youthful female voice answered,

"I'm here."

"Your mother is sleeping, and your father is worried."

"I'm sorry," said Becca in a monotone, barely moving her lips and maintaining her gaze straight ahead.

Johan followed her line of sight southward. The peak of Gibraltar was awash in morning sun. An orange disk hung in the sky to the east. A few traces of clouds graced the horizon.

Becca sat stiffly, teary eyed. Johan was struck by Mother Nature's canvas and the poignancy of the situation. Johan stayed quiet as he sat down beside her, continuing to gaze in the same direction.

After what seemed a long time, but was only a minute or two, Becca remarked factually, "It is beautiful."

"Yes, it is."

"Why does this have to be?" she asked rhetorically.

But Johan responded, "It is the destiny of your people, sad to say. You have so many blessings, yet many burdens."

"You were attacked and you're not Jewish."

"True. But I was a victim because of what I said to some strangers. It doesn't matter what Jews say."

She contemplated that then said, "How do you know so much?"

"We are not so backwards in Amsterdam. I had to study from Moses to Moses."

"Moses to Moses?"

"Ja, from the one who parted the Red Sea to the one some people call Rambam. I didn't like it at times, but some of the stories were just as interesting as the ones traders told when they came to make deals with my father."

"You're sounding like Ben in some ways."

Johan smiled, took her by the forearm and gently coaxed her up. "Now come, before your mother wakes up and your father loses his mind."

13

On the Western Mediterranean Sea
Saturday, May 12, 1492

Captain Pinzon was angered when Mino revealed Ben's presence. Pinzon was adamant he would not tolerate a stowaway. Mino made a compelling case, positioning Ben as a person that could help the crew in more ways than physical labor. Over the next two days, as Pinzon observed the ease with which Ben interacted with his crew, his feelings waned to minor irritation.

Ben earned the respect of his mates by applying his mathematical skills. He provided instantaneous calculations of sail areas and triangulated distances that would have taken others as much as an hour if they could make them at all.

Fortunately for Ben, he established his value away from the commissary. His intermittent nausea was compounded by the noxious odor, at least to him, of food prepared on the *fogón*, a small oven used shipboard. While the provisions were first rate, he stayed as far away as possible from the wafting of gibbing herring and cooking meat.

As the ship tacked through the strait between Morocco and Spain, Ben was pleased he fared with most of the crew, only heaving occasionally. The funnel created by the extended points of Africa and Europe often accelerated the prevailing westerly winds making seas quite rough. For a day and a half, the crew struggled with little progress and little sleep.

The winds finally dissipated into a mild breeze allowing the captain to set his sails and proceed slowly but smoothly in a north by northwesterly direction. Following the mid-day meal, the crew relaxed, scattering about the top deck.

Luke, the ship's chief navigator, opened a box at his feet. He lifted a brass astrolabe, eight inches in diameter, one of two aboard.

"Ben," he shouted. "Help me inspect these instruments."

"Happy to help, but I don't know the first thing about them."

"It's about time you learned, and I suspect you'll be teaching us shortly."

Luke handed him one of the astrolabes and removed the second one, larger at twelve inches across.

Ben held the instrument by the ring at its top, dangling a circular disk with four pie-shaped cuts pointing to the center. From there, two attached clock-hands radiated, opposite one another.

Ben gave Luke a smile.

Luke smiled back, "You are a man of angles are you not?"

"Well yes," replied Ben as he pensively rotated the device. He noticed a few star names were etched on the device's perimeter and what looked like an aiming mechanism. Ben continued, "May I see the other one?"

"Surely," said Luke as they exchanged.

Ben noticed that various earthly locations had been etched on an inner disk on the one he held. Lisbon and Lagos were spelled in their entirety. Ben was able to discern *Cabo V* represented Cabo Verde. But *PdlF* confused him.

Luke prompted him, "What is going through that mind of yours?"

Ben speculated, "It appears you aim it at specific points in the sky to find your latitude. I can't figure just yet why the locations on land are marked on a single plane. They are not in a straight line from here, or from anywhere, as far as I can tell."

"Excellent reasoning. I expected nothing less from you. Let me give you a hint. We use the sun and the North Star, as it never moves in the heavens."

Ben theorized, "The instrument in my hands can give us a relative position to points on land, but the one you're holding can't do that because you don't know those points when you cross the ocean."

"Lord," muttered Luke, closing his eyes and shaking his head. Now raising his voice, "Men, we have a genius on board."

"Another Luke," stated Mino from across the deck. "Just what we need," he continued sarcastically. Ten crew members were above deck, within earshot of Luke. Nine laughed.

Then Ben fired off a series of questions to Luke on daylight navigating, using heavenly objects which changed their position, and steadying the instrument when windy. After a few more minutes, Luke tried to close the conversation. "Enough for lesson number one. As I said, soon you'll be the teacher."

Luke's backup navigator promised himself under his breath, "Not if I have a say."

"One last question, for now," implored Ben. "What does PdlF mean?"

"Palos de la Frontera. It's the place we will meet the Santa Maria and the La Pinta, our sister ships."

14

Near Merida, Kingdom of Castile, Spain
Monday, May 21, 1492

While travel by sea could be dangerous, both Benjamin and Johan were acutely aware that a land journey of such magnitude could be even more challenging. The relative civility of Gibraltar and Amsterdam did not permeate throughout the countryside. They would have to be extremely careful.

The group fell into a regular routine. Stop traveling by early afternoon. Rest and set-up camp. Rest some more. Review maps and plans for the journey's next segment. Eat and pack before dusk. Rise while still dark. Make final preparations and break camp at dawn. Following this regimen, they were able to travel during the coolest and the safest time.

Johan performed the heavy lifting and tended to the oxen. Benjamin assembled and disassembled the sleeping areas. Esther prepared the meals. Becca did odd jobs as orchestrated by the other three. Keeping Becca busy on a variety of tasks was the best way to assuage her grief and maintain what little morale remained within her. Leaving her beloved Gibraltar and her best friend, Ben, weighed heaviest.

The convoy made good progress in the first eleven days, averaging about fifteen miles each day. They would take a day on the banks of the Guadiana River to wash clothes, rest the animals and make minor repairs. A slight breeze across the water tempered the heat in the campsite.

With the work done, Benjamin asked Johan, "Do you play chess?"

"*Natuurlijk*. It is very popular in Amsterdam. I did expect that you play."

"And why would that be?"

"Is it not true those who have forced you to leave, Ferdinand and Isabella, are avid students of the game?"

"And I didn't expect you would know about their chess prowess. Shouldn't I practice so that one day I can defeat them?" continued Benjamin in the rhetorical duologue.

"Indeed," replied Johan with appropriate sarcasm.

As the rules of chess varied in different parts of the world, Benjamin inquired, "Do you move the queen one square at a time, or any direction as far as she can go without obstruction?"

"Either way is fine with me, but I prefer more mobility for her."

"Me too," said Benjamin. "What about bishops and pawns?"

"Diagonal for the bishops and two squares for pawns on the first move if you'd like."

"I can see you are familiar with some of the new ways to play."

"Let us engage."

Benjamin retrieved the board and placed it on a makeshift table. As he handled the sack containing the pieces, it felt bulky and noticeably heavier than expected. Benjamin reached in. He furrowed his brow when his grasp yielded more than chess pieces. Suddenly, he jerked his hand out as if bitten by a scorpion.

Johan jumped in response, "What is it?"

"Pardon my reaction," said Benjamin. "Nothing seems to be alive in here, but equally surprising." He concluded, "There are indeed chessmen but there seem to be coins as well."

Confused by Benjamin's seemingly contradictory reactions, Johan interjected, "Coins are good."

"A blessing or a curse?" Raising his voice, "Esther, Rebecca, please come here immediately."

Mother and Daughter dutifully responded from across the campsite. As they approached, Benjamin carefully and quietly emptied the bag onto the table. He then separated the contents into three groups, gold, silver, and combatants.

"Do either of you know anything about this?"

Esther and Becca looked at the table, stunned to see a display of gold and silver coins. Both said, "What?" at almost the same time, sounding almost comedic. Benjamin did not find any levity in their reaction. "Becca, could Ben have anything to do with this?"

"I swear I don't know anything about this. Ben and I played chess a few weeks ago. There were no coins in the sack."

Benjamin devised a plan to conceal the silver and gold, at least the thirty-two coins smallest in size. Johan and Benjamin carefully whittled out the bottom of the chess pieces. Johan carved the white pieces which would receive silver inlays while Benjamin tackled the brown counterparts.

Meanwhile, the women concocted a makeshift glue from cooking ingredients, primarily flour and boiling cow bones. An hour later, not long after the men had completed their woodwork, Esther found the right proportions, temperatures, and timing to form the glue.

As the men supplemented the pieces in their royal armies, Rebecca and Esther sewed the remaining thirteen pieces into various garments.

After the work was completed. Esther suggested to Johan he tell them about the place that would be their new home.

There was much to convey about Amsterdam. Figuring there was no rush given the length of their journey, Johan proceeded slowly. He explained, "The core of the city is its harbor, on the Ij Bay. It is linked to the Amstel River by a canal, called Singel. There are large earthen walls behind this moat, providing a ring of protection for the city from both man and nature. As the city grows, additional canals are planned, surrounding the city, like the rings of a tree."

The city's layout stimulated many questions, primarily from Becca. She wanted to know if the water froze in the winter, how wide was this Singel, did people live on boats on the water, how do you cross it, do people swim in the canal and the bay and the river?

Johan's passion for his homeland's beauty helped ease the fears of the unknown for his companions...destined to live beneath sea level rather than above it, in humidity rather than dryness, in coolness rather than heat.

15

GIBRALTAR, KINGDOM OF CASTILE, SPAIN

WEDNESDAY, MAY 23, 1492

The intense pace continued for Roberto Méndez and his employees. With the surge in shipping traffic and some forty thousand Jews mobilizing in Spain, there was no relief in sight.

The long spring days allowed work to continue into the early evening. Méndez walked the warehouse floor, spot checking the inventory, as he did at the end of each day. A man stood motionless in the doorway, blocking the setting sun. Méndez immediately noticed the stationary figure since the rest of those around him looked like a colony of ants, seemingly moving at random.

As Méndez began to move towards him, his foreman approached, "Sir, there is a messenger for you from the North."

"Thank you, Manuel. Please tell him to meet me in my office."

"Very well," replied Manuel.

Méndez entered his office. Within a few seconds the messenger arrived. He silently extended a small scroll of paper. Both standing, Méndez untied the small closure and began reading. He sat down. Keeping his eyes fixed on the document, he motioned to the messenger to be seated. He read the text of some 200 words.

"Did you stop in Seville?"

"Yes sir, as requested. I got here as fast as I could."

"No doubt."

Méndez then unrolled the document on the table in front of him and placed some polished rock weights on its corners. On his second pass, he studied the verbiage more carefully. Meanwhile, the messenger closed his eyes, trying to remain erect.

Méndez, now laboring over each word, sighed then said, "I was afraid this might happen."

The messenger, now lingering on the edge of sleep, heard the utterance and snapped forward, "Sir?"

"I'm sorry. It sounds dangerous for the travelers."

"Yes sir. It appears that way sir. Sir, I am expected to return immediately."

Without hesitation, Méndez commanded, "You will eat and rest properly. I will make the appropriate notations in my instructions."

Méndez stood up from the table. He leaned out the doorway into the warehouse and ordered the first person who passed by, "Ali, will you tell Matias we have a visitor for the night."

"Right away, sir."

"Also, we will need to dispatch a second messenger tomorrow morning with our guest."

Communications were a vital part of the Méndez enterprise. Méndez closed the office door. With lodging and transport arrangements in progress, he turned to his desk preparing to consume another scarce resource, paper. Made primarily from cloth and discarded garments, he would use two small pieces, one for each messenger.

Méndez lit a candle and placed it into a lantern. He sharpened a quill, then filled its hollow stem with ink. He fidgeted, placing the quill in its holder. He wasn't ready to write, so he prepared a second quill.

Five minutes expired until he began to write meticulously. One document would travel by the returning messenger to his trading partner in Seville. The second document would be carried by a messenger to Christoforo Colombo.

16

ATLANTA, GEORGIA, USA
MARBELLA, PROVINCE OF MÁLAGA, SPAIN
FRIDAY, JULY 26, 2002

About 2:30 p.m. local time, Delta flight 56 began its descent into Hartsfield-Jackson Atlanta International Airport. The lead flight attendant diligently recited a canned script, slowly enunciating the airport's full name. The former mayor and city's charismatic black leader, Maynard Jackson, was memorialized by adding his name to that of his predecessor and member of the white establishment from decades ago, William Hartsfield.

O.T. anticipated a day when the name would be elongated to acknowledge a civic leader from the area's burgeoning Asian community. He imagined something like *the Hartsfield-Jackson-Phan Atlanta International Airport.* Then leave it to a clever journalist to invent an acronym for it.

On the descent to runway 27-left, Rusty and O.T. had a view of downtown. Its tall structures were split horizontally by a layer of light brown haze.

While Rusty could afford to fly private, it was an expensive proposition, and another worry he didn't think he needed. He recalled Payne Stewart's untimely demise when everyone, including the pilots, fell asleep and subsequently died due to an oxygen leak. Besides, Delta could take him practically anywhere from Atlanta. After hundreds of flights, most with O.T., the airline treated them very well.

Rusty preferred the window with O.T. next to him, providing another layer between the occasional obnoxious fan or the paparazzi.

On the final approach, the first-class flight attendants began distributing the few garments they had collected during boarding.

"Here's your sport coat Mr. Stephens and yours too Mr. Sills," said a lanky blond in her thirties. She then leaned between them, smiled, and whispered,

"The co-pilot wanted me to wish you good luck at the PGA Championship."

O.T. laughed, "Autograph requested?"

"He didn't say anything..."

Rusty handed her a signed Delta cocktail napkin before she could finish the sentence, "Thanks for the great service."

O.T. needled Rusty, commenting that their lawyer and agent, Brent Lattimer, would not be too happy with the unauthorized autograph. Brent was a partner at King and Spalding, an elite international law firm based in Atlanta.

Rusty responded in kind, "Yeah, they certainly run a tight ship at K and S. I'm sure I have just dealt a crippling blow to the Rusty Stephens franchise."

Five minutes after the tires on the 767 scorched the runway, the aircraft crawled into gate E-3. In twenty minutes, Rusty and O.T. deplaned, collected their luggage, and navigated through customs then immigration. *Ahead of schedule* thought O.T.

They dumped their luggage for transport to the baggage claim, hardly breaking stride to the transportation mall, a mile long subway, connecting the concourses of gates with the main terminal facility. After stops at D, C, B, A, and T, the train pulled into the baggage claim stop.

Their driver awaited as they ascended the long escalator. The typical livery sign was not needed. O.T. looked around for a second, spotted a young man in khakis and a white Ralph Lauren polo shirt. He waved and walked towards him, calling out, "Hey Nguyen, how are you?"

"I'm great. Welcome back. Sure is fun waiting for you guys."

O.T. followed, "Yep, this has to be one of the better places for people watching."

Rusty handed Nguyen his carry-on, "How's everything? Not eating too much at the Varsity?"

"Not much, but hey, don't knock it. It's still a great place for a burger and now there's a room that broadcasts only sports with Georgia Tech athletes. They show highlights of Salley, Geiger, Anderson, Price, Marbury, and the golfers with a lot of Bobby Jones."

"I didn't realize you're such a hoops fan."

"More than football. By the way, I made the inquiries for you. No problem."

O.T. shot Rusty a curious glance as they hoisted themselves into the spacious stretch Hummer. They hadn't been in the vehicle more than a minute when Rusty's pocket buzzed. He eased out his phone, smiled and said, "Speak of the devil."

O.T. listened to Rusty's side of the conversation.

"Hi Brent. How are you?... ...Great... ...Anything urgent?... ...We need to change that. Any problems?... ...Good, I'll explain later. Thanks."

"Change what?" asked O.T. barely a second after Rusty closed his phone and replaced it in his pocket.

"I forgot to mention it."

With a wide grin on his face, O.T. fired back, "All this with Nguyen and Brent has something to do with Sandy, doesn't it?"

"Sort of," confessed Rusty. "I had Brent postpone our meeting Monday."

"Fine with me," said O.T. biting his tongue.

Nguyen waited for the southbound traffic to clear then made a left opposite Peachtree Way, easing the elongated Hummer under the entry structure fronting Park Place, a high-rise at 2660 Peachtree Street.

Skeptical at first, Rusty warmed to his condo. Terrific location. Great views from the thirty-sixth floor. Most important, it was ultra-secure and private, due to a large extent on the building's high-profile clientele like his neighbor, Elton John.

As Rusty shifted his body to exit the limo, he said to O.T., "I almost forgot. Sandy and I were on the Internet the other night. She showed some genealogy sites. We typed in your name for shits and giggles. There were too many related names, so we tried with a dash. Can't remember what came back but if you're interested, let me know and I'll send her your email address."

"Might be kinda fun. You may not be able to call me a mutt much longer."

Rusty laughed, "Enjoy a couple days of R&R."

By the time their conversations concluded, Nguyen had Rusty's bags unloaded. A uniformed doorman moved the luggage to a waiting elevator.

"Welcome home, Mr. Stephens. Let me help you up."

"I got 'em Tim, thanks. But could you arrange a ride for me over to Tech at nine tomorrow morning?"

"Will do."

Just as Rusty had a pre-shot routine on the course, he had a routine for returning to his condo after a trip. First, carry his bags to the large walk-in closet off his bedroom. Next, turn on the stereo to Tech radio, open the shades in the living area and take in the view for a few seconds. Then scan the fridge for future reference, to see what his housekeeper had provisioned. Finally, he would peruse the mail, as laid out in order of importance by Brent Lattimer's assistant.

Today, he broke with the pattern. Barely through the door, he dropped his bags on the floor with a thud, making a beeline for the study. He switched on his computer and took a seat while the Dell booted up. He launched AOL. After entering his screen name password, Rusty looked at his stack of magazine arrivals placed on his desk. He was disappointed when he did not hear the robotic prompt of "You've got mail."

He slumped his shoulders. He wondered if he gave Sandy the other email address. He made the switch then continued to sort through the magazines, anticipating the familiar phrase. Rusty knew he had mail as he left some unopened entries when he departed for Spain.

"Damn," yelled Rusty not as a curse but as a revelation. He remembered he turned the computer's speakers off the last time he used the machine. When he reverted to his private account, he spotted an email from scole@columbia.edu.

He opened it. A message appeared indicating an electronic greeting card awaited him. Rusty clicked on the link. Five seconds later, a brief animation began. A pixie girl and a preppy boy run towards one another in a high school hallway. They stop a foot apart, slowly lean over, smack each other on the lips, then do an about face and walk in the opposite direction. All done to the sixty's classic, *Will I See You in September*. It ended with a customized message, "Missing you already, Sandy."

Rusty's grin stretched from ear to ear. *Not only was the e-card cute, but Sandy had spent time searching for the proper way to express her feelings. Either that or she was having a bunch of one-nighters and mounting an excellent follow-up campaign.* He laughed out loud at the very idea.

Rusty tapped the "reply" button, saw Sandy's email address filled in, and typed, "Missing you too. And yes, before September."

He hesitated on the closing. He couldn't say love, could he? And sincerely sounded a bit disingenuous after the intensity of their encounter. Then he remembered O.T. had once shown him some emoticons. He knew there must be a drop-down list but had no idea how to access it. He would have to make one up. First, he typed :-) which he has seen before. That seemed too plain. He typed 8-! thinking an exclamation point was in order. He hit send.

Fifteen seconds later, a response appeared on Rusty's screen. "Now that's funny. I haven't seen a ! in any emoticons and I didn't know you wore glasses."

"I don't."

"Sometimes an 8 instead of : means glasses."

"Oh."

"Don't worry, I won't tell the press."

Ironic, thought Rusty. *How am I going to tell her about the press, among other things?"*

17

Manhattan, New York, USA
Sidney & Waterville, Maine, USA
Saturday, July 27, 2002

Spain was great but returning to Manhattan always exhilarated Sandy, even during the oppressive summer heat. She wasn't too crazy about trudging up two flights of stairs, suitcase in tow, to her Upper West Side walk-up on 87th Street. But then again, she wasn't on the fifth floor and her apartment faced a street rather than a noisier avenue.

Sandy enjoyed interacting with her fellow tenants beyond the occasional "Have a nice day." It all started with the anti-graffiti task force, as the building's super liked to call it.

A year ago, just after the landlord's maintenance team applied a fresh coat of paint to the common areas, some mischievous teens slipped into the building and couldn't resist the canvas. Perhaps due to the freshness of the surface, the "Fuck You" above the banister on the first staircase was neatly inscribed. Its companion, also neat and halfway up to the second floor was "Fuck You Too."

This inspired Tamara Wright, a talented graphic artist with the apartment across the hall from Sandy. No stranger to graffiti, having grown up in Spanish Harlem, she masterfully closed off some loops and extended the other letters to create "Book You" and "Book You Today." And so, the task force was born and traipsing up the steps always elicited a smile from Sandy.

Sandy entered her 500 square foot studio. As usual, the first thing she did was say hello to Katoo, a small soapstone sculpture which resembled Katy as a puppy. Sandy was hungry and needed sleep. She fought both urges, extracted her laptop from her carry-on, and snapped it into its docking station.

While starting the computer, she called her parents.

Herman picked up the ringing phone, "Hello."

"Hi Daddy. How's Mom?"

"Mom's fine. Tell me about Cameron."

"I will, but what's going on with Mom?"

Herman explained the way in which he found Beth. He tempered the seriousness of his explanations by detailing how man's best friend turned out to be woman's best friend. Sandy listened patiently. Finally, Herman asked, "Still there?"

She answered tersely. "I'm here," clearly passing the buck back to Herman. Knowing his daughter's forthright nature and genuine concern, he spoke candidly. He couldn't be 100% sure about his wife's condition. Therefore, he had insisted on some follow-up.

She then asked for her mother. "Hi Mom. How ya feeling?"

"Great, really. Now tell me how you're doing."

Once Sandy heard the positive tone of her mother's voice, she felt comfortable responding.

"Mom, I really like this guy. He's nice, good looking, seems to have a good career, and he's different."

"How different?"

"They say opposites attract. He's different in a good way."

"Jewish?"

"No," letting the word linger, as if to say, "Do you have an issue with that?"

In the spirit of guidance, Beth concluded, "You just met this fellow. Remember, opposite and different are not the same thing. But you better tell your dad about him. He's always complaining that Katy knows more about your love life than he does.

Beth handed the phone back to Herman. Sandy provided her father the details of her meeting with Cameron and Brian in the nightclub and an abridged version on her subsequent evening with him.

"Sounds like a long-distance relationship. When will you see him again?"

"We haven't figured that out yet, but hopefully soon. Keep me posted on Mom. Bye Daddy."

"Bye sweetheart."

·••◆••·

She did have another email from Cameron but was disappointed it wasn't more personal. Cameron wrote that he was going to be traveling and very busy. He closed with a "hope to see you soon," which seemed encouraging yet standard. Sandy rationalized in her head, *at least it was more thoughtful than typical emails, with their abbreviations, choppy phrasing, and standard salutations.*

He also provided Brian's email address saying , "My half-breed (ha ha) friend is interested in investigating his lineage." She set up an address book entry for Brian, started to sign-off, when an instant message arrived from Sally.

Salinmaine: Hi sis, on-line on a sat nite?
Sancole917: just got in from spain.
Salinmaine: howz cameron
Sancole917: k I guess
Salinmaine: guess? Things cool off
Sancole917: too early to tell, why are you home
Salinmaine: Just about to leave for you know whose pub
Sancole917: have you gone sleaze
Salinmaine: sat night summer colby single profs come in
Sancole917: all 3 ???
Salinmaine: ha ha, more like 15, some cute
Sancole917: pls call a cab if you drink, btw whats with mom
Salinmaine: says she's fine, MRI next week, luvya
Sancole917: u2 ttfn

Sandy looked at the clock in the kitchen, or rather the area in a corner of the apartment with the appliances. It was just after 10:00 p.m. which translated to 4:00 in the morning in Spain, where her day had started. But she felt a sudden jolt of energy brought on by the noise of the city. In stereotypical New Yorker fashion, she decided to hit the streets for a cup of coffee, the Sunday Times and perhaps some noshes for the morning.

Closing the door behind her, Sandy pushed back on it to ensure it was locked. As she began to fumble for her keys to secure the deadbolt lock, she heard the distinctive slide of shoes on the staircase. The sound was quite different from the older tenants and men, who tended to clomp their way up.

Still facing the door, Sandy called out, "Tam?"

"San?" replied Tamara, elongating her monosyllabic nickname.

Sandy turned to see a stunning woman, 5'8" in heels, Capri pants, a midriff top exposing a firm mocha belly decorated with a half inch chain hanging from a small piercing. Her hair was pulled back severely with a pair of goggle style glasses resting on the forehead of a subtly painted face.

"Wow, look at you. Home so early?"

"You know, first date, dinner at eight, not great..."

At which point Sandy finished the expression, "last date."

They laughed and Sandy continued, "I'm going for coffee, come on."

"Why not," said Tamara rhetorically as she stopped two steps short of the landing to wait for Sandy.

A warm breeze ruffled the paper place settings on the table at the outdoor café where they dropped anchor.

"So, how was your trip?"

"Okay, not wonderful, maybe wonderful," monotoned Sandy.

Tamara leaned forward, "Girl, you want to try that again?"

Before Sandy had a chance to respond, their order was delivered.

Sandy immediately attacked her Cobb salad, stabbing at a piece of turkey. Tamara sipped her latte and listened attentively as the encounter with Cameron was revealed between bites. Every thirty seconds or so, Tamara furrowed her brow slightly just to indicate she was absorbing the story.

"Sounds like you have a case of like at first sight."

Puzzled, Sandy bounced back with, "Love at first sight?"

"Sister, you can't tell if you're in love until you go through some shit together. You're deeply in like. Nothing wrong with that. And besides, you don't even know when, if ever, you'll see this guy again. So be cool."

"I don't know if I can ... be cool."

Tamara could see her friend was fading from the long day and time change. "Don't think about it until you've gotten some sleep."

"Thanks for listening." Reaching for the check, "Let me get this. Share the *Times*?"

"Sure."

"I'm sleeping as long as I can. You take it. And you can trash the ads and sports section if you want."

The women entered their respective apartments. Despite Sandy's exhaustion, she decided to take a final check of her email before collapsing on her Murphy bed. A message was marked as new in her in-box. A surprise but not the one she wanted. The sender was not Cameron Stephens but his colleague, Brian Sills.

Brian detailed his curiosity about the family name. He recalled that his grandparents referenced a longer name from time to time, but he wasn't sure if it was hyphenated. As she typed her response, she mumbled sarcastically, "Well that certainly clears things up."

18

ATLANTA, GEORGIA, USA
MONDAY, JULY 29, 2002

As the cab approached Tech, the Georgia Institute of Technology, Rusty could see the building commonly known as the tit. The domed symmetrical athletic arena was topped with a circular windowed area and a fixture at the pinnacle that very much resembled a nipple.

The four-mile drive from his condo could take anywhere from ten to forty-five minutes depending on traffic, now discussed in the same breath with L.A., New York, Boston, and Chicago. Much of the traffic had cleared by 9:00 a.m.

With time to spare, Rusty decided he could enjoy a leisurely walk through the grounds, checking out the never-ending construction in progress. Shortly after he first arrived in Atlanta, O.T. took him to see Jerry Farber, a local comedian who insisted the state bird of Georgia should be a crane rather than the brown thrasher.

After entering the faculty office building, Rusty scanned the directory. He then bypassed the elevator for the staircase to his right. He ascended, taking two steps at a time. A plaque indicated that offices 200 - 250 were located on the left corridor.

The door was open to office 248.

"Professor Washington?"

"I am," responded a black woman, fifty-ish, looking more like a newscaster than an academic. "You must be Mr. Stephens. Please come in. Do you prefer Cameron or Rusty?"

"Cameron's fine."

"I understand from President Clough that you'd like to audit my comparative religions class."

"Yes, I would."

"Why don't you wait until the start of the next quarter?"

"My travel schedule is pretty challenging. Quite frankly, I just met someone of a different faith who I like a lot. Made me realize I don't know much about religion, other than the one I was given."

The professor fiddled with her pen for a moment before responding, "I appreciate your candor and the modesty on your travel schedule."

She rose from her chair and extended her right hand, "Actually, you picked a good day to start."

"Great," shaking her hand. "Just out of curiosity, I didn't think the so-called trade school on North Avenue had religion classes."

They both smiled. Professor Washington said, "I think it was Albert Einstein who said, 'Science without religion is lame, religion without science is blind'. I'll see you in a few minutes."

Rusty arrived at the classroom about ten of. The small auditorium, with stadium seating, was already crowded. Rusty couldn't remember summer classes being this full. He took a seat to the side. A few of the students glanced his way possibly recognizing him. Any golf aficionados in the room knew Rusty was an alum but this was such an unlikely place for him, they had trouble connecting the dots.

At precisely 10:00, Professor Washington entered the room. The students settled almost instantly. She placed her attaché next to the end seat on the first row of chairs. She stood to the left of the podium and launched into a brief monologue.

"Good morning. I hope everyone had a nice weekend. I realize it's hard working on your team presentations during summer session. This concludes the section we have been doing on Moses Maimonides, or Rambam, as he was also known. Let me set the stage for this morning."

Moving away from the podium she continued, "Maimonides was born a Spanish Jew. The year of his birth is in dispute, perhaps 1135 or 1138. To avoid religious persecution, he fled with his family to Morocco then to the area now called Israel, and eventually to neighboring Egypt. Many believe his plans for a lifetime of religious training were interrupted when his brother, David, a jewelry merchant, perished on a voyage in the Indian Ocean, with much of the family fortune. Maimonides died in 1204. With that, let's have your presentations fill in some of the blanks."

From the initial skits and speeches, Rusty learned that Maimonides became a physician, one of his patients being the Sultan of Egypt. One team provided a quote Rusty found particularly interesting. On the 850th anniversary of his birth, Vitaly Naumkin, a Soviet scholar, observed, "Maimonides is perhaps the only philosopher in the Middle Ages, perhaps to this day, who symbolizes a confluence of four cultures— Greco Roman, Arab, Jewish, and Western."

When it seemed like all the presentations were over, five gangsta looking students moved to front and center wearing baggy clothes and sunglasses. The two girls wore hijab style hair coverings. One of the guys wore a Jewish prayer shawl, a tallit, with a yarmulke head covering, while another wore a chain necklace with a heavy silver cross hanging from it.

The last member of the group detached the microphone from the podium, cupped his hands around it and began spitting out a rap rhythm. After a few measures, the group began hopping and waving their arms from side-to-side. The rap began.

Pointing at themselves, "We be 'plexed."

Pointing at the audience, "You be 'plexed."

Pointing at the ceiling, "They be 'plexed."

The gestures repeated with, "We need Rambam. You need Rambam. They need Rambam."

Waving their left arms, "He scribed the Guide."

Crossing with their right arms, "He scribed the Guide."

Then opening both arms as if to welcome, "He scribed the Guide, *The Guide to the Perplexed.*"

The last word was screamed for emphasis and the second verse started.

"We can't do the law."

"You can't do the law."

"Call Moses."

"Moses ben."

"Ben Maimon."

"He scribed the code, he scribed the code, he scribed the code."

"It be the Mishnah Torah."

It was obvious the team was having fun, growing more confident with each verse.

"We can see the doctor."

"You can see the writer."

"They can see the leader."

"Rational for the Hebrews," spoken loudly by the Judaica clad member, as he hopped forward onto his right leg.

"Rational for the Muslims," spoken more loudly by one of the girls in a hijab as she dropped to both knees.

"Rational for the Christians," shouted with even more gusto with the crucifix extended to the heavens.

Then together, "Better be heeden' Rambam."

The group rapped three more verses before receiving a whooping ovation from the other students.

Professor Washington returned to the podium. "That's a hard act to follow. All of you did a great job today. But there was one thing you likely came upon but didn't touch on in your presentations. Rambam is often identified with the hierarchy, or ladder, of giving. Look it up if you haven't already. Think final exam."

"Finally, for you engineers and mathematicians that know Pascal, he said something remarkably similar, about four hundred years later, 'Noble deeds that are concealed are the most esteemed'. See you in a few days." She packed up her attaché case. She glanced at Cameron, sensitive to his desire for a low profile, and closed with, "Have a good afternoon, all."

19

RANCHO MIRAGE, CALIFORNIA, USA
TUESDAY, JULY 30, 2002

Last week's sales momentum vanished. Perhaps Tommy was pressing too much now that Sonya's scholarship had taken a substantial hit. He was exhausted, both mentally and physically.

As if on autopilot, he entered his apartment and flopped down on the couch. What to do about dinner? Out of the corner of his eye, he saw the kitchen phone flashing the numeral 1. With the kids and business using his cell phone, it couldn't be very important, so he ignored it for the moment. He snatched the remote from the coffee table and turned on the Golf Channel.

When the show broke for commercials, Tommy said authoritatively, "Okay, we're going with Healthy Choice," as if someone was listening and endorsing his positive intention. On the way to the freezer, he pressed the messages button on the answering machine.

"You have one new message."

The machine paused for a second. A male voice came on, "Hello, I'm tryin' to reach Thomas Torres. This is Hootie Johnson calling from The Augusta National Golf Club in Augusta, Georgia. Please call me back at your earliest convenience. My number is 706-667-7877. Thank you."

Tommy let out a loud laugh, thinking the southern accent wasn't half bad, wondering who Carlos conscripted for the gag. Caddies had far too much idle time while waiting to pick up a game. They were always cooking up new practical jokes or remodeling old ones. And Carlos was one of the best. Tommy dialed his mobile.

"Hey Tommy."

"You are one funny dude. Whoever you got did a great imitation of Hootie."

"Who?"

"Hootie!"

"And the Blowfish."

"Now that's even funnier."

"Tommy, I haven't got a clue what you're talking about. Come again. You called me. Need some help or something?"

"You already did it. I was feeling down. Your crank call cheered me up."

"I'll say it again buddy. I don't know what you're talking about?"

"You didn't leave me a message?"

"Nope. I make my fake calls to radio jocks."

"And you're sure none of your compatriots at the course left the message?"

"Absolutely."

"Okay, listen to this."

Tommy held the phone's mouthpiece near the answering machine's speaker and replayed the message. He transferred the phone to his left hand and grabbed a pen with his right. He looked for a scrap of paper. None within reach. When the so called Hootie recited the number, Tommy wrote it on his hand.

When the message completed Tommy asked Carlos, "What do ya think?"

"If that's a fake, it's a damn good one. Why don't you dial the number? It's after work hours in Georgia so if it's the real deal, you'll probably just get a recorded message or the ground crew."

"Good idea. Can you hold on for a few seconds?"

"Sure."

Tommy dialed the number. A smile took shape as he heard the recorded message of Augusta National.

"Carlos, can you come over tomorrow on your way to work?"

"Why?"

"I can't call Hootie back without my caddie."

20

ATLANTA, GEORGIA, USA
WATERVILLE, MAINE, USA
THURSDAY, AUGUST 1, 2002

The brim of his baseball cap, embroidered with "Yellow Jackets," protected Rusty's forehead from the summer sun. He angled his beige BMW rag top into a slot in the Gold's Gym parking lot, a mile north of the perimeter, the fifty-five-mile loop around Atlanta, officially I-285.

Gold's had several locations closer to his condo but drive-time wise, it was a push. Besides, he enjoyed the ride up Roswell Road. Perhaps the rapid transition through a half-dozen micro communities appealed to Rusty, at least subliminally.

The BMW was almost inconspicuous due to its relative modesty. Parked on his right was a black Hummer, to the left, a red Ferrari. Professional athletes frequented Gold's. Since Rusty was shorter than basketball players, smaller than most football players and had more teeth than the average hockey player, the occasional stare and odd remark were rarely directed towards him.

The gym was relatively empty on weekday mornings after yuppie rush hour.

As he entered the large facility a perky receptionist looked up from her workstation, "Morning, Mr. Stephens."

"Hi Kelley."

"Ran left you a message." She punched the keyboard and read, "Couple minutes behind schedule. Warm up and meet me in the aviary. He said you'd know what that means." She looked up at Rusty with a puzzled look. "If you don't mind me asking, I'm trying to figure out what it means?"

Rusty smiled and pointed across to the balcony on the other side of the gym, an area with many bench presses, "It's shorthand, where the Falcons and the Hawks work out."

Kelley mouthed an "Oh." Rusty wasn't sure if she didn't understand or just wasn't amused.

Rusty changed. With Ranjit running late, he decided to do some additional stretching.

A tall Indian appeared, topped in a muscle shirt bearing the Gold's logo. "Sorry I'm late. I was researching some high energy foods I thought you might like. Let's get going."

They methodically worked through presses of varying weights and bench angles. Ran spotted for Rusty and recorded the results.

Fifty-five minutes later Rusty was back on the road, invigorated and armed with Ran's food recommendations.

Next stop, Brent Lattimer's satellite office, conveniently nearby. King and Spalding added offices in the suburbs over the last thirty years as metro Atlanta burgeoned from less than one million inhabitants to over four. At this time of the morning, the ride to Brent's offices, near Perimeter Mall, would take less than ten minutes.

Rusty's mobile phone erupted along the way. Rusty let O.T. program the phone with a unique ring for himself. When the opening riff of *Smoke on the Water* sounded, Rusty simply answered, "What's happening?"

"Just checking in. On schedule for this afternoon?"

"Yes. Wait a minute. No. Hold on." A Barnes & Noble bookstore caught Rusty's attention. "Can you do me a favor?"

"Sure, name it," said O.T. routinely. These confirmations were perfunctory. The only time he replied to Rusty with anything other than yes, was two years ago when a teenage driver, late for school, rear ended him.

"Call Brent and tell him I may be a few minutes late."

"And what about the practice session?"

"I'll call you back. Thanks."

Rusty clicked off as he made a left into the shopping mall. He parked, raised the top on the BMW, locked the door with his key fob, and walked towards the bookstore.

One of the customer service reps saw Rusty walk in, then stop to scan the signage hanging over the tables and rows of books. The young man, with thick black glasses sashayed over to Rusty, "May I help you?"

"I'm not sure whether I should look in philosophy or religion?"

"It sounds like you have something particular in mind."

"Moses..."

The rep raised his hand, cutting off Rusty, quick to help but also to show off his intelligence, "Neither. You want Judaica."

Rusty continued, "As I was saying, Moses Maimonides."

"Well, you got me there," waving his hand away back to his hip. "I don't know who that is, but let's look it up. Right this way." Rusty followed him about twenty paces to a counter close to the store's center. The rep spun one of the computer terminals around on its dolly. "Is that the Author's name or the subject?"

"Both," replied Rusty, which further befuddled the clerk.

The screen displayed dozens of matches for Moses, a handful with the combination of Moses and Maimonides, but only one of those was in stock. As he was led through the maze of racks, it occurred to Rusty that they could have tried an inquiry on Rambam. Then again, that would probably have produced no matches whatsoever.

Rusty was about to sit down and browse the book over a latte. However, he realized that might be like trying to eat one potato chip. So, he headed for the checkout line. While waiting to make his purchase, he reached into his pocket, retrieved his earphone, unraveled the wire, pressed the tiny plug into his phone, and inserted the earpiece.

He scrolled down to his father's work number and pressed the green key to dial. He heard ring tones as he handed the cashier the book along with his Amex Centurion card.

"Sir, are you a member of our discount book club?"

Rusty shook his head, indicating no, pointing to his earpiece.

"Stephens Pharmacy Services."

"Carlton Stephens please. Is that you Anita? It's Cameron."

"Hi Cameron, let me see if I can find him for you."

"Thanks. I can see the old man won't let you retire."

Before she could respond, the phone connection clicked.

"Hi son, how are you? Anything wrong? You hardly ever call in the morning."

"Thank you."

"What?"

"Sorry Dad, I was just checking out of a bookstore."

"You sure you're okay?"

"Fine. I was just picking up a book on Moses Maimonides. Ever heard of him?"

"The name sounds vaguely familiar. Wasn't he a doctor or something hundreds of years ago?"

"Among other things and more than eight hundred years ago. Most people don't even know that much."

"What brought this on?"

"Just curious. I'm on my way to see Brent. I'll explain later. Love to Mom."

·••◆••·

A shiny black Steinway graced the seventeenth-floor lobby of the King and Spalding offices on Ravinia Drive, just outside the perimeter. The former managing partner acquired the instrument a few years ago to host a reception for one of the practice's marquis clients, the ASO, Atlanta Symphony Orchestra. Brent Lattimer liked to needle his peers responsible for the ASO— Rusty paid for the eighty-eights while ASO fees were de minimis. Lattimer called them low-bono. As Rusty entered the lobby, a well-groomed receptionist greeted him, "Good morning Mr. Stephens."

"Good morning. I'm a little late for Brent."

"He'll be with you in a moment. May I bring you something to drink?"

"Coffee would be great."

"How do you take it?"

"A little of both, thanks."

Rusty took a seat in a supple leather couch across from the piano. He grabbed a golf magazine from one of the tiled rows splayed on the long coffee table in front of him. Peeling back the cover, he scanned the table of contents to the left of the masthead. He noticed an article he hadn't seen before, entitled, "Jim Flick analyzes Rusty Stephens." No doubt his mother would include this in her scrapbook. As he flipped to the indicated page, he heard high heels pinging the finely polished parquet floor, moving towards him.

Rusty turned and stood up immediately. A handsome woman, in a tailored Michael Kors suit approached, mid-forties, not a hair out of place, carrying a silver coffee tray with all the accoutrements. He smiled and let her place the service on the table before they embraced in a professional hug.

"I didn't know the managing partner delivered coffee."

"When I come up from town, they put me to work. Are we treating you well?"

"Just fine."

"Brent will be with you in a few minutes. Good to see you."

"You too."

Lydia Huxley turned with the precision of a runway model, returning behind the pair of heavy doors from which she entered the lobby area. She walked twenty feet down the hall and entered a small conference room. Brent Lattimer was arranging a small stack of documents. He looked up over the top of his reading glasses. "Well?"

"He seemed perfectly normal to me."

"Did he say why he had his caddie call me?"

"No."

"Thanks Lydia."

"Maybe you're overreacting?"

"Rusty is very precise, never late. Ever since his parents introduced him to us, when he started at Tech, he has never had O.T. call us. The only thing I could get out of O.T. was that a woman, as my teenage son might say, is 'sweating him'."

Lydia quipped, "If that's true then you don't have to worry about him coming out of the closet."

"I just don't want to lose the Rusty franchise."

"Correction. We don't want to lose the Rusty franchise."

"Point taken. I don't want to keep him waiting too long, but if you have another minute, let me run this idea by you."

"You've got my attention."

····◆····

Beth Cole entered the MRI waiting room of the magnetic resonance imaging unit at Thayer hospital. She found a seat, after retrieving a recent issue of *Better Homes & Gardens*. Its spine had barely been cracked, in stark contrast to issues of *People*, many of which with missing or torn covers.

Within a minute, a door opened. A stocky nurse bellowed, "Good morning, Mrs. Cole. Nice to see you. It's been some time. Come back please."

Beth walked across the room, passing several other patients and their significant others, before responding. In a low voice, "Nice to see you too Francine. Did Dr. Cole tell you I was coming? I insisted that I come in by myself. I don't want to cause a fuss."

"Dr. Cole didn't give you away. And not to worry, you aren't cutting ahead of any other patients. We have a lot of new staff, so you just got a bit unlucky with me here."

"Unlucky?"

"Just kidding. The only fuss you cause is when you bring in your potato pancakes over for the holidays."

They laughed.

Despite never having an MRI, her years of casual dinner conversations with Herman gave her a basic understanding of the protocol. They entered a relatively large bathroom with a few lockers.

Francine surveyed the lockers, "I think all of the lockers are available. This shouldn't take long since you've done the paperwork already. When you're ready, just come through the far door and don't forget to take off all the jewelry Dr. Cole has bought you." They laughed again.

Beth opened a locker, retrieved a hospital gown, and changed. She was impressed as she slipped into comfy disposable slippers. She entered the room housing the MRI machine.

Francine reviewed the process before turning Beth over to the tech team. Beth was gently guided onto the MRI's patient platform. After nudging her into position and checking the flow of her IV drip needed to add image contrast, two technicians eased her into the closed-bore tunnel. They exited the room.

The banging and clanging started shortly thereafter. Beth found the MRI more interesting than intimidating. She wasn't inherently claustrophobic but grateful one of the techs suggested she keep her eyes closed. It reminded her of a Moog synthesizer demonstration she happened onto when visiting Chicago's Museum of Science and Industry in the late sixties.

Thirty minutes later, Beth dressed, thanked the MRI staff, and headed towards her husband's office. After a short walk, a two-floor elevator descent and another short traverse through a tunnel to the doctors' offices, she peeked around the corner of the doorway.

Facing an empty office, Beth was only slightly disappointed as Herman had said he would be waiting for her. She conjectured *no doubt some kind of emergency*. She roamed around his office as she hadn't set foot in it for years. She lingered over a picture of Sally and Sandy. While admiring her favorite, the girls playing with Katy, she thought she heard Herman's voice in muffled conversation with some other people.

As Beth edged back towards the doorway, the volume increased, although still suppressed from normal levels. She could discern only a few words, none of which were meaningful to her.

She continued towards the sounds, exiting Herman's office. Beth stepped across the hall and noticed five people were talking and staring at a wall of x-ray images in a narrow alcove.

"Herman?"

The conversation halted immediately.

"Herman, what is it?"

21

Rancho Mirage, California, USA
Augusta, Georgia, USA
Friday, August 2, 2002

Carlos knocked on the door, then entered without waiting for a reply. He made a beeline for Tommy's makeshift bar. He grabbed the Tequila bottle and two shot glasses. He quickly filled both glasses and placed them in the middle of the kitchen table.

"We're celebrating," announced Carlos.

"What?"

"We're going to The Masters. I had my boy do a search."

"CJ?" questioned Tommy, referring to Carlos Junior. "He's only eleven."

"Loves to surf. Internet and Ocean. He found some blogs saying invitations may be sent to Latinos, mi amigo."

Tommy knew there had been some negative press in recent years regarding minority and women membership at Augusta.

Carlos lifted his glass to toast.

Tommy reached for the phone instead. "We need to call first. It's not official yet."

Tommy punched the number on his cell phone, touched the speaker button and placed it in the middle of the table so Carlos could hear. From opposite sides, they hunched over the phone, heads almost touching. They looked like they were locked in some sort of prayer ritual.

"Augusta National Golf Club. How may I help you?"

"Mr. Johnson please. This is Tommy Torres returning his call."

"He's expecting your call. I'll put you right through."

"This is Hootie Johnson. How are you today Mr. Torres?"

"I'm fine sir, and you?"

"I'm the same and hopefully we'll make your day finer. On behalf of the members, we'd like you to play in our tournament next April. You should be receiving the official letter shortly."

With a big smile on his face, Carlos mouthed, "I told you so."

"Definitely, I would be honored sir."

"Excellent. Get yourself to Augusta and we'll provide lodging Sunday through Thursday night. I'll put my assistant back on the line to go through the details with you. Next April will be here before you know it. Have a nice weekend."

Tommy barely got out another "Thank you sir," before audible tones signaled the call transfer.

Carlos continued to smile, as Tommy whispered, "Fuck that Thursday stuff." With both middle fingers extended, flipping two birds at the phone, Tommy smiled back at Carlos continuing, "We'll be playing on the weekend. I'm leaving it to my caddie to make reservations for Friday and Saturday."

22

RANCHO MIRAGE, CALIFORNIA, USA

SUNDAY, AUGUST 4, 2002

Carlos focused his binoculars on an aluminum marker 200-yards away, as Tommy launched balls downrange with a five iron. There was no wind to speak of. As Tommy's projectiles landed, Carlos called out the direction and distance from the target.

"Three short. Two right. Three long." They heard a clang. "You nailed that one bro." They heard another ping but not as loud. "Give you half credit for that, hit after one bounce. Hold on."

"What?" said Tommy as he moved the next ball into position.

"This is perfect. About the same time as dusk in May and just about the same time you will be marching up the 18th at Augusta in the final pairing."

"Let's practice the winning putt. I don't think I'll be chipping in like Larry Mize when he snagged The Shark," referring to Greg Norman.

They adjourned to the putting area. As Carlos set up markers on the practice green for a putting drill, Tommy's cell phone rang. Tommy answered and just listened. The blood seemed to drain from his face, which winced as he listened.

Carlos reacted, "What's wrong?" All Tommy could do was put his hand out to silence Carlos as his knees began to buckle. Falling to both knees as if in Church, Tommy finally said, "I understand sir. Thank you for calling. When can I talk to him?"

Carlos raised Tommy back to his feet. Tommy stared blankly forward. In a monotone, almost robotic in sound, Tommy said, "Louie was forced to eject from his plane. His primary chute didn't open. The backup deployed. He broke both legs on impact. Concussion too. He burrowed into the sand to evade the insurgent forces. Two days later he was extracted. He's on his way to Germany now."

Carlos eased him to a bench, sitting him down. "I'll get you some water."

Head down in his handkerchief, Tommy was wiping away tears as Carlos extracted a bottle of Evian from the golf bag. He twisted off the top and extended the bottle. The cool surface touched Tommy's hand.

"Gracias. I'm not sure I'm crying because he's hurt so badly, or he is alive, or we're just wasting good blood over there."

23

NEAR SALAMANCA, KINGDOM OF CASTILE, SPAIN
THURSDAY, JUNE 7, 1492

For two weeks Benjamin, Esther, Rebecca, and Johan eked out steady progress in a north by northwesterly direction. Their maps and instructions proved reliable. This reassured Benjamin. Over the years, he had heard traders exchange tales about the desert, most of which he was sure had been embellished. However, the stories about water scarcity seemed real and concerned him the most.

After a long day Benjamin stretched out on a blanket and studied the sky. He scanned the blue canvas, stopping to study each cloud, sparse as they were. As if contemplating one of the oil paintings he had been privileged to view at Casa Méndez, he wondered *what is the omnipotent artist trying to say about life and existence? Why were he and his family in this place at this moment*?

Across the campsite he saw Esther busying herself mending a shirt. He heard Johan explaining to Becca the necessity of commanding the four squares in the middle of the sixty-four square chess layout. Benjamin smiled as he drifted into a light sleep. *Typical Becca, she didn't need much help to trigger her competitiveness.*

A rustling sound followed by muffled voices stirred Benjamin. With visions of a knife-brandishing bandit, he opened his eyes fully. Realizing he hadn't been dreaming he jolted upright, shouting, "What is this?"

The next few seconds seemed like eternal silence as his eyes absorbed the scene and his mind tried to process it.

Johan sat in an extended position with his hands and ankles bound and tied together. A trickle of blood oozed from his forehead. His face showed a look of frustration, so Benjamin figured he was not seriously hurt. A rotund man, bald with a scraggly beard, pointed a long wooden spear at Johan.

Another man, tall with huge forearms, controlled Becca upright. With her hands tied, Becca stubbornly thrashed as her captor's left arm held her around her waist and his meaty right hand covered her mouth.

A deadpan Esther stood stoically facing a short young man with a dirty face and barely the beginnings of some whiskers. He too had a crude weapon.

A few feet from Benjamin, the bandit with the crafted sword and the trimmed beard, sat quietly, manipulating a plant stem that he'd been chewing on. Clearly the leader, he interrogated Benjamin, "What are you doing here?"

"We're on a journey to the north."

"You have crossed into our land."

Benjamin knew this was a lie but had no choice but agree. "We didn't know. What is the tariff to cross your land?"

As if having a quiet chat over coffee, the leader said, "I'm asking the questions, Señor. Your daughter?"

"Yes."

"Tell her to settle down."

"Becca," was all Benjamin said, letting his face communicate the remainder of the message.

Only after Becca stopped moving did the interrogation continue.

"You know, for trespassing, we can kill you?"

Upon hearing this, Esther collapsed to her knees. She extended both hands, reaching at the crude poncho of her guardian. Grabbing a handful of cloth with one hand, she broke her fall as she collapsed to the ground.

"My wife needs some water. Please."

"Go ahead. Help her. Quickly." He waved his hand nonchalantly as if to brush off the request. "My men know what to do if you try anything."

As if placed in a still life, Benjamin moved within the frozen scene. He dipped a jug into the water barrel, returned to Esther, sat on the ground crossed his legs, elevated Esther's head onto his lap and tipped some water into her mouth.

While Benjamin tended to his wife, the leader continued, "Now I want some direct answers. Where did you come from?"

"Gibraltar."

"What is the purpose of this journey?"

Benjamin felt that whatever he said would be wrong, no matter how truthful. But he had to answer.

"We are relocating to Amsterdam."

"Why?"

"My son had been unjustly accused of a crime. The accusers are following us."

"You have saved the lives of you and your family, at least for the moment."

Becca's guard reacted, "We should take care of them now before the others catch up with us."

The leader walked over towards Becca, stroked his beard as if contemplating the idea. He then placed his hand on his comrade's shoulder. With a swift movement, he pressed his fingers into the guard's scalene muscle and pinched it severely.

The pain debilitated his comrade, who flinched and reacted with a strained, "*Mierda*!" Becca was involuntarily released and ran immediately to her parents, huddling with them on the ground. The dog submitted to his master and awaited his next command, which didn't take long to emanate.

"Tie them up," pointing around the campsite to various locations. "Not together."

Five minutes later the four travelers, bound and helpless, watched the intruders rummage through their provisions and their possessions. While the bandits stopped to examine certain objects in detail, tools were tossed into a sack without hesitation. Extraneous items, like the game pieces, were simply ignored.

About fifteen minutes later, after whispering to each of his cohorts, the leader called a halt to the proceedings. He approached Benjamin, brandishing his weapon.

"Señor, you don't have much clothing but what you have is high quality." He studied his weapon, rotating it in the glistening sun. "My men didn't find any money. You have some. I want it. Now. I'm going to save you the trouble of negotiating with me."

The weapon was raised. As he began to thrust it downward, blood spurted all over Benjamin. Becca, the only prisoner with a partial view of Benjamin screamed, "No."

Like calling into the caves of Gibraltar, a fainter "No" echoed, but it wasn't Becca's voice. The leader doubled over, dropped his weapon, and crumbled to the ground. As he tugged at the projectile lodged in his neck Becca realized it wasn't her father's blood gushing forth.

Six well-appointed men, dressed as militia of some sort, moved swiftly to secure the bandits. They had little problem as the body of the serpent had just been separated from its head.

The apparent commander addressed Benjamin in several languages to ensure he was understood, "You are *joden, judíos, juifs*, Jews, correct?"

Benjamin looked at Johan who subtlety hunched his shoulders, implying he didn't want to guide Benjamin's answer. A split second later, surmising that the new arrivals were educated, Benjamin replied in Ladino.

Upon hearing this the commander instructed, "Come with us."

"May I ask where?"

"I don't think it should matter. You can continue by yourselves, and you will likely be killed within a few days. Or you can travel in our protective custody."

Without a moment's hesitation, Benjamin opened his hand and extended it. When it was clasped by the commander, Benjamin said, "I'd like to introduce your new traveling companions. My wife, Esther, daughter Rebecca, and our friend Johan. I am Benjamin. We are fortunate you arrived when you did."

"It's our destiny. I am Paulo. Stephano and I will guide you."

"Did someone send you?"

"None of your concern," said Paulo, as he motioned to his brigade's members to take the bandits away. Then he and Stephano graciously accepted food and drink.

24

CALABOR, KINGDOM OF CASTILE, SPAIN
TUESDAY, JUNE 19, 1492

"What are you doing?"

"You startled me Becca," said Johan, sitting up abruptly from his hunched over position on a makeshift seat from a fallen log. "I'm carving."

"I can see. Carving what?"

"I'm not sure how you would say it. I suppose it's something like a mallet."

"It looks like a cane of some sort."

"Almost, but I will make the bottom of it larger."

Becca bent down over Johan's shoulder to get a closer look. Her head was close enough to his to feel its radiance. Johan stopped his cutting strokes and turned to Becca. An awkward moment.

Feelings of warmth spread within Becca. She reacted quickly, "If it's not a cane, what's it for?"

As the tension dissipated, Johan responded, "It's called a *kliek* and we use it for a sporting contest we call *kolf*."

As inquisitive as ever, Becca asked a lot of questions. Johan explained the basics of the sport and its history as best he knew it. He promised Becca that after they arrived in Amsterdam, he would take her to see paintings, from two hundred years ago showing *kolf* sportsmen.

He extended both hands, forming a circle by touching his index fingers together and his thumbs together. He illustrated the approximate size of the ball struck by the *kliek* two centuries ago.

Johan explained that contests progressed from one landmark to the next. The man whose ball hits the designated targets with the fewest number of strikes is the victor.

Johan then revealed, as he closed the tips of his index finger and thumb on his left hand to form a small circle, that over the years the ball has become smaller to reduce wind resistance.

"Do you play well?" inquired Becca.

"Fair."

"Ben will show you?"

Johan looked puzzled, "Does Ben play?"

"No but he could help you be better than anyone else."

"Really, how?"

"At figuring distances."

"This I want to see."

"Show me how to play."

"Women don't."

"I expected as much, but can you just show me?"

Johan picked up his semi-finished handiwork and stood up. He instructed Becca to stand and bend slightly at her waist placing her feet shoulder length apart. Johan then placed the mallet in her hands and fumbled trying to get them in the proper position. He then placed a stone in front of her and placed the mallet behind it.

"Just a moment," said Johan, as he moved behind Becca and put his arms around her, placing his hands on top of hers.

Becca breathed more rapidly.

"Becca, Johan," interrupted Paulo. He spoke seriously but free of judgment, "I'm pleased I arrived before Señor Solomon. We are preparing for dinner. Your assistance is required."

25

PALOS DE LA FRONTERA, KINGDOM OF CASTILE, SPAIN
WEDNESDAY, JUNE 20, 1492

The Niña dropped anchor near her two sister ships. The harbor's dimensions paled in comparison to Gibraltar, so Colombo's triad dominated the scene.

Ben missed his family but the barrage of activity around him was exciting. It didn't matter that the astrolabes were in perfect order. Ben busied himself checking, re-checking and polishing them.

The captain walked over to Ben and placed his hand on Ben's shoulder. "Nice work. You cannot possibly do any more so you can take me ashore."

"As you wish."

"Let us depart then."

Ben rowed the small craft. The short journey passed in silence. Ben had learned over the last few weeks that conversation, if any, was initiated by the captain.

After Ben beached the craft, he offered a hand to the captain. In no danger of getting wet, the captain waived off Ben. "I'll be back in an hour." The captain walked briskly up the hamlet's main pathway.

Ben secured the boat and sat down facing the water. He scanned the horizon, anticipating the adventure ahead. Lost in thought for a moment, he jerked when he felt a strong grip on his right shoulder. He shifted quickly.

"Ben, I didn't intend to alarm you."

"Sir, you surprised me. You said an hour. I wasn't expecting you."

The captain spoke calmly, "There's been a change in plans. Come with me."

They retraced the route the captain had taken just a few minutes ago. They approached the inn and tavern in the town's center. Ben was prepared to wait outside, expecting to be tasked with another errand. The captain motioned Ben inside and pointed at a chair for him to sit.

The captain then turned to the counter and returned in less than a minute, placing two glasses of Jerez sherry on the table. The captain sipped his then studied the remaining liquid for a moment.

"Ben, you're a smart young man and an asset to have on my ship. However, you're not going West with us. I have met with Commander Colombo and my brother, Martin, the Pinta's captain. We've made a business decision. Your skills are more valuable for coastal navigation. You'll be going on another ship which will set sail from Portugal for points North. My navigator will be fine, thanks in large part to you."

The captain laughed lightly and continued, "I have sent a messenger to the ship to collect your possessions. Your shipmates are learning of your situation as we speak. I didn't want to create any more anxiety for them or you. Perhaps you will see them again someday."

Ben absorbed the words. The force and conviction with which they were delivered made it evident that an appeal would fall on deaf ears. He gained his composure and began to form his question. The captain held up his finger, "Drink up. I will explain, as best I know."

Ben learned he would travel by land to Portugal. He would then travel to Lisbon and sail north or make a land journey through Portugal and re-enter Spain. The captain raised his glass, "To your health."

Caught in the moment, Ben did not know what to say or do. He parroted the captain, in tone and enunciation, "To your health." His composure impressed the captain, now having second thoughts on acquiescing so quickly to Colombo's bartering.

"Ben, you'll have success. Your guide will be here momentarily, so we shall enjoy this fine sherry while we wait for him and your possessions."

26

Santander, Kingdom of Castile, Spain

Friday, July 4, 1492

Benjamin welcomed the sight of Paulo's arms outstretched over his head, signaling the group to stop. Benjamin dropped to the ground, rapidly but under control. Esther, who had been walking arm in arm with Becca, released and rushed to wipe his brow.

Paulo could see Benjamin struggling as the temperature climbed over the last few days. However, Paulo stated firmly that he had a specific place in mind, and they would have to continue for a short time. He stressed the importance of reaching the destination.

After a brief respite and a few sips of water, Benjamin declared his readiness. Esther took his arm without protest. Johan, who had been trudging solo, offered to escort Becca. She protested to deflect her parents from possibly noticing her interest in him. Johan noticed the small curl of her lips as she tried to suppress a devilish little smile. He tried to do the same and turned away to walk on Benjamin's other side.

The heat rose in waves from the sunbaked terrain. Some dust kicked upward. Despite minor eye irritation the breeze provided a welcome relief. They had become so accustomed to following the sound of Paulo's gait that closing their eyes did not impede their progress.

The wind increased in force rustling their clothing and causing their pots, pans, and tools to collide in a welcome cacophony of new sounds. However, like an orchestra warming up before a symphony, the random sounds quickly became boring.

With the increase in head winds, Paulo moderated the pace slightly. After about an hour and a half, the worst gusts subsided. Full visibility returned.

Paulo noticed a small movement on the horizon slightly to the left of their projected path forward. He made eye contact with Stephano. The entourage continued ahead. Over the next fifteen minutes, the fleck on the horizon gradually enlarged and the position shifted slightly towards the line of Paulo's direction.

The breeze subsided almost entirely. Raised heads were now able to identify human, not animal, shapes moving in the distance. Paulo made subtle adjustments to his march so that the groups would eventually intersect. A few minutes later, two discrete figures danced among the upward waves of heat.

"One of those people looks like Ben," said Becca wistfully.

"Just a mirage," replied Johan, "You haven't..."

Before Johan could end his sentence, Becca sprinted ahead.

She stopped abruptly after fifty strides and screamed, "Ben! Ben!"

The approaching figures continued, obviously not hearing Becca's wails. She exploded forward.

"Ben! Ben!"

The men stopped, looking towards the sound.

Becca ran another ten steps closer, screaming Ben's name.

The sound was returned with a long "Becca!"

When Benjamin, Esther and Johan heard the reply, they took off towards Becca.

In full stride, Ben hardly had time to move before Becca reached him. They hugged for twenty seconds before Johan embraced both simultaneously. Then a group hug, with tears rolling off chins and popping the dusty soil by their feet.

For several minutes they all asked question after question not waiting for responses. Ben calmed down first, catching his breath, he said, "Let me introduce you to Pedro, who brought me here and is taking me, I mean us, to Amsterdam."

Benjamin replied, "Pedro, Ben," turning behind him. "You should meet Paulo and Stephano, who...."

Benjamin scanned the landscape. It was barren. He turned back to Pedro. "Did you know these men?"

"None of your concern."

27

GIBRALTAR, KINGDOM OF CASTILE, SPAIN

TUESDAY, JULY 17, 1492

Periods of calm, though rare, allowed Méndez to stroll through some of the less traveled walkways and paths around town. It was normally a relief to take a break from the frenetic activity in the warehouse. But this walk wasn't as satisfying as usual. He took his time packing the bowl of his Meerschaum pipe with a new tobacco from Amsterdam. He inhaled the vapors, thinking this would calm him in anticipation of lighting it later. It didn't.

While the physical environment hadn't changed, the community's soul had. Méndez couldn't stop thinking about the world's condition. *Could there be an end to the paranoia? Why couldn't people learn from Maimonides' wisdom, around for nearly 300 years? Perhaps one day soon, everyone in the world would understand his Guide to the Perplexed and practice biblical principles with rationality and compassion.*

As Méndez ambled along, he thought he heard a faint echo.

"Señor Méndez."

Probably nothing since it was the two words he heard most often. He stood still and heard the sound again, this time increasing in volume. Someone was screaming and approaching rapidly.

"Andreas, what is it?"

"Señor... ...," he said while exhaling, gasping for air. "...Méndez, I..."

"Andreas, catch your breath, please," placing his hand on the boy's shoulder to calm him.

Still short of air, the boy was eager to speak.

"There are two messengers sir."

"Where are they?"

"In your office sir."

"Did they say anything?

"First, I heard 'three to Biscay'. Then I heard, 'one to Biscay'."

The next instant Andreas was wrapped in Méndez's arms, receiving a big bear hug.

The expression on Andreas' face conveyed shock and disbelief.

"Andreas, both are right. Thank you for running so hard to find me."

They walked back to office, both pleased for different reasons.

"Ah Paulo, Stephano, come into my office," said Méndez as he stepped between them tousled them affectionately. "You both look well. I trust your cargo is the same."

"All were together in Santander, but the elder Solomon is weakening. It is unclear if he will endure the remainder of the journey, but his son's arrival may bolster him."

"I pray you're right Paulo. It's good that your brother has two weeks to board them for the voyage to Amsterdam. Thank you both. Please report back when the family reaches its destination."

"By all means."

28

Above Athens, Georgia, USA
Manhattan, New York, USA
Monday, August 12, 2002

O.T. closed his eyes as the pilot completed her welcome aboard message. He snored quietly.

The flight leveled off in a crystal-clear sky. The ride was smooth. Rusty brought a plastic coffee cup to his lips without taking his eyes off the page. The book was divided into a substantive introduction to Rambam's life followed by a modern translation of *The Guide to the Perplexed,* which was written as three books.

Maimonides was born in 1135 and raised in Cordoba, Spain. Jews, Christians, and Muslims enjoyed a peaceful life in this vibrant city.

In 1147, when the fanatical Islamic leader of the Almohad Caliphate, Abd-al-Mumin, came to power, Maimonides witnessed horrifying violence and intolerance. Riots were incited. Jews were attacked and synagogues destroyed.

A proclamation was issued that anyone in Cordoba refusing to adopt Islam could leave, and have their property confiscated, or be put to death. When the Jews assembled at the royal palace requesting mercy, the king responded, "It is because I have compassion on you that I command you to become Moslemin, for I desire to save you from eternal punishment."

Rather than give up their faith, Maimonides' family chose exile. They roamed about Southern Spain, avoiding the Almohads, eventually settling in Fez, Morocco, around 1158.

There Maimonides wrote his commentary on the Mishnah, the Oral Torah, committed to writing about 1,000 years prior. The Mishnah codified laws, duties, and rituals not contained in the Hebrew Bible's first five books.

But life was difficult for Jews in Fez. They tried to blend in, feigning belief in Islam, and studying in secret. There were executions. In 1168 Maimonides left Fez in the middle of the night, emigrating to the Middle East.

Rusty was hard pressed to understand how a young man could rise above such brutality to inspire the oppressors as well as the oppressed.

He dug into the words written 300 years before Columbus set sail to the New World. Not the easiest read, Rusty took his time to absorb each word. What started as laboring morphed to savoring as Rusty resonated with Maimonides' premise that God should not have human traits. Expressions like the hand of God should be interpreted metaphorically.

An hour later Rusty pushed the button on his armrest, moved his seat back, and closed his eyes. His thoughts drifted to Sandy. A few minutes later he opened his eyes when offered more coffee.

He undocked the phone from the seat back in front of him, extricated a credit card from his wallet and passed it through the magnetic stripe reader on the side of the handset. He dialed Sandy's number. No answer. Her answering machine engaged after the third ring, with the manufacturer's default message, "I can't take your call..."

Cameron left a message saying he had business in the New York area which would most likely consume much of the upcoming weekend. He'd very much like to see her Sunday evening as he wasn't heading out until late Monday morning.

He reopened his book on Maimonides.

Sandy returned with a deli lunch to Columbia University's Schermerhorn Extension building. She entered just south of 119th Street's dead-end into Amsterdam Avenue. Opting for the steps, she exited on the fourth floor, leaving twenty feet to her office.

She unwrapped her sandwich and began eating as she awakened her computer.

During summer, the offices were quiet at the Department of Anthropology, particularly for those who worked in applied anthropology. Not only an opportune time to take vacation, but summer was also the best time for field work.

Sandy put her sandwich down, sipped her iced tea, and responded to a few emails. She swiveled to look outside and smiled as she mentally replayed her Spanish chair share with Cameron Stephens. Then she remembered talking with him about Brian's surname.

Turning back to her computer, Sandy clicked on her favorites list and launched Internet Explorer. Just for fun, without any scientific rigor or forethought, she entered the words 'genealogy Sills' which she placed together in single quote marks to ensure the search included both words in the results. She tapped the Enter key.

29

RANCHO MIRAGE & SAN DIEGO, CALIFORNIA, USA
RAMSTEIN, GERMANY
THURSDAY, AUGUST 15, 2002

Hold music played. A few seconds of *Baby Elephant Walk,* performed on a calliope and blasting directly into Tommy's ear, was enough. He pressed the speaker button and set the phone down on the coffee table. He fidgeted with a copy of *Golf Digest*, thinking about what he would say.

A minute later, "Sonya," in her own voice was concatenated with the machine generated, "has joined." Before Tommy could toss the magazine, "Louie has joined."

"Are you both there?"

"Yep. Yes."

"How are you feeling son? What's it been, about two weeks?"

"I'm fine, bored, stuck in plaster, hobbling around on crutches, tired of watching what little TV we have over here. What's going on Papi?"

"All good. Kids, I want to run something by both of you at the same time. First off, I have been invited to play at The Masters, and..."

"That's incredible," yelped Sonya.

"Wow," said Louie. "How did that happen?"

"I'm not sure. That brings me to the next point. It is..."

"Papi," said Louie, interrupting, then taking a few seconds to carefully consider his words, "Could this be some attempt at political correctness?"

"Probably, but I'm not sure I care. Here's the kicker. I was contacted by someone from SI."

"SI?" queried Sonya.

"*Sports Illustrated*."

"Oh, and?"

"They want to do a story on us, interview both of you and take photos. They said they'd travel to meet with you. I can't make this decision on my own. On the one hand, it sounds exciting. On the other hand, I've got to concentrate on my game. So, the fewer distractions the better."

Louie piped up, "Can you hear me?"

"Yes," said Tommy. "We can hear you fine. This isn't the best service, but it's free. What were you going to say?"

"I was going to ask if you talked to Carlos about this?"

"I did and he's for it. Said it could be helpful, later on, or at least until I can play on the Senior tour."

Tommy interrupted a short silence, "Did I lose you?"

"I'm here."

"Me too, just thinking," said Sonya. "Okay. If it isn't a distraction, would you do it?"

"Probably but it sounds like you are cooking up something," said Tommy.

"Just an idea. We'll all come to you, get it done at once. We'd have a short visit. I can coordinate everything, so you don't have to worry."

"I guess they're teaching you something down there in San Diego. Louie? Can you get some leave?"

"Heck, with my busted legs I can just as easily sit on an airplane as in the barracks here. But I'd like to add to Sonya's idea. We should be able to join you at the tournament, too."

"Now we're talkin'," chimed in Sonya. "Papi, what do you think?"

"Worth a try. Sonya, I will send you the contact info for the writer at SI. Name's Hank Hersch. I'll call Carlos. He's working on arrangements in Augusta. Louie, you just work on getting yourself over here as soon as you get some dates from your sister."

"Wilco. This has been one helluva call."

"Let's not get too excited. We all have lots of work to do."

"Okay Papi," said Sonya, "Gotta go. Love you."

"Me too," echoed Louie.

"Me three," concluded Tommy. "Talk to you guys soon."

"Sonya has left the call."

"Louie has left the call."

Tommy smiled at the phone as he cradled it.

····◆····

Sonya usually enjoyed meeting her study team at the campus Coffee 'n' Talk, a two-minute walk from her apartment at Paseo Place. On alternate weeks the group used a conference calling service. Today, she was happy to be on a call as it bought her some additional time to multitask.

While waiting for others to join, Sonya dashed off an email. *Dear Mr. Hersch, I am Thomas Torres' daughter, Sonya. My dad asked me to reach out to you regarding a possible article for your magazine. We could meet with you in Rancho Mirage, including my brother, who will be coming in from Germany. What are some possible dates? Sincerely, Sonya Torres.*

Ten minutes later, a pop-up notice of Hersch's return mail flashed on her screen. Sonya opened it and noticed his suggested dates. She replied, adding a request for reimbursement of Louie's expenses should the government not cover them all.

Nervous that she may have asked Hersch for too much, Sonya immersed herself in her study group. As the team meeting concluded, she received a noncommittal response.

30

MANHATTAN, NEW YORK, USA
FRIDAY, AUGUST 16, 2002

Hank Hersch pushed the bagged croissant into his backpack, grabbed his coffee, and exited Au Bon Pain. He jaywalked across West 50th Street angling toward the entrance to the Time-Life Building on Avenue of the Americas.

"Good morning, Hank," said a security guard, who had worked the lobby for twenty years and knew all the old-timers, many on a first-name basis.

"Morning, Johnny."

"Have a good day, Hank."

"You too."

On the elevator to the *Sports Illustrated* offices on nineteen, Hersch couldn't help but wonder about Johnny's story— *how was he the same upbeat person since they met thousands of mornings ago?* Then again, Hersch's business was stories and the one at hand was Tommy Torres.

Waiting for his Mac to boot, Hersch picked up the handset on his office phone and dialed Jim Drake.

"Hello."

"Jim, it's Hank. How are you?"

"Great. To what do I owe this pleasure?"

"Can I coax you out of retirement for a few days?"

"Haven't you got a stable full of shooters? And unless things have changed, I don't think you get to make the assignment."

"I've got a contact in the photo department, owes me a favor but I know they'd love to have you on this one. It's special."

"Aren't they all. But try me."

Hersch summarized what he knew about Tommy Torres. He was about to draw a parallel to the *Book of Job* but didn't want to overdo it with Drake. He never had.

Drake listened patiently, with the occasional, "Uh huh."

Hersch went for the close. "We'll have a nice time in California. Bring Jean. Make a minivacation of it. There won't be any crowds. Then we'll go to The Masters next spring. It'll be forty years since you shot Nicklaus on his first win there. The Torres story could rival that."

There was a long silence on the line.

"Well?" said Hersch tentatively.

"I'm just messing with you Hank. I'm in. I'll look for an email from the photo folks on possible dates and details."

"Thanks, Jim."

Hersch then opened an email from the finance department with the subject line, "Torres Story - Louis Torres expenses."

Admittedly, Louie was ancillary to the story, but Hersch was disappointed by the expense cap. Writers, editors and photographers never reached into their own pockets to cover expenses. But somehow Hersch knew he'd help Louie make up any shortcomings by Uncle Sam.

31

SPRINGFIELD, NEW JERSEY, USA
MANHATTAN, NEW YORK, USA
WATERVILLE, MAINE, USA
SUNDAY, AUGUST 18, 2002

The Hooters' blimp appeared to be grounded for the remainder of the PGA Championship's final round. Thunderheads boiled to the west. The clouds moved quickly. It wasn't the rain as much as the threat of lightning that might postpone the tournament's completion. The television broadcasters relayed the network meteorologist's assessment.

The final pairing, which included Rusty, stepped onto the 1st tee box a little past three following a multi-hour delay. Two hours later, as they made the turn to the 10th tee on Baltusrol's upper course, O.T. remarked, "If the skies clear a little and the guys in front of us don't go on the clock, we might be able to wrap this up today." Rusty acknowledged with a slight glance. O.T. was happy with the response as it meant Rusty had immersed himself in the business at hand.

With a narrow lead over his playing partner, Justin Leonard, concentration was paramount. Justin's putter could get red hot at any moment, and it had been warming since the 1st green. The field in front was not able to mount a serious charge, now fighting for third place.

Rusty and Justin, though friends off the course, intently focused on the business at hand, truncating courtesy to a minimum.

Justin had the honors, having cut Rusty's lead on the 9th hole. Justin hit a slight fade over 290-yards ending up in the middle of the fairway.

"Nice," said Rusty, in a matter-of-fact tone.

"Thanks," replied Justin, as he picked up his tee.

Hitting a slight draw, Rusty's result was a few yards longer than Justin's.

"Good," continued Justin as he and his caddie started down the fairway.

"Thanks," echoed Rusty.

Justin played onto the green in regulation within eight feet of the hole. Rusty did the same, two feet closer to the pin.

Both caddies and golfers walked around the green to study the situation. Including the dozen or so putts each golfer made on this green during Wednesday's practice round then three competitive rounds, and the topological maps in their pockets, all were familiar with the green's layout. But humans and Mother Nature conspired to make green conditions like snowflakes. Flag stick locations are moved each day, grass grows, the greens are mowed, the wind alters moisture content, spike marks multiply around the pin, pitch marks are not always repaired properly, and often insects lurk nearby.

Justin finally took his position, performed his pre-putt routine, then drained it.

"Nice," acknowledged Rusty, barely discernible above the cheering crowd, reacting to the potential equalizer.

"Thanks," said Justin as he touched the tip of his cap to acknowledge the gallery.

Rusty and O.T. re-checked their speed and line assessments while Justin stepped back and did a light fist touch with his caddie.

The crowd's last rumblings dissipated. Rusty was ready. He curled his six-footer in over the high side lip of the cup.

"Good," said Justin stoically as the gallery cheered.

"Thanks," said Rusty, acknowledging the fans with a slightly elevated right hand for a half wave.

The applause continued for both golfers as the entourage of security personnel, officials, sign carriers, and caddies walked through a roped corridor to the 11th tee box.

Two hours later, as the group marched down the 18th fairway, Justin's caddie tried to whisper to O.T., "Boring."

O.T. agreed, "No argument here."

However, Rusty overheard it, "Boring?"

Justin's caddie replied, "Sorry. Boring in a good way. Like we're watching *Groundhog Day*. As you guys traded shots, it's 'Nice. Thanks. Good. Thanks.' O.T., that about it?"

O.T. nodded, "You got it."

They all laughed, breaking the tension that had been building for the last two hours.

Some thirty thousand spectators had coagulated around the 18th green. Justin and Rusty walked up the fairway, grins on their faces and caps raised.

The crowd erupted in a cacophony of whoops, hollers, and applause.

Justin's caddie and O.T. gave each other a high-five.

The drama continued as both golfers had left themselves with makeable putts, just over ten feet. Again, Justin was away and first to play. His read was perfect. The ball left his putter face clearly on the proper line. The crowd stood. Many had raised their arms skyward as the ball dropped into the cup's center.

Rusty smiled with a "Nice."

Returning a grin, "Thanks."

The crowd settled as Rusty took the stage. Everyone knew what the television commentators were saying, "Miss it for a playoff, sink it for the win."

Without hesitation, Rusty executed his routine and drained the putt. O.T. hugged Rusty. Handshakes were exchanged among the golfers and the group that had accompanied them most of the day.

Judy Rankin, golf commentator and former professional herself, quickly made her way on the green with her cameraman and producer in tow. The interviews would have to be conducted quickly as the rain delay had cut into the network's evening programming. Normally, the runner-up would be handled separately, but Justin was accommodating despite the dramatic loss.

A quick question for Justin on his final putt and a congratulatory remark was followed by a few questions for Rusty. Both golfers were on their way to the scoring tent as the sun slipped toward the horizon, coloring the clouds left behind by the earlier storms.

Rusty sipped a Pepsi as he checked his scorecard, adding from left to right, then right to left, then calculating variance versus par, the triple check as he called it. But this was the PGA, so he added even holes then odd holes and did a final check. He signed his card, but the day was not over as there was a short awards ceremony followed by a press conference.

Dusk settled in as O.T. and Rusty got into the courtesy van back to the hotel. Rusty leaned back and closed his eyes, decompressing from the day's events.

He snapped forward, "Darn."

O.T. reacted, "What's up?"

"I left Sandy a message that we would go out around eight tonight in the city."

"That ain't gonna happen."

"No kidding. I don't have her number on me."

"Here. Take my cell phone. I have her number."

"You do?"

"She's investigating my family tree."

O.T. typed in "s" then "a" which narrowed the list to five entries. He scrolled down to "Sandy" and pressed the send key, handing the unit to Rusty.

Sandy recognized the number flashing on her phone.

"Hi Brian, how are you?"

"This is Cameron. I'm sorry I couldn't call you earlier."

"I got your message. You probably had something better to do."

"Well sort of, let me explain."

"That's okay Cameron, some other time. Take care. I'm hanging up now."

The Sox rarely played on Sunday night. A rain out earlier in the year, resulted in a doubleheader today. Sally liked watching the Red Sox play the Yankees. She got into the habit growing up. It was her special "Dad" activity as Sandy had no interest in spectator sports. Besides, her favorite shows were in summer reruns.

Sally picked up her phone and punched Sandy's number. The pre-recorded message started after a few rings. After the tone, Sally began speaking, "Hi sis, you and Cameron must still be out having a..."

"Hi, it's me," Sandy interrupted somberly.

"Well?"

"Well, nothing. He finally called me a half hour ago. Wish I hadn't answered the phone."

"Could he be going out with someone else?"

"Who knows," continued Sandy. "It was weird. He called me on his business partner's phone, apologizing for standing me up."

"So maybe they had a business outing or something."

Sandy's phone beeped in her ear. She told Sally to hold on for a moment as a number with a New York City area code, 917, flashed on the small screen.

Sandy answered and listened to the message. "Sally, you're not gonna believe this."

"What?"

"There is a delivery guy in the lobby from Flowers 24 by 7. Says he has a special delivery from Cameron Stephens, and he was instructed to just call and leave the delivery by the front door."

"Sally concluded, "The only thing I can say is this guy may not be Jewish but at least he's feeling some guilt. Go ahead and go. Talk to ya later."

"Okay, love you."

32

MANHATTAN, NEW YORK, USA
NEWARK, NEW JERSEY, USA
MONDAY, AUGUST 19, 2002

Sandy's co-workers ogled at her in good fun. None had seen the girl from Maine in full makeup, heels, and a dress. She didn't cover her sexy cleavage. The summertime heat, coupled with the University's need to conserve energy, relegated Sandy's shawl obsolete for the morning.

Cameron's cell phone beeped twice showing Brian's number in the display, "Everything okay?"

"You're all set."

"Thanks. See you later."

Cameron ended the call and scrolled to Sandy's number.

From down the hall, Sandy heard the *William Tell Overture* emanating from her office. She couldn't reach her phone before the music stopped and her voicemail kicked in. She retrieved the message on her office speaker phone so she could tidy her desk at the same time.

"Hi, it's Cameron. I was able to pick you up. I'm in the black Lincoln in front of your office. Come on down when you're ready. Take your time."

Sandy stopped arranging her desk. She opened her purse and fumbled for lipstick and mirror. Three heads peeked around her doorway and laughed. Sandy caught herself and joined them with a giggle.

"See you in a couple hours," said Sandy, regaining her composure.

Her colleagues looked at one another. One shot back, "We've already signed you out for the day."

The livery driver stood outside the car in a long sleeve white shirt with a thin black tie. No jacket in this heat.

With little doubt in his mind, he affirmed her identity with a "Miss Cole" as she approached. He opened the door and Cameron stepped out to greet her. As if he had been posed for a Paul Stewart catalog, Cameron froze, a smile on his tanned face, dirty blond hair naturally in place, silk slacks, linen jacket, light blue shirt and foulard tie.

They kissed politely on the cheek.

"You look great," said in unison and they began laughing.

Cameron helped Sandy into the limo and the driver closed the door. With tinted windows and air conditioning in full force, Sandy immediately donned her shawl.

The limo headed south on Amsterdam. Barring a political protest or emergency, they would make the seven-mile trip comfortably by noon.

They sat awkwardly for a few moments. Just as Cameron began to declare a *mea culpa* on the previous evening's botched schedule, Sandy inquired as to his business. Cameron didn't want to lie but he didn't do much better at cogently explaining his clothing venture. He welcomed the distraction of a half dozen drummers banging on inverted plastic cannisters, as they moved through Times Square.

Sandy wasn't satisfied with Cameron's explanation. But she sloughed it off, rationalizing that her business was difficult to understand too.

With zigzags by the driver to keep pace with the timed traffic signals and the one-way cross streets, they arrived at Bouley in twenty minutes. Sandy didn't unwrap her shawl as the restaurant was literally ten paces from the curb and equally as chilly as the limo.

The maître d' greeted them, "Welcome Monsieur Stephens. We have your table waiting. This way please." He led them around a corner to the side of the restaurant with the darker decor.

"Is this a regular haunt of yours?" said a quizzical Sandy.

"The last few days have been very busy. I've had to deal with lots of people. Brian made the reservation. He told me it would be relaxing as well as tasty."

Again, Sandy felt the response was somewhat evasive but let it pass. When the maître d' approached and indicated per Mr. Sills' request that the tasting menu be provided, Sandy dug her heels in, insisting on seeing a menu.

Sandy received the menu but didn't open it. She placed it on the table and turned to Cameron, "This place is beautiful, but I feel like I'm in the mezzanine watching Brian conduct."

"That wasn't what I intended." Cameron then summoned a menu for himself.

After studying the a la carte menu for a minute, they both looked up and simultaneously said, "The tasting menu." Again, they laughed.

The conversation settled down as they talked about their families. Cameron was an only child, so his siblings were dogs. Sandy thought *at least we're both dog people.*

The first course was beyond superb and the service attentive yet unobtrusive. Cameron listened as Sandy talked about life in Maine. She spoke about the beauty and desolation of winter and the tourist onslaught in the warmer months. At a lull in her monologue, Cameron interjected, "What was it like growing up there Jewish?"

Sandy paused, looked down and circled the rim of her wine glass with her index finger. "That's an interesting question." She tried to verbalize that at times she felt special and at other times isolated and lonely. With Rosh Hashanah, the Jewish New Year, as an example, she contrasted the warmth of family gatherings and the frustration of missing school. "You were either excused from your assignments when others weren't, or you had to catch up, neither of which I liked."

Then Sandy volleyed back, "Growing up in Georgia, what was your exposure to Judaism?"

"I only saw horns once," said Cameron. She laughed more at his feeble attempt to maintain a straight face than the joke itself.

Cameron continued, explaining that the only Jewish students in his high school were a grade or two ahead of him. When he was young, his parents told him, "They kept mostly to themselves."

The conversation lightened up as they couldn't help raving to one another as the cuisine continued to arrive table-side at a properly orchestrated pace. Coupled with the effects of a wine selection for each course, two hours seemed to slip away in a heartbeat. They lost track of time.

Brian entered the restaurant and approached the table. With a comedic flare, trying to speak English with a French accent, Brian leaned over the table, "Monsieur and Mademoiselle, it is necessary for you to depart shortly."

"Brian?" said Sandy. "Uh, nice to see you."

"You too. "Sorry to interrupt but we're pressed for time. I wanted to give you this." Brian handed her a small, folded piece of paper. "I was going to email you. I asked my grandfather about our family name. Maybe it can help."

"I'll check it out."

Turning to Cameron, "I'll settle the bill here, do the hotel check-out, and meet you at the airport."

Cameron closed with, "Thanks, see ya in a few."

As they entered the limo, Sandy said, "I didn't know you had such a tight schedule today."

"Well," hesitated Cameron, "I didn't want to put a damper on lunch."

"You didn't."

The conversation ended as they headed uptown, not able to keep their hands off each other.

····◆····

Rusty entered Virgin's Upper-Class lounge in Terminal B at Liberty International Airport. After check-in at the reception desk, he spotted O.T. nestled in a corner away from the televisions and departure monitors, eyes closed, earphones on. Rusty tapped him gently on the leg. O.T. twitched from his light sleep, extended his right arm, hand in a fist, thumb extended, pointing up, then horizontally, then downward, back to horizontal then upward.

Rusty responded with his thumb up.

O.T. smiled and closed his eyes as Rusty placed his bags next to O.T's. and returned to the bar and buffet area.

With wheels up projected for 8:30 p.m. Rusty planned to sleep on Virgin flight 01 from Newark to Heathrow. On prior flights, he was able to catch some shuteye during the seven-hour flight. His pre-flight regimen consisted of a light meal, one Stoli on the rocks before exiting the lounge for the departure gate, finishing with a Tylenol PM just before takeoff.

The flight crew was attentive as usual. Rusty crammed into the bathroom to slip on the Virgin pajama top. The sweatpants were too much of a hassle. On his way back to his seat a flight attendant asked Rusty if he was interested in a fifteen-minute in-flight massage. If so, did he want to be awakened if a slot became available. He smiled, "That's a yes and a no, thanks."

Rusty settled in, glancing at the safety card and a pamphlet illustrating the flat bed pods coming soon to Upper Class.

The Boeing 747 turned the corner on the taxiway, second for takeoff on runway 4R, a northeasterly heading. Following a smooth takeoff, a cabin announcement was Rusty's cue to roll his seat back to a horizontal position. A flight attendant reached overhead to help Rusty with the duvet.

Blindfold on, earplugs in, Rusty configured himself as best he could. He had learned a few positions, not quite twisting him into a pretzel. He was fully expecting his next conversation to be about breakfast on descent.

However, his protocol betrayed him tonight. Each time he drifted towards sleep, Sandra Cole's image distracted him, as if a rubber band bracelet was tugged and snapped back. *Was it her outspokenness? Her brains? Was it her hands? Her upbringing? Was it her smile? Her body? Was it her unabashed physical attraction to him? Was it their synchronous laughter when they blurted out the same thing?*

33

LONDON, ENGLAND
ATLANTA, GEORGIA, USA
TUESDAY, AUGUST 20, 2002

About 5:30 a.m. UK time, Cameron adjusted his seat for a neck and shoulder massage. At 6:00, he drifted into an uneven sleep until the cabin lights were turned on by the crew an hour later. Had he not dreamt of Sandy as his caddie, in a white jump suit at Augusta National, he would have sworn he was awake the entire flight.

Cameron and Brian took a pass on using the arrivals lounge but did take advantage of Virgin's private limo downtown. They arrived at the Savoy and immediately checked into their rooms, which had been guaranteed for the night before. They agreed to meet for lunch at 1:30.

Cameron unpacked a few items, showered, and flopped on the turned down bed. Exhaustion finally won and he fell asleep, still thinking about the girl from Maine. Fortunately, he left a wake-up call just in case.

Brian spotted Cameron entering the lobby. Brian belted out, "Isn't this place great? So full of history. The concierge was just telling me that Marconi made his first broadcast to the U.S. from here and Monet painted views of the Thames from his room."

With tongue in cheek and still a bit groggy from his nap, Cameron said, "I can smell a cloud of smoke from Churchill's cigars."

"If you change the tone slightly you will endear everyone who catches your BBC interview tonight."

"Okay, I'll keep that in mind. Let's eat something."

The Savoy had several dining options, but Cameron and Brian needed some fresh air. Sunglasses on, they crossed the Strand and ambled up the hill towards Covent Garden. Within ten minutes they settled at an outdoor café.

After they ordered, Brian began to review the itinerary. Cameron leaned his head back and closed his eyes to enjoy the sunshine. Cameron knew the plan but figured it was good for Brian to repeat it, just so there weren't any cockups.

They finished lunch. Brian suggested they walk around some more as they had plenty of time before they needed to be at the BBC studios. Cameron declined as he wanted to relax, perhaps work out in the hotel gym.

Cameron entered his room with purpose, retrieving his *Guide to the Perplexed.* He opened the front cover and removed a piece of paper with some names and numbers on it. He looked at his watch, still set to East Coast time, to ensure that he would not be calling too early.

The receptionist answered with a tinge of a southern accent, "Shalom. This is The Temple. How may I help you?"

"Rabbi Sugarman, please."

"May I say who is calling?"

"Rusty Stephens."

"Just a moment."

"Hello, this is Alvin Sugarman."

"Rabbi, this is Rusty Stephens. Thanks so much for taking my call. Professor Washington suggested I get in touch."

"No trouble. She's a good friend. What can I do for you?"

Rusty explained his interest in Sandra Cole and his desire to learn more about her religion.

The rabbi responded, "I assume Sandra is Jewish, and you are..."

"Episcopalian."

"And you can see yourself in a long-term relationship with her, maybe marriage?"

"I suppose in the back of my mind."

"If your relationship does progress, would either of you want to convert?"

As the question hung in the air, Rabbi Sugarman explained his purpose in asking it was to ensure Rusty was aware that marriage was a journey and not a destination, be it interfaith or intra-faith. The rabbi mentioned some issues he had addressed with mixed marriages in his thirty-five-year association with The Temple, a bastion of Reform Judaism in Atlanta and the South.

They conversed a few more minutes and agreed to meet upon Rusty's return to the States.

"I really appreciate your time, Rabbi."

"Again, my pleasure but I do have a simple request."

"Sure"

"Before we meet, please watch *Driving Miss Daisy* even if you've seen it before. You'll catch a glimpse of me in my one and only motion picture appearance. Seriously though, the film is relevant to our conversation today."

"Will do. Thank you, Rabbi. When we get together, can we talk about Rambam?"

"For sure."

"One more thing if you have another minute?"

"Sure."

"Aren't there lots of temples in Atlanta?"

"There are."

"So why is your temple called The Temple?"

"Our formal name is the Hebrew Benevolent Congregation. But since we were the first synagogue in the city back in 1867 people started referring to it as The Temple and the name stuck."

"Okay, so I'm not crazy. Thanks."

"I look forward to meeting you."

34

AUGUSTA, GEORGIA, USA
SIDNEY, MAINE, USA
WEDNESDAY, AUGUST 21, 2002

The original hitching posts provided a rustic facade for the entryway to Dixie Drugs. A family business for six generations, the store had expanded over time in a unique way. The store's older parts were left intact alongside the new additions. The Double D, as the locals called it, had more than survived amid convenience stores, pharmacy chains and buying clubs. The spinning stools, at the Fifties soda fountain, were often occupied by people sipping their premium coffees bought elsewhere.

Carlton Stephens picked up his prescription, signed the charge slip and turned to his right, almost bumping into another customer.

"Excuse me," said Carlton looking up. "Oh, Hootie, how are you?"

"I'm fine. How's your wife?"

"She's got a little bug, otherwise just fine. Thanks for asking." Carlton transferred the small bag to his left hand so he could shake Hootie's hand.

Hootie looked at the package and asked, "Doesn't your company supply all the medications to this place?"

"These days we're so mechanized, I can't just step into my warehouse anymore and grab 'em. Besides, the Double D is one of our oldest customers. Always a pleasure to stop by." Carlton segued, "It looks like you've added a few hundred yards to the course. I know our club sold you some land to lengthen the 13th."

"With the distances these young guys are hitting, we had to. Can't have Tiger playing his second shot into the 18th with a sand wedge ever again. Hootie continued, "Looks like Rusty is having a sensational year which I trust will continue into next spring. It certainly would be a thrill to have another local boy win our tournament."

Carlton responded lightly, "Christina will insist he is near the top of the leader board after Saturday's play. I don't know if she is more concerned about his success on the course, as much as a late tee time on Sunday so he can go to church in the morning."

Hootie laughed and patted Carlton on the shoulder, "Excuse me. I've got to get to a meeting at the office. Nice to see you. Please give Christina my best."

Sally tried to enter the Cole home quietly, but the screen door creaked. Katy barked once and ran to the door. As soon as Sally entered, Katy took to her hind legs and enthusiastically greeted her.

"Is that you Sally?"

"Hi Mom. You too Katy. Down girl. I was trying not to disturb you if you were resting."

"Sweetheart, I'm feeling fine. Don't worry. Lunch is almost ready. Can you set the table?"

Sally had executed this chore so many times, she continued the conversation unabated. Opening the cupboard, she queried, "Did you speak to Sandy yesterday?"

"Well..." said Beth. "Her prince charming visited. With all the nice Jewish boys in New York City, go figure."

About to place napkins and silverware on the table, Sally stopped and turned. "Mom, when you were growing up in Detroit, did you ever think you'd be living in rural Maine?"

Slightly miffed, Beth replied tersely, "How did you get from Sandy's date to my childhood?"

"Things don't always go as planned. Mom, are you sure you're okay?"

"Sorry I snapped at you. I'm actually looking forward to seeing your father's med school friend at Sloan Kettering, so we can get on with it, one way or the other. Let's eat."

Other than Sally complimenting the meal, they ate quietly and quickly. As they finished up, Beth began clearing the table. As she got up to help, Sally said, "Why don't you start packing for New York. I'll clean up and join you in the bedroom."

35

RACHO MIRAGE, CALIFORNIA, USA
THURSDAY, AUGUST 22, 2002

The *Sports Illustrated* travel department did a nice job provisioning rooms at the Westin near the Palm Springs airport.

At 8:30 a.m. Hank Hersch and Jim Drake tapped the coffee urns the hotel staff had placed in the conference room alongside some continental breakfast items. They sat down to review the day's game plan.

Drake would take photos of Tommy with his children while Hersch chatted with Carlos. Then Drake would adjourn to the golf course with Tommy and Carlos, giving Hersch ample time to interview Sonya and Louie. They'd meet back at the hotel for lunch and wrap up by mid-afternoon.

Hersch reviewed his notes while Drake set up equipment at the room's far end for a few indoor shots. As scheduled the Torres clan and Carlos arrived at 9:30.

The first few minutes together were awkward with six people introducing themselves to one another, shaking hands and fumbling with names. Hersch motioned to the food and beverages, at which point the intro logjam dissipated.

As planned, Hersch started by collecting some insights from Carlos while Drake commenced some feature shots of Tommy, Louie, and Sonya.

Hersch was intrigued by the dynamic between Carlos and Tommy. At first it seemed unusual for a caddie to have so much influence over a golfer. It began to make sense as Hersch got a glimpse into Carlos' preparation, methodology and most important, their history together.

Other than some confusion by the hotel staff with the lunch delivery time to the conference room, the day went as planned.

At 3:30, Hersch and Drake sat down to debrief. "Jim, you look like you can hardly contain yourself."

"Yep. Gimme a sec," said Drake as he pushed a small button and dialed the tiny wheel on his Canon EOS-1Ds. After locating the desired image, he carefully positioned the camera, heavy with the three and a half pound EF70-200 zoom lens attached, to give Hank a look. "Check this out."

Hersch squinted at the camera's small display. "It looks like Carlos and Tommy are touching their foreheads together. And those are Carlos' hands on Tommy's shoulders?"

"Indeed. When you see the image blown up, there's no way this could have been planned or posed."

"It looks like something you might see during an actual event, maybe basketball or football. If it's happened in golf, I haven't seen it."

Drake just shook his head. "I know, crazy."

"But it makes sense," said Hersch.

"It does?"

Hersch sorted his thoughts for a moment. "As you'd expect Carlos is preparing Tommy with repetition and practice. But at the same time, he's rehearsing himself. Maybe some caddies with similar techniques, but this looks unique, at least to me. And we're over six months away from The Masters."

"Interesting. That might explain the photo."

"Great shot, Jim. Thanks again for doing this."

"It worked out well. But I'm curious what else you found out about the family?"

"Funny. I enjoyed every minute with them but there was nothing to enjoy. You and I are used to seeing people, especially athletes, with their share of good breaks and bad breaks. Well... this family has had nothing but bad luck. I mean for years on end."

"But he did get invited to The Masters," countered Drake."

Hersch pondered that. "Hope it's a good thing."

36

MANHATTAN, NEW YORK, USA
FRIDAY, AUGUST 23, 2002

Sally, Sandy, and Herman sat quietly in the waiting area at the Memorial Sloan Kettering Cancer Center x-ray clinic. They turned magazine pages halfheartedly. Sandy dropped the *Cosmopolitan* into her lap and turned to Herman, "Daddy. Is Mom going to be okay?"

Herman reached over, patting her gently on the knee. "Why don't you girls go downstairs and get some coffee. I'll wait. I should be able to get the details from the radiologist. We were classmates in med school."

"Want something?" asked Sally as she stood up.

"No thanks."

Sally and Sandy walked down the hallway, vanishing into an elevator bay. Sally looked quizzically at the sign declaring it a Sabbath elevator. Sandy read her look and explained that observant Jews are not allowed to do certain types of work on the Sabbath. Pressing elevator buttons is on the list, so the elevator stops at all floors, up and down from Friday sundown until Saturday sundown.

They reached the lobby and Sally said, "I saw a Starbucks on the way over. It's close by. The coffee will be better than here, and I get the employee discount." Sandy agreed. They returned with their beverages less than fifteen minutes later. When they spotted Herman, they picked up their pace.

Herman said, "I figured I would see the doctor as soon..."

Sally interrupted, "How's Mom?"

"Inconclusive. So that's not bad, but we will need to come back for a follow-up visit."

"How is she handling it?" continued Sally.

"She's fine and getting dressed now."

All three headed back to the elevator to collect Beth. They arrived at the waiting room as Beth finished providing contact details to the administrative staff. She turned from the counter and gave her daughters a quick kiss on their cheeks.

As they left the hospital Herman advanced forward to hail a cab. With hardly a cloud in the sky and a pleasant 73°, Beth insisted they walk. They headed west on 65th Street and turned left on Third Avenue.

Sandy interrupted the small talk, "Dad, I think you're in trouble. We're just about at Bloomingdale's."

"Sounds ominous," said a sarcastic Herman.

"I'll give you a break Dad. I need to stop at the office, and I've got some errands I need to run, so you'll have one less shopper with you. But watch out at dinner. What time is our reservation?"

"Not my job," said Herman.

Beth said, "7:30."

"Mesa Grill, right?" said Sandy.

"Right."

Sandy looked at her watch. "Great, so I'll see you guys in a few hours. I'll walk through the store with you and get the subway from the basement there."

When the 2-express pulled into the 96th street station, Sandy decided to skip the office, as she exited onto Broadway. After a quick stop at the corner bodega for tampons and Q-tips, Sandy entered her apartment building. She pulled the plastic grocery bag up her arm making it easier to retrieve her mail from the lineup of brass mailboxes. Sifting the good mail from the credit card solicitations and catalogs addressed to her roommate, Occupant, she dumped the junk. Less to carry upstairs.

Sandy hung her keys on the decorative hook by the door, tossed her bag with the Verizon bill onto the kitchen counter, and immediately sat down at her PC. She scrolled through her in-box. Nothing from work. Good. She passed over an e-bill from Con Ed and a promo from the Pottery Barn. There was an email from BSArtist345.

She chuckled out loud at Brian's user ID as she launched his message. He provided some background information on his parents, grandparents, and as much as he could remember about his great-grandparents. She scanned the data. Nothing unusual or special. She surmised she wouldn't find too many rings in Brian's tree.

Sandy continued through her in-box. She passed two spam items for penny stocks and discount drugs. Next was a letter from Whisperwood Camps in Maine, a no-frills lodge with private cabins on Salmon Lake, about halfway between Augusta and Waterville. Practically every summer the four Coles escaped for a long weekend at Whisperwood, just to be together away from home and work.

This summer might be tough for Sandy. She opened the email if only to see what she would be missing. She perused the customary intro from the owners, "We're going to have another great season..." There was a short article on the early inhabitants near this small lake, and hence, the original name, Ellis Pond.

"YES," yelled Sandy out loud. She felt like her father staring blankly into the refrigerator looking for something right before his nose. "Ellis Island." She returned to Brian's email, zeroing in on his great grandparents' lifespans. They coincided with Ellis Island's operational dates for immigrant intake, beginning in the early 1890's.

Sandy delved into various sites related to Ellis Island, both official and unofficial. She printed Brian's email so she could compare his data with that on the screen. Brian had scribbled the dates were guesstimates. He had also denoted some names with (sp?), unsure of the spelling.

It was slow going for Sandy. She entered phonetic spellings and then used soundex capabilities to search for similar sounding names. With so many hits, the software responded back with a request to refine her search.

In two hours, Sandy had searched seven of the surnames belonging to Brian's eight great-grandparents. Her day planner software sounded the alarm for dinner. As if emerging from a trance, Sandy grunted, "Shit, shit."

She stood up from her chair, hovering over her PC, typing while trying to slip out of her shoes. She typed Brian's last name, Sills, which she had saved for last. As she anticipated, a simple name would have thousands of duplicates. Sandy turned to grab a summer dress from her closet as the screen filled in. She turned back and entered some target first names. Stripping off her jeans and shirt, she was delighted as the list narrowed to just a few names.

Now we're getting somewhere. Down to her bra and panties, Sandy hovered over the screen. She couldn't wait to investigate further. She jiggled the mouse until the cursor arrow morphed into a hand, at which point she launched the link to the first record. Nothing. Second record. Back arrow. Third record. "Whoa."

Her cell phone rang. She looked at the display. "Shit, Shit, Shit." It was her sister. "Sally! Don't say it. I'm sorry. I'll get there as soon as I can."

Sandy started the shower. While the water heated, she selected some clothes, practically throwing them on the bed. As if she was a video clip on fast forward, she got ready. Fifteen minutes later, she grabbed her purse and keys, heading for the door.

She ran back to her PC and toggled to a Compose panel where she typed "B" then "S" then "A" when the system auto-filled the remainder of Brian's email address. She typed into the subject line, "Progress." She tabbed to the body then entered "Your GGG-father most likely named Solless. Does that ring a bell?" She hit the enter key and ran out of her apartment.

····◆····

Thankfully, traffic was thin, and she had an aggressive cabbie. He popped the accelerator to make several lights as they barreled down Broadway through Times Square. Sandy leaned forward to look at the credentials posted over the glove box, intending to complement her driver by name. She smiled, reminded of Seinfeld's stand-up when he claimed to see a surname comprised of five consonants followed by the symbol for Boron.

With the sliding partition open between the front and back seats, the driver reacted, "Okay Miss?"

"Yes, thank you Zykl. I'm running late and amazed at the time you're making."

The cab slowed as it approached the Mesa Grill on Fifth Avenue, a block west of Union Square Park. Sandy looked at the meter as it ticked up to $14.85. She already had a twenty-dollar bill in hand. She reached her hand through the portal. "Keep the change," as she popped the door and darted out just as the cab stopped.

She entered the restaurant and spotted Sally sitting to the right at a table next to a vacant tangerine colored chair with her parents masked slightly by a waiter. Sandy walked past the hostess, pointing at the table, trying not to be too rude.

"Sorry I'm late," as she took a seat.

Herman said, "We decided to order."

"No problem." She looked at the waiter and said, take one of their appetizers, one of their entrees and one of their desserts, and make my order from those. Thanks so much."

As if this was totally normal, the waiter responded, "Something to drink?"

"A Cosmo would be great, no rush."

Beth queried, "Surprise, surprise. I didn't know you were this adventurous in the food department."

Sandy responded, "It's easy here. Everything's great."

Sally contributed, "I think I saw Bobby Flay in the back cooking."

Sandy continued, "I rest my case."

As they chatted about the city, Sandy's drink arrived. They continued for a few more minutes. Blue corn pancakes were placed before Sandy and her mother. Another waiter brought roasted corn soup which was delivered efficiently to Sally and Herman.

A rehearsed "Bon Appetit" was uttered with an echo, barely audible, as both waiters retreated.

Sandy practically inhaled her appetizer, "Good choice Mom."

Beth responded rhetorically, "Hungry, are we?" She placed a calming hand on Sandy's wrist. "Okay, my New York City girl. Aren't you supposed to savor the drinks, food, and the company at a fine restaurant?"

"Sorry, I've gotten caught up in somewhat of a mystery. It's hard to stop because every clue leads to another one, almost like a genealogy scavenger hunt."

"Aren't they all when it comes to family trees?"

"I suppose you're right Dad, but this one is really intriguing."

"In what way?"

"Cameron's assistant, Brian, asked me to look into his family tree. He's such a blend of physical characteristics that he was curious, and it made me curious."

Sally chimed in, "And you like Cameron a lot."

"Duh, but I think I would've been interested anyway. Makes me wonder if I like genealogy more than anthropology."

Herman responded, "Any other ologies we need to know about?"

Whatever direction the conversation was headed, it ended as Sixteen Spice Chicken, the Fire Roasted Veal Chop and the Steamed Halibut were served to Beth, Hermann, and Sally respectively.

"I think our waiter is pranking me," said Sandy. "Go ahead and start."

The others tasted their food, immediately acknowledging the goodness with facial expressions and closed mouth purrs.

A minute later Sandy's Halibut arrived.

Again, she polished it off well before everyone else. Sandy, oblivious while consuming, looked up, and became aware of the situation. "Is it that bad? I guess I'm not my usual self."

Beth consolidated, "We all are a bit off. Don't worry about it. Relax. We know what you're having for dessert. We all ordered the same thing."

····◆····

Sandy stepped inside her apartment, kicked off her shoes, and plopped on the couch. She slid a manila folder from her carry bag. The edges were slightly tattered, but the tab was inscribed neatly with S-I-L-L-S in block letters. This file had become one of her inventory items, transported back and forth to the office. Brian's lineage had become her persistent puzzle, her Rubik's cube, with each twist demanding a look around, inevitably followed by another twist.

Most of the contents were web page printouts. There were some hand-written notes Sandy recorded when she debriefed Brian on his heritage. Stapled on the inside of the cover was the beginning of a family tree, print-ed from a software program template. She triumphantly printed S-O-L-L-E-S-S in a box five levels above Brian's name. She fumbled through the pages in the folder to add as many missing names and dates as she could.

Sandy didn't know how far back she would be able to trace Brian's lineage, but at least she had a trail back to Europe. The first hundred plus years had been relatively easy. The next century would be exponentially more challenging, and beyond that, almost impossible. Sandy leaned back, closed her eyes, and thought about calling Cameron, Brian, her parents, and sister.

She dozed off.

37

ATLANTA, GEORGIA, USA
ORLANDO, FLORIDA, USA
MONDAY, AUGUST 26, 2002

Typically, Monday was the quiet weekday for Brian and Cameron. Tournaments usually ended on Sunday for a same day return to Atlanta.

Brian felt around for his toast, found it, then moved it to his mouth as he concentrated on the blog he was reading. He indulged himself with a few select blogs on Mondays, his high-tech way of reading the tabloids.

The phone rang. Brian returned the toast to the plate. He didn't recognize the number on the handset's small display, so he answered plainly, "Hello."

A perky voice came on enthusiastically, "Hi, this is Clarissa calling from the Golf Channel, trying to reach Mr. O.T. Sills."

For a moment O.T. thought one of his caddie buddies had arranged a prank call, but it was a little early in the morning for that.

"This is he."

"Mr. Sills..."

"O.T., please."

"Okay, O.T.," hesitantly. "We are starting a new segment on *Golf Talk Live*, featuring pros and their caddies together. We'd like you and Rusty to be our first guests."

"Have you been in touch with Rusty's agent?"

"I'm not sure. My job is to get in touch with the caddies."

"I don't know if Rusty will go along with this but if he does, I'm in."

"Thank you, Mr.... O.T. Can you please give me your email address?"

This raised O.T. suspicions. "If it's okay with you I'd rather not."

"No problem. If you have something to write with let me give you our website information so you can review the material there."

O.T. took the information and the call ended. He immediately punched up Rusty's number.

He answered, "Hi, not so quiet Monday, huh?"

"Then you already know about the Golf Channel thing."

"Brent called to tell me about it, thinking I would decline."

"And?"

"I thought you might want to. Besides, you need to experience going through makeup, so you know what a pain in the butt it is."

O.T. silently pumped his fist but tried to keep his cool, "So when do we do this?"

"That we will leave for Mr. Lattimer, Esquire."

PART II

"You must accept the truth from whatever source it comes."

Moses Maimonides
(1138 - 1204)

38

AMSTERDAM, BISHOPRIC OF UTRECHT

THREE YEARS LATER - SATURDAY, MARCH 21, 1495

The spring equinox seemed to awaken lowlanders from hibernation. The bitter Easterly winds off the North Sea gave way to gentler breezes and the promise of days longer than nights. Today was welcomed with its unseasonably warm temperature and cloudless sky.

At midday, the town looked like a confused bee colony with what appeared to be fifteen thousand Amsterdammers buzzing around on the canals' edges, traversing small bridges, and stepping onto frozen earth piles, all waiting to be shaped according to the city fathers' plans. The city was finally achieving some growth and stability since stone buildings were mandated following the last devastating fire, fifty years prior.

In about two hours Ben completed the inventory of goods destined for Scotland. As he often did the day before a ship's departure, he paused for a moment, leaned on a gunwale, and listened to the water slush around the hull. He closed his eyes, faced the sun, and wondered *does God have a purpose for me or am I just a creature...*

"Ben! Ben! Are you up there?"

"Up here, Johan."

"I need your help. It's urgent," waving Ben down the gangplank.

"What's wrong?"

"Nothing," confessed an excited Johan. "Sorry to startle you. I've been challenged to a big match this afternoon. The layout is difficult, and the wind is picking up. Two guilders when we win. One will be yours."

"What's this all about? I don't play very well and wouldn't be much help on your team."

"There are no teams today," explained Johan. "It's just me and Meneer Dijkstra. You will be my adviser. I want to beat him so badly after someone from his company said we could have done better on our last shipment. With all the angles and canal crossings, I need you to guide me."

The contest route was explained to Johan by Dijkstra. There were seven targets in total. They would start at the Begijnhof, the Beguine Court of almshouses. From there to Saint Nicholas Cathedral, the Newer Church, then over and back across the Oudezijds Voorburgwal canal, finishing at the Cathedral of Saint Mary and Saint Catharine, the Older Church.

Starting twenty paces away, both contestants would hit their opening volleys from the grassy area towards the front door of the house occupied by the oldest widow in this lay convent. Both men were expected to hit this initial objective on their first strike.

Polished wooden balls were carefully covered with a mixture of sap and precisely cut flower pedals to minimize damage to the targets and bystanders who might get in the way.

However, only Dijkstra, Johan and Ben entered the quiet sanctuary of the Begijnhof. One after the other, they genuflected slightly as they each placed three pennings, about one hundredth of a guilder, on the stoop below the first target.

As customary, the challenger, Dijkstra, played first and knocked the door with a thump, pretty much dead center. After each strike, the player was to call out his score relative position to his opponent. Dijkstra turned, smiled at Johan, and said emphatically yet muffled given the surroundings, "Odd," indicating he had taken one more shot than his opponent at this point. Ben, standing behind Johan, placed his hand on Johan's shoulder to calm him. Johan did not flinch.

Johan's effort whooshed low to the ground just brushing the lower right door panel. Dijkstra muffled his laugh in the name of sportsmanship. Johan remained stoic and glanced at Ben. Their eyes acknowledged that he had performed his opening salvo as planned. Johan calmly said, "The like."

The second target was a stone marker halfway to the Newer Church, about 250 paces from the starting point next to the widow's door. Dijkstra's strike exited the Begijnhof, as he declared, "Odd." Ben placed his hand in the small of Johan's back for just a moment, but long enough to be noticed by Dijkstra. Johan made his strike, also exiting the courtyard and calling his position, "The like."

They crossed the small bridge across the Begijinensloot, where a crowd of spectators awaited them.

Two hundred paces remained to the small target, Johan, made a good approach, "Odd." Dijkstra followed suit, "The like"

With an unintended deflection, Dijkstra hit the target with his next strike and proudly strode to his ball, waiting to proclaim "Odd" until he picked it up. Johan's third strike was close, "The like," but he needed another to hit the mark. With no visible emotion, Johan called out, "One more."

Onto the next target, the Newer Church's cornerstone. Dijkstra played, declaring, "Even," Ben leaned forward and whispered in Johan's ear, "Don't look at me and don't doubt me. Aim your strike twenty paces to the right of his path. I need to do some measurements while he continues to think you are playing badly."

Johan shrugged. *I asked Ben to guide me, so I should heed his advice.* Johan delivered his next strike as he was told. The spectators, growing in number, gasped at the result. After Johan's ball touched the third marker, he called "two more."

They walked to Dam Square, the starting point for the next target. Their scores did not change after hitting the designated section on the near side of the rampart, Oudezijds Voorburgwal. Johan and Dijkstra called out, "Two more" and "Two Less," respectively.

The fifth target required crossing the water. Dijkstra followed those who had taught him the game. He aimed his ball directly across the hazard to prevent its loss in the event of a wobbly flight.

Ben placed both hands on Johan's shoulders and adjusted him so that his strike would cross more open water. He leaned forward and whispered, "I have considered the precise angles and distances. Make your strike as you did for the third target, please."

Johan hit the ball with the force and direction as instructed. The flight was not perfect, but it cleared the far bank safely with five paces to spare. The gallery, now numbering over seventy-five people, erupted with cheers. More demonstrative to Dijkstra than the crowd's outburst was Johan and Ben's even demeanor.

Dijkstra played his next strike which came to rest about three paces past Johan's. From there they made a like number of strikes before their balls touched the gate fronting the Gothic Chapel, Agnietenkapel. Johan closed the gap to "one more."

Following the penultimate target, they were like, even. They prepared their shots back over the water to the final target, the Older Church's cornerstone. Dijkstra made a powerful pass with his next strike. His mallet made an impressive sound. However, it scraped the hard earth slightly behind the ball, reducing its impact velocity. The projectile advanced less than half the distance to the church, barely clearing the water.

The crowd waited anxiously for Johan's strike. Ben walked off five paces directly to Johan's right. He stopped and asked some spectators to move back. Ben did this to provide Johan a clear field of vision as the strike would not come near the spectators.

The crowd jostled as Ben continued to walk another fifteen paces. All eyes were now on Ben as he turned ninety degrees to his left and stared ahead, soldier-like, at attention. He walked ten paces towards Johan and stopped again, now turning ninety degrees to his right.

Becca joined the gallery but didn't need to look at her brother. She knew he was just verifying the triangulation which his brain calculated in seconds. She reflected on their childhood musings on Gibraltar's slopes, the images melting into a sporting contest in a different world.

Ben returned to his supporting position behind Johan and leaned in, "There is no aiming point so I will nod when your feet are aligned properly."

Johan took his stance and turned to look back. Ben nodded ever so slightly to affirm.

The projectile behaved as Ben had anticipated. It rode the wind, which also prevented it from going too far right. The strike sailed the longest many had ever witnessed, over 150 paces. The crowd erupted.

The pressure reverted to Dijkstra. He made a respectable strike. However, his limited ability to anticipate the wind's action on his ball, left him in an untenable position.

Dijkstra conceded and handed Johan the winnings. Applause erupted along with a few hoots. The crowd dispersed quickly.

····◆····

Ben and Johan were jubilant, walking and replaying each strike in detail. Ben noticed two men walking together, not far behind them, at a brisk pace.

Johan said, "What are you thinking?"

Ben shrugged his shoulders, "I don't know. Maybe they know us from Gibraltar."

Instinct took over as Johan blurted out, "Follow me."

Ben followed Johan who was running as fast as he could down the narrow path adjacent to the canal. Johan ran over a small bridge, made a right by the intersecting canal, and ran into a building on his left. Forcing a word between each breath, "Where... are... we?"

Johan, also struggling for air, "Let's go."

They walked through a small entrance way. Johan opened a door to his right and led the way.

"Hello Father," said Johan.

Dijkstra entered the room from the left. Ben gulped and barely mustered a good afternoon, "*Goedemiddag*, Meneer Dijkstra and Meneer Rasch."

Dijkstra bellowed in laughter, realizing the awkward situation he created. "Johan, you played admirably. And Ben, your guiding skills were most impressive."

Johan's father added, "I confess that I wanted Meneer Dijkstra to witness Ben's skills."

Dijkstra continued, "I have an opportunity that could be very lucrative for all of us. And Ben, from your demonstration today and your navigation skills I have heard so much about, you are the man to make this work."

39

ST ANDREWS, SCOTLAND
SUNDAY, MARCH 22, 1495

Anticipating the sunrise, Artair's flock began to stir gently, not far from the River Eden's banks, just upstream from its dissolution into the North Sea. He looked East as the orange disk peeked over the horizon. The spires of St Andrews Cathedral cut into the sun as it continued skyward. *A beautiful sight indeed.*

This would be an excellent time to practice with a new wooden cleek he had fashioned while tending his flock. He looked forward to golf with his mates during the long summer days ahead.

Seen as a distraction to military readiness, the parliament of King James II had banned golf for the general populace. Over the years the ban was sporadically enforced. Fortunately, Artair was a proficient archer so no one could accuse him of shunning his duty to Scotland.

He didn't have much money for fancy cleeks and balls, but he did have the opportunity to strike often. Artair transformed the tedious work of herding sheep by aiming balls to move them. The more accurate, the less work he had to do. It was enjoyable and helped pass the time.

He also had some experimentation to do. Most cleeks were made to be one ell, the distance from an average man's elbow to index fingertip. He would reduce the cleek's size slightly until he felt most comfortable trying to preserve as much length as possible.

Artair positioned his makeshift wooden sphere on the ground. He noticed a lamb beginning to stray from her mother. Artair thought he could draw the lamb back into the herd. He hit the ball to the creature's far side. It landed too far from the target to create a reaction. While walking to retrieve the ball he whistled at the lamb, which complied by ambling towards her mother. This was encouraging as he had to move his flock to higher grounds with spring approaching.

40

AMSTERDAM, BISHOPRIC OF UTRECHT

SUNDAY, MARCH 29, 1495

Ben and Johan seated themselves at the dining table. A plate of marinated herring, sparsely covered with chopped onions, set stomachs growling. Becca entered the room and placed some vegetables in the table's center. She took her seat.

Becca glanced down and gathered the small bundle near her feet. Lifting it up, she said, "Be a good girl. Say hello to your Uncle Ben. And your father too."

"Other than Johan's light hair, I think she favors you Becca." Ben transitioned, "Johan, did you tell Becca about our meeting with your father and Meneer Dijkstra?"

"I told her we met after the contest but didn't give her any details."

As Ben explained the trade expedition's purpose and timing, Becca maintained a stoic face. Ben finished. They ate in silence. The tension was palpable.

Johan broke the silence, "*Lieve*," dear. Turning to Becca, "Of all people, you know how skilled your brother is with calculations. He is the best navigator in the territory."

Becca responded, "I hear what is going on. It's not the waters or the North Sea, it is the pirates. Am I wrong?"

Ben reached for his niece, "*Liefje*," little dear. "Tell your mother, I will be fine."

41

ON THE NORTH SEA
NEAR BERWICK-UPON-TWEED, ENGLAND
TUESDAY, APRIL 14, 1495

Rarely did an early morning on the North Sea offer a warming breeze with enough energy to power a ship. Regardless, sailors did not want to be on these volatile waters any longer than necessary, particularly in early spring, when storms could rise with little warning.

Ben ordered the *Koninklijk-Rasch*, the Royal Rasch, to tack frequently, altering its direction seemingly without purpose. The crew showed signs of restlessness and frustration. Despite Ben's armband signifying his importance to the Rasch Company, one of the veteran sailors asserted himself with the captain.

"Sir, it's Tuesday. We should be anchored in Dundee."

"Do you have a question, sailor?"

"Why are we wasting time crisscrossing when the seas will certainly get rougher. Shouldn't we be in port by now?"

The captain gave a simple answer, "We are making sure we stay safe. Please pass this along to the crew."

What the captain didn't elaborate on was the increased likelihood of pirate attacks. The Dutch navy, not even ten years old, could not cope with the demands of the burgeoning commercial trade in the region. Although many merchants opted for convoys, they took time to organize and added substantial cost to a voyage.

The captain was proud of his ship, a Caravela Latina, with two large triangular sails, and a more modern hull construction than the widely used Clinker design, still prevalent on the seas.

He was impressed with the way in which Ben navigated, heading the Rasch closer to the wind than square rigging would allow. Little did the captain know Ben had trained on a Caravela, the Niña.

The captain took a deep breath, enjoying the spring air and the soothing slushing rhythm of the water caressing the hull. He gazed towards the west with Berwick-upon-Tweed barely discernible in his peripheral vision to the northwest. He closed his eyes and inhaled again.

When he focused again, a fleck on the horizon, not seen before, caught his eye. With a northerly course and what little he could see of Berwick-upon-Tweed, it should not be changing in shape or size. He rubbed his eyes.

"Ben," shouted the captain with urgency.

"Sir," replied Ben calmly.

"Possible ship approaching from the west."

Ben, standing next to the helmsman, looked at his compass, then commanded, "Turn westerly forty-five degrees, heading two hundred seventy degrees."

The captain yelled, "Ben, Ben." With the wind coming from the north and the ship's northwest course, there seemed to be no reason to fall off to the west. "Why did you change course?"

"Sir. If you have sighted a hostile ship, I am plotting a course in the event the criminal has a companion."

The breeze was strengthening, now pouring directly over the starboard side. The blip on the horizon grew rapidly as both ships approached one another on beam reaches.

The helmsman noticed that Ben's sight line was towards Berwick-upon-Tweed. Ben, cupping his hands around his eyes to sharpen his attention, did not respond. The helmsman then called out, "Captain?"

Ben calmly put up both arms, palms out, towards the helmsman and the captain. "Apologies, I was just making some calculations. Ben addressed the helmsman directly, "How much time, on the present course, until we meet the ship coming towards us?"

Both the captain and the helmsman hesitated. "Please gentlemen, your best estimate will suffice." The helmsman deferred to the captain, allowing him to answer first.

After Ben absorbed the two responses, he stood with one arm extended towards Berwick-upon-Tweed and the other towards the approaching ship. He looked like a preacher welcoming his flock. Little did the crew know, he was creating an obtuse angle. He closed his eyes as he adjusted his footing to ensure he didn't topple as the ship pitched. The crew stood and watched silently in amazement, as Ben moved his head slightly along the arc he had created with his outstretched arms. The captain remained focused on the oncoming vessel.

For the next ten seconds Ben concentrated on the triangulation. To the others on-board it seemed like an eternity. Ben opened his eyes and calmly turned to the helmsman, "Prepare to come about."

The helmsman, repeated in as loud a shout as he could muster in the wind, "Prepare to come about."

The crew scampered into position and waited. And waited. And waited some more.

Ben had again closed his eyes, moving his head from left to right to left to right. He visualized the timing device he learned about as a youth, invented some 600 years before by the engineer, Abbas ibn Firnas, in Ronda, not even a three day walk from Gibraltar.

Other than rhythmic waves slapping the Rasch, there was silence. The crew was unsure if they were in the presence of an idiot or a genius. Ben's head continued to move consistently for seventeen more repetitions. He looked rather odd as the wind kept his hair on the left side of his head. As if waking from a refreshing slumber, he opened his eyes and quietly said, "Hard to leeward."

The helmsman shouted, "Hard to lee" as he turned the rudder to initiate the turn to the Northeast. The sails luffed loudly, snapping to-and-fro as the bow passed directly into the wind. The crew knew the vessel had more than enough speed to finish the traverse through what some called the dead zone. Accordingly, they were ready to trim the sails and cleat the sheets which controlled them. Following a 130° change, the helmsman began tacking on a 40° heading.

The ship cut through the chop gracefully. The captain assigned a crew member to keep an eye on the approaching ship to the west. After Ben's tacking maneuver, the distance between them changed at a markedly slower rate.

The captain commenced a slow walk around the ship's perimeter, admiring the crew's good work. He stopped to peer over the starboard gunwale. Expecting the open sea, he took a deep breath, "Ben, ship on the horizon East by Northeast." Trying to hide the concern in his voice, he continued sarcastically, "I suppose it would suit us better if I kept my eyes closed."

Ben requested the captain to estimate three distances— to the ship on their starboard, to Berwick-upon-Tweed, and the ship on their port.

The captain wanted to express confidence and control to his crew, so he responded rapidly with the numbers, which he believed were accurate. The crew watched as Ben took his stance again.

This time Ben only closed his right eye, pushing his head forward, concentrating on Berwick-upon-Tweed. He held the position. Two deck-hands looked at each other, smiled and began moving their heads from side to side. Ben saw the pair in his peripheral vision, laughed and said, "Gentlemen, our last maneuver was all about timing. This one is all about position." And as he had done before he calmly repeated, "Prepare to come about."

Twenty seconds later, Ben commanded the maneuver. After the helmsman tacked to North by Northwest, Ben challenged the helmsman to sail as close to the wind as possible. The entire crew could see the ship bisecting the routes of two potentially hostile vessels. Smiles were exchanged and all would be well at the pub tonight in Dundee.

The air of excitement didn't last long. A third ship was spotted, moving directly towards them.

Ben called out, "Captain, if these ships are conspiring among one another, they are trying to box us in."

The captain replied, "We need to make that determination. Let us fall off to a more Westerly heading and watch their movements."

"Agreed," continued Ben, turning to the helmsman, "Make your heading three hundred degrees."

The captain's eyes moved from the ship off to the west, then to the north then east. He repeated the surveillance then called back to Ben, "All three have altered their course. Options?"

With full confidence Ben replied, "Stay on course. We have speed but need to determine their armaments."

Time seemed to slow as the three ships converged on the Rasch. Some crew members busied themselves by tidying slack in the lines and sheets. Others just fidgeted. The crew watched as Ben and the captain gathered in the bow to huddle, obviously talking about possible scenarios. The only audible part of the conversation was Ben's conclusive, "Aye sir."

Ben ordered the Rasch to come about, taking a course directly in line with the ship to the East. Ben and the captain had agreed to lure them out into the open sea and then outrun them back to the West. The Rasch closed rapidly on the ship to the East. A cannon blast crackled in the air. The shot from the oncoming ship's bow fell short, but not by much. As the cannon was likely being reloaded, Ben screamed in one continuous command, "Prepare to come about, hard to lee."

Fifteen seconds later, the Rasch was closing rapidly on the pirates to the West with cannon fire barely out of range to the stern. As the vice was about to close about the Rasch, Ben commanded the helmsman to head up to a 320° heading, just 40° off the wind, now coming from due North.

Ben knew the other two ships, now closing, could not head up as much as the Rasch. As the Rasch changed course, a lead ball pierced the hull right on the water line. Wood crunched, deceptively muffled by the water.

No one was below deck. The two closest crew members went below and immediately screamed that they were taking on water intermittently as the waves pummeled the ship. The captain yelled, "Ben will take the helm. All below, We will move as much cargo as possible from aft to fore."

Instinctively, Ben knew that he had lost the slight advantage of speed. To make the situation worse, the enemy ship to the North hovered in position.

Ben called out the captain, "Dundee is now in jeopardy. I believe we can make our alternate site."

The captain replied, "Aye, sail for Kirkcaldy."

As he adjusted the rudder, Ben confirmed, "Course set for Kirkcaldy."

42

KIRKCALDY, SCOTLAND
WEDNESDAY, APRIL 15, 1495

Exhausted from a long night of baling and fashioning temporary patches, the crew hardly moved as the first light colored the eastern sky. The captain roused two sailors to ferry Ben ashore, as he was the logical choice to make the trek to Dundee.

While the captain and Ben were disappointed by the turn of events, there was a mutual respect in that they had worked together to prevent loss of cargo and life.

As Ben prepared to board the rowboat, he confirmed with the captain, "I have the merchant documents you scribed. Is there anything else?"

"No. But remember, as you head... never mind, you can probably find your way with your eyes closed. Have a safe passage."

Once on dry land Ben started walking methodically, undoing his brain's desire to compensate for the Rasch's continuous bobbing, pitching, and rolling.

After a few minutes he began to walk steadily. Based on the sun's position, it seemed obvious which path he would take as he departed Kirkcaldy.

To be sure, he hailed a woman collecting vegetables from her garden. Extending his arm and pointing, "Pardon, Dundee?" Ben had learned a fair amount of English from traders visiting Amsterdam. It wasn't necessary as the woman acknowledged his direction, half waving, and half pointing.

In contrast to flat Amsterdam, Ben relished the subtle changes in elevation under his feet. He continued to climb, imagining he was exploring Gibraltar with Becca, until a gust of cold wind from the North slapped him in the face.

The sun gained elevation as did Ben for the first few hours. He seemed to be making good time, almost feeling guilty that the altercation with the pirates brought him to this beautiful terrain.

With the sun warming the late morning air, Ben decided to find a spot to rest and eat some rations he brought from the Rasch.

Ben was about to bite into a piece of cured meat, when he heard a thunk. There was hardly a tree nearby. Besides, a falling branch would not make such a sound. He looked up to see if any birds had released some overweight prey. An empty sky. A second thunk. Then another and another. The sounds were spaced out evenly, so something strange was happening. He quickly wrapped his food and ran towards a small hilltop.

Ben stopped. A big smile broadened across his face. He stood watching a shepherd attempt to gather his flock of sheep by launching rounded objects at them with a long stick. *Not bad*, thought Ben, though the sheep weren't responding with any regularity as some of the projectiles were carried off-line by the wind or flying too far.

The shepherd, oblivious to Ben walking towards him, continued to make strikes. If it were possible, Ben's smile widened further as he noticed the shepherd making practice swings before striking a ball.

Finally, the shepherd noticed Ben about sixty paces away. He yelled. Ben couldn't discern if he was barking in English or Scots. Ben halted, then waved his right hand towards himself to encourage the shepherd to make another strike. He did, resulting in a thunk twenty paces to Ben's left and a good fifteen in front of him. Ben then extended both arms, motioning both now, yelling back, "Hit me!"

The shepherd understood the challenge, took a practice swing, then made a strike. Less than ten seconds later it hit, with a similar sound, ten paces to Ben's right and a few behind him. Ben could tell the projectiles were about the same size. Impressive. The shepherd appeared to be finding his aim and launched another. Four seconds into flight Ben took one step casually to his left. The thunk was just two and half paces to his right. The shepherd set up again and launched. Again, only a few seconds into flight, Ben took a single pace to his right. The thunk was almost in Ben's last footprint.

Ben then removed a white cloth from his pocket and waved it in mock surrender. The shepherd acknowledged. Even at a distance they had established a rapport, regardless of their potential to communicate verbally.

As they started walking towards each other, Ben yelled "*halo*" in Scots and was delighted to hear the shepherd respond in English. Ben zigzagged, stopping to pick up some balls and inspecting them. Eventually, they converged, shaking hands.

"I'm Ben."

"Artair."

"Does the golf help with herding your sheep?"

"Sometimes."

"After several launches you almost hit me."

"That's the problem. I use too many balls before I close on my target."

"Maybe I can help," said Ben pointing at a few sheep which had meandered from the herd.

Ben aligned Artair's feet properly, then pointed to the way in which the wind might influence the missiles' paths, and finally showed him how to overlap his hands when gripping the shaft. As the day waned, they continued to hit balls and retrieve them, hit and retrieve, and hit some more.

When dusk approached, Artair said, "You've earned dinner. You didn't tell me where you are headed."

"Dundee."

"Then you'll need to stay overnight lest you fumble in the dark for the next six hours, likely get lost, but more likely, break an ankle going over the rough terrain."

"I grew up on cliffs in Southern Spain, so I think I can find my way," replied Ben. "But it is not worth the risk, so I accept. Thank you."

They chatted amiably as they walked to Artair's campsite.

·••◆••·

A light smokiness filled the air, which roused Ben from an unintentional nap. Artair noticed and spoke, "It appears your journey has tired you. No doubt you're hungry."

"I am. Smells good. Thanks again for the hospitality."

"It is only fair. You helped me with golf."

Ben took a deep breath, stretched, and scanned the horizon, soaking in the end of a beautiful and interesting day.

Artair tended the small fire. He continued, "I should be much more competitive now."

Ben smiled, held up his right hand, and wagged his index finger, "Aha! I suspected you were using your skills for more than herding sheep.

You said competitive. Two traders I met in Amsterdam told me golf was banned in Scotland."

"It's been that way for over thirty years. As long as we practice archery and the King thinks we're ready for battle, no one seems to mind. However, interfering with day labor is another issue so we typically get together on Sundays after church and evenings, especially during the long days."

Ben sipped from a communal cup. "It is nice to have clean water to drink, a welcome change from beer and mead."

"Do you have golf where you're from?"

"Once in a while we have a match in Amsterdam, very similar to golf, called *kolf*, but nothing regular or organized."

Staring at the fire, Artair took a bite of coarse dark bread. After chewing vigorously for a few seconds, he queried, "How did you learn the sport?"

Ben chuckled, "Mostly by accident, but I am not really skilled in playing. Somewhat a long story."

"Is there enough time before I go to sleep in a few hours?"

"Good point, but I will try not to put you to sleep right away," said Ben laughing and enjoying Artair's sarcasm.

Ben took a deep breath and scratched his head "Where to start? As a child, the only parts of the Bible that interested me were the mathematics. My father was simply happy I wasn't totally disinterested. And I had to look after my sister, so I devised numeric games for us to play."

"Go on."

"When I was about eleven, my father's most important client had a patron who wanted to do better at golf. Father recommended that I help him with distances and angles. I did help. I enjoyed it. And I made a little money for it. So, I did that as much as I could. But I have hardly played, so I suppose I am good with your King James." Ben hesitated. Feeling comfortable with his new friend, he continued, "Or as good as King James could be with a Jew."

Artair jerked slightly in disbelief, "Are you saying you are a Jew?"

"I am."

"I thought Jews were fictional characters in the Bible."

"Really?"

"I was raised as a good Catholic, but no one, at least in my family, believed the heavens and earth were created in six days, or Noah actually gathered one male and one female of every animal onto a boat. I have trouble organizing a hundred sheep."

"So, what did you learn about us Jewish characters? That we grew horns, that we killed Christ?"

"We didn't talk about it much in our home and I never spoke with other children about Jews when I was growing up."

"Interesting."

They sat in silence for a minute as the fire crackled. Ben then summarized, somewhat tongue in cheek, "So you are a golf-playing shepherd who doesn't take the Bible literally. What about your family?"

"It's only my mother now. My father died when I was thirteen, so I had to look after his flock. I didn't care for it at first, but we needed the money, and I didn't want to let Mum down."

"What changed?"

"Golf."

"How did you learn about it?"

"My Mum actually."

"Outstanding. This is a better story than mine."

"Mum works at a place called the Goat Heid Inn, near St Andrews, where we live. Supposedly one evening she was talking to a few regulars about how badly she felt for me, taking on work I detested so much. One patron said I needed something to pass the time and gave Mum a club he was no longer using. And thus, a golf club was passed from a goat head to a sheep herder, simple as that. I have been striking ever since... Why don't you stay over tomorrow and go with me to play tomorrow night? I could use the help."

"Unfortunately, I have urgent business in Dundee."

"How long will that take?"

"Could take a few hours or a whole day. I have to arrange for ship cargo movement."

Artair poked the fire with a stick a few times, needlessly concentrating on the task at hand. He looked up and said, "I have a plan. We will get you going at first light. The ferry crossing River Tay from Seamylnes is unreliable. The ferryman at Tayport is my mate. He will take you back and forth to Broughty Ferry without delay. Dundee is four miles from there. I will give you a few shortcuts to Tayport. With any luck you can finish your business promptly and meet me in St Andrews for golf."

"How far away is St Andrews?"

"About the same distance as Tayport, so going to Dundee will add some distance to your journey. Altogether, about twenty-two miles. Correction, about twenty-five miles for you as our miles are longer than yours."

Ben started laughing hysterically.

"What's so funny about that?"

While catching his breath, Ben uttered, "It looks like... I'm not the only one... intrigued by... mathematics."

Artair's wide smile was visible even in the scant firelight.

Ben continued, "I will do my best to make it. How will I find you?"

"Easy, when you see the castle, look towards the ocean or ask anyone you might come upon."

"And your flock takes care of itself when you're golfing?"

"Wishful thinking. A couple lads help me."

They sat in silence, fire crackling, until Ben piped up, "One last thing. Will there be any problems if they suspect that Ben Solomon, a Jew, is helping you?"

"We're good-natured people, but let's not take a chance, particularly after I'm beating them badly and they've had a lot of mead. How about we make Solomon into Solley, a good old Scottish name? Ben Solley."

Ben extended his right hand, "Ben Solley, nice to meet you."

"Artair Spalding, you as well."

43

ST ANDREWS, SCOTLAND

THURSDAY, APRIL 16, 1495

In mid-afternoon Ben forded the River Eden. From what the locals told him, he estimated that he had another hour of walking before he had to slow down to look for Artair and the other golfers.

Usually, the air settled as the evening approached. Not today. Though not gusting, the wind velocity increased steadily. Ben imagined about the challenges Artair might have in aiming his strikes. He stopped to observe the true wind speed. Now anticipating his new friend's need, Ben picked up his pace almost to a trot.

Not an hour passed when Ben heard some loud voices. That was all the directional guidance he needed. As he homed in on the chatter, he was able to make out a few words.

A voice right behind said, "They're arguing about the first strike."

Ben pivoted quickly, "Artair! You practically scared the life out of me."

"Glad you got here. The guys always mix it up, in one way or another, before we start."

They put their arms around each other's shoulders and marched towards the group.

····◆····

Artair took the lead, "I'd like you to meet a new friend, Ben Solley."

Perfunctory greetings did nothing to break up the debate on whether the projectile for the first strike should be dropped or placed on the ground."

Ben leaned toward Artair, cupped his hands, and whispered into his ear.

Artair piped up, "Gentlemen, Ben has a suggestion."

"Ben who," said a bystander, a tall and substantial man.

Artair continued, "Hah, Davis, you and Ewan are too busy arguing. This is Ben. He knows something about golf. He might have a way to resolve your disagreement."

The four men stopped almost instantly, shifting their gaze to Ben.

"I'm afraid Artair has put me on the spot. Where I come from, we play in the streets, and we have no choice but to place the ball on the ground to start at each target. But you have this beautiful earth."

"Artair, you say this man knows golf," said Davis. "Sounds to me more like a peddler."

Everybody laughed. Davis, clearly the leader, opened his palms to Ben, "Go on lad."

Ben continued, "It seems to me everyone should start without undue disadvantage. Neither of the ways you are talking about would accomplish that. What do you think about making a small pile of dirt with your hands and placing your ball on top of it?"

The men looked at one another. Davis shrugged his shoulders, bent over, looked up at his mates and said, "Well, on with it."

As Davis shaped a launch area, Ben said, "Who declares the target?"

The remark was met with laughter.

"Ben, is it?" said Davis. Then pointing, "See the post about a hundred paces that way?"

"I do."

"It is placed behind a hole. The man with the fewest strikes to put his ball in the hole, wins."

"Very practical," said Ben.

"Would you like to compete?"

"No thank you. I am here to help Artair if you permit me."

"Is that fair with our wagering?" questioned Ewan, another competitor.

Davis, "Surely it makes no difference. Don't we put all the winnings together for our food and drink at The Heid?"

Ewan agreed. He knelt, cupped his hands on the earth and brought some soil together. He patted it down then looked up. "Gents, is this acceptable to place my ball for the first strike?"

Nods followed. Ewan slid his hand into his pocket and pulled out a sphere. Ben noticed it had a slight sheen.

Artair noticed and whispered to Ben, "He applied sap to the balls and polished them."

Ben nodded his understanding. Ewan made his strike and the other three did likewise. Then two marched toward the left, one walked straight away as Ben and Artair walked to the right. Artair turned his head slightly to speak to Ben. He hesitated as he could see Ben was in a deep state of concentration. Artair slowed his pace. Ben stayed in sync while Artair shifted his eyes downward to spot his ball.

They stopped. Ben pointed to the right and suggested, "Take some practice swings over there."

Ben then took a stance immediately behind Artair's ball, extending his right arm towards the target post. With his left arm extended back to their starting point, he inhaled deeply feeling the breeze on his face. He turned to Artair, "You should make an attempt to fly it exactly forty-three paces forward taking aim five paces to the post's right."

"Really?"

"Trust me."

A few minutes later, the group converged on the area surrounding the post. All four were within ten feet of the post. Davis, the closest at six feet, proudly declared he arrived in three strikes. The others grumbled. Hamish led a chorus of, "four."

Davis continued, "Artair?"

"Two."

"Two?"

"I am lucky but not for the strike. Ben told me where to aim and how far to send it."

Ben chimed in, "But he still had to strike it properly."

The four golfers needed two more strikes for their balls to drop into the hole. At that point, with Ben in tow, they started trudging back to the original starting point.

About halfway, Ben inquired quietly to Artair, "Is there only one post?"

"Aye."

"This could be tedious after a while. How many times do you walk up and back?"

"It depends on the night, who can play, what is going on at their homes. In late spring and early summer, sometimes we can make more than ten trips."

"Why not plant a few other posts in so you can play back and forth or loop back to the start?"

Artair piped up to the group, "I think we need to hire this man."

Ben put up his hand, palms out, in protest.

Davis placed his arm around Ben, "Let's talk about it at The Heid."

44

St Andrews, Scotland
Friday, April 17, 1495

The morning light slipped through the shutter boards covering an opening in the small room. Awaking to a throbbing head, Ben suspected he was at the Goat Heid Inn. His last vivid memories were singing and eating *powsowdie*, a soup made with sheep heads, which tasted quite good when masked by generous portions of a potent liquid he heard the locals calling Scots whisky.

The bed was more than comfortable, an indulgence, compared to the Rasch or fireside with Artair. Ben's head throbbed. He rolled away from the slivers of light. With no glass in the window, the room stayed a wee bit darker.

It could have been five minutes or hours later when he heard two knocks on the door, followed by a soothing female voice, "Mornin' to ya."

Ben rustled.

Three knocks then with increased volume, "Mornin' to ya."

Ben managed, "Am I in the Goat Heid?"

"Indeed, you are. Artair's mum told your mates to help you upstairs when the pub closed."

Now sitting up, Ben responded more cogently, "I will clear out soon."

Cracking the door so she could speak normally, "First, you tidy up and have some breakfast."

Ben stood, but needed to steady himself, holding the bed with his left arm. "Thank you, but I have to return to Kirkcaldy."

"From the looks of it, you will not be going very far today, let alone on a twenty-mile hike. I'll bring you some fresh water."

"Thank you..." with an uptick of an incomplete phrase.

"Evina. Everyone calls me Evi."

"Ben."

Ben walked gingerly downstairs into an open room, took the seat at a table set with a single plate.

"Now you're lookin' spry," said Evi as she placed a mug of milk aside the plate. She expected to smell a gamy guest but apparently Ben has used the small water basin to its fullest.

Ben took a sip, mumbling "hmmm" in approval.

Evi retrieved Ben's plate. He noticed the ease of her movement in the kitchen, reminding him of Mother. He closed his eyes, visualizing Gibraltar. A minute later, his stomach growled as the smell of cooked eggs, hot bread, and onions brought him back to the moment.

Ben used his right hand to lift a forkful of egg to his mouth. "Delicious." He noticed a stare from the corner of his eye. Turning to Evi, "Something wrong?"

Evi hesitated, "No, not really."

"Go on."

"This may seem silly, but I have never seen anyone use their right hand for a fork."

"I come from a small group. A rebellious sort. We had no weapons, so we learned to fight with forks."

A moment of silence then Evi erupted with a belly laugh.

Ben smiled, pleased with Evi's reaction to the jest. "Let me ask you something. What is this drink called Scots whisky? You certainly can't drink it like beer."

"You're right no doubt. Some folks around here don't know it yet. Just last year, the Lindores monastery, not far to the west, started making it. Supposedly the University got some for a big celebration and the leftovers ended up here, not sure how. Good thing they're not making much of it right now, but I suspect that will change."

"No doubt" echoed Ben. "Do they serve Jenever at the pub?"

"I've never heard of that it."

"It's made from juniper berries. It's so strong that some people use it for medicinal purposes. If I had known this whisky would have the same effect, I would have used more restraint."

"You're a funny man."

·••◆••·

Later in the morning, with the castle off his right shoulder, Ben walked the short distance to a bluff overlooking the North Sea. He spotted a smooth slab of stone just a few feet away and moved to it. Evi was right. He wasn't going very far today. He inhaled the salty air, dense with moisture, very much reminding him of Amsterdam. The nip in the air took him further back to the winter days in Spain.

Ben surveyed the endless palate of small waves. He knew there was motion, but the surface seemed fixed from his vantage point. Dark patches made their journeys across the surface as the clouds blotted the sunlight, seemingly at random.

For the moment, the sun warmed Ben. He sat down, continuing to stare eastward, enjoying the quiet. The wind was not strong enough to speak. The few birds cruised in silence. He closed his eyes. *Is there a reason I am here at this time in my life?*

A cloud masked the sun. The breeze picked up slightly. Ben laid back and put his hands in his pockets. As the cloud passed, the warmth returned. Ben dozed off.

"Taken in some more sleep, I see, Mister Solley."

Ben twitched from his light sleep, recognizing the tenor, "Ben, please. Hello Evi. How did you find me?"

"Now you don't think you're the first to get a headache from a long night in the pub."

"I suppose not."

"Well, this is a popular place to get the cobwebs out. You're in my uncle's spot."

Ben returned the jest, "So you had nothing better to do than wake me up?"

"Davis wants to see you. He will come back around to the Heid in mid-afternoon. I told him I would give you the message as I had a fair notion of your whereabouts. And here you are."

"Thanks, I'll walk back with you."

·••◆••·

Davis entered the Heid, and spotted Ben at a table with a beer in his hand. With rhetorical sarcasm, "Sure you wouldn't like a taste of Scots?"

Ben smiled, "How goes it?"

"Good, good," said Davis, taking a seat. "I'll get right to it Ben. All the golfers you met last night, to a man, want you to be our adviser."

"What do you mean?"

"You would work for us. You help us set up the holes, guide us as we play, fix the rules, and resolve disputes. We will pay you well."

"You know I live in Amsterdam?"

"Aye but stay for six months."

"I can't."

"You like golf."

"True."

"You like Artair and the fellows."

"Also true."

"And you like Evi."

Ben crinkled his face. "What do you mean?"

Davis extended his hand to Ben's shoulder and shook it in a brotherly way, "Well, she fancies you."

"How do you know that?"

"You're the only one, other than her own Da, she would help after too much drink."

Davis closed with, "Please think about it."

"I will."

Davis may or may not have attempted to add to the job's enticement but now Ben couldn't help thinking about his instant attraction to Evi. He admitted to himself, *this woman fascinates me.*

45

AUGUSTA, GEORGIA, USA

SUNDAY, SEPTEMBER 1, 2002

"Here Mother, take my arm," offered Cameron. "The steps are wet."

"Thank you, son," replied Christina as she smiled and grabbed hold.

They walked towards the rear of the Saint Paul's Episcopal Church of Augusta. Carlton held the door for them.

The cumulus clouds, having thundered serendipitously during the sermon, were carried away by a comfortable easterly breeze. Several parishioners gathered in the churchyard to catch up on the latest local goings-on.

"Hello Christina, Carlton, Cameron," bellowed Paul Grant. He guided his wife, Julie, towards the Stephens group.

"Mr. and Mrs. Grant, nice to see you," replied Cameron.

Paul asked Cameron about life on the tour. Julie and Christina delved into their latest civic project.

Carlton broadened the conversation with Paul as he knew the last thing his son wanted, however innocent, was to talk about golf akin to a press conference. This gave Cameron the opportunity he was looking for. Politely but commanding, Cameron placed his hand on Paul's shoulder, "Will you excuse me? I need to speak with Reverend Portman."

Betraying his surname, the Reverend was tall and slim, almost a Cameron knock-off, though his parents' generation.

"Hello Reverend Portman."

"Nice to see you, Cameron. Great that you could take a Sunday morning off from your schedule to worship with us."

"Not by choice," replied Cameron with a slight frown. "I missed the cut on Friday."

"Oh, sorry. I know that doesn't happen often." Shifting the topic, "Do you like living in Atlanta?"

"I like it. Do you have a few minutes?"

"Sure," replied Reverend Portman as he motioned with his head away from the crowd. They walked several steps to separate themselves. "What can I help you with?"

"How does the Church view the teachings of Moses Maimonides aka Rambam?"

Reverend Portman furrowed his eyebrows and smiled, "Now there's a question I don't hear every day, or every decade for that matter. Thirty seconds might be the most you would get from the majority of my colleagues. But I just happened to attend a seminar not too long ago on Christianity in the Middle Ages. To answer your question, I'm not aware the Church has a view. Any particular reason you're asking?"

"I audited a comparative religions class at Tech recently. A full unit was dedicated to him. I was intrigued as to why his teachings, eight hundred years ago, seem to apply directly to our lives today and hardly anyone knows about him."

The priest rubbed the side of his face as he concentrated and looked down momentarily to focus. "My opinion, and only my opinion, is that it requires thought and reflection. The average person in our society, unfortunately, doesn't seem to have the time or patience. However, there are several modern adaptations of his hierarchy of giving, which is encouraging."

"These seem at odds with each other. Average people go to church and synagogues and mosques. Shouldn't they be hearing about Maimonides in those places?"

"I can see you have a strong interest in this. How did that happen?"

"As I said, I heard about Maimonides at Tech, just by chance. I went there to learn about other religions and became intrigued. Perhaps because people talk to me all the time about doing good so I can increase the value of my name and my brand."

"Interesting. I think we ought to talk about this further at some point."

With the precision learned from hundreds of media interactions, Cameron looked the Reverend squarely in the eyes, "I look forward to it. Really nice seeing you again."

46

North Belgrade, Maine USA
Orlando Florida, USA
Tuesday, September 3, 2002

As much as he hated to admit it, Herman was glad cable had finally come to the Maine woods. It was nice to have on a rainy day or just for background when his eyes were too tired to read.

Whisperwood, true to its name, had placed regulators on the TV volume controls. The lodge also blocked many channels, including those dedicated to infomercials and sensational news. Fortunately, the Golf Channel wasn't one of those. Herman stopped surfing and placed the remote down on the small end table gently, as Beth had fallen into a light sleep next to him on the couch.

A commercial faded as a deep, polished voice took over. "Peter Kessler back with more *Golf Talk Live* and our chat with Rusty Stephens and his caddie, O.T. Sills. Right before the break, you were about to tell our audience how your nicknames came about."

Rusty and O.T. looked at each other, motioning for the other to tell the story. After they shared a short laugh, Rusty leaned back, deferring to O.T.

"The names sorta happened together," started O.T. "Rusty has a sixty-three-degree wedge that can be very difficult to hit, but Rusty does it very well. It was stamped Trusty Rusty. It's supposed to tarnish over time so that's the rusty part. I think Cobra, can I say the name on the air...wanted to give you confidence by calling it trusty. Many years ago, when we got into tough situations around the green, I started saying, 'trusty rusty,' as I handed him the club, and Rusty would grab it saying, 'one time,' for good luck."

Kessler, the experienced journalist, contributed, "Golfers are a superstitious bunch but I'd say anything if it helped me hit a lob shot like Rusty."

Herman mumbled, "You got that right."

Rusty picked up the story, "As time went on, 'trusty rusty' became Rusty and 'one time' became O.T. When reporters started following us around, one of 'em must of overheard us, thought those were our names, and used them in a broadcast. They just stuck. I don't mind, do you... Brian?"

O.T. pointed at Rusty. "Me neither."

Kessler continued, "Well that explains a lot as O.T. is a far cry from Brian. I must admit, when my producers booked you guys for the show, I did some research. I called a good friend, Carrie Coleman, perhaps the first professional female caddie and a great one at that, male or female. She confessed she assumed O.T. stood for overtime."

They shared another short laugh, then O.T. contributed, "Makes sense. I met Carrie a few years ago, at a pro-am, when she was on Lee Trevino's bag. We were both logging pretty long hours that week."

The camera panned back to capture all three as Kessler turned to Rusty, "Let me close out this segment by putting you on the spot now, Rusty. Please let us all in on your given name."

"Cameron."

Kessler, ever quick, responded, "Do you use a Cameron putter."

"I do."

"How ironic," concluded Kessler. "With all due respect to Scotty Cameron, your nickname came from a wedge."

Kessler's final sign-off was drowned as Herman shouted, "Oh my God!"

Beth lurched up, "Herman, what's wrong."

"I'm sorry, nothing really."

Beth flopped back down from her involuntary push-up, "So why did you scare me half to death?"

"Well, you know Sandy has been seeing Cameron Stephens."

"Of course. And you yelled because of that?"

"Turns out his nickname is Rusty Stephens."

"He's a golfer, yes?"

"Yes, but he's not just any golfer."

Beth rubbed her eyes, "I just don't understand why she had to hide this from us."

47

SIDNEY, MAINE, USA
MANHATTAN, NEW YORK, USA
ATLANTA, GEORGIA, USA
WEDNESDAY, SEPTEMBER 4, 2002

Sandy sat up in her bed, grabbed her mobile phone, removed it from its holster, and tapped her parent's number.

"Hello."

"Hello Daddy. How is..."

Herman handed the phone to Beth, "Hi honey," bellowed her mother.

"How are you feeling? Is everything okay? What's with Dad?"

"Slow down sweetheart. I'm feeling good. Everything's okay," said Beth as her voice trailed off.

"It doesn't sound that way."

"Honestly, I'm feeling fine. Your father is upset."

"Why?"

"Something to do with your boyfriend."

"What about him?"

"He saw him on TV the other day."

Increasing the volume and tempo in her voice, Sandy practically screamed, "Why was he on TV? Did something happen to him?"

"Not at all. I didn't mean to give you a start. He was on the Golf Channel."

"Why was he on the Golf Channel?"

"I'm not sure. Something to do with his name."

"What do you mean his name and what does that have to do with golf?"

"Your dad says he's a golfer."

"Dad's a golfer. Can I just talk to Dad?"

"I'm not sure he wants to talk about it, but I'll try."

Sandy heard Beth yell out, "Herman, can you please pick up the phone and talk to your daughter...please?" A few seconds passed. "Hold on, I'm trying. He's just staring out the window. Let me see if I can get him to call you back."

Resigned, Sandy said, "Okay, thanks Mom."

Ten seconds later, Sally's cell phone rang. "Hi Sandy."

"Do you know why Dad is so upset with me about Cameron."

"I'm fine, how are you?" said Sally sarcastically.

"I'm sorry. I called to see how Mom was doing. Dad answered the phone and wouldn't even talk to me. Mom says she's okay, but she really couldn't tell me why Dad was so angry; something to do with Cameron on the Golf Channel."

Sally responded, "Mom says she feels well, and I believe her. The thing with Dad, as much as I can piece together, has something to do with Cameron's nickname."

"Cameron's nickname?"

"Wish I had more for you sis, but I'm sure you'll figure it out."

"Thanks Sally. Talk to you later." She hung up.

Sally looked briefly at her phone, shrugged her shoulders, and closed the clam shell.

Sandy started her PC and opened a browser window. She typed "golf channel cameron stephens."

In less than a second, 741,000 results were returned with the top ten displayed on her screen.

She clicked on the first link. Her screen filled in. Leveraging her research skills, she quickly parsed the article, scrolling to the salient sentence, at least for her. She read, "In his typical style, Peter Kessler cleverly closed out the interview with Rusty Stephens and his caddie, O.T. Sills revealing their nicknames' origins."

Sandy leaned in closer to Cameron's image and Brian sitting side by side, in two armchairs, opposite Kessler.

Sandy dialed Cameron's cell phone.

"Hello."

"Hi Cameron."

"Hey."

"May I please speak to Rusty?"

"Uh Uh Uh Well Uh Err Uh."

"Bye." Click.

•••◆•••

The staccato knock upon Rusty's condo door identified O.T. He used his key to enter. He walked into the living room, where he found Rusty slouched in a chair by the window, expressionless, eyes fixed on Buckhead's sprawl of mansions and the acreage leading up to them. Rusty hardly moved his head as he mumbled, "Thanks for coming over."

"No problem."

"I messed up really bad." He explained what happened. "Total brain fart. I feel like Van de Velde cratering at The British Open."

"There's a big difference. Jean made one bad decision after another, compounding the problem. You might be able to recover from this if you want to."

"Why wouldn't I want to?"

"We've talked about this before. Maybe you two aren't meant for each other."

"I think we are, but even if it turns out we aren't, I'd regret it for the rest of my life if I let it end this way."

O.T. was glad to see Rusty perk up, talking about the future. "I think there are a few parts to this, like what do you want to say, how do you say it, and when. I could reach out to..."

"Thanks, but I have to make this shot."

48

MANHATTAN, NEW YORK, USA

FRIDAY, SEPTEMBER 6, 2002

Sandy tightened her robe's sash, almost swaddling herself as she began to proofread her email draft. She sipped her tea.

Cameron,

When we met, I was totally amazed. At the risk of using an old cliche, you swept me off my feet. As we got to know each other, I thought we could deal with the differences in our upbringing.

But I don't see how we can sustain a relationship, when you have to hide your very self from me. I now know you are a professional golfer. Over two-thirds of pro athletes get divorced (it's the researcher in me). I found a sad story about Fred Couples' ex-wife. And Linda Rubin divorcing Tom Watson after twenty-five years. Then there's the Bible-thumpers, for lack of a better word.

With your profession's culture, its extremes, and your need to hold back from me, it is almost impossible to imagine a future together.

I wish you nothing but the best,
Sandy

She was satisfied with the email but needed something on the subject line. Blank wouldn't do. She took another sip of tea. She savored it, as much as she could, then put her mug down and typed "Different Worlds" into the subject. She inhaled and clasped her hands underneath her chin, focusing on the screen. One last read. Her hand then embraced her mouse.

She closed her eyes as tears started to form. She clicked. Swoosh.

She heard a ping almost instantly. "Oh great," she muttered to herself, thinking she mistyped Cameron's email address resulting in a message bounce back. She opened her eyes.

She couldn't help but cast an ironic smile, with moist eyes, as she saw an email from Cameron which crossed with hers. She opened it.

Dear Sandy,

I'm sorry. You had every right to hang up on me. I will try to explain myself.

You know me well enough to understand why I don't like to tell people I've just met, what I do for a living. I don't want anyone to like me just because of that. But I let it go too far. Brian warned me, but I was selfish. I was enjoying not having to talk about my public life.

Early on, I knew you were someone special. After we first met, I wanted to understand our respective religions. I wasn't intending to go on a spiritual journey, but I was intrigued when, somewhat by accident, I learned about Moses Maimonides, his ladder of giving, and his writings on the Bible.

I would like to meet you somewhere away from the public eye or talk on the phone when you are ready. If you'd rather not, I would respect that too.

Miss you,
Cameron

Sandy closed her laptop. She opened her front door, took two steps across the hall, raised her hand to knock on Tamara's door and froze as if she was playing a child's game. The sturdy door hardly muffled the unmistakable sounds of passion. Sandy returned to her apartment, pulled a piece of paper from her printer, scribbled, "Tam, Need your opinion on something. Didn't want to interrupt, San." She finished, added a smiley face, folded it while she walked back across the hall, then slipped it under Tamara's door.

Sandy stepped back into her apartment and dialed her sister's number.

"Hello"

"Sally. Am I messed up?"

49

PORTLAND & SIDNEY, MAINE, USA
FRIDAY, SEPTEMBER 13, 2002

Sandy exited the airport terminal, phone to her ear. "Thanks Tam. I appreciate you telling it like it is. Gotta hang up. Just about to get into my sister's car."

She walked past the pick-up area, into the parking lot towards a few spaces where the family rendezvoused for years, dubbed the Cole-ection area by Sandy as a precocious nine-year-old.

Sandy opened both doors on the passenger side of Sally's Subaru. She heaved her duffel in back then slid into the front seat. They leaned in and kissed, left cheek to left cheek. "Thanks for picking me up."

"No problem. I have a good crew that's really stepped up since Mom's scare."

"How's she doing?"

"Let's get going and I'll fill you in."

Sally fumbled for the parking ticket. Sandy noticed and pulled a five-dollar bill from her wallet. Sally backed out and drove towards the attendant station. She continued, "You know Mom. No problem as far as she's concerned."

"What about Daddy?"

"He doesn't seem overly concerned but I think he's struggling between being a doctor and a husband."

"Is he still pissed at me?"

"He's not pissed. I think... disappointed more than anything. Glad you came up. Where did you leave it with Cameron?"

"It just sort of ended. I called you right after he and I exchanged emails. We haven't communicated since. You said give it some time. I took your advice."

"What about Brian? Have you talked with him about the situation?"

"Not really. He said he'd understand if I didn't want to help him anymore with his family tree. It was nice of him. But he was so excited when I located his great great grandfather. And it's interesting for me, so I told him I'd continue to investigate. I traced the family name, which was changed five generations ago in the United States and may have a link back to Europe."

"Wow. Maybe we should do our family tree."

"We'd probably hit a dead end in Anatevka."

"*Fiddler on the Roof*?" asked Sally.

"Yep, let's go see it next time you visit."

With hardly any traffic Sally was able to zip right through Portland on I-295, which shortened the trip by several miles over the loopy I-95. The one-hour trip went by quickly as the sisters caught up on the latest goings on, including the most important topic, a new ice cream flavor at Gifford's.

As Sally drove up to the house Katy ran over in a flash. Both women opened the car doors about the same time. Katy didn't know where to go first. As Beth and Herman followed, they ended up in a four-person hug surrounding the pooch. Dog heaven.

The greeting continued until Katy settled down.

Herman spoke up, "After I get your bag into the house, I need to run up to Oakland for a few minutes. If you're not too tired from the trip, why don't you come with me?"

"Sure," said Sandy, thinking positively that her father wanted to address the proverbial elephant in the room. They could get that out of the way.

Beth piped up, "Great, Sally and I will start dinner in a few minutes."

Hardly a second after Herman put his Pathfinder in Drive, Sandy said, "Dad..."

"Let me go first since I called this meeting."

She smiled, "That you did."

"I know you need to have a private life. I get that. But we've had such a close relationship, I suppose I was upset you couldn't tell me you were dating Rusty Stephens."

"I wasn't dating Rusty Stephens. I was dating Cameron Stephens."

"Was?"

"We aren't seeing each other for the same reason you got upset. He couldn't be honest with me. I didn't think it was going to be a fling, but it looks that way."

"I know I'm sounding like your grandmother, but things happen for a reason."

"So I'd like to know the reason Cameron and Brian got such crazy nicknames."

"It has to do with golf," said Herman. "Let me try to explain. Rusty, or I guess I should say Cameron, has a rusty club."

Sandy interrupted, "Why would he want a rusty club, when he can afford any club he wants?"

Herman explained a rough surface imparts more backspin which can help a ball stop on the green.

"Interesting. What about Brian?"

"O.T. stands for one time. For good luck, some golfers and caddies say it once in a while to add positivity. It seems that as Brian hands Cameron the club, see I said their names right, he would say 'rusty' and then Cameron would reply 'o and t'."

"That all sounds pretty convoluted."

As he pulled into a parking spot, Herman said, "There are plenty of strange names out there. I just need to drop off these papers for our accountant. Be right back."

····◆····

Herman and Sandy pulled up to the house. They could hear laughter emanating from the back porch. As they angled towards the kitchen, they could see a bottle of Chardonnay, halfway drained, sitting on the counter.

By the time Herman lifted the bottle and inspected the label, Sandy had retrieved two more wine glasses from the shelf. A second bottle was uncorked a few minutes later.

Like old times, everyone was upbeat and helpful. With the wine consumption, any cooking errors wouldn't be noticed.

After dinner and more wine, the evening unfolded when they nestled into the couch and cushy chairs in the living room. Katy joined them, nuzzling Beth for attention. Unlike old times, the dishes remained in the sink.

Sally and Sandy tried to pick up the conversation when Beth and Herman peeled off to bed with Katy in tow. Struggling to keep their eyes open, hardly getting a sentence out, they both fell asleep.

50

SIDNEY, MAINE, USA

SATURDAY, SEPTEMBER 14, 2002

As the sun came up, Beth traipsed into the kitchen, smelled the aroma of coffee brewing. "Sandy, honey, what are you doing up?" Noticing Sandy with her head down, resting on her hands, elbows on table, staring into her steaming mug, "You alright?"

"I'm afraid Bacchus got the best of me."

"We did have almost two bottles of wine, but it's not like we were drinking martinis all night. And you've never had a problem with wine from what I remember."

"I fell asleep, woke up a few hours later, dehydrated, drank a glass of water then started thinking about Cameron and couldn't go back to sleep."

"Want to talk about it?"

"I talked to Sally."

"That's good but I'm sure she didn't have a magic bullet for you. No one does. All you can do is talk to people you respect and make your own decisions."

"Mom, I know you're right, but I feel like I'm drifting without a rudder. I've never been indecisive, or second guessed myself so much."

Beth sat down on the other side of the table. As Sandy looked up, Beth extended her arms, grasped Sandy's hands and gently lowering them to the table. "Don't be so hard on yourself. I think it's the grapes weighing on you right now. Not your gray matter."

"There's something else."

Beth lightly massaged the tops of Sandy's hands with her thumbs, knowing Sandy would spill the beans when she was ready.

"I got a voice mail from Cameron. He invited me to go away with him for a few days."

"Is that a good thing or a bad thing?"

"Not sure. Maybe both. I sort of expected he'd get back in touch with me after we traded emails last week."

"So, what's the good part?"

"He's so easy to be with."

"Do you mean physically?"

"No, but that too."

"What's the bad part?"

"The long-term. Like I'm home raising kids and he's traveling the world, with women throwing themselves at him all the time."

Beth yanked her head back and blinked, "Sandy, sweetheart, aren't you ahead of yourself, imagining a bad marriage, when you hardly know him, really?"

Sandy pulled her hands back gently, grabbed her coffee with both hands and took a gulp. "You're right."

"I am?"

Sandy smiled, "And there's one more thing."

"I'm afraid to ask."

"Nothing bad. Cameron wants to meet me at the Waterville airport."

"There haven't been commercial flights there for years."

"I know. I guess I should have said Cameron wants to pick me up there."

Beth pondered for a few seconds, "Does that mean what I think it means?"

Sandy smiled and nodded.

51

ATLANTA, GEORGIA, USA

MONDAY, SEPTEMBER 16, 2002

Driving towards downtown on Peachtree Street, Rusty was on the lookout for the Equifax building on the right as it would indicate he'd gone too far. However, after watching *Driving Miss Daisy*, he had no trouble spotting The Temple. When the traffic gapped, Rusty turned left into the narrow driveway past the building, pulled around back, and parked.

Upon entering the offices, he was greeted with, "Shalom, Mr. Stephens, Rabbi Sugarman is expecting you. Right this way. May I get you something— coffee, tea, water?"

Rusty declined as he was shown into the rabbi's office. "Welcome Rusty."

"Rabbi, nice of you to see me. May I have your autograph? You'd be my first movie star."

"You beat me to the punch. You'd be my first golf star."

They laughed as the rabbi continued, "Have a seat and tell me where you'd like to start."

Rusty wasn't sure why he found the rabbi's appearance unusual. Perhaps he was expecting a stereotypical long beard, yarmulke, and robes. What he saw was a man in a button-down shirt who looked like he could be Wolf Blitzer's brother.

Rusty began, "I do want to talk about interfaith relationships, but can we start with Moses Maimonides?

"Certainly."

"This may sound silly, but he was way ahead of his time; he had an acronym, Rambam."

"True. It was used by Jewish people," said the Rabbi, smiling at Rusty's observation. "I suppose Rabbi Moshe ben Maimon was a mouthful even back then."

Rusty continued, "I've found his life and history fascinating. It's impressive, at least to me, that there's so much information on someone who died over eight hundred years ago. Anyway, I read parts of *The Guide to the Perplexed*. I doubt I'll read all of it. I found it very challenging."

"It is. You could spend years if not a lifetime studying Rambam."

"I got interested in his ladder of giving, which seems to be relevant in today's world. Can you tell me about that?"

"Sure. Traditionally there are eight rungs on the ladder. The lowest rung means giving a token amount with reluctance. The next rung is giving something willingly. Next is giving a meaningful amount, whatever that is, but not until asked. About halfway up the ladder is giving without being asked. Moving upward on the ladder is giving anonymously to an unknown recipient, then ultimately giving to help people so they are no longer in need, and in turn, can become givers."

"That's a lot."

"I agree. I think it's easier, at least for me, to simplify it as the need for recognition at the bottom and anonymous empowerment at the top."

"I think I can get my head around that. Thanks."

"Rusty. Almost all religions manifest this concept in some way. Do you have a sense on why it captured your imagination?"

"Good question." Rusty smiled. "I was asked a similar question after church with my parents two weeks ago. I said it has something to do with people telling me how being charitable will help me. But I think it's more than that."

"Do you have a sense how?"

"Not exactly sure. Maybe a power that isn't being used."

"I know it's new to you. Keep digging. Now tell me about this person who came into your life recently. Is there any one thing you think best describes her?"

Rusty looked up as he concentrated, "Rabbi, beyond the instant chemistry, if I had to put it into a word, Sandy's authentic."

Rusty summarized the impulse to learn about Sandy's religion, how that took him back to his alma mater and then his misstep in trying to hide his occupation. He then explained he was going to meet Sandy privately to the extent that was possible.

"Did you have a chance to watch *Driving Miss Daisy*?"

"I did. Great cast. Jessica Tandy and Morgan Freeman were phenomenal. So were Dan Aykroyd and Patti LuPone."

"Their intermarriage doesn't feature prominently in the film, as far as screen time, but it masterfully reveals three important topics— parental pressure, traditions, and beliefs."

Rabbi Sugarman went on to contrast traditions, like lighting a Menorah on Hanukkah or caroling at Christmas. He then contrasted beliefs in Jesus, as one of the most influential humans in history, or a God in human form, who died for mortals' sins.

The rabbi confirmed Rusty's awareness that the worldwide Jewish population was minuscule. What sparked Rusty was the religion's diversity on so many levels— from beliefs on interfaith relationships and marriage, from Ashkenazim of Eastern European lineage to Sephardim of Iberian ancestry, from Reform to Liberal to Conservative to Orthodoxy with dozens of Hasidic dynasties, like the Lubavitch and the Satmar, based in Brooklyn.

"Rusty, my point in all this is that I recommend you and Sandy, if you move forward together, thoughtfully come up with a game plan, so to speak, just for you and her."

"Makes sense."

"Those of us who started officiating mixed marriages decades ago, had always wanted to bring the non-Jewish partners into the fold, perhaps part of a survival instinct. Some people still believe this, but attitudes shift, even from one generation to the next."

Rabbi Sugarman leaned closer to Rusty and continued, "In fact, I recently spoke with a terrific rabbi, Randi Musnitsky. I tried to recruit her here, unsuccessfully, many years ago. She told me most interfaith couples, in her experience, have a substantially higher degree of success when they select one religion for their children and raise them with those beliefs. This overrides whether the parents worship differently, or even mixing traditions in the home."

Rusty gazed at the wall, internalizing what he had just heard.

The rabbi broke the short silence. "There's a lot to think about. Is there anything else I can help you with?"

"Not right now. Thanks for your time."

"Rusty, I know you're busy but how about a short tour so you can at least see where I preached to Jessica Tandy."

"Sounds good."

After the tour, Rusty thanked the staff and had his picture taken with the rabbi. He exited the building, calling O.T. as he walked the few steps to his car, "All set?"

"Good to go."

"Have fun and the rest will take care of itself."

Rusty pulled out of The Temple driveway, making a right on Peachtree Street. He was aware that dozens of streets around Atlanta were named Peachtree this or Peachtree that. As he headed towards the DeKalb-Peachtree airport, he figured the name fit right in, as everyone he knew called it Peachtree-DeKalb, or by its three-letter code, PDK.

In a half a mile Rusty punched the M5 as he entered I-85. Four minutes later, he exited onto Clairmont Road, which would bring him directly to PDK in less than ten minutes.

A young woman, in a peach-colored, button-down shirt, and black slacks greeted Rusty as he stepped from his car. "Good morning Mr. Stephens, you're ready to go. Mr. Sills brought over your luggage and credentials. Keys in the car?"

"Yep."

"We'll take good care of her. Please follow me."

A pilot, professionally dressed in a short sleeve white shirt, seemingly from central casting, replete with epaulets, black necktie, and aviator shades, leaned from the doorway, extended his hand for both courtesy and safety.

"Welcome aboard. Have a seat and buckle up. If you need anything before we take off, let me know. This can be a busy place, but I think we can take off within fifteen minutes if you're ready."

"Great, let's go."

Rusty stepped up and in, then hunched over to accommodate the low ceiling. He sat down in the left seat of the pair facing forward. The pilot slid into his seat up front, also on the left, and began confirming his instrument and radio settings per the pre-takeoff checklist.

Leaning slightly right, turning back towards Rusty, the pilot said, "Mr. Stephens..."

"Rusty, please."

"Okay. I'm Bart, Bart Emerson, your captain for the trip. My co-pilot today is Ken Stafford."

A hand quickly came into view from upfront. Rusty smiled as it looked like Thing from *The Addams Family* reruns he watched at Tech. At least Cousin Itt wasn't in the cockpit.

Bart improvised the remainder of the standard script, "This is a Cessna Citation. I never get tired of flying this baby. We should land in Waterville about three hours after takeoff. The cabin can be a little tight but with only you and one other person, you should be able to spread out a little."

"Sounds good."

"We'll be taking off to the Northeast, so you should have a nice view of Lake Lanier on the climb out. Let me know if you want more flight info, otherwise we'll shut up and let you relax."

"No problem. Thanks."

Bart put his headphones on. As he communicated with air traffic control and began to taxi to runway 2R, Rusty was rethinking his resistance to private air travel. It was hard to believe that less than forty-five minutes ago, rabbi Sugarman was showing him a Torah scroll with a silver pointer, a Yad, for reading it.

Rusty noticed that O.T. had also dropped off some reading material in a brown expanding file, a post-it note attached with "Cameron" scribbled on it. Included were the current issues of *Atlanta Magazine* and *Sports Illustrated.* Rusty smiled as he found *Down East* and *New York Magazine* in the stack. Brian also threw in a reproduction of a book published in 1892, *Golf in the Year 2000*, which he had been encouraging Cameron to read.

Rusty gently tossed the magazines and book on the chair to his right. He closed his eyes and listened to Bart's side of the conversation with Air Traffic Control, "Affirmative, Citation November Seven Niner Eight Whiskey Alpha, line up and wait, runway 2-right."

Bart turned his head back. "Another few minutes Mr. Stephens, uh Rusty."

When he brought the jet to a gentle stop, Rusty opened his left eye to see a prop plane to his left on final approach to the runway. A few seconds after it passed, Bart eased the plane forward turning it ninety degrees to the right. As the engines spun up, Rusty heard, "Citation Whiskey Alpha cleared for takeoff."

Rusty perked up, as he was thrust back in his seat. The plane accelerated down the runway, lifted off, and gained altitude quickly. He took a brief glance out the window then leaned over to the right, picking out the *Sports Illustrated.* He typically turned the pages without stopping at the table of contents, occasionally digging into an article.

About halfway through flipping, he paused when he noticed an article titled, "Tommy Torres Plays the Game of GOLF." Starting on pages fifty-six and fifty-seven, was a rendering of the old Milton-Bradley board game, *THE GAME OF LIFE, A FAMILY GAME.* The colored letters, L, I, F and E were replaced with G, O, L and F. Rusty remembered playing LIFE at a young age with his parents.

The GOLF game board snaked over several pages with squares tailored to Torres and his family, including— Timeshare salesman, earn $35,000 a year; Daughter loses scholarship, pay $12,000; Son has horrific accident, pay $7,000 for rehab; Attempt qualifying school, pay $3,500; Cut back your caddie's hours, save $500; Remove basal cell from sun damage, pay $750; Miss the cut, pay $3,000 expenses; Wife dies from illness, pay $6,000 for funeral; Special invitation to play at The Masters, lodging provided; and travel to Augusta, pay $1,500.

The game's spinning wheel, used to advance the pieces, was replaced, symbolically, with a roulette wheel. Photos of Tommy in his younger days, as a newlywed, a teen, and a baby were dropped into the bends and curves as the track meandered across the pages.

The article prompted Cameron to think about the difficulty in playing golf for a living. No such thing as long-term contracts. Injured or don't play well, no purse. No such thing as half your games at home. Every week, a different place. Pay your caddie and your coaches from your own pocket.

Sure, Rusty had worked extremely hard. With a loving family, successful parents, good friends, and athletic programs growing up, Rusty realized he had the odds stacked in his favor. Tommy Torres didn't have a chance. A widower, single parent, limited means growing up, and a never-ending stream of obstacles sapping his energy at each twist and turn.

There were many personal sports sagas but this one caught his attention. Rusty then did something he had never done with an SI issue. He dogeared the page. He set the magazine down, closed his eyes, and drifted off.

52

WATERVILLE, MAINE, USA
FARMINGTON, PENNSYLVANIA, USA
MONDAY, SEPTEMBER 16, 2002

The Citation taxied to a stop on the tarmac at Waterville's LaFleur airport. After the co-pilot unfolded the stairway, Cameron descended to greet Sandy with a hug. She reciprocated, holding tight. By the time they released, her bag had been stowed. Cameron guided her up the narrow staircase.

After they took their seats, Cameron extended his hand. When Sandy took it, he said, "I'm glad this worked out."

"Me too."

They sat quietly as the engines revved. In less than five minutes, they were rolling down the runway.

As Sandy sensed the plane begin its descent, Bart leaned out from the pilot seat, and said, "Good news folks. We don't have to go to Pittsburgh. The weather's great. We have excellent visibility and plenty of daylight. Shouldn't be too bumpy on the way down."

Sandy turned to Cameron, "We're not going to Pittsburgh?"

Cameron smiled, "We were just stopping there but we don't have to now."

"I don't know if I can take too many more surprises today."

"This is just a short cut."

"I'm sure," said Sandy, winking as if playing along as she leaned to her left and kissed Cameron on the cheek.

Bart tuned his radio to 123.0 Megahertz in preparation for contacting Nemacolin Security. He was required to communicate at least ten minutes prior to landing to ensure the runway was clear, not so much from other traffic, but free of debris, branches, or rocks from weather or wildlife in the area.

Bart called out, "Folks, sorry to interrupt. The FAA says I must. We'll be landing in a few minutes. Please make sure your seat belts are fastened and your seats are upright. Stow any loose items. Thanks."

Already belted, Cameron and Sandy adjusted their seats.

Sandy wasn't sure what warp speed was, but this might be it. As predicted the flight was smooth as silk. The plane hardly leveled off during the descent, approaching the narrow runway heading southwesterly.

Bart skillfully landed the plane, rolling it to the runway's end then guiding it left to park in the turnaround. He shut down the engines, while Ken tended to the hatch. "Enjoy. See you in a couple days."

"Thanks, a real treat," said Sandy.

Cameron echoed, "Much appreciated."

Within fifteen seconds a limo pulled onto the tarmac alongside the plane. The driver popped the trunk, exited the limo, and held the door saying, "Welcome to the Nemacolin Woodlands Resort." Meanwhile, a colleague loaded their luggage, with a partial assist from Bart, while Ken moved chocks into position in the front and back of the aircraft's tires.

The check-in at Nemacolin's Chateau started with champagne served in a crystal flute with a hearty welcome from an all-smiles receptionist. She handed them a folder with information about the property and a printout listing various pre-bookings for meals and activities. She informed them their room had been upgraded.

A timid voice emanated from below Rusty, "Mr. Stephens, may I please have your autograph?"

The receptionist tried to interject. "I'm sorry, Mr. Stephens."

"No problem," He bent down and asked, "What's your name?" as he accepted a Nemacolin hat and pen from the boy.

"Michael."

Rusty had no trouble spotting his parents, supervising from about twenty feet away. Figuring he was about nine, Rusty continued, "Well Michael, is this your hat?"

"No, but my dad said that if I got your autograph, I could have it."

"I see. Here ya go," as he signed and returned the hat and pen.

Sandy took Cameron's hand and squeezed it. "Pretty cute."

The receptionist introduced them to a concierge, handing her the Presidential Suite's passkeys. The concierge politely insisted she take them to their room. As the elevator slowed to the fifth floor, the Chateau's top, she informed them that their luggage had already been delivered to their suite and their golf clubs to the Mystic Rock course.

As they entered the room, they were introduced to their butler, who inquired if they would like him to unpack their bags. They declined. After a quick demonstration of the thermostats and curtain controls, they were finally alone.

Taking Cameron by his right hand with her left, she led him to the window, "I didn't think anything could top the plane ride." With a giggle, "The President has a lovely suite."

"I have to admit, this room is outrageous. I've heard the owners are trying to organize a PGA golf tournament here. That's how Brian found out about it and probably scored us the upgrade. His skills transcend the golf course."

"PGA?"

"Sorta sweet you don't know that. It's the Professional Golfers Association."

"Sorry. I'm slow when it comes to golf acronyms."

As they continued to enjoy the view, Cameron unhooked his hand from Sandy's and reached under his left arm where he stashed the welcome folder. He opened it and looked at the pre-bookings. "Nice. Looks like we have a couples massage in the spa, in uh, not quite three hours. I guess O.T. figured we might have to land in Pittsburgh."

"Three hours, hmm," said Sandy, as she gently extricated the folder from Cameron's hands, closed it, and set it on an end table next to them. She placed her forearms on his chest, with her hands on his neck. She lifted herself a few inches, just enough to barely touch his lips with hers. She lingered for a few seconds, then pulled her head back slightly and lowered her hands to Cameron's belt buckle, as she whispered with a sly grin, "Whatever shall we do?"

····◆····

Sandy and Cameron walked across the expansive foyer of the Chateau to Lautrec, Nemacolin's five-star restaurant. They were expected and seated without hesitation. The hostess walked away. Before they could adjust their seats, two glasses of Veuve Clicquot, Yellow Label Brut, were poured. After the afternoon of urgency followed by unwinding, they just looked at one another and clinked their glasses.

Cameron said, "Let's drink to the Spa."

Sandy added, "And skipping Pittsburgh."

Cameron echoed, "And skipping Pittsburgh."

Sandy returned her Baccarat flute to the table, "After this afternoon, I'd be more than happy with a burger."

"This place looks amazing. We don't have to make any decisions on ordering and we're only a few minutes from the room."

"True." Looking down and nervously twisting her bracelet, "Can I ask you something?"

"Sounds ominous."

"Well, I'm not sure how to say what I'm feeling. It's just that..."

As Sandy hesitated, two waiters simultaneously placed filled shot glasses before them. One waiter retreated while the other piped up, "The chef has prepared an amuse-bouche, a cucumber shooter, with ingredients sourced locally. Enjoy."

Rusty said to Sandy, "I guess we're even. You didn't know what PGA stood for and I haven't got a clue what amuse whatever means. This is delicious."

"It's just French for amusing your mouth, getting your taste buds ready for more. We had one in New York, but we didn't get all the fanfare when it was served. Seriously, in all your world travels, you didn't know this."

"It's more like a cold beer, a steak and a Caesar when we're on the road."

On a practiced cadence the waiters continued to deliver small, delicious plates with a matching wine taste for each. Cameron and Sandy talked about growing up in their respective geographies and cultures. They debated sitcoms. Sandy liked *Friends*. Cameron liked *Scrubs*. Sandy liked *Will & Grace*. Cameron liked *The King of Queens*. Neither liked *The Bachelor* and agreed it wouldn't last. They both liked *Seinfeld*, although Sandy watched the original airings and Cameron was catching up in syndication.

When Nemacolin's founder, dining alone across the restaurant, finished his meal, he stopped by their table. "Rusty, I'm Joe Hardy. Nice to have you here. Hope it's the first of many visits."

Rusty began to push up from his chair, "Thanks for having us."

Hardy politely placed his hand on Rusty's shoulder gently pressing down. "Don't get up, please enjoy your dinner."

"I'd like to introduce you to Sandy Cole."

"Nice to meet you, Miss Cole."

"You too, Mr. Hardy."

"Hope to see you both here next year. We'll be hosting the Pennsylvania Classic on Mystic Rock."

"Congratulations," said Rusty, tactfully non-committal, as Hardy exited.

"You were right about the tournament," concluded Sandy.

That interaction created a lull in the conversation. Cameron broke the silence, "I think you were about to bring up a heavy topic."

Sandy smiled, "You were saved by the amuse-bouche. With all the wine we've had, maybe we should talk about it another time."

"Maybe the wine will help."

"I'd rather when our heads are clearer. But I did want to ask you about something else. After we got up from our nap, so to speak, and I went to the West Wing to my OWN bathroom, thank you, I passed your stack of magazines and took a look. Do you really read *Down East* and *New York*?"

"O.T., I mean Brian, just being thoughtful or his sense of humor, not sure which."

"Funny, but I actually noticed you folded a page in *Sports Illustrated*. I wouldn't normally read that magazine, but I knew you had read a specific article, or were going to come back to it again."

"I read most of it," Cameron interjected.

Sandy continued, "I did too. What made you mark it?"

Cameron rubbed his chin for a few seconds. "I found it interesting that he and I both have a knack for golf. But, I was blessed to get where I am while it feels like he's cursed. I wonder why that is and why it has to be like that."

"And golf has something to do with this?"

"That's the strange part and maybe the reason I just didn't chuck it after I read it. This man's life is so much more than achieving anything in sports."

The dessert course was almost too much, but they managed to savor a couple bites before stepping away from the table.

Holding hands, they entered the empty elevator, on the short trip back to their suite.

Sandy turned to Cameron, "Thank you again for a wonderful day."

"You're welcome. Thank you."

They kissed passionately until the elevator doors opened on the fifth floor. As they opened the door Sandy said, "I'll meet you in bed."

"Sounds good to me."

Sandy diverted to her bathroom, stripped, slipped on a plush hotel robe, washed her face then brushed her teeth. She dimmed the lights, entered the bedroom, laid her robe on a nearby chair, climbed into bed, and spooned her man.

Cameron twitched slightly, already sound asleep.

53

FARMINGTON, PENNSYLVANIA, USA
TUESDAY, SEPTEMBER 17, 2002

A shaft of light pierced the gap in the curtains, hitting Cameron directly on his face. Wrestling with the tangled sheets, attempting to cover his head, he heard a knock at the door. He slid from the bed, slipped on a robe, walked to the door, and looked out the peephole. He opened the door to a butler, perfectly starched, who wheeled in a breakfast cart. "Good morning, sir."

"Thanks. We're not moving much. You can just leave it."

"Let me know if you need anything else."

Cameron bolted the door. He poured a glass of fresh orange juice, took a sip as he returned to the bedroom.

He sat on the bed, stroked Sandy's hair, "Good morning."

Sandy rolled gently onto her back and fluffed a pillow behind her. Barely opening her lips, she said, "Hi," motioning with her finger across her mouth indicating she should brush her teeth.

"Try this," as Cameron passed her the glass of juice. She drank slowly and handed the glass back to Cameron, saying, "Tastes good."

"Good. Because I can't wait after wimping out on you last night."

"Then put the damn glass down and do me."

···◆◆◆···

In the afterglow, Sandy found herself happily draped across Cameron's chest. She purred, "I could stay here all day."

Cameron stroked her hair. "I hate to say this, but I have some business I need to take care of."

Somewhat resigned, Sandy responded, "Well, okay. I'm sure I can find something to do."

"I'm sure you could but I'd like you to help me. C'mon, let's try to get moving. I'm going to take a quick shower and throw on some golf clothes."

"I don't have any golf clothes."

"Anything casual is fine. My casual clothes are golf clothes. We can get you some golf clothes if we need to."

Within twenty minutes, Cameron was dressed and picking over food on the breakfast cart. He turned towards the other wing of the suite, elevated his voice, "How ya doing? The eggs got cold." He bit into a strawberry. "The fruit's delicious and there are some croissants that look good. I think there's a microwave. Happy to heat one up for you. Coffee?"

"Coffee and a croissant would be great. Gimme a few minutes then I'll grab some fruit and we can go."

They exited the suite, as Cameron put on his sunglasses and his golf hat backwards, rim protruding behind him.

Sandy laughed, "Now there's a look I didn't expect."

"Helps lower my profile."

"Okay, I'll get with the program." She flipped her hat to follow suit.

Cameron put his arm around her as they walked towards the elevators.

Sandy continued, "You look adorable in your disguise."

"Thanks, I think."

The staff at Nemacolin's Links Golf Course was enthusiastic, trying its best to act nonchalant as Rusty and Sandy entered the pro-shop.

Sandy surveyed the golf attire and equipment, both women's and men's, covering just about every square inch of available space.

When Cameron completed the sign-in at the counter, they exited the side door, hopped on the electric golf cart which had been prepped for them, and drove to the driving range.

As Cameron braked gently, he spoke to Sandy in his best corporate tone, "Welcome to my office."

"Sure beats mine," replied Sandy.

"I know you don't play golf, but have you ever hit balls at some point?

"Hundreds."

"Have you been holding out on me?"

"Mini-golf."

It was surreal to Sandy. Here she was, receiving her first golf lesson from one of the best players in the world.

To minimize her likely frustration, Cameron asked Sandy to reflect on the muscle memory she had to acquire when she learned to ski on icy New England slopes. After a few dozen attempts with Cameron's guidance, Sandy launched three consecutive balls into the air with a 7-iron.

Stopping her on a good note, Cameron extracted binoculars from his bag and handed them to Sandy, requesting she estimate the distance and direction that his shots landed from a red flag, 100-yards downrange. Cameron hit twenty balls then repeated with Sandy reporting, relative to a white flag 150-yards away and then a blue flag 200-yards away.

Sandy didn't have to do much work, as Cameron predicted each shot's landing right after he struck the ball. Sandy stammered, "Holy shit," on just about every shot. At the beginning she was amazed at Cameron's accuracy in predicting the landing spot. As the distance was increased to 150 and then 200-yards, she was blown away when the shots were landing just as close to the flag as they did at 100-yards.

That was the start of a fun day with the bonus of near-perfect weather. They scouted the Mystic Rock course, stopping occasionally to play an open hole. They also looped around The Links course, admiring the views and incredible sculptures punctuating the layout.

After lunch, they parted company for a few hours. Sandy headed to the spa and Cameron to the gym.

At 6:00 they stepped up to the bar at the back of the Chateau's foyer, placed a drink order, then settled in the small adjoining room, facing the runway and the woods behind it. Sandy's Grey Goose martini was served, followed by Cameron's Negroni. They carefully lifted full glasses and carefully touched them.

"Thanks for a wonderful day."

"My pleasure, for sure."

They reminisced on the day's activities and tried to spot the Citation. Cameron speculated, "Maybe they had another job, went to refuel, or we're driving to Pittsburgh tomorrow morning."

Taking a sip, Sandy continued, "Either way's fine. I'm feeling no pain."

"You were going to bring up something last night at dinner, something serious. Maybe now's a good time to talk but something's been on my mind too."

"Okay, you first."

"Actually, it's a reaction to something you said about golfers in your email. Yes, there are the so-called Bible-thumpers with their Wednesday night fellowship. And yes, there's the party people, and the philanderers and there's plenty of alcohol around. But, and admittedly I've been on the tour for a limited amount of time, I think you'd find that the golfing community is a microcosm of the population at large."

"I get that and sort of expected you might feel that way. I've been thinking about how money impacts relationships. It made you hide the real you from me. In some ways, I understand you have a public side that needs protecting."

Sandy took a sip to organize her thoughts, "Most couples struggle with money, how to get it, how to save it, what sacrifices are needed, and what are the most important things to spend it on. It becomes part of their journey together. From what I know now, unlike most people, that might be irrelevant to us, or anyone who has a long-term relationship with you."

"No doubt. The money part of the journey, as you say, is replaced with weekend work, excessive travel, time away from family, and endless demands away from the course. I guess that's what got to me about Tommy Torres—losing his wife, his daughter struggling, son seriously injured, and a second job to make ends meet."

"It does put things in perspective." Sandy put her drink down and extended her hands to cover Cameron's left hand. "Cameron, the last day and a half has been wonderful, a fantasy. I care deeply about you. I'm glad you didn't give up on me."

Cameron rotated his hand under hers, squeezed, and smiled, "Likewise."

54

TETERBORO, NEW JERSEY, USA
MANHATTAN, NEW YORK, USA
WEDNESDAY, SEPTEMBER 18, 2002

As the Citation wound its way towards Teterboro airport, the trip from Nemacolin felt more like a commercial flight. Bart guided the aircraft to successive lower altitudes, making intermittent turns. The descent was choreographed by Air Traffic Control to accommodate the morning rush-hour traffic at several municipal airports, as well as LaGuardia and Newark, about fifteen nautical miles to the East and South respectively. Ken called out items from the landing checklist, which jiggled from some turbulence. The prevailing winds necessitated that Bart fly the craft east then double back to the west for a landing on runway 24.

Brian was waiting by the door in the flight support area as Bart taxied the Citation back to the terminal on runway 6. As Sandy and Cameron approached, he held the door, grabbed Sandy's carry-on baggage. "Well?"

"Glorious. Hi Brian," said Sandy, pecking him on the cheek.

"What she said," echoed Cameron. "Waiting long?"

"My flight into Newark was early. Hardly any traffic getting over here. Killed some time visiting the aviation museum on the other side of the field. Kinda cool."

"What's the plan?"

"It's going to work out better if you guys say goodbye here. I've arranged a car to take Sandy to Manhattan. Then, we'll head to Southampton. We need to be at Shinnecock by one for a practice round. I'll get the cars loaded up. See you out front in five."

As Brian walked away, Sandy and Cameron faced each other. Sandy took Cameron's hands and looked him in the eyes. Starting seriously and evolving to a smirk, "Thank you for a wonderful escape, Mr. Stephens, Rusty, Cameron, or whatever your name is."

Cameron retaliated, "My pleasure, Sandra, Sandy, SC. Can I see you next weekend?"

"Your place or mine?"

"Mine, if I make the cut, otherwise yours."

"Sounds like a..."

Cameron kissed her deeply before she could finish the sentence.

Rusty and O.T. had hardly settled in the limo when Rusty queried, "Did you see the article in SI on Tommy Torres?"

"I did. I met his caddie, Carlos, a few years ago at an event sponsored by The Caddie Association. Good guy."

"Torres was invited to play at The Masters."

"Yeah, I saw that."

"I was thinking we should see if there's anything we can do for him?"

"Maybe they could stay with your folks," said O.T. in jest.

"Very funny."

"Why don't I reach out to Carlos?"

"Why not."

••••◆•••

Sandy dumped her luggage, turned on the AC, and made an about-face back downstairs to the bodega. She returned to a cool apartment and placed a salad in the fridge. Still energized from her trip, Sandy unpacked, answered a few work emails, and opened two pieces of snail mail which might need attention. She ate then called her mom and her sister.

About to recheck her email late in the afternoon, she heard a voice at the door, "San?"

Opening the door to a hug, "Hi Tam, come on in. You're home early."

"Corporate event last night. We knocked off early today. After I found your note, I knocked on your door a bunch of times over the last few days. Had the feeling you were away. What's happening?"

"Got home this morning. Something to drink?"

"A drink drink?"

"I think there's some wine in the fridge. Not sure if it's any good."

Sandy retrieved the Chardonnay and twisted the cork from the previously opened bottle. Tamara located two wine glasses on a shelf.

They sat down on opposite ends of the couch. Sandy started at the point where she and Cameron crossed emails. That prompted the note to

Tamara on her way out the door to visit with her family in Maine. Sandy then detailed the whirlwind trip to Nemacolin, and the duality of Rusty/Cameron and Brian/O.T.

Tamara listened patiently. When Sandy concluded and sipped her wine, Tamara smiled. "You left out something."

"Yes, Tam, the sex was amazing. The last few days have been incredible, for sure. But I can't help thinking about a future with him traveling all the time, me at home with kids, his family, my family..."

"Let me see if I have this right. You like him. He likes you. He's intelligent, good looking, open minded. He has more money than almost everyone else on the planet. Your family knows about him. And the sex is great. That about cover it?"

Sandy examined her wine glass for a few seconds. "When you say it like that..."

"I'm just sayin'. This all reminds me of my grandparents, who constantly played records by The Tams. Ever heard of them?"

"No, should I have?"

"Maybe you've heard their music. My favorite is *Be Young, Be Foolish, Be Happy*. Check out the lyrics sometime."

"Will do."

Tamara then changed the subject, "Are you back in the office tomorrow?"

"Since I didn't know my exact schedule, I had already extended my time-off. No one knows I'm here so I'm not going back in 'til next Tuesday."

After finishing the previously opened Chardonnay, they upgraded to a delicious Sauvignon Blanc which Tamara retrieved from across the hall.

They continued to gab for another forty-five minutes. While Sandy knew about Tamara's master's degree from Columbia, she didn't know Tamara earned her bachelor's at Spelman College in Atlanta. In turn, Tamara discovered Sandy's passion for genealogy and the side project for Brian.

After Tamara left, Sandy sent Cameron a text message, thanking him again. He called her after completing his practice round. They talked for a good half hour.

55

MANHATTAN, NEW YORK, USA
THURSDAY, SEPTEMBER 19, 2002

With the late summer sun sneaking in, Sandy awoke shortly after 7:00 a.m. She puttered around the apartment while her coffeemaker dripped.

Sam Champion, a local meteorologist, warned Sandy and a million other people in the ABC viewing area that today would be hot and humid.

She set out for the subway shortly after 9:00. Exiting at 42nd street, she stopped to enjoy coffee in Bryant Park before the day turned sticky.

Early in her student days at Columbia Sandy learned to navigate the New York Public Library's special collections. She walked up the steps, passing the two stone lions, through the Corinthian columns, and entered Astor Hall. She made a right, walked as far as she could, then continued left into the expansive genealogy research room.

Sandy quickly discovered that the extensive document archive was predominately domestic, including census data, passenger lists, newspaper archives, and naturalization records. She found some external databases which could be accessed on the Internet from the library's workstations. Sandy took note of these for further investigation, which she could do on breaks and off hours directly from her office. Most interesting was the emergence of two new companies that had begun to offer consumer genetic DNA testing.

She made the decision to focus on the likely connection between Sills and Solless, even though Brian couldn't recall anyone in his family mentioning the latter surname.

Sandy wasn't sure where to dig next. Maybe there was a documented name change. Could it have been a nickname that stuck? If one name was dropped and another came into use, how could she ever connect the two? Before she got too worked up about this puzzle part, she decided to locate a staff member who might be able to assist.

A librarian, at a nearby reference desk, listened patiently, then picked up the handset on her phone. As she punched in a four-digit extension she asked Sandy to wait a few minutes. Sandy nodded.

A professional woman, mid-forties, extended her right hand as she approached. "Hello, I'm Mary-Kate. How can I help you?"

Sandy introduced herself and re-explained the challenge. Mary-Kate outlined several approaches, indicating the necessity to narrow them down. As a researcher, Sandy understood. They sat down at a workstation to do some searches.

Once Mary-Kate determined that both Sills and Solless were not common names, the next step became clear. She suggested Sandy look at census records starting from 1920 and use the address as the common factor. If the Sills family didn't change residences, Sandy might be able to find a Solless at the same address a decade earlier. Mary-Kate indicated she was hesitant to recommend a brute force approach. However, she conjectured that given the uncommon names and known geography, it just might work.

Mary-Kate closed with a caveat, "Don't get your hopes up too high. Most surnames are changed at immigration intake, often connected to a person's trade."

"Do you have a thesaurus?"

"On-line, right here." Mary-Kate moved the mouse and clicked.

"Please type in Sills."

They watched as the screen filled in with a list— beam, billet, block, brace, ledge, pile, post, ridgepole, splint, stake, stave.

"Holy you know what. Thank you so much."

"Not sure what I said or did but you're welcome."

"I'll be back soon I'm sure," said Sandy. She quickly scooped up her possessions and walked briskly towards the exit.

56

SOUTHAMPTON, NEW YORK, USA

FRIDAY, SEPTEMBER 20, 2002

With a cloudless sky, there was still plenty of light at 6:42 p.m. when the LIRR, the Long Island Railroad, engine slowed to a halt, bell clanging. Sandy had a good idea who would be meeting her but looked for a placard with her name as she walked through the one room station. Ten steps later she said, "You must be Nguyen."

"And you Sandy. You pronounced my name much better than Rusty and O.T."

"Isn't Nguyen your last name?"

"I'm impressed. So, you know family names come first in Vietnam. Nguyen's just easier here. If you said it in the Hanoi market, half the people would look up."

"I might call you Mr. Nguyen, at some point, just to goof on the guys." Nguyen smiled and took her bag.

The four-mile drive to the house on Middle Pond Road took less than fifteen minutes, helped by advice Nguyen received earlier in the week, avoid Route 27. As they turned onto the gravel road into the property, Nguyen picked up the conversation, "Rusty and O.T. are still at the course."

Sandy surveyed the manicured hedges. "This place is huge."

"Rusty's travel agent outdid herself, but we actually need the space. You'll see. It can be hectic around here at times. Let me know if you need anything. O.T. calls me his 'Girl Friday'."

"Okay. You're now my man Friday, Mr. Nguyen."

"Cool. Let's get you settled."

Nguyen led Sandy to the palatial master suite and lifted her suitcase onto a luggage rack. He suggested a quick tour and then Sandy could unpack and relax. Sandy agreed but insisted on brevity as she knew Nguyen was busy. He pointed down a hallway to six bedrooms with en suite bathrooms.

When they entered the expansive kitchen, Sandy was introduced to Danielle, the catering coordinator and chef, available 24/7. Danielle requested Nguyen make a pickup at the Lobster Factory on Montauk Highway. He agreed. It would be the next stop after retrieving Rusty and O.T from Shinnecock and returning them to the house.

Sandy suggested, "We can finish the tour later. I can see you've got a lot going on."

"Almost done. Let me show you how to get to the pool. Then you can find your way back to your bedroom."

"Deal."

They passed Brent Lattimer, Rusty's attorney from Atlanta, seated in the den with Barb Pappas, Rusty's marketing agent. They stopped their conversation, stood up, and introduced themselves.

Sandy returned to the bedroom. As she opened her suitcase, it started to sink in. All the people she just met were staying at the house. This chill environment was more like an active commerce zone.

···◆◆◆···

Cameron came into the suite shortly before 8:00 to find Sandy in a robe, sound asleep on the bed.

"Hi sleepyhead." He gently stroked her hair from her face.

Rolling on to her back and propping up to kiss him, "Long time, no see. How did it go today?"

"I don't tee off until one-fifty tomorrow."

"Is that good?"

"Not bad, I'm in the second to last group, tied for second right now, playing with Matt Kuchar, my teammate at Georgia Tech."

"Should be fun. Are you sure this was a good idea?"

"What do ya mean?"

"Me being here. It's great to see you but it feels like serious business around here."

"It is. But I play best when I am happy. And I'm very happy."

Cameron explained the way in which a major tournament impacted a small community. Only a few times a year did all the big golf manufacturers, charities, international media, and tens of thousands of fans converge. It clearly made sense to Sandy that this gorgeous home eliminated hotel hassles, restaurant reservations, and limited the exposure to paparazzi and invasive fans.

Cameron stood up. "Dinner should be ready in fifteen to twenty. I am going to take a shower. "

"You sure?" Sandy then got up, opened her robe revealing a cute pink bikini, "Just kidding. My quickie will be in the pool. Let's not rush the good stuff."

Cameron smiled, kissed her lightly and headed to the bathroom.

Sandy felt as if she had been welcomed to someone else's family dinner. It was a laid-back meal with Danielle and Nguyen joining them at the long table. Barb and Sandy fell into stereotypical roles insisting they clear the table with Danielle. They returned with ice cream and sherbet to follow the seafood. Danielle let everyone know coffee was ready. O.T. asked if they wanted to grab coffee and move somewhere else to plan for Saturday. Rusty suggested they just hang at the table for a few minutes. No one objected.

Sandy started to stand. "I'll leave you to it."

Rusty smiled and reached out to settle her, "You're part of this."

O.T. started, "Nguyen, we need to leave here at around ten tomorrow morning."

"No problem. I'll come back and bring others to the course when they're ready."

Brent chimed in, "Barb and I have some meetings here at the house. We'll move Nike back to ten-thirty, so you guys aren't rushed to get outta here. I'll come over after our meeting with Cobra, which should be over around two."

Barb added, "As long as it's not pouring, I'd like to come over with Brent."

Brent continued, "Sounds good. Rusty, are your parents coming up?"

"I told them not to. There's too much going on, which there is."

"Right," said Brent non-judgmentally. Everyone smiled except Sandy. She had a gnawing feeling that she was now interfering with Cameron's family and business.

O.T. picked up the conversation, "Sandy, we have passes for you Saturday and Sunday. Come over anytime."

Barb looked at Sandy, "No pressure, the media hasn't been notified that Rusty has a girlfriend and I doubt very many people know."

Rusty piped up, "So you can roam about the course just like any other fan. Nguyen, you went over yesterday, didn't you?"

"I did."

"If the schedules work, maybe you can show Sandy the course before we tee off?"

"That should work."

O.T. turned to Sandy, "Tiger Woods is in the last group tomorrow, which is good news and bad news. There will be less people following us, but there'll be crowds waiting for him at upcoming holes. Don't get too frustrated. Leave extra time to get anywhere."

"I'm sure my Man Friday will show me the ropes, won't you Mr. Nguyen."

"My pleasure."

"Well played," said O.T. Other than Nguyen and Sandy, everyone looked confused. "Inside joke," said O.T. He then turned to Rusty, "I talked with Carlos just before dinner."

"Carlos...," questioned Brent.

"Tommy Torres' caddie."

"Who's Tommy Torres?"

Rusty turned to Sandy, "You wanna take this?"

Sandy responded, "Is this my first press conference?" Everyone laughed. "Rusty, O.T and I..." she hesitated, realizing she could context switch between golf names and real names. "We all read this incredible article in *Sports Illustrated* about this man and his family. He's a pro golfer who's had a tough go of it. His wife died leaving him to raise two kids. His son was almost killed in combat, severely injured. Daughter struggling to make tuition. The article has an upbeat ending as he's been invited to play next year at The Masters."

Rusty jumped in, "I've never met Tommy, so I asked O.T., actually it was his idea, to reach out to Carlos to see if there's anything I could do for him. And..." turning to O.T.

"He did have a request."

"What's that?" said Rusty.

"For you not to show up next April in Augusta," said O.T.

Rusty laughed, "Anything else?"

Negative nods all around.

"Great."

As the meeting broke up, Sandy asked O.T. if he had a few minutes. They followed Danielle into the kitchen, poured two coffees and found their way to a quiet nook, passing Rusty who had tuned to the Golf Channel on the giant screen in the den. O.T. held up his hand with index finger extended, indicating he'd join Rusty shortly.

Sandy was excited when Brian told her that his grandfather used to describe the impressive window woodwork and craftsmanship of Brian's great-grandfather. She explained her epiphany in the library, leading to her suspicion that Solless could have been shortened to Sills based on his grandfather's occupation. This realization didn't immediately help with investigating Brian's family in Europe, but it would help eliminate hundreds, if not thousands, of dead ends.

"I know Cameron is waiting for you. Tell him I'm going back to the suite to relax."

"Will do. See you tomorrow."

They stood and hugged.

····◆····

Sandy cleaned her face, pulled her hair back, brushed her teeth and climbed into bed. She suppressed her first instinct to go on-line. She opened *A Good Walk Spoiled* and started reading. An hour later, Cameron entered the bedroom quietly.

Sandy greeted him, "Hi, I'm up. This is fascinating."

Noticing the book, " It's bound to be a classic. Feinstein writes well. What possessed you to get that book?"

"Pretty simple. Wednesday after I went to the library to research Brian's family tree I went to The Strand, a massive bookstore in Greenwich Village. I asked a salesperson to recommend something to give me insight into professional golf."

"He, or she, picked a good one."

"They know their stuff there."

"Be there in a few minutes," as he turned to the bathroom.

Cameron slipped into the king bed. They turned to each other.

"I'm glad you're..."

They kissed.

"...Here."

Sandy felt movement on her leg. "You sure I won't sap your strength for tomorrow."

"Golfers need to be calm. Adrenaline doesn't help golfers."

"Okay, Doctor Stephens," said Sandy as she rolled on top to straddle him.

As their breathing settled, Sandy stroked Cameron's chest. She teased, "Do I handle your balls as good as Brian?"

Trying to keep a straight face, "He marks them."

"I forgot my Sharpie."

"That's a relief."

Teetering on sleep, Sandy said, “You seem to have a good team.”
“I know. And you’re on it now.”
“Are your parents going to be okay with all this?”
“Uh huh,” said Cameron as he drifted off to sleep.

57

AUGUSTA, GEORGIA, USA
SOUTHAMPTON, NEW YORK, USA
SUNDAY, SEPTEMBER 22, 2002

Christina and Carlton Stephens returned home immediately after church. They prepared to spend the afternoon glued to two televisions. Carlton tuned the large screen, affixed to the family room wall, to network coverage. A portable set was positioned on a bookshelf to the right. It would carry The Golf Channel. Sandwiches, snacks, and drinks were ready in the refrigerator and kitchen counter, for self-service. Christina opened two snack tables.

They had traveled to several tournaments where Rusty made the cut, contending on the weekend. They didn't expect to be dis-invited after they had made their plans. However, supporting Rusty was more important. So be it if this is what he wanted. Christina and Carlton tried to rationalize the situation—not enough room for them at the house—logistics too complicated.

At noon Carlton tipped back in an easy chair with remotes for the two TV's. Christina spread out her knitting on the couch. The Golf Channel commentators, Billy Kratzert and Stephanie Sparks, detailed the course set-up at Shinnecock Hills, almost 7,500 yards, from the tips of the tee boxes to the greens, with challenging pin placements. Carlton remarked to Christina that should they ever have a chance to play the course, he'd be happy to join her on the forward tees.

The Saturday round, often referred to as "Moving Day" by the media, as players jostled to position themselves for Sunday's final round, lived up to its moniker. The breezy conditions took their toll on the field. The nearest contenders to the top four were six strokes behind going into the final round. Bunched together were Tiger Woods, Matt Kuchar, Rusty, and the elder statesman, Bruce Fleisher. Sunday would be an exciting round with Rusty and Bruce starting at one over par and Tiger and Matt, immediately behind them, tied at even par.

The broadcasters discussed the contenders' strengths and possible weaknesses. Tiger Woods always garnered airtime. Then there was a segment on Georgia Tech golf, from Bobby Jones to Matt Kuchar and Rusty. The biggest story was Fleisher's performance the last three days. Kratzert segued to a piece that ran on The Golf Channel the night before talking about Fleisher's single win on the PGA tour and his emergence on The Senior PGA Tour, including back-to-back wins at the Royal Caribbean Classic in 1999 and 2000.

The Golf Channel transitioned to NBC at 1:00 PM. When Carlton returned from the bathroom and the kitchen, Rusty's tee time was less than fifteen minutes away. All but six players were on the course, none making headway against the leaders.

Bruce and Rusty shook hands on the first tee. After the P.A. announcement and gallery cheers, they hit their tee shots, then commenced their four-plus mile walks, side by side. Both landed in the fairway on the relatively short par-4 with Rusty landing fifty yards in front of Bruce. As Carlton gave a thumbs up to Christina, he noticed Rusty interacting with Bruce. Usually, it was O.T. jabbering.

"Nice ball," said Bruce.

"You too."

"Sure you'd rather be back there with Matt."

"I practically lived with the guy for three years at Tech," replied Rusty. "He can be in the ring with the Tiger today."

The short conversation broke the first hole jitters which even pro golfers experience. Bruce and Rusty made good approach shots, followed by two putts for routine pars. They vacated the 1st green and stepped out of earshot near the 2nd tee box, facing a wait at the long par-3. To be expected with the fans clustering for Tiger, a gusty breeze, and hardened greens.

O.T. sensed that Rusty wanted to engage with Bruce. Okay to have someone else smooth Rusty's emotions on the course provided Rusty stayed focused on the task at hand.

As they waited, Rusty continued, "I enjoyed the piece on you last night."

"Thanks. Should I call you Rusty or Cameron?"

"I guess you saw my segment with Kessler. Rusty's fine. Flash or Bruce?"

"Bruce is good," smiling as they continued to walk to their balls, talking with heads facing forward.

"Back-to-back wins at Royal Caribbean, nice."

"Great tournament. Goldstein and his team do a terrific job. Winner gets a cruise too."

"Key Biscayne, not too hard to take?"

"Crandon is a beautiful track. Some of the guys aren't happy with the locker room. I heard the golf gods can't do anything about that."

Two volunteers stretched out their arms to settle the crowd. Brad Faxon flew into the left green-side bunker leaving him a difficult, short sided, sand shot. Bob Tway followed with his ball running up to the green's edge. He'd have a lengthy putt.

Bruce turned to Rusty, "Looks like we'll be waiting a few more minutes."

"Mind if I ask you a personal question?"

"Not at all."

"What was it like growing up Jewish in all those small towns you lived in?"

"My mom, who was Orthodox and smart as a whip, is the only reason I had a Bar Mitzvah and know anything about Judaism. I thought you were going to ask me about being Jewish on the tour."

"Well that too."

"Hang on. Looks like we're up."

After Rusty and Bruce completed the 2nd hole, speed of play accelerated. Like a traffic jam unwinding after a fender-bender clean-up, everyone in front started to move. Rusty and Bruce focused on their games, one shot at a time. Other than the occasional "good shot, nice ball and great putt," discussion was between caddie and player.

Carlton and Christina settled into the rhythm of Rusty's round. They always worried about a disaster hole, the so-called dreaded snowman, or 8, which many golfers marked with animus on their scorecard, scribing a small circle on atop a larger one.

While Christina and Carlton's stomachs churned with each of Cameron's shots, they could see, even on television, that today he was steady. Superstitious by nature, Carlton feared the announcer curse, hoping no one would say, "Rusty is in the zone." Carlton felt calm enough, at the next commercial break, to grab a sandwich and an iced tea.

Bruce and Rusty approached the 9th green, avoiding all eleven bunkers on the hole. Rusty was even for the round. Bruce was one over. Considering the event's importance and the Shinnecock Hills course conditions, their performances were commendable.

After completing the 9th hole, O.T. dug into a pocket on Rusty's bag for a Snickers and a water. He handed them to Rusty as they rounded the clubhouse to their right. Bruce caught up to Rusty as they waited to cross the two-lane road onto the tee box to start the back nine. Bruce gave a quick wave to his left. Rusty's head followed Bruce's. He saw a reply wave from a tall, attractive, middle-aged woman. A younger woman to her left then waved.

"My wife, Wendy. I have no idea who the other person is."

Rusty waved as did O.T., "My girlfriend, Sandy, but we're trying to keep her out of the limelight."

"Good luck with that. If the girls didn't know each other five minutes ago, I'm sure they do now."

They checked the scoreboard as they waited for Faxon and Tway to clear the 10th tee.

Carlton and Christina listened attentively as Dick Enberg, the play-by-play announcer, segued to Judy Rankin for a back nine analysis. The course concluded with three exciting finishing holes. The challenging par-4 18th was most recognizable from Corey Pavin's dramatic approach shot on the way to a US Open victory in 1995.

Rankin made it clear that Bruce and Rusty would need to attack the short par-4's, the 13th and 15th, if they wanted to persevere over Tiger and Matt, who were playing brilliantly behind them.

With four holes to play, Rusty and Bruce continued to play well. But they were running out of holes to close the gap on the leaders. As they walked the 15th fairway to their tee shots, Bruce piped up, "Looks like we're now competing for third place."

"Guess so."

They both acknowledged the reality and smiled. Tension dissolved.

"I wanted to ask you earlier, what it's like being Jewish on the tour."

"I've rarely experienced overt antisemitism during my career but it exists behind closed doors. With me mostly golfing, Wendy received the lion's share of snide remarks. Many years ago, I played a round with Herman Barron, the first Jewish golfer to win on the tour. I wish I had asked him about it."

"Is it just you? I mean, are you the only Jewish person out here?"

"With Corey's conversion, I think it's just me on the Senior Tour. You may want to talk to the guys out here with you on most weeks, Jonathan Kaye and Skip Kendall. Skip and I had the same agent for several years. I take it you're not Jewish."

"No. Sandy is. Shortly after I met her, I was turned on to Moses Maimonides. Long story."

"Funny you say that. My mom used to talk about his thirteen principles of faith. But the ten commandments were drilled into me more."

"What about his ladder of giving?"

"She never said anything about that."

As they walked up the 18th, Rusty inquired, "Did you see the SI article on Tommy Torres?"

"I did. At first, I assumed it was Tommy Tolles until I got into it. I thought I had problems growing up, but nothing compared to what life handed him."

"Sandy and I were both struck by his story."

With only two twosomes left on course, spectators not lining the fairway were clustered tightly around the 18th green. Rusty and Bruce finished to thunderous applause. The handshaking commenced, golfer to golfer, golfers to caddies, caddie to caddie. Rusty and Bruce navigated the roped alleyway, attended by volunteers every twenty feet, as they made their way to the scoring tent.

Wendy and Sandy were chatting like old friends when Rusty and Bruce approached. They talked for a few minutes, at which point Rusty and Sandy headed back to the 18th green to support Matt Kuchar, now fully immersed in Tiger-mania.

While disappointed for Cameron, Carlton was a golfer and a golf fan, as well as a father. They heard the decibel level increase as Tiger and Matt covered the last fifty yards to the 18th green.

Dick Enberg, channeling Howard Cosell, described their duel as a heavyweight fight in the last round with combatants alternating punches. While the golfers and their caddies settled on the green, the network cameras scanned the crowd. The camera stopped on Rusty.

Rankin spoke up, "There's Rusty Stephens apparently waiting for his Georgia Tech teammate, Matt Kuchar."

Enberg followed-up, "He appears to be holding hands with a young lady. Do we know who that is?"

"I don't think we do."

"Let's see if our director, can find out. We may have a scoop."

Carlton belted out, "Christina..."

58

Kirkcaldy, Scotland
Saturday, April 25, 1495

Ben had worked diligently with the captain and crew over the last few days. Today, he planned to complete preparations for his departure. He very much wanted to walk back to Dundee on Sunday, a quiet day for the masses.

The captain assigned Ben two crew members to count the inventory of all goods remaining on the Rasch, after removing those damaged beyond use from the skirmish at sea.

He helped the captain calculate any adjustments needed for the documents previously delivered to the merchants. The Dundee community was tight-knit. It was crucial that product allocations be done properly when more than one merchant, ordering the same item, was impacted by a loss. Although child's play for Ben, he was very methodical, instilling confidence in the captain. In turn Ben was empowered to negotiate further as needed.

Ben checked with the crew on turning over his navigation chores before approaching the captain. "Do I have your permission to depart in the morning?"

"Did you double check inventory and the allocations?"

"Yes sir."

"And the crew is ready to navigate without you?"

"They may even get your ship there without a new hole."

The captain laughed, "We could have been at the bottom of the North Sea. Make sure you take enough provisions. We'll see you there in about a week."

Ben disembarked from the ship.

59

DUNDEE, SCOTLAND
MONDAY, APRIL 27, 1495

When Dunhope Castle came into view, Ben took a seat on a toppled tree. Based on his visit ten days prior, he knew he could be more efficient with his follow-up visits. He took a few minutes to calculate his route to the twelve stops.

Ben chewed on some sea kale he brought from the ship. He couldn't decide if he liked it, but he had gotten accustomed to it.

His initial stop went well. Ben was offered mead which he gladly accepted. The merchant had taken the time to review the document in advance. Given the circumstances, delay and loss, some data needed to be added before it could be agreed and signed. Ben reviewed the revised quantities for each product and the pricing concessions for the delays. There would be further concessions if the Rasch was not in Dundee within a week from tomorrow. When Ben handed the document back, it was folded in such a way that the buyer could apply his seal.

That Ben could rattle off various pricing scenarios imparted confidence in the transactions. Ben had an abacus with him, which he used only when a counterparty insisted.

The first stop was not a good predictor of the challenging day ahead. From there, Ben encountered the gamut of obstacles— locating only two other merchants, documents not reviewed in advance, dickering over a penning on a large order. However, he did secure some new prospects Johan's father had told him about.

The day ended well, thanks to the Gardyne clan, merchants he met on his first visit. The patriarch, Patrick Gardyne, upon learning Ben had not arranged lodging, welcomed him into his home.

60

AMSTERDAM, BISHOPRIC OF UTRECHT
TUESDAY, MAY 21, 1495

After crossing the North Sea, sailing through the Frisian archipelago and the Zuider Zee, then navigating a short stretch of the Ij river, the Rasch docked in Amsterdam.

Immediately, the captain dispatched a crew member with the sealed documents. The courier walked briskly, less than 500-yards on the Damrak canal, to the Rasch offices.

Johan, Dijkstra, and Rasch were meeting around a table when they heard a knock on the door. Johan walked down the narrow hallway to answer it. When handed the document stack, Johan recognized the markings. He gave the crew member a hearty handshake and requested the captain visit the offices after the ship off-loaded.

The documents were handed to Meneer Rasch. He quickly counted them, handing them one at a time to Dijkstra on his right, "There should be twelve, correct?"

"Yes," responded Dijkstra.

"There are sixteen."

Dijkstra studied them, one at a time. "It looks like Ben has added two new prospects. Excellent. And two letters from his own hand, one to Meneer Rasch and the other to Johan and Rebecca." He handed them to Rasch and Johan.

Rasch opened his letter. "This is surprising," which froze Dijkstra and Johan. He continued reading, set the paper down and looked up. "Ben is taking a leave of absence. It is unclear how long he will stay in Scotland." Turning to Dijkstra, "Perhaps there is a way to have Ben remain our agent there." Turning to Johan, "There may be more details in your letter. I think you should be with your wife. Come back tomorrow."

Johan mumbled, "Thank you both," He departed quickly, letter in hand, worrying not only how Becca and his mother-in-law would react, but already missing his friend and his daughter's uncle.

····◆····

Tineke was napping when Johan entered the house. Speaking softly not to wake her, "*Dag*." Hello.

Becca turned, "What are you doing home so early?"

He went to hug her.

She accepted it but quickly pulled back. "You have news?"

"Everyone is fine. It's Ben. All I know so far is that he is staying in Scotland for some time. He sent a letter to us. I thought we should open it together."

They unfolded the documents on the table. Becca acknowledged Ben's writing. The letter was dated May 1st.

Becca and Johan,

By the time you read this, it is likely you know I have chosen to remain in Scotland, at least for a while. After the last three years, we are blessed that we have choices.

Sister, you understand my passion for mathematics and physics. Perhaps their predictability comforts me in this turbulent world.

Brother, I cannot call you brother-in-law for our blood was joined on the fateful day on the Gibraltar docks.

I find myself conflicted by the flowing and ebbing tides of free will and fatalism. Had my ship not been damaged in battle, I would be in Amsterdam today. Had we followed our Jewish brethren to Portugal, you would not have created a beautiful child.

The people here have embraced me for reasons that are not fully clear. They do not know my entire history, nor do they seem to care. They certainly don't see me as a wealthy nobleman or a warrior. They are not suspicious of my ideas. They seek my knowledge, analysis, and criticism. Perhaps, I err in thinking the people here are different.

I have been hired by a group of men, not for their vocation, but rather for their avocation. They will compensate me extreme-

ly well for assisting them with golf. There are two parts to this endeavor— first, to organize golf as a sport, not unlike contests for war but peaceful, which appeals to me so much, and second, to coach the men with their shot-making and sportsmanship. You both know how much I intensely relished those opportunities, though sparse, in Holland.

There is no doubt I will miss you during my extended stay here. I will do my best to visit, as it will be difficult for me not to see you, Mother and little Tineke.

I have reflected a great deal on the difficulties Mother may have with my decision. Please comfort her with the words of our namesake, King Solomon— There is a time and a purpose for everything in God's kingdom.

Please give Mother and Tineke a long embrace for me. Your loving brother,

Ben

Postscript— As I was about to seal this letter, I realized I almost forgot to mention that I have met a wonderful woman.

61

St Andrews, Scotland

Friday, July 19, 1495

Evi couldn't sleep. At first light, she quietly dressed so as not to disturb her parents. The morning chill was quickly vacated by early sunshine and a slight breeze from the southwest. She walked the short distance from their modest stone house towards the shoreline, hoping to catch the rising sun spread its fingers across the crags.

About an hour later, her mother hugged her tightly upon her return. They relaxed their embrace, looked at each other, eyes watering.

"Let's have some porridge," said her mother as she eased Evi towards the hearth. "Then we'll do some spinning to pass the morning."

"Thank you, Mam."

They sat silently for a few minutes, sipping on beer, between bites of smoked fish and thick porridge.

Taking Evi's hand, "It is early for you to marry, my darling."

"Mam, I am eighteen. Many are married for years at my age."

"Those come from nobility."

"They marry to protect their lineage. I will marry a man who is noble in heart and deed. And Da won't have to give a dowry."

"He could easily do so."

"Bonnie may need it when she grows up."

"That she may."

Evi sensed uneasiness as her mother busied herself with the hearth, and topping up their tankards, both unnecessary.

"Mam? Are you alright?"

"Have you considered your wedding night?"

Evi laughed, "I think you're more nervous than me. You didn't have the benefit of working at The Goat Heid when you married Da. Don't worry, Mam."

····◆····

Ben rolled over in the bed at the Goat Heid. He flopped his right arm across his eyes attempting to mask the sunlight. He wanted to sleep. It would be a long day. He tried to dream about the first night with his bride. The thought aroused him. He then tried to count the houses he and Evi had visited to invite townspeople to the wedding. When that didn't work, he resorted to counting sheep. That made him think of Artair and work. He finally resigned himself to rise.

Mid-afternoon, Artair entered Ben's room at the Heid. "How are you feeling?"

"Better after bathing and shaving."

"Look at you in your leather jerkin."

"My sister made it for me after we settled in Amsterdam. I cleaned it earlier today."

"Her craftsmanship shows well. I'm sure you are missing her and others, but you have so many people here that care about you."

"Indeed. I think it's the waiting which is maddening."

Artair knew his friend. "What do you say we leave now and stop at the University before heading over to the church?"

"Excellent idea. I'll meet you downstairs."

Ben took a few minutes to tidy the room.

They exited the Heid, heading east on Market Street. They walked a hundred paces, turning left into Muttoes Lane, crossing North Street onto the University grounds five minutes later. They settled on a bench, posturing to point their faces towards the warming sun.

A few minutes later, Ben patted Artair's knee. "I'll be back in a few minutes." Ben passed the Chapel with the opulent tomb of archbishop James Kennedy, in favor of St Salvator's College. He passed through the foyer and entered the book room.

He lightly ran his index finger across the spines, one by one, remembering his first book, his family, Gibraltar, and Fridays. Three years ago, he and Becca were helping Mother prepare for Sabbath dinner.

Today, he would take his vows in a wedding Mass, as a marrano, a secret Jew. Though Ben was sure his parents would not favor marriage to a gentile, he also knew they had seen evil and good in both Jew and gentile.

Ben emerged from the College's dark halls into the bright light, rousing Artair from a nap, as he reclaimed his seat on the bench. "My turn," said Ben, as he closed his eyes.

"Go ahead."

A half hour later, they walked to North Street, and headed east.

As afternoon gave way to evening, congregants began to assemble outside St Mary's Church upon Kirkhill. While anticipating the evening ahead, they enjoyed a cloudless view of a calm sea to the East and the majestic St Andrews Cathedral, less than 200 paces to the West.

Artair and Ben entered the church, waving as they passed the gathering crowd. They were immediately greeted by James Allardice, the provost, who would officiate. They confirmed the planned proceedings then continued with some small talk. Unbeknownst to Ben and the populace, the archbishop, William Scheves preempted the provost's inquiry into Ben's baptismal records. Scheves knew the community wanted this union and would benefit from it.

Ben took his position by the altar as Artair marshaled the witnesses into the church.

Evina looked radiant as her parents escorted her down the center aisle. Her white dress, with raised floral patterns, was complemented with a green bodice and beige stitching. Her hair was gathered in a headpiece interspersed with white heather. The gregarious barmaid had morphed into a demure princess. As he took Evi's hands, Ben fought to control a flood of emotions.

The service commenced by binding the bride's and groom's wrists with a satin sash. Vows were then exchanged after which the provost released the slip knot. A ring ceremony was followed by three scripture readings. After blessing the couple, the provost concluded the ceremony by sharing a dram of whisky from a wooden quaich. Evi took a sip, at which point, as coached, Ben downed the remainder. They were hardly pronounced husband and wife when cheering broke out.

Arm in arm, Evi and Ben walked down the aisle. As they exited the church, the bagpiper commenced. Everyone marched joyfully to town.

····◆····

The Goat Heid was ready. On each table were pewter flagons of wine, pottery flagons of mead, and bowls of nuts. Within minutes, total silence succumbed to high volume, modulated periodically when food was brought to the tables.

Over the next two hours the guests enjoyed fish, rabbit, peacock, fruit fritters, and of course, goat meat. Silence returned for a brief spell about nine. The wine, mead, beer, and ale drinking stopped for an Atholl Brose toasting, led by Evi's father. Artair and Davis followed. Ben and Evi kissed after each speaker.

As the sun set, close to 10:00, Ben took Evi by the hand and started upstairs. The crowd noticed and protested by going silent.

Ben and Evi halted halfway and turned to the revelers. Evi spoke, "Don't stop on our account."

"It's too early to leave," one of the guests yelled.

Evi waved goodbye as she said, "My wedding day is today, not tomorrow. Maybe we'll be back."

Davis chided, "Ben, we'll see you back in ten minutes."

Boisterous laughter enveloped the room as the newlyweds continued to Ben's room.

Ben opened the door to his room. They held hands, stepping over the threshold together. Ben closed the door, "Finally. Are you..."

Evi kissed him passionately before he could finish the question. She pulled back, turned around, "Help me with my dress."

Ben obliged. She turned back around, in her undergarments, "Now, I will help you."

Ben stood still. As Evi was about to remove Ben's leggings, he took her hands, "Have you seen many men?"

"I only want to see one."

He brought her hands to his lips and kissed them.

"I ask because I am different from your father or others you may have seen. I've had a brit milah as God first commanded Abraham."

Evi looked more curious than mystified. Ben looked down and continued, "Some extra skin on my manhood was removed a week after I was born."

Still holding hands, she rolled her hands on top of Ben's, taking them to her lips, with a devious smile. "Last week my girlfriend told me about a man's foreskin. One less thing to worry about."

She released his hands. They tore at their own undergarments. Facing each other, naked, they hugged as they collapsed on the bed. They stopped momentarily, breathing more rapidly, quiet but for the partygoers' muffled sounds. Evi brought her hands down Ben's torso, taking hold of him. As Ben expanded even more in her grasp, she explored with her fingertips, then squeezed gently. "I love that you are different."

62

AMSTERDAM, BISHOPRIC OF UTRECHT

EIGHT MONTHS LATER - TUESDAY, APRIL 7, 1496

Evina joined Becca and Mother in preparing the table. For the afternoon, Johan and Ben were tasked with Tineke, now a feisty one-year old.

Johan was happy to take his daughter along with Ben to visit the trading company offices. After a few other stops, the dank skies let loose with a heavy downpour. They took refuge inside the *Haringshoek*, the Herring Corner, for a warming drink. They returned home when the skies began to clear in late afternoon.

The table looked beautiful, sparkling in candlelight. With Johan's parents, seven places were set formally. A diminished eighth place was reserved for the prophet Elijah. Should he arrive, he could sit there with little Tineke cradled to the side. Becca asked everyone to be seated. She prompted her mother, "Do you want to start the Haggadah?"

An emotional aura permeated the room as Mother spoke, "It is wonderful that we can all be together. Here. Tonight."

"You are right Mother," echoed Becca as she turned towards Johan's parents. "We are very happy to have you on this day, the 15th of Nisan, in our year of 5256 and look forward to being in your home this Sunday, on Easter."

Becca smiled, "For my brother, the man of books, well at least two books." She handed them to him.

"She's making fun of me." Turning to Johan's parents, "Growing up I had little interest in the Bible. It was this book I was obsessed with." He held up his mathematics book. "But I must admit, this book," holding up the other, "which Father bought from a trader from Toledo in 1490, is almost as good.

"Better," chimed in Mother. "It is almost biblical, extracted from the Jewish law Rambam scribed three hundred years ago."

Ben continued, "I can't disagree Mother. We will read it, or some of it, to help our Haggadah service. It is written in Hebrew. I will read short passages in Hebrew. Mother, I'd like you to repeat them in Ladino, Becca in Spanish, then Evi in Scottish. Johan, we're leaving you and your parents with English, Dutch, and Flemish. By the time we complete a round, everyone should understand it."

Johan jested, "I'm not sure about Tineke."

After a laugh, Ben continued, "Repeating in seven languages will leave us eating the Seder meal tomorrow morning, so Becca and I have decided which parts to read."

The abridged service honored the basic traditions, consuming the four requisite cups of wine and blessing the special foods like matzo and bitter herbs. Despite intermittent interruptions of a gurgling Tineke, the readings brought forth much emotion. Most of all, the story of Moses leading his people on the exodus from Egypt. Ben made the linkage to his father, remembering that three millennia later, Benjamin followed in the tradition of Moses, bringing his family from Spain but never reaching the promised land, Amsterdam in this case.

The service ended in a couple hours. Becca and Evi insisted on serving the Passover meal while everyone else stayed at the table. A delicious rice dish was served. Unlike their Ashkenazi brethren, Sephardic recipes for Passover allowed rice, seeds, and corn, which Mother mixed masterfully.

The Haggadah carried over into the dinner conversation. Johan mentioned that a trader from Italy brought news. Jews were expelled from a small town in Austria, Caritha, about a month ago. The trader also spoke about an odd genius from Tuscany, an eccentric named Leonardo, who had painted a mural on a wall, over 100 square feet, of Jesus at his last meal, a Passover Seder. Furthermore, he used mathematical calculations to make a machine to fly like birds. Ben's ears perked to that reference, "Did it work?"

"Not according to the trader."

"Nonetheless, incredible. Whatever happened to Abraham Zacuto? His navigation tables are in my book."

Becca contributed, "I suspect he went to Portugal like most of the Jews from Salamanca. It's so close to the border."

"I didn't know all that," said Johan. "But what I did hear is that he is in Lisbon, helping a Portuguese explorer, Vasco da Gama, prepare navigators for a trip to India."

"That's a shame," said Mother.

"Why is that?" said Ben.

"I'm sure he was accepted by King John, but I'm not sure King Manuel was as welcoming. I don't expect it will be long before Señor Zacuto will have his exodus or be forced to convert."

Becca could sense the dour mood, "Let's celebrate our blessings. Evi, how long are you and Ben going to stay? You've been a little evasive."

Evi took Ben by the hand and placed them visibly on the table. "We think about two more months. We're glad to tell you all together, we decided to have our baby born here."

The room erupted in joyful kissing, hugging, questions trampling on questions. Silent speculation on Evi's billowing clothing gave way to friendly debate about who knew what and when.

63

ST ANDREWS, SCOTLAND
SUNDAY, JUNE 28, 1496

In the two weeks since their return from Amsterdam, Evi and Ben struggled to seize control of their lives. Between baby Benno's demands and the work backlog in Ben's business, sleep was a precious commodity.

Finally, Ben found a workable cadence. He carried Benno with him to the golf fields in the afternoon, swaddling him, and walking him from launching area to post to launching area to post. He would bring Benno home for an early dinner before returning for coaching in the evening.

With Artair looking after the laborers, Ben was pleased with the progress grooming the land, despite the wet spring. New posts extended the layout to just about fifteen acres. Artair had worked hard. Ben rewarded him with a variety of wooden balls he brought back from Amsterdam. Some were smooth, some rough and others carved with shallow patterns. Artair was excited to be the first to try them.

Evi and Ben roused at first light, about 4:15. They edged closer, relishing the silence outdoors and inside. As dawn slithered into the room, they hoped to steal a few more quiet moments.

Ben whispered, "How are you feeling?"

"Exhausted but safe," speaking softly. Stroking Ben's hair. "I loved everything about our trip— your family, Johan's family, Amsterdam, our first wedding anniversary on the North Sea, and even the, am I saying this right, the *mohel*?" The person who performs the Jewish rite of circumcision.

Ben kissed Evi hard to muffle his loud laugh. Catching his breath, "You can say it anyway you like."

Evi reached below the covers, gently rubbing him, "I want him to look like you, at least in some places."

Her touch aroused him. “It’s only been five weeks.”

“Sorry. I want you but I’m not yet ready to carry another.”

“We need to track your monthly.”

Pecking him on the lips, “Spoken like a true mathematician.” Evi looked at Benno, yet to stir. “I can’t tell if he will be fair like me or darker like you.”

“We’ll have to see. He certainly won’t see the sun as much as I did in Gibraltar.” Ben stroked her hair. “I see my father in him. I wish you could have met him.”

“Benno will have the strength of Solomon. Of that I am sure.”

Evi looked over at Benno who yawned then cooed. “He will need me in a few minutes. Are you looking forward to today?”

“I am. You have honored my traditions. I will honor yours. Our Benno should have his own traditions, as long as he follows the Ten Commandments...and Rambam.”

“And Rambam.” Evi retrieved Benno from his cradle and brought him into bed between them. They admired their creation. “We’ll make sure he does.”

···♦◆♦···

With the burgeoning community Evi knew so well, and the widening circle of Ben’s acquaintances, Benno’s baptism would be in the cathedral, a very short walk from St Mary’s.

During the long summer days, the ringing of St Andrews Cathedral’s bells began with Matins, early prayers, well before sunlight. Then Prime bells at dawn with a final ringing at Compline, for evening prayers, shortly after sunset. Today was a special occasion, as most baptisms were conducted as soon after birth as possible, ideally on the day of birth. Today, the bells chimed at mid-morning, the midpoint between Terce and Sext.

A brisk breeze drove the congregants inside. Many arriving early took the opportunity to meander among the nooks and chapels of this religious castle, covering one and a half acres, over a hundred feet high, and anchored by a tower and six turrets. The stained-glass windows sifted the morning sunlight into colorful shapes, randomly decorating columns, pews and flooring.

Benno’s baptism would be held in the nave with William Scheves officiating. Though in failing health, he looked fit for the occasion. After the assembly quieted, he met the baptismal party halfway to chancel, welcoming them with a special acknowledgment to the three godparents— the head of the shipwright's guild and the dearest friends of Evi's parents, who she knew as *antaidh* and *uncail*, aunt and uncle.

Scheves led the group to the baptismal font. The baby was baptized then blessed. Latin prayers were then offered, with some squirming among the congregants as the archbishop struggled intermittently with the large book of illuminated manuscripts. The Lord's prayer, the Credo, and Ave Maria were recited in turn by one of the godparents.

The archbishop consecrated Benno with holy oil, making the sign of the cross on his forehead. The baby didn't seem to mind. The godparents carefully wrapped him in a white gown and raised him. They proceeded the short distance to the altar. At this point, the archbishop then requested everyone to join the godparents in professing faith for Benno.

The ceremony concluded with the archbishop recording the Baptism on a vellum page in a quire for registering the church's baptisms, marriages and burials. Then, on behalf of Benno, Evi and her parents, the archbishop invited well-wishers to partake in drink and food outside in the courtyard. The archbishop led the way, followed by Evi and Benno, Ben, godparents, and Evi's parents.

Evi heard, "Your Grace." With her eyes focused on a gurgling Benno, she assumed it was someone addressing the archbishop. When she heard Scheves respond the same way, she jerked her head up, assessed the situation, and reacted with, "Your Grace," which started a cascade of manly neck bows and feminine curtsies. "Your Grace" echoed as the crowd emerged from the building.

Evi whispered to Ben, "It's King James."

"I know. Who is standing next to him?"

Handing Benno to Ben, she cupped her hands to her mother's ear.

Her mother returned the communication.

Evi leaned back to Ben, "His brother, James, Duke of Ross."

"Ross?"

"North in the Highlands."

"Oh."

King James spoke directly to Evi and Ben, "Congratulations on the birth of your son."

Evi piped up, "Thank you, Your Grace."

Ben followed, "Your Grace, I thank you as well. He was actually born in Amsterdam."

Switching from Scots to Flemish, James continued, "May he lead a long and prosperous life. Please excuse me. I do not speak Dutch."

Ben fumbled a response.

James laughed, "Let's all try English."

The archbishop, somewhat bewildered by the King's direct engagement with Evi and Ben, "Your Grace, what brings you to St Andrews?"

"Twofold William," addressing him informally. "Brother James and I wanted to see how you were fairing. We also wanted to attend the Baptism."

"This baptism?"

"William. Of all people to think this is below us."

Addressing Ben in Spanish so only Ben would understand, "He doesn't like me." Turning back to face the archbishop, "I need to talk to Mr. Solley about archery."

With that, the King placed his hand on Ben's shoulder, guiding him away. The royal entourage split to attend to the King and the duke.

Archbishop Scheves was happy to visit with the King's brother. He knew the three boys from birth— James, the King; James, the Duke of Ross; and the youngest, John, the Duke of Mar. Though Scheves had an up and down relationship with James III, they eventually reconciled. They both preferred the middle son, regretting that he would not ascend to the throne. But James IV turned out to be a popular royal, the opposite of his father.

Though Ben had learned much about the King over the last year, he never could have imagined having a private conversation with him. He waited for the King to address him.

"I know much about your golf endeavors."

"Your Grace. Made possible by the people here. Sir. May I ask you how you knew to speak Spanish to me?"

"As a learned man, I felt compelled to investigate a so-called golf mathematician. You are a learned man. What have you discovered about me?"

"Your Grace sponsored the new College in Aberdeen."

"That is true. I hope there will soon be books in the library for you and your son. What else?"

"Your Grace. People speak with respect for what you have done since you became King at age fifteen. Your mother was Margaret of Denmark, rest her soul. People speak fondly of her."

"My people favored her more so than my father. I think most everyone is hoping I take as admirable a bride. I must play golf as much as possible before then."

····◆····

Once the King put Artair, Davis and the other men at ease, the afternoon of golf was quite lively and enjoyable. Royalty didn't enjoy any special benefits when it came to making strikes. The King made his share of good and bad strikes. The changing winds added to the challenge but also provided an opportunity for Ben to demonstrate his expertise with angles, distances, and trajectories.

Ben and the King got on well. They were close in age. They possessed a thirst for sharing knowledge. They could communicate in several languages.

The day passed quickly. Ben had planned to spend time with the family, but he was sure Evi would understand. He was overjoyed when a commissary was assembled. Arranged by the King, the bounties were displayed in mid-afternoon which included lamb, pheasant, and mead.

Naturally, the meal would not commence before the King could partake. He addressed the group in Scots Gaelic, thanking them for their hospitality and sportsmanship. He raised his tankard, "To Ben and Benno Solley." Motioning to enjoy the food and libations, "Enjoy."

As the King prepared to depart, he approached Ben, "My appreciation for a delightful afternoon."

"Your Grace, it was my good fortune."

"I need you to do something else."

"As you wish, Your Grace."

"I can see from watching, you make suggestions to the men on the angle of their stick. It is indeed challenging to make all strikes with a single stick. Can you make me a set of sticks so that I can use different ones for different conditions?"

"Your Grace, it would be my honor."

"Excellent. I will have my treasurer provide you advance funding."

"Thank you, Your Grace."

64

Kirkcaldy & Edinburgh Scotland
Monday, July 27, 1496

Ben updated Artair on his earlier journey to Edinburgh a few days after Benno's baptism. On that trip Ben hired two bowyers, makers of wooden bows, for the King's commission. He chose to divide the work among them— John Mayne for shafts, and Brodie MacThom for club heads. From the King's four-pound advance, he paid them each five shillings to build a few experimental versions. The remaining seventy shillings would cover construction, travel expenses, and a modest fee for overseeing the work.

Ben welcomed Artair's companionship and collaboration on this follow-up trip. They stopped near Kirkcaldy for a rest, their fatigue compounded after a long weekend on the golf fields. With spitting skies and a new work week Ben was confident that Davis could handle a diminished number of golfers over the next two evenings.

As they relaxed, Ben shared his nostalgic feelings on the events which brought them together. Artair reminisced too, recalling their first meeting over a year ago, when they decided to change Solomon to Solley.

Artair then inquired, "Has there been any adverse impact due to your Jewish past? If so, I haven't witnessed any."

Ben responded, "Very interesting how you posed your question. Firstly, Jewish is not in my past. Evi and the children understand that the religion we practice together is built on mine. Did you know that the word catholic was not used until many decades after the death of Jesus?"

"You are indeed a scholar."

"I don't think my mother and father, rest his soul, would agree. But thank you. And like you, I have not seen any overt animosity." Ben attributed this to benefactors, some anonymous, who had helped him.

·••◆••·

On the ferry across the Firth of Forth, Ben updated Artair on the bowyer arrangements. Ben contracted Mayne for two shaft types, white ash, and yellow birch, and MacThom for two club head types, holly, and beech.

Though forewarned by Ben, Artair twitched his nose and mouth as he inhaled the city's fetid smells.

They entered Brodie MacThom's shop, a stone's cast past St Giles' Cathedral.

Artair looked empathetically at MacThom's sickly daughter, about ten years old, sitting in the corner, pale faced, blanketed, and almost catatonic. When they departed with the club head samples, Ben subtly placed a shilling behind the quill stand.

A steady breeze mitigated the stench as they continued east past the Wahenbooth tenements on High Street. Artair was amused, as Ben prepared him for John Mayne, a non-stop talker. When they first met, Mayne had rambled about how the royals had impacted his business—from the public ban on golf, to the affinity for cannons over bows, to the limits on tree cutting. While Ben did find some of his patter interesting, he told Artair to insist, at the earliest opportunity, that they needed to depart.

Ben was shocked. The stop was short. After they departed Mayne's shop Artair jested, "Are you sure he is the same person you met before?"

"Indeed. It must be the shepherd's solitary existence rubbing off on him."

As they circumvented the hunting grounds to the southwest, they agreed that Mayne had the better knowledge on wood flexibility and MacThom on hardness. They also agreed that Mayne would perform the final assembly.

By mid-afternoon, Artair and Ben had secured lodging at the Sheep Heid Inn. They each imbibed a tankard of ale while planning their testing. Ben checked the supply of leather stripping to affix club heads to the shafts. They had two different types of wooden balls and two variations of leather balls which Ben had brought back from Holland.

Ben sipped and said, "So my golf friend, I hope you have your strength. We have much work today."

"It should be enjoyable."

"You should only say as much when we are done tomorrow. I will need you to make one hundred and ninety-two strikes today and the same tomorrow."

"No doubt you can explain."

"Simple. Two shafts times two club heads times four ball types times six strikes with wind from the right and six strikes with wind from the left."

"Simple for you. We better start as it will take time to re-tie when we change heads with shafts. Hopefully, none will snap while I am hitting."

"Hope not, but we do have spares. We have almost two miles to the sea or maybe we can find a place in the hunting grounds behind us."

They exchanged tired looks. Ben asserted, "Hunting grounds. Seaside tomorrow."

They didn't have to go far to find amenable conditions, a flat field with crags and hills jutting out nearby, which would help funnel wind. As Artair attached a white ash shaft to a holly head and a yellow birch shaft to a beech head, Ben laid out the balls in four groupings— wood, smooth and grooved; and leather pouches stuffed tightly with animal hair, exteriors smooth and rough.

Ben recorded as Artair made twenty-four strikes, twelve with each club, striking the four ball types three times. They walked down range, retrieved the balls, and repeated in the opposite direction. After the next round trip, Artair reversed the club heads and shafts placing the ash with beech and birch with holly. Two more round trips, no damaged clubs, only minor tightening of the leather bindings. They completed their task in less than three hours.

Over dinner they discussed the day's results. Ben talked about the data. Artair talked about feel. They found themselves in total agreement that it was more about the balls than the clubs, at least today. They had no doubt that the smooth balls flew less distance on a more jagged path, as if they were following the line of a kite string, being tugged at random.

Ben tweaked the plan for Tuesday's testing. Artair would still make one hundred ninety-two strikes, making half with crosswinds and then forty-eight downwind and forty-eight into the wind. Ben was also sensitized to Artair's animated discussion on feel. Tomorrow Artair would comment on each launch after his follow-through on the strike.

A beautiful orange sunset capped the day. Artair said, "Red sky at night, shepherd's delight."

"You mean golfer's?"

"That as well."

"Rest well. We must start early tomorrow."

65

EDINBURGH, SCOTLAND
TUESDAY, JULY 28, 1496

As much as Ben missed Evi and little Benno, he slept solidly for the first time since returning from Amsterdam. He rose early as did Artair. They downed some bread and cheese. Without much conversation they started out shortly after sunrise.

After walking a half-mile to the east, then hiking for another quarter mile, they settled on a field like St Andrews, with sandy soil, fescues, and lavender patches.

While they had established a testing rhythm the day before, today Artair's commentary on each strike added thirty minutes to the testing. As anticipated, the hair stuffed balls outdistanced the wooden balls by fourteen paces, on average.

On the way back to the Sheep Heid, they debated the club composition. They settled on the white ash and beech combination.

Just after high sun they ate, collected their overnight belongings, and settled with the innkeeper. Heading west to the ferry they first stopped at John Mayne's to order twelve ash shafts and the final assembly to be done immediately after he received the club heads.

Brodie MacThom looked extremely pale and drawn. He was grateful to receive the order for two sets of six club heads, to be shaped on various angles, including one with a flat surface. He would deliver them to Mayne when complete.

Ben noticed the shilling he deposited the day before had not been discovered, so he added another one and moved them slightly so they would be found during the next dusting.

66

St Andrews, Scotland
Friday, August 7, 1496

About halfway from the solstice to the equinox, sunlight would persist past 9:00. A warm summer day had beckoned twenty golfers to the fields, many of whom were still playing. The busy day was compounded by a delivery from the King's courier.

With little daylight remaining, there were just a few making strikes, including Davis. Under Ben's tutelage, Davis was striking with much more consistency. Watching the men of various shapes and sizes, along with their degrees of sobriety, Ben had come to realize that good arm movement could not overcome a bad grip and stance.

Ben waved when he sighted Evi and Benno. He loved what had become their summer ritual—strolling by the sea to what felt like a private Sabbath locale. As they converged, Evi handed over Benno, who continued to slumber. Evi then took Ben by the arm. As usual they started with small talk about the day's events, or lack thereof.

However, Ben's pace was jerky today. Evi could feel tenseness in his biceps. Breaking their stride and leaning her head on his shoulder, "Tell me *mo ghaol*." My lover. "Something is troubling you."

"James has requested I deliver his new clubs within two weeks."

"They will be ready, won't they?"

"Yes."

"Where must you take them?"

"To the Palace at Linlithgow."

"That's not far from Edinburgh."

"Less than twenty miles."

"And you're being paid well."

"Yes."

"And you've taken the journey many times. Something else must be on your mind."

"When you are a nobody, people do not care if you're different. I stick out already. Just look at my brown eyes."

"I love your eyes."

"People have come to realize James befriended me, of all people. And they see that I am prospering."

"And?"

"People are jealous by nature. They blame others for their own problems. In Spain, they blamed the Jews. How will we be treated if my heritage becomes widely known?"

They continued walking arm in arm as she considered her response. "I have seen men at their worst and at their best." She squeezed his arm. "We all have angels and demons inside. All we can do is fight the demons and help others find their inner angels."

"There aren't too many women as circumspect as you."

"We will stay humble, despite our many blessings."

67

EDINBURGH & WINCHBURGH, SCOTLAND

TUESDAY, AUGUST 18, 1496

The two-day trip progressed on schedule. Ben and Artair had hoped for passage across the Firth late Monday afternoon. However, their horses needed more rest than anticipated. When they stopped at St Bridget's Church in Dalgety late Monday afternoon, the parish priest insisted they share a meal and spend the night.

With a start shortly after sunrise on Tuesday, they boarded the day's first ferry at North Queensferry. After crossing to South Queensferry, the ten-mile trip to John Mayne's was uneventful. When they entered the shop, two customers milled around while Mayne adjusted their bows. Noticing Ben, Mayne stopped what he was doing, located the sack containing the clubs and handed it to Artair. Ben counted out the coins for the balance due. They were back on their way within ten minutes.

By mid-afternoon, they had passed Kirkliston, following a short break on the banks of the River Almond. As they approached the small hamlet of Winchburgh, Artair spotted some downed trees across the road, about a hundred yards in front. He galloped ahead. As he approached, two more trees crashed to the ground. His rouncey reared, throwing Artair from his saddle. Ben could see him splayed on the ground. He dismounted and started running towards him.

When Ben saw four men surrounding Artair with face coverings and knives in hand, he stepped into the woods on the road's left side. As much as he wanted to help Artair, he was outnumbered. He crept closer as the bandits inspected Artair and his cargo. They didn't know what to make of the golf clubs. One bandit tried to use a club as a walking stick. It flexed to the point where the others laughed.

Ben was hoping this was just a robbery. If he waited, Artair might be harmed or even murdered. He looked around to see if he could create a distraction, something to frighten them.

The lawless reivers continued to search. Ben's rouncey sauntered forward to meet his four-legged companion. The leader went to inspect the arriving horse. He took one look at its tack and signaled to the other three. They dropped everything and scampered into the forest.

Ben called to Artair as he ran to him. No answer. Ben could see he was breathing. He placed his right index and middle fingers on Artair's wrist, immediately below his left hand. He counted out loud to reinforce the cadence. When he reached fifteen, he repeated with Artair's right wrist. He then counted his own pulse. All three measurements were about the same. He spoke to Artair. No response. He wrapped Artair's right thumb over his index finger and squeezed them as hard as he could. There may have been a faint response.

Artair was not a small man, at least thirteen stones by Ben's estimation. With six miles to Linlithgow Palace, Ben could not carry Artair. Trying to get him on horseback, behind Ben or on a mount by himself, was not feasible.

Ben selected two sturdy branches from the fallen trees, each about ten feet in length. He bound them at the top, laying out an isosceles triangle for a makeshift stretcher. He collected six branches of varying lengths for the ribs. He needed to secure Artair's head in a way to minimize movement. To that end, he used the golf clubs to fashion a cradle for Artair's head near the closed top of the open-ended triangle.

Ben prepared the lashings from the back of both saddles that would secure the stretcher. He rehearsed connecting them. Then he placed the improvised bed next to Artair. Ben was able to lift him by the feet, just enough to clear the poles to position his lower body. Then he tucked his hands under Artair's arms to move his upper body, gently lowering his head onto the golf clubs.

Ben dug two indentations in the road at the base of the long polls to prevent them from sliding. He then gathered the straps taking the ends in his mouth. Ben used his legs to lift the structure with Artair. He put his head through the opening at the top, almost collecting a mouthful of Artair's hair. He secured both horses to the straps and slowly lowered himself.

Finally, Ben covered Artair with a light blanket, tucking in the sides as much as possible. He was still breathing normally. Ben assured Artair, hopefully not on deaf ears, that he would be alright.

Ben fed each rouncey a carrot, turned around and led them, slowly at first, to ensure the structure would hold. Dragging Artair for the next few hours was sure to be bumpy, even on this well-worn road.

68

LINLITHGOW, SCOTLAND

WEDNESDAY, AUGUST 19, 1496

Artair opened his eyes. He felt as if he was floating. The scent of fresh flowers permeated the room. He gently turned his head to the right, looking through a window, catching the sun reflecting on a serene loch. He eased his head to the left. A beautiful young woman, seated not more than fifteen feet away, appeared to be reading. She was adorned in a hoop skirted dress with a white hennin, a half foot high cone covering her head and hair.

"Am I in heaven?"

Placing her book on the side table and rising, the woman said, "I'm pleased you have awakened. You have been sleeping for nearly a day."

Trying to prop himself up, "Where am I?"

"You are in the Palace at Linlithgow." She approached the bed, placed her hand on his shoulder to suppress his movement, "I am Margaret Drummond, mistress to King James."

"Your Grace."

"The doctor departed not long ago. He said that when you feel like you want to move, proceed very slowly to make sure you have your balance."

"What happened?"

"You were thrown from your rouncey."

"I'm such a *gowk*." A fool.

"You are too hard on yourself, I'm sure. According to your companion, you were ambushed by bandits. There were four masked men. They intentionally spooked your mount. Your head took quite a knocking. Do you remember who your companion is?"

"Ben Solomon, I mean Ben Solley."

"That's encouraging. The doctor said you might not remember things and there would be nothing he could do about that."

"How did we escape?"

"Apparently, Ben took cover on the roadside. As his horse rejoined yours on its own, the criminals saw the King's red and yellow lion rampant. It is fortunate His Grace provided his coat of arms to you, and wise of your mate to drape it over his pony."

"Do you know where Ben might be?"

"He is with James, trying the new clubs." Margaret smiled. "Where did you expect him to be?"

Artair tried to rise quickly, "Can I be taken to them?"

Laughing, "Ben predicted this would be your first request when you awoke. But the royal doctor insists you rest and move slowly."

Dejected, Artair slumped back onto the bed.

"Don't despair. They will be back for a midday meal. The doctor will be back about that time to check on you."

····◆····

Late morning, a boisterous voice erupted as James entered the palace. "How is our patient?"

The doorman snapped into action. "I'll fetch Lady Drummond." Before he could do so, Margaret said, "Your Grace," addressing the King publicly as she descended the staircase. "He is making excellent progress."

She made an about face as James passed her on the stairs. She followed with Ben trailing her. They entered the room. Artair was gazing at the loch, slightly leaning forward, bracing himself with both arms on the windowsill.

"Artair, you're up."

He turned, "Ben... Your Grace."

James spoke. "Ben and I needed you this morning." Turning to Margaret, "Did the doctor bleed him again?"

"He told me that he had taken enough blood from the swelling on the back of his head. He didn't need to take more from his arm."

"Good that you looked after him."

Lady Drummond acknowledged with an abbreviated curtsy.

"If we gain the doctor's permission, I will see you both at the midday meal and then we will take some further practice." James turned to exit. Margaret followed. Artair and Ben bent their heads.

Ben was ecstatic. "Look at you. A miracle." Not receiving the return of emotion, "What's wrong?"

"I betrayed you."

"What do you mean?".

"I had just woken up. My head ached. Lady Drummond tested my memory."

"And?"

"She asked me if I knew you. I said, 'Aye, Ben Solomon' and then I corrected myself."

"Under the circumstances, you did absolutely nothing wrong."

"I certainly hope that it is so."

"Let's get you walking. I'd like you to strike balls next to the King this afternoon."

Ben placed his hand on his hip. Artair took hold of the loop Ben created and they started to pace the room. They walked the room's length and back.

Ben asked, "How do you feel now?"

"Very well. Can I ask you something?"

"Anything."

"I understand that you wanted to help MacThom. But why didn't you just hand him the coins?"

Ben laughed, "Now, I've betrayed you."

"Impossible."

"Well, not really. I intended to leave the coins anonymously."

"Why?"

"Rambam."

"Rambam?"

"Short for Moses Maimonides. He was a philosopher." Then adding, "But practical." He said the highest form of giving does not oblige the receiver, nor bring praise to the donor."

"Have you met him?"

"I wish. He was born in Spain over three hundred years ago. Like me, he had to leave because he was Jewish."

Their conversation shifted to the clubs they delivered. Artair wanted to know every detail on each of the King's swings. Ben elaborated for twenty minutes. By the time Ben stopped, they laughed joyously when they realized Artair was no longer using Ben as a crutch.

They stiffened when the doctor entered. He placed his hands under Artair's chin, looked him in the eyes and pronounced, "There is much to learn about medicine, especially the head, where most of our senses are located." He asked Artair to look at points in the room without moving his head.

Releasing his hands from Artair, he asked him to stand and balance on each foot with eyes closed. He checked the small wound he created to bleed Artair. "If I didn't know better, I'd say you are more fit than your friend."

····◆····

Ben and Artair entered the dining hall and were seated according to protocol. Placed at the back and off to the side among thirty others, they were happy to consume a hearty meal as inconspicuously as possible.

After eating a few bites of boar and a swallow of mead, James motioned to a courtier to begin with the wise old owl, William Elphinstone, the Bishop of Aberdeen. He had come to discuss the Education Act, passed by the Parliament two months prior. At sixty-five years of age, Elphinstone had boundless energy for education. While James didn't believe the recently adopted act requiring compulsory learning was enforceable, even with a twenty-pound penalty for non-compliance, he acquiesced to Elphinstone's request for additional funding.

Ben leaned over to Artair and told him about the King's collaboration with Elphinstone in founding the University of Aberdeen. Artair remarked on the bishop's finery. The room went silent as Ben was about to remark that royal and church garb are simply different uniforms for two related armies.

The man immediately to James' left stood. He announced, "His most Reverend Excellency Gavin Douglas."

Douglas took two steps forward to ensure the King's bodyguards stayed between them. He tipped his head forward towards James, "Your Grace." He began reciting his latest poem. He started in classical Latin meter, dactylic hexameter.

Six stanzas later he transitioned to English in a cadence of dactylic pentameter. At that moment, Ben and James made eye contact from across the room, tacitly acknowledging the creativity and the underlying structure. Five stanzas later, he returned to Latin. Each word chosen carefully, weighting them neither more nor less than normal conversation.

When he concluded, the room echoed with applause. Douglas bowed his head to James and sat down.

While James enjoyed the poetry of Walter Kennedy and William Dunbar, he found them hard cast in tradition. He saw the future in Gavin Douglas.

Ben couldn't help but notice the King's efficiency as he held court while eating, commanding detail and dispatching orders.

A courtier then announced John Damian, seeking funds for two projects— Building an alchemy factory to convert copper and nickel into gold, and a flying machine which could be used in war. James knew these projects were far-fetched. However, he kept a straight face, as if he were playing a high stakes card game. *Perhaps someday Damian might eventually happen onto something useful.*

After Damian was dismissed, the courtier formally announced, "Representing Ferdinand the second and Isabella the first of Castile, Señor Don Pedro Lopez de Ayala." The King and Ayala rose, walked to one another, and embraced. They weren't far from Ben and Artair when they began speaking rapidly in Spanish.

"Your Grace, wonderful to see you."

"Don Pedro. I trust you are finding Edinburgh welcoming."

"Indeed. The house you leased for our embassy is second to none. Niddry's Wynd is an excellent location Your Grace. Muchas gracias."

"Are you prepared to accompany my army to Northumbria next month?"

"Without a doubt. Will your grandfather's cannon be deployed?"

"I believe in cannons. You know that. However, at well over seven tons, moving the Mons is not trivial. And each ordnance is nearly four hundred pounds. But I will let my commanders make the decision. Shall we make a wager on their decision?"

Ayala bent his hands upward in resistance to the offer. They continued to make small talk in Spanish for several more minutes. By that time, everyone in the room was distracted, talking softly, eating, drinking, or looking around. Except Ben. Ayala looked over. Ben was enveloped by the same uneasiness as he and Becca experienced passing Señor Méndez in Gibraltar over four years ago. A few seconds later, a courtier signaled to James. He returned to Margaret, and they exited the hall.

James selected the third club from the set. Its head was not flat but not severely angled. He struck five balls. Their distances ranged from forty-five to sixty yards. The first two flew straight for the most part with a nice arc in the air. Ben could see James visibly attempt to apply more power to the next three. They traveled off-line, lower to the ground, one to the left and two to the right.

James turned to Artair, "Similar to yesterday."

Artair was about to respond, when Ben interjected, "Sir, with your permission, can you have the balls retrieved? I'd like Artair to make strikes with the same club and same balls."

A dutiful servant retrieved the balls as Ben was making his suggestion. Artair set-up for his first strike. James stopped him, "Wait a moment."

"Sir", said Artair, tipping his head slightly forward.

"People in my court want to please me. I understand that. They also want to serve their own interests." Raising his right hand, forefinger extended upward, making small circles, now speaking sarcastically, "I should not consort with Lady Drummond. I should marry Catherine of Aragon. No, I should marry Henry's daughter. Apologies for my digression. My point is this— make your strikes with all the skill you have."

Artair made his five strikes. They all veered slightly from a straight path, though in a similar arc, outdistancing James, by an average of fifteen yards.

"Your Grace. If we only had Artair yesterday. It is now obvious after watching you both, one after the other."

James was eager to learn the prescription, "Is it my stance, the arc of my swing, the way I hold the club?"

"Sir, it is your billowing clothing."

"My clothing?"

"They restrict your movement. To compensate, you are exerting yourself more than you should. Applying extra muscle will not make your ball go further. You simply need to make each strike freely and let nature's laws take care of the remainder."

Artair contributed, "Never in my wildest dreams did I ever think a shepherd's tunic would give me an advantage over a nobleman."

"An excellent observation," said James. "I will return shortly."

James returned, not quite looking like a shepherd. He had removed his jerkin in favor of a *leine*, a flattened linen shirt with narrow sleeves. Ben was optimistic, as he sensed the clothing change would positively impact the King's performance.

The King and Artair alternated shots. While making perfect strikes, one after the other, was elusive if not unattainable, James had improved significantly.

As they continued to enjoy the moment, Ayala approached.

"Your Grace. I came to say farewell for now."

"Don Pedro."

They approached and embraced.

Ayala whispered in his ear, "Be careful with these two."

"Why?"

"The darker one may be a Jew. We know how to deal with them in my country."

"I appreciate the warning. Have a safe journey."

"Your Grace."

69

Coldstream, Scotland
Monday, September 21, 1496

Mid-morning, Bishop Don Pedro Lopez Ayala rode west with 1,300 men of the Scottish army along River Tweed's North Bank. Starting upstream at the confluence of the River Till, 900 troops had been positioned over the last four miles.

Ayala mused as he led the company past the Church at Lennel. For hundreds of years, royal marriages spanning Europe's borders resulted in wars. Skirmishes filled the time in between, as if playing Noughts and Crosses endlessly, with each side fantasizing the other would forget how to counter the first move.

As a diplomat, Ayala had a variety of duties. He reveled in the work, from negotiating treaties, to playing cards with James, to managing Perkin Warbeck's claims to the English throne, to executing orders from Ferdinand and Isabella's palace in Cordoba. Little did he know, maturing as a young noble in Toledo, that much of his work would revolve around encouraging, and in certain cases discouraging, sovereign fornication.

The most important perquisite of Ayala's position was his staff of guards and servants, twelve of which rode in his entourage today. In the main body with Ayala were just over 200 men-at-arms. A generation ago, 700 archers and crossbowmen, half on foot, would support the men-at-arms. Today, more than half the archers were replaced by soldiers with culverins, small bore handheld cannons, three feet in length. While easy to carry at four pounds, the challenge was orchestrating the ordnance, gunpowder, and ignition tools.

A scout reported that the vanguard just established full control of the 300-acre thumb created by a ninety-degree bend in River Tweed.

Now a crew of 350, responsible for forty-two wrought iron cannons, their transport horses, and munitions carts, was allowed to advance to the front. The 250-pound falconets, just under four feet long, were easy to maneuver into position compared to the Mons, which had already killed two horses en route.

The drone of clacking walking sticks and pounding hoofs dissipated as more positions were established along the River, ending at the river's bend in early afternoon.

Late afternoon, Ayala sighted Warbeck and the red banner, with silver and gold leaf, which James had commissioned for him. He approached, "May I interrupt the Duke of York?"

"You may. How are you, Don Pedro?"

"I am well. Pleased the ride has been completed. How is Lady Catherine?"

Warbeck smiled, "She is a wonderful woman. I could hardly imagine that I would marry a Scot. She was honored to wear the wedding gown that James presented to us."

"She looked radiant. You are a fortunate man."

"Indeed. She will make England proud when she is crowned."

"First things first. Are you comfortable with the preparations?"

"We've had false starts before. The plans are sound. The foot soldiers all look clean-shaven. They will certainly not be held by the face. And my allies are ready. Thank you for your support."

"I believe James is already marching to take down Twizel Castle."

"He is." Noticing a distressed look on Ayala's face, he inquired, "Something bothering you?"

"That obvious? Tell me something. Do you have any Jews in England?"

"Edward expelled them over two hundred years ago, around 1290 I believe. Why do you ask?"

"When I visited Linlithgow last month, James was practicing golf with a Jew."

"Are you certain?"

"Not a hundred percent." Ayala continued, proud of his worldly connections. "But I've seen many of our Lord's killers over the years. We removed them from Spain last year. When Isabella and Ferdinand's son married Maximilian's daughter in Austria, also last year, I spoke with The Emperor. He told me a hundred years ago the Jews had been cleared from the major cities, including Nuremberg and Frankfurt."

Warbeck returned to the prior thread, "Did you tell James about the Jew?"

"Surely."

"And how did he react?"

"He thanked me for the warning."

"I'm confident we can do our part to protect him from that evil."

They continued to relax, talking about other targets of interest including Norham Castle, further downstream on River Tweed. Cannon fire from a distance didn't bother them in the least. It was the loud explosion nearby which startled them.

Horses snorted and raised their heads in fear. Men began scampering about, like a colony of threatened ants. Warbeck and Ayala, trying to assess the situation, were surrounded by Ayala's Spanish servants. Arrows struck three, one in the leg and the other two critically, head and groin. They started to mount their horses but thought better of it, lest they be more exposed targets with no time to don armor.

With reins in hand, they ran towards Coldstream. Cannon fire increased but so did the incoming arrows, striking four more guards, two of which were immediately disabled. The chaos dissipated as Warbeck and Ayala's group distanced themselves from the fighting and the rear-guard support.

Just as they reached the village, James arrived on horseback with his protective entourage.

"Your Grace," shouted Ayala. "We heard you were marching on Twizel."

"I changed course after a messenger reported. Lord Neville will be here in a few days with the English army. We have time to raze Twizel and I've sent Cochrane and his miners to collapse the Castle at Heaton. You two must head back to Edinburgh immediately. I will clean up the mess you have left me."

"Apologies, Your Grace," said Warbeck, bowing his head. "May I inquire as to what happened?"

"The English sent a forward party to attack our flank. That happens in battle. It was the inept response by the cannon brigade which we were counting on to counteract those types of maneuvers."

Ayala offered, "The brigade is well trained, Your Grace."

James, in his wisdom, offered praise and criticism, "Your men did indeed fire rapidly and with purpose. They need to be better educated on tactics and trajectories. There is a man who can help, Ben Solley."

Stunned, Ayala said in disbelief, "The Jew?"

James concluded, "I don't care what he is, if he can help us prevail."

Ayala and Warbeck bent their heads and looked at each other from the corners of their eyes as the king rode off.

70

Amsterdam, Bishopric of Utrecht

Sunday, December 6, 1496

Becca awoke early, as usual. She moved deliberately in the pitch-black darkness. Today there was no reason to rustle Johan. Their Tineke, now two, had turned into a good sleeper. Becca resisted the temptation to adjust their blankets.

After exiting the room, Becca lit an oil lamp. As a beneficiary from Amsterdam's emergence as a trading center, Becca was able to reduce her dependence on flickering candles. She relished the steady light and the sliver of time, as Mother would not rise until first light.

She smiled when she noticed the fragrance box and wine cup from last night's household tradition. Saturday nights, at dinner, they celebrated Havdalah, which Johan and Becca adapted to honor the end of Becca's Sabbath and the start of Johan's. Now seemed like the perfect time to write a short letter to Ben.

She quietly located quill, inkwell, and a small piece of linen paper.

Greetings to you brother,

We are all well. As you would expect, Mother is moving more slowly. She has found joy with Tineke, singing, playing, feeding, and napping with her. It has allowed Johan to work hard and for me to help him. Some of your passion for numbers must have found its way to me.

I suspect you have not yet heard the painful news from Portugal. King Manuel has expelled the Jews and the Muslims. From what we understand, it was a condition of his marriage to Isabella of Aragon, daughter of Ferdinand and Isabella. No doubt you will be concerned about Mr. Zacuto, as are we. He was so openly welcomed by Manuel's brother, King John, when we all had to leave our beloved homes in Granada and Castile. We do not know if he has departed or become a New Christian.

There are rumors that many Jews will come here. I can only hope it is true. We could start a congregation and someday have a synagogue. It would be wonderful to have enough men for a regular minyan. Until then, we will celebrate our traditions as best we can.

I find the situation in Portugal ironic on this day. People here are celebrating the generosity and kindness of Saint Nicholas, feasting, and helping others.

Please come back soon, or better yet, come back forever. I know there is a place for you to work with Johan. We miss you. Evi became a part of our family when you visited. We know Benno will make a great playmate for Tineke.

May you and your family be safe. Your loving sister,
Becca Solomon Witte

She dated the letter, then let it sit for a few minutes, ensuring two small unwanted ink splotches dried thoroughly. She prepared an envelope and inserted the letter. Johan would take it to his office to seal and arrange delivery through the shipping company.

Becca leaned back, inhaled deeply, and closed her eyes.

Mother entered the room with a halfhearted, "Good morning."

No response. Mother approached from behind, noticed the addressee, then placed her hands on Becca's shoulders. "I miss him too. Did you tell him you're pregnant?"

71

ST ANDREWS, SCOTLAND
SUNDAY, MAY 16, 1497

The death of the beloved Archbishop Scheves, in late January, plunged his congregants into a state of purgatory, leaving no spiritual leader and a mediating voice between the regimes of James III and James IV.

It was common knowledge that James III, unpopular with his constituents, fueled the sibling rivalry of his three young princes, leaving them rudderless when Queen Margaret died at age twenty-eight.

James Stewart, Duke of Ross, projected a hardy "Pax vobiscum," as James IV concluded his brother's installation as Archbishop of St Andrews. The congregation's boisterous response, "Et cum spiritu tuo," echoed throughout the imposing structure.

James IV took the hand of his brother, James, to his right, and the hand of their youngest brother, John Stewart, to the left and raised them. Cheers broke the solemnity.

John, the youngest but wise beyond his years, innately understood his eldest brother's brilliance. James IV had mastered family politics, consolidating his parents' divergent wishes to forge a practical path forward.

With spring in full force, the show of unity was uplifting and couldn't have happened at a better time. The pomp did not go unnoticed. Ben saw Don Pedro de Ayala in the processional, walking behind the three brothers. He gently elbowed Evi. Looking up from a fussy Benno, she saw Ayala glancing at them. She proudly straightened her posture.

A blustering wind, punctuated with strong gusts, helped to dissipate gatherings outside the cathedral. After exiting the west doors, some parishioners took protection behind the northern wall and began to gossip. The brothers, along with Ayala, entered the North Porch room, dismissing their guards to wait in the nave aisle.

The King turned to his brother, the new archbishop, "Did Don Pedro inform you of a Jew here in St Andrews?"

"He told me he suspected as much."

"Good. Do you know the individual?"

"Aye."

"Please take John to retrieve him, though I doubt there will be trouble. Make sure to bring him to me unharmed."

The younger brothers left. James continued, "Don Pedro, thank you for providing the warnings to James and John. It is better we use him to our advantage rather than vanquish him or kill him at this time."

Ayala nodded in agreement, "Your Grace."

There were rumblings in the remaining crowd, as Ben, with John at Ben's right, and James opposite, walked back into the building, returning to the North Porch.

Ben entered, stopped, bent his head forward, "Your Grace."

The King stared at Ben sternly. James remained motionless, as did the others, allowing the suspense to build. "You are Spanish. My advisers tell me you are a Jew. I was present for your son's baptism. You may be a Jew, or you may be a New Christian. It does not matter to me. What matters is that you serve me as I see fit. Do you understand me?"

Ben nodded, "Aye, Your Grace."

"You are to deliver to the archbishop, no later than the sixteenth of every month, the sum of twenty shillings for God's work. Should you fail to meet this obligation, unless you are at war, you will be obliged to pay an additional sum of five shillings. Again, do you fully understand what is required of you?"

Again, Ben nodded, "I do, Your Grace."

"Then you are dismissed."

Ben exited at which point the King turned to his brothers and Ayala, "If ever this man is not helpful or fails to meet the obligation I just established, I expect to be notified immediately, before any action is taken."

The King extended his hand to each in turn. He initiated a single, emphatic up and down stroke with each, to seal the agreement. "Have a good day. I have to attend a land inspection." The King turned and departed.

Ayala and James were pleased Ben had been put in his place, properly. They muted their excitement with gentle pats on one another's shoulders.

Ben walked Evi and Benno home. He assured her that he would explain what had transpired with the King when he returned home from work at the golfing fields. It was not his day of rest.

As usual, Davis and Artair left church at the earliest opportunity. Ben found them in an impromptu contest for the longest strike. They had learned from Ben how to place a mark on their balls in a way which would not impact the flight.

In some cases, their strikes traveled over 150-yards, downwind on this blustery day. After they retrieved their balls, Ben watched them hit into the wind. It was almost comical when the strikes sailed half the distance before seemingly falling from the sky.

Davis and Artair both knew that strikes flying closer to the ground would be more effective in combating the wind. Ben helped them adjust their stances in relationship to the ball and suggested slight modifications to their hand position on their club shafts. After several trials, men were launching lower with results over 100-yards.

They were thanking Ben when they heard, "Can you help me make the same adjustments?"

Turning to the voice and almost in unison, "Your Grace."

James had walked about a hundred paces from his mounted entourage. Despite the chilling winds, the King had removed his jerkin, to maximize his freedom of movement.

Ben gathered the King's clubs as the players moved toward the cleared area to launch their first strikes. Davis, Artair, and Walter had been schooled by Ben, well in advance, that the worst thing one could do was let the King win. They all hoped James would do well, which would also bring credit to Ben.

No one noticed when Ben had picked up some pebbles as they made the short walk to the first launch area. Ben then said he had from one to four stones in his hand and each golfer should make a guess. The correct selector would determine the initial striking order. The ball reaching the target with the fewest strikes will determine who strikes first on the next. Ben asked James how much time he had allocated to play. When James responded, Ben determined they should play up and back twice, a total of twelve targets.

The men were nervous at first, including the King. By the time they reached the first post, they had all relaxed, each making some good strikes, often laughing, as their expectations were lowered in the wind conditions.

Davis and James made the same number of strikes, with Artair and Walter one additional. However, as they walked to the second launch area, James piped up, "Gentlemen, if I understand the honor of this game, one must make a strike where the ball lies." The group all nodded, like a marionettes line, in the affirmative. "I accidentally moved my ball, so I concede to Davis."

"Thank you, Your Grace," said Davis, thinking, perhaps as the others, that a man truly reveals himself when he plays golf.

The day proceeded with the contestants comfortable when splashed with sunlight, warm when walking, and cool when stationary under cloud cover. With the King's permission, Ben offered suggestions to all players. In the King's case, the challenge was self-imposed and centered on confidence, as opposed to technique and competition which he saw in most other men.

When play completed, all exchanged handshakes. When it appeared that the final "Your Grace" had been uttered, James spoke, "Ben, may I see you privately?" It was more a command than a request, obvious to all, with no need for Ben to answer.

"How is your new son getting along?"

"Very well, thank you for asking, Your Grace."

"Ben, I encounter many men of small minds." He let that sink in, then continued, "Do you not agree?"

"Aye, Your Grace."

"It is easy for weak minds to convince themselves that Jews have money illegally. So you will continue to pay the archbishop regularly. You will show no emotion when you do so."

"Aye, Your Grace."

"Did my messenger deliver the coins to you last week?"

"Forty shillings. One month is twenty."

"Good, twenty should be delivered every month, but I want you to have a month's contingency."

72

ATLANTA, GEORGIA, USA
FRIDAY, SEPTEMBER 27, 2002

Shortly after 5:00 p.m. Rusty entered The Temple offices in the same manner as his first visit. This time no one noticed. The place was buzzing with activity.

"Ahh, Mr. Stephens," bellowed Rabbi Sugarman as he stepped from his office. "I did hear a car pull up. Apologies. It's rather busy around here at the moment."

"No problem."

"Come on in Rusty. We have a few minutes before I have to get ready."

Following the rabbi to his office, Rusty inquired, "Is it always this busy on Friday afternoons?"

"Today more than most. We have the Bat Mitzvah of a young woman tomorrow morning and after tonight's service a somewhat more elaborate reception, what we call an Oneg Shabbat. Have a seat. How is business?"

Smiling, Rusty responded, "Well. Most people don't ask me about that."

"Sorry, I'm not sure I'm following."

"Most people talk to me about the sport. I'm usually asked about my last tournament or about the next major championship or how I got started in the game or a bunch of other things. Rarely is it about my business."

"Oh, I see. After we first met, I did a little research as I really don't know much about golf. I play, if you could even call it that, mostly at charity outings. From what I can tell, most athletes that make their living playing sports are paid by teams or big companies. Golfers, on the other hand, have their own businesses and you only earn when you play well for several days in a row."

"True. But we do get paid for promotions, ads, appearances, and sponsorships."

"I understand, but correct me if I'm wrong, when you're not in the spotlight, so to speak, those are worth much less."

"Rabbi, you're a quick study."

"There is something else that struck me in a cerebral, dare I say, almost spiritual way."

"Sounds intriguing."

"You play an honorable game. You are your own judge, calling penalties on yourself, sometimes asking an opponent or official if in doubt."

"And that's religious?"

The rabbi laughed, "Perhaps a stretch, but I believe there is an aspect of Godliness in golf. It emanates from within you rather than coming to you."

"I had never thought about it that way. But I think you can tell a lot about a person's soul by the way he, or she, behaves on the course."

Rabbi Sugarman stood up. Rusty bent forward to follow.

"Stay seated. I just have to change into a robe for the service."

Walking over to his closet he said, "I took the liberty of finding some people you can sit with. If you'd rather not, it's okay."

"That'd be nice, thank you."

"Great. They're old friends, Dick and Thelma Wolf. I went to high school with Dick. But watch out for Thelma. From what I understand, she recently made a hole in one."

"Thanks for the heads-up."

"They're lovely people, here tonight on the anniversary of Dick's mother's death."

"Would that be *Yizkor* or *Yarhzeit*?" When the rabbi raised his eyebrows, Rusty continued, "I did some research on Jewish lifecycle events."

"We've only got a few minutes, but yes, *Yarhzeit* is Yiddish for observing the anniversary of a death. *Yizkor* is Hebrew, meaning memorial prayers, probably added to various services back in the time of Maimonides. Listen for the Kaddish prayer tonight. By the way, you don't need to wear a head covering for our services. C'mon. Let me introduce you."

The rabbi made a brief, low key introduction and walked away. Dick noticed some stares, whispering, gentle elbows nudging adjacent congregants. He suggested Rusty take a seat between himself and Thelma. They settled into the dark wooden pew on upholstered maroon cushions.

In the fifteen minutes before the service started, Thelma and Dick learned that Rusty grew up in Augusta, was raised as an Episcopalian, went to Tech, and now lives in Buckhead. Rusty learned that Thelma was a transplant from Pennsylvania. Dick's mother, Hermina, or Hum as many people around town knew her, was remembered tonight as a compassionate character with a wicked sense of humor, Miss Daisy's opposite.

Contrary to the expectation set by Rabbi Sugarman, Rusty had to ask Thelma about her ace. She hit a seven iron on the Par-3 17th at the Standard Club. Rusty remembered the outcropping behind the hole as he had played a charity event there on the Tuesday before the PGA Tournament held down the road at the Atlanta Athletic Club, in 2001. As Rusty pointed out, golf is a sport in which they can share experiences, whereas neither he nor Thelma was going to hit a Greg Maddux fastball or slam dunk a basketball like Dominique Wilkins.

Rabbi Judy greeted the congregation with a "Shabbat Shalom," which the seventy or so congregants echoed in the large chapel. Then she invited the Bat Mitzvah's mother and grandmother to come forward. They initiated the service by lighting two Sabbath candles while reciting the blessing they had learned as children.

The service proceeded with responsive reading in English. Other than a few cantor melodies, the Hebrew portions were translated. Several prayers seemed familiar to Rusty, like recitations by Reverend Portman. Intuitively this made sense. In Sunday school, he studied the Old Testament as well as the New Testament.

Shortly after the service started, Rusty noticed that God was only referenced in gender neutral terms. He suspected it wasn't always this way.

About twenty minutes later, Rabbi Judy, elbows at her waist, extended her arms, palms up, raising them slightly as she gently commanded, "Please rise for the Shema, the cornerstone of our faith." Rusty expected the proclamation of a singular God. However, it was the juxtaposition of the phrasing "One God" with "Sovereign of the Universe" rather than "King of the Universe," that struck him. He made a mental note to talk to Rabbi Sugarman about it.

Rabbi Judy took a seat after she charged the congregation to pray silently. Rusty inhaled deeply and closed his eyes, trying to quiet his mind, as he does on the links. But he was not on the course. As if he was clicking through photos on the viewfinder toy he found years ago in his parents' attic, he imagined Sandy, click, Mother, click, Father, click, Magnolia Lane, click, Tommy Torres, click, Reverend Portman, click, Marbella, click, O.T., click, Sandy, click, Jesus, click, Seve, click, Professor Washington.

Three minutes later, Rabbi Sugarman stepped up to the pulpit to deliver a short sermon, tailored to the Bat Mitzvah's posse of thirteen-year-old friends in attendance, some not Jewish.

Rusty made another mental note, near the service's end, following the Mourner's Kaddish prayer and the recitation of Temple members' names who died recently or the anniversaries of their passing. Rusty resonated with the words the rabbi spoke about eternal life, suggesting it is achieved by performing acts of goodness while on earth.

The Temple's lay President was invited to the pulpit to make a few closing remarks before the closing hymn and the rabbi's final blessing.

After the "amen," Dick stood, extending his hand to Rusty, "Good Shabbos. Thelma quickly gave Rusty a peck on the cheek before he could react. "Good Shabbos. It was a pleasure meeting you. We'll see you at the Oneg?"

He didn't know whether he should say Sabbath, Shabbos or Shabbat in response. His mental notebook was filling up. "Thelma, Dick, thanks for welcoming me. It was nice to meet you. I'm sorry but I have to run."

Dick responded, "We hope to see you again."

"Likewise."

A small group had gathered around Rabbi Sugarman. Rusty was able to catch his attention, with a half wave. He then signaled with his fist to his ear, thumb and baby finger extended, that they would talk. The rabbi acknowledged with a nod as Rusty made a beeline for his car.

Rusty cranked the ignition and called O.T.

"Hello."

"What took you so long? Your phone didn't even ring."

"I just sit around on Friday nights waiting for you to call. Aren't you going to The Temple."

"I did. The service was short, but I didn't want to deal with a crowd of strangers at the reception."

"So, you're hungry?"

"I am. If you're free come on over. We can order something in."

"Sad to say, I've got no plans. But let's go out," implored Brian. "No one will bother us at Kiyo Ya. Great Sushi. Gimme fifteen minutes. We can meet there."

"Where is it?"

"Pershing Point. I'll text you the address. Where are you now?"

"Not far, maybe five minutes. I'm still in The Temple parking lot."

"Drive slow."

"I'll try to get a table."

"Sounds like a plan."

····◆····

Rusty was seated in the back, facing a small fountain gurgling peacefully on a floating wooden shelf. O.T. followed the hostess, down a few steps, past a long Sushi bar with four chefs at various workstations.

"Obviously you had no problem finding the place," said O.T. taking the seat opposite Rusty facing the room. "Did you talk to Sandy?"

"I knew it would take you a few minutes, so I called her."

"Did she know you were going to The Temple tonight?"

"Not in advance."

"What was her reaction?"

"I think she was glad I was interested. I told her I enjoyed the service. But I think she wondered if my reaction may have been the novelty of the experience."

A hostess arrived with a bottle containing hot sake, poured two cups and walked away.

Brian raised his cup, "*Kampai.*"

Cameron reciprocated.

Brian continued, "Was it?"

"Was it what?"

"The novelty of the experience?"

"Perhaps that's part of it. But there was something weird about the service, the meeting with the rabbi and the people I met."

"Weird?"

"Like, there's something very appealing about Judaism."

"No shit? Because of Sandy?"

"Granted, we wouldn't be talking about this if I hadn't met her, but this has nothing to do with her. I might look into taking a Judaism orientation course."

"Really?"

"The rabbi said there's a weekly class in the evenings."

Their attention was diverted for a few minutes when miso soup and salad arrived.

Brian spoke up, "It might be tough with our schedules, but I'd go with you if you wouldn't mind?"

"Sure, I don't mind," replied Cameron. "I'll say the same thing to you, 'really'?"

"The only time I ever went to church was on Christmas Eve and Easter Sunday. Never went to Sunday school. I'm sorta curious. Might as well start at the beginning."

73

MANHATTAN, NEW YORK, USA
SATURDAY, SEPTEMBER 28, 2002

Upon hearing Tamara's distinctive knock, Sandy shimmied to the bed's edge. She suppressed "Not a good time," yelling, "Just a minute." She pushed her pillows aside, sat up and reached for her robe. She loosely knotted the sash on her way to the door.

Now a careful New Yorker, Sandy looked through the peephole. She verified it was her neighbor. She uttered a sleepy "Hi Tam," as she unbolted and opened the door.

"Rough night?" said Tamara, extending coffee to her in a small blue thick paper cup with a plastic top, inscribed with, "We are happy to serve you" in Greek style gold lettering.

Sandy took it and sipped. "Thanks."

"Iqbal's finest," referring to the street vendor who had garnered a spot for his cart outside their building years ago. "It'll get you started until you get in gear. It's beautiful out."

"Why don't you come back later. I'm just exhausted. After I came back from the Hamptons Monday, I had to play catch up at work. I need to sleep."

"You'll sleep when you're dead."

"Funny. My bubbe used to say that."

"Bubbe?"

"My grandmother. It's Yiddish."

"Cool. I'm with her. Take your time. I'll wait."

Sandy went to the bathroom with her coffee. Tamara heard the shower start as she plopped down on the couch. She sipped her coffee and picked up *New York Magazine*. She put it down when she noticed a small pile of papers sitting on the table. A yellow post-it note was affixed, with, "Brian, Ellis Island" written on it.

Calling out to Sandy, "Do you mind if I look through this stack about Brian?"

"Help yourself. I was excited when I found out his great grandfather came through Ellis Island. But I'm stuck now trying to find his ancestors in Europe."

The phone rang. Tamara was thinking about answering it, but Sandy had her answering machine set on two rings.

"Hello, this is Sandy, you know what to do at the tone, so do it."

The beep sounded and Cameron's voice came on, "Good morning beautiful..."

Sandy bolted from the bathroom in a towel with her hair in a turban fashioned from a second towel. She yanked the phone from its cradle in the kitchen, "Hi handsome...Miss you too."

Tamara motioned with her hand, pointed to the door, to see if Sandy wanted some privacy. Sandy signaled her to stay then continued the conversation as she stretched the long cord into the bathroom.

Tamara flipped a few pages, stopping intermittently to read some details. Fifteen minutes later, Sandy exited the bathroom, then shimmied into a pair of jeans and a light sweater. Still nursing her coffee, she sat down with Tamara. "You're still reading that?"

"It's not the most exciting stuff but I can certainly see why you can get addicted to it. Almost like a scavenger hunt."

"Sort of," said Sandy, her head bobbing in agreement.

"One thing in your scribbles caught my attention."

"What's that?"

"You have a squiggly line with an arrow pointing from Brian's great great great grandfather to Europe."

"True."

"And didn't you tell me Brian has a dark complexion?"

"Probably."

"What about South America, Africa, or even Asia."

"I asked Brian about that. He's insistent on Europe."

"And you're stuck?"

"I'm not ready to give up, but..."

Tamara put up her hand to stop Sandy.

Sandy reflexed, "What Tam?"

"Maybe the prior generation was already here."

"Whaddaya mean?

"My Bibi told me she came over long before her mother."

"Bibi?"

"My grandmother. It's Swahili. I've got some Kenyan blood in me, supposedly."

"You may be on to something. Do you have any plans now?"

"Not really."

"If you don't mind helping me research, then let's go. Brunch is on me. Jewish soul food, okay?"

"Sounds good. I'll go pee, grab a jacket and meet you in the lobby."

As much as they both liked Iqbal, Sandy insisted on buying Tamara a latte at the Starbucks around the corner. They continued south five blocks on Broadway to Zabar's with their umbrellas extended.

Late morning on Saturday, they expected to wait but were seated right away. Sandy suggested Tamara order matzo ball soup and she would take kreplach soup. Sandy explained that kreplach was first cousins with wonton soup. They could trade if Tamara didn't like balls.

The double entendre did not go unnoticed. They giggled. Tamara started dishing with Sandy about Cameron and their recent travels culminating in Southampton. The soups arrived. The conversation stopped temporarily. Tamara liked the matzo balls.

Waiting for their bagels and nova to be served, Sandy came back to Tamara's Bibi, fascinated that her grandmother could share stories with Tamara about her great grandmother. Tamara explained that she tried, to no avail, to find out more about her ancestors on that side of the family.

When Tamara's cousin visited New York, they hit the typical tourist attractions. At The Battery, on Manhattan's southern tip, most activity centered on the Statue of Liberty. Tamara told Sandy she visited Castle Clinton, used for over thirty years for immigrant intake before Ellis Island. She had felt a connection to her relatives when walking around but couldn't find any information about them there.

When their plates arrived, the conversation shifted to the optimal cream cheese schmear and whether to top the fish with capers and onions. They stopped talking and dug in.

Close to finishing their bagels, they noticed customers beginning to queue for table seating. As expected, their waiter approached their table, left their check, and politely asked if they would like him to add coffee to their Starbucks cups. They declined. Sandy grabbed the check, saying excitedly, "Tam, I've got an idea."

Now inspired and ready to go, Sandy dropped a pair of Jacksons on the table. "Let's go." With Tamara in tow, she walked immediately to the curb, raising her right arm to hail a cab.

With sparse traffic on a Saturday morning, they arrived at the library ten minutes later. Sandy assured her they wouldn't be cooped up too long, now that the rain had stopped and it had turned into a beautiful, fall day.

Sandy walked quickly into the building. Tamara noticed, "You look like you know what you're doing."

"I was here a couple of weeks ago. Everyone's very helpful."

Mary-Kate happened to be there and remembered Sandy. After a brief introduction to Tamara, Sandy asked about Castle Clinton. Mary-Kate explained that a building on the site was first constructed by the Dutch in the early 1600's when New York was New Amsterdam. Eventually demolished, it was replaced by a new structure, a fortification following the Revolutionary War, only to be used as a social venue, called Castle Garden.

Tamara inquired, "When did it become Castle Clinton?"

"Good question," responded Mary-Kate. "In 1817, it was renamed in honor of DeWitt Clinton, who had been New York City's mayor the same year he secured funding for the Erie Canal, aka DeWitt's Folly. The bad news, many of the hard copy records, transferred to Ellis Island were lost in a fire there. The good news, we have a database you can access. I can set you both up on workstations if you'd like."

Sandy attacked the keyboard with vigor, sounding like a woodpecker. Tamara looked over, covering her mouth to stifle a laugh, then gently tapped on Sandy. Self-aware, Sandy grimaced and lightened up. But Tamara became entranced in the moment. After ten minutes of typing, clicking, and scrolling, Tamara asked, "Find anything?"

"Maybe, you?

"Me too."

74

ATLANTA, GEORGIA, USA
THURSDAY, OCTOBER 10, 2002

As eager as she was to see Cameron, Sandy opted to stand patiently on the escalator, rather than climb the moving stairs with her carry-on. As she crested, she saw Brian.

"I know you were expecting Rusty, uh, Cameron."

She intentionally replied in kind, "O.T., uh, Brian, nice to see you." She leaned forward for a quick hug. "What happened?"

"Last minute conference call with his attorney."

"Brent?"

"Yep, something about ensuring his endorsements weren't tied to his stats on the course. Didn't seem like a crisis but I think a renewal came up on one of his contracts. Anyway, he should be done by the time we get to the condo. Nguyen's waiting in the car. Luggage?"

"Just this."

"Great, let me schlep that." Brian grabbed the suitcase's handle.

"Thanks," replied Sandy. "I think you know more Yiddish than I do."

"Huh?"

"Schlep."

"Oh. Anyway, Nguyen was going to solo but together it'll save a few minutes. Also, I was hoping you could tell me about any new branches you found on my tree, so to speak. It's incredibly nice of you to do this. I want to reimburse you for any expenses, so please let me know."

"No biggie. At this point you owe me a couple lattes and a few cab fares in New York."

"No problem."

Leaving the air conditioning for a warm, humid night, Brian sighted Nguyen, who had found a spot to hover by the curb. As they approached, Nguyen exited the car. Like old friends, Sandy and Nguyen hugged and exchanged greetings.

As Nguyen merged the vehicle onto I-85 North, Sandy began to explain how her friend, Tamara, had prompted her to alter course. Her explanations were confusing with great great this and great great that. With her fatigue and some stop and go traffic at the end of rush hour, she was hesitant to pull out her notepad, sensing some nausea.

Sandy tried to simplify. "Your grandfather's grandfather, as you know, arrived at Ellis Island. However, many years earlier, his father came into the U.S. through Castle Clinton in Manhattan just before the Civil War. Great that I found him, but if it hadn't been for Tamara, I would still be looking for him in Europe. And here is the incredible news. I think I've found the father of your ancestor, who arrived at Castle Clinton."

"Where?"

"Somewhere in the U.K. Most likely England or Scotland, probably not Wales but still checking that part out."

"I can't believe you got this far."

"Me neither."

Nguyen turned the car into the circular drive fronting Cameron's building. After stopping, he removed her bag from the back while Sandy said goodbye to Brian. Nguyen extended the arm of her suitcase, taking it to the front door. The doorman said, "Good evening Ms. Cole. Mr. Stephens is expecting you."

Alerted by the doorman, Cameron greeted Sandy at the elevator. Once inside the condo, they kissed lightly, hugged then kissed again passionately. Sandy pulled him close, purring as she felt his arms envelop her and his package expand.

"Somebody missed me."

"It's been almost three weeks."

"Too long. You better take advantage of me before I crater."

Pulling back slightly, "Hungry, something to eat, drink?"

"How about...let me see...how about I raid your fridge while you start a bath for me."

"Scavenge rather than raid but have at it."

"How about making it a bubble bath for two?"

"Even better."

····◆····

They languished in the steamy, soapy water, lying opposite each other, heads resting comfortably on rolled up towels which Cameron thoughtfully placed. They caught up on the basics— family, weather, and plans for the next few days. They took turns soaping and rubbing each other's feet. Hard to tell who needed it more, a golfer who knocks off twenty miles in a golf tournament or a New York City pavement walker. Eventually, Cameron asked about Sandy's foray into Brian's lineage.

Sandy provided the short version of what she'd covered in the ride from the airport. She concluded, "There's one more thing." She hesitated.

"Well?"

"You can't tell Brian."

"Your secret's safe with me."

"Pinky swear. No, let's make it a little piggy swear."

"Haven't heard that one."

"Just made it up," as she reached her right hand across herself to squeeze his right baby toe with her thumb and index finger. Cameron followed suit with his right hand, "Okay, little piggy swear."

"I think Brian's ancestors had something to do with golf."

"Are you serious? That would be insane."

"I know. That's why I don't want to say anything to him until I prove it one way or the other."

The bubbles dissipated exposing Sandy's wet soapy chest. Cameron let his eyes fall, then reached his left hand across to Sandy's other foot, "One more thing...little piggy swear...you won't fall asleep on me."

Sandy smiled. "I'll double swear," as she crossed her arms mischievously framing her chest, inhaling deeply to accentuate her breasts, and simultaneously squeezing and pinching his baby toes.

75

Atlanta, Georgia, USA
Sidney, Maine USA
En route to Augusta, Georgia, USA
Friday, October 11, 2002

With a mug of coffee in hand, Sandy puttered around the condo while Cameron pumped iron at the gym. She repacked a few items, then savored an English muffin with blueberry jam, watching the morning traffic move like a caterpillar as it inched downtown on Peachtree Street.

As Sandy entered the kitchen to top-up her coffee, she noticed a snow event warning for the northeast crawling across the Weather Channel ticker. For obvious reasons, Cameron tuned to that channel daily. She found the remote on the counter and un-muted to hear Jim Cantore's storm analysis.

Twenty seconds later, Sandy called her mom. Beth answered. Sandy inquired about the storm. As expected, her mom recited the Scandinavian expression, "There is no such thing as bad weather, only bad clothes." Sandy joked that airplanes don't wear clothes as she segued to the call's real purpose, her mom's upcoming visit to Sloan Kettering, in New York. Beth informed Sandy that they were driving down and given the time of year, early snows didn't hang around too long, even in Maine. They continued to chat until Sandy heard the front door unlocking. They said a quick goodbye.

"How was your workout?" queried Sandy.

"Good, did you run?"

"No, I just hung out."

"Can we leave today?"

"I suppose. Did you speak with your parents?"

"We're still on schedule with them tomorrow. I have something else in mind, a surprise."

"Do I still have time for a run?"

"If we leave at three, that should give you plenty of time."

"Great."

With the help of Philip, the weekday morning doorperson, Sandy planned her route. She told him she'd like to run about three miles. Off she went, Philip's sketch in hand, phone in pocket.

Sandy stretched as she walked from the building. She jogged left onto West Wesley, then left onto Rivers Road. Seven minutes later she made a right on Peachtree Battle just after passing Habersham.

She stopped, jogging in place, looking up and down the road at the beautifully groomed mall of flowers and trees, serving as divider for opposing traffic. After three cars passed, she crossed to Nacoochee with nice views of Peachtree Creek. She looped back on Woodward Way past Peachtree Battle. She slowed slightly to admire some impressive homes as Woodward Way Park transitioned to Sibley Park.

Sandy returned to the building and checked her pedometer. Three miles on the nose. She put her hands together and bowed to Phillip. "Thank you. Thank you."

"My pleasure."

"I could do this every day." As she walked to the elevator bank, she turned and smiled, "Keep your pencil sharp."

When she returned from her run, she found Cameron busy setting place mats, napkins, and flatware on the kitchen counter bar.

"Look at you."

"I thought we'd go out for lunch to a great little Italian place, Pasta Vino, just down the street. I called for a reservation. Little did I know they're only open for dinner. Then I figured you might need some time to wind down and shower. How was your run?"

"Terrific, Philip is the man. Look at the map he drew," as she uncurled it.

Cameron examined it, as he flattened it further pressing out the edges, "Nice. Let's keep it in the drawer with the takeout menus." He opened the drawer, shuffled through the stack of papers, pulling out the menu for Henri's Bakery and Deli. "Their food's incredible."

Sandy studied the menu for the thirty seconds. "Is it as good as it looks?"

"Better."

"I'm thinking Po-Boy, turkey or roast beef?"

"You can't go wrong with either."

Sandy smacked him on the lips, "You decide, and a cronut pretty please."

"For sure. Be back in a few."

····◆····

After lunch, which lived up to Cameron's hype, they headed south on the downtown connector, exiting east onto I-20. As they passed the perimeter, Cameron relaxed his right foot as he engaged the cruise control.

What seemed like leveling off in a plane after breaking through the clouds, in this case traffic, Sandy tilted her seat back about six inches. She closed her eyes and said, "Are we heading towards Augusta?"

"We are, but we're not staying with my folks tonight. I didn't want to hide anything from them, so I told them we weren't sure of our plans, which is kinda true. I'll update them later."

"Okay..." elongated Sandy, now curious. "How much do we, or should I say you, know about our plans?"

Now seemed like a good time to detail his burgeoning curiosity about Judaism. He explained the chain of events, from meeting her, to Professor Washington at Tech, to Rabbi Sugarman at The Temple.

Cameron didn't know much about the Jewish community in Augusta. There were only a few hundred Jewish families in a city of well over a hundred thousand. He remembered that many times over the years, he passed a small, beautiful city government building with Greek columns on Telfair Street. A few weeks ago, he learned it was a synagogue built shortly after the civil war, called the Children of Israel. The congregation moved to Walton Street, a hop, skip, and a jump from the Augusta Country Club and The Augusta National Golf Club. "We're on our way there for Sabbath services."

After Sandy absorbed the short monologue and its conclusion, she reacted with, "Wow, that is so cool, Cam." Then she laughed.

"What's so funny?"

"It seems like I've created two monsters! Brian's really into his family tree, and now you're exploring religious history and Judaism. Actually, very cool. Why didn't we just go to services tonight in Atlanta?"

"I had that experience, met some nice people, but I wanted to see what's happening in my hometown, and thinking it might be more like your congregation in Maine."

Sandy extended her left hand on top of his right. He took the steering wheel in his left hand as Sandy took his hand back to her lap and closed her eyes, thinking *this is going to be one interesting weekend.*

76

Aiken, South Carolina, USA
Saturday, October 12, 2002

About 8:30 AM, Sandy and Cameron exited their suite at the historic Willcox Hotel. They found the staircase, descended one flight to the main floor, then traversed the lobby to the restaurant. As usual they requested a table on the room's perimeter, allowing Rusty to face away from most guests. They both nodded as a waiter on one side of the table offered coffee and the waitress on the opposite side orange juice.

Sandy tipped a small amount of milk from a warm silver pitcher into her cup and took a sip. "Mmm, that's good. After the three hours on the road, then the service and dinner, I wasn't looking forward to driving another twenty miles to get here. Again, you surprised me. This place is beautiful."

"I surprised myself. I used to play golf here several times a year, sort of an interstate rivalry. We never stayed overnight. Never even thought about it. The place was sorta rundown. When I heard it was reopened earlier in the year, I figured why not give it a try. Plus, we wouldn't run into any Augustans."

"What time are we meeting your folks?"

"One."

"Good. Now I have a surprise. I booked a couples massage for us at ten. Thought it might mellow us out for the afternoon."

Cameron took her hand and squeezed it. They continued to talk about the property and some historical trivia they had read on a wall display.

Breakfast arrived, and the waitress reversed the meals, serving the bagel and cream cheese to Sandy and the scrambled eggs and grits to Cameron.

Sandy and Cameron raised eyebrows at each other, both opting not to correct the server. As they exchanged plates, Cameron said, "You think she was driven by our accents, our gender, dyslexia or just a typical error."

Sandy laughed, "Maybe a combination." She took a bite of her eggs, "Are we going to talk about the big elephant in the room?"

"Elephant?"

"The service last night."

Cameron deliberated for a second, "Maybe it's a dog tugging on you but hardly an elephant."

"Good point, but I was bored for the most part. You?"

"It was interesting."

"Even the sermon?"

"Well," said Cameron. "The guest speaker didn't show so I suppose my expectations were lowered."

"Maybe you're enjoying it because it's new and different?"

"Maybe. I'm sorry. I thought you'd like it."

"I like the holidays— Purim, when children dress up like biblical characters; Sukkot, where we celebrate the harvest in a shack outside; Hanukkah, a miracle after a battle; and even Yom Kippur, where we reflect for twenty-four hours while fasting. The rest is just rote repetition, like saying the same prayers before eating on Friday night, which we did until I was a teenager."

Cameron was silent. Sandy took his hand and squeezed it. "What is it?"

"I have all these thoughts going through my head. It feels a bit strange. I don't know where to start or how to get them organized to make any sense."

"Go on, try." Sandy smiled, "I've sequestered the press in the media tent outside."

Cameron expressed that he too liked the religious holidays, not because they were based on a man's divinity. Rather, they brought the family together. With no siblings, he looked forward to spending Christmas and Easter with his cousins, aunts and uncles and grandparents.

He also confessed that in his late teenage years, he kept a big secret, thinking others wouldn't understand. When looking upon images of Jesus on a crucifix he wanted to see God. Instead, he saw a human being and philosopher, who died violently as he struggled for justice. He wondered how Jesus was different from Gandhi or Martin Luther King.

Sandy wanted to respond but held back. She didn't want to interrupt his near stream of consciousness.

"Right after I turned twenty, a few golf buddies dragged me off the putting green one night. They took me to see *Godspell* at a summer stock theater. I wasn't expecting much when I entered a huge tent near the local community center. It kinda blew me away. I remember keeping the program, which was just a piece of paper, xeroxed and folded in half. I had quite a different reaction to the show than my friends and I wasn't exactly sure why. Maybe something to do with the meaning of the Messiah."

After sipping his orange juice, he shrugged his shoulders, and started talking about hatred in the world throughout history, starkly manifested by the events on 9-11. He wondered why Muslims, Jews, and Christians, with their common roots, couldn't stop killing one another.

Cameron apologized if he gave the impression that he was heading to the so-called dark side. He concluded, "Until now, I never felt comfortable telling anyone about these feelings. Am I totally freaking you out?"

Eyes locked on Cameron's, Sandy smiled, remaining silent. This had been an incredible moment of intimacy. She let it soak in before speaking. A minute elapsed, which felt like an hour. Cameron finally broke the trance. "What are you thinking?"

"No way are you freaking me out. When you started talking, I was reminded of the never-ending tugs-of-war, or maybe it's tug-of-wars, between, you know, good and evil, politics and religion, nature and nurture. But I'm just one person, and you're just one person. That made me think about the movie, *Pay It Forward.* It came out not too long ago. Did you see it?"

Cameron hadn't seen it. Sandy summarized the plot. A teacher gives a seventh grader an assignment to come up with an idea to change the world. The young student starts doing favors for strangers and then they start doing favors for other strangers and it cascades from there.

At this point, Sandy stopped. Now Cameron's mind started turning back to Rambam and charity. He refocused on Sandy's face. "Okay, there's that smile again. Do tell."

"Rusty Stephens isn't just any person." That hung in the air for a few seconds. Sandy took a final sip of coffee, "C'mon, we don't wanna be late for our massages."

77

AUGUSTA, GEORGIA, USA

SATURDAY, OCTOBER 12, 2002

As Cameron pulled up to the clubhouse at the Augusta Country Club, two valet attendants stood ready to open doors.

"Nice you see you Mr. Stephens," said a lanky young man as he pulled back the car door.

"Lee, is that you?"

"None other."

"I didn't recognize you at first. You've shot up. How're your folks?"

"They're fine."

"Please give 'em my regards."

"I will. Your parents are already here."

"Thanks. See ya later."

Cameron walked around the car to Sandy, gently taking her by the arm to guide her. No coats to check on a warm autumn day so they proceeded directly to the dining room. They followed the hostess to the table. Some members, trying to acknowledge their local hero, but at same time giving him some space, flashed a hand in an abbreviated wave with a muted, "Hey Rusty" or "Hi Cameron."

As she absorbed the scene, Sandy giggled to herself, reminded her mother warned that despite Talbot's roots in New England, she should expect to see its catalog on full display at the country club. Thankfully, she listened to her mom, careful not to dress like she'd just stepped off Madison Avenue.

As they approached, Carlton stood as Christina remained seated.

"Hi son."

"Hey Dad." They hugged. "Meet Sandy Cole."

"Nice to meet you, Miss Cole."

"Sandy, please."

"This is my wife, Christina."

"Nice to meet you Mrs. Stephens."

"Christina."

Not too awkward thought Sandy. She smiled as Cameron went to the other side of the square table and kissed his mother on the cheek.

Small talk ensued after the waitress recorded drink orders, distributed menus, and delivered a monotone recitation of today's specials.

Carlton suggested to Rusty that after lunch they watch the football game between his alma mater, the University of Georgia, and Tennessee. With UGA ranked sixth in the country and UT ranked tenth, it should be a good game. Cameron agreed, thankful Georgia Tech was not playing today.

The most vibrant, but rarely publicized rivalry between UGA and Tech was golf. When Carlton witnessed these matches, he was an ardent yellow-jacket fan, leaving his red bulldog sweater in the closet.

With the sports banter in full force among the men, Christina queried Sandy about her impressions of Georgia. Sandy, ever honest but careful to ensure she didn't come off as patronizing, responded by comparing Atlanta and New York City, and the feel of small-town Maine with what little she had experienced of rural Georgia.

Both pairs finally realized their waiter was ready to take their lunch order. As expected, all eyes turned to Sandy.

"I'd like the BLT please."

Carlton and Christina froze.

Sandy turned to Cameron, a confused expression on her face, "What?"

Cameron sized up the situation in a few milliseconds, stifled his laughter, "Mom, Dad. Sandy isn't Kosher."

They let it pass. Christina ordered, followed by Cameron and Carlton.

"Mr. and Mrs. Stephens..." continued Sandy.

Carlton cut in, "Carlton, please."

Christina followed suit, "Christina."

"Carlton, Christina," echoed Sandy as naturally as possible. "I am Reform. Most of us do not follow the dietary law. There is an Orthodox congregation in Portland, and I suspect they keep Kosher. Hard for me to imagine growing up in Maine and not having a lobster."

Sandy hoped the levity would end this part of the interaction, but it turned out to be a great conversation starter.

Christina didn't know that lobster, and all crustaceans, as Sandy informed her, were not allowed. She was aware of the prohibition on consuming pork. Ten years ago, Carlton learned that dairy and meat could not be eaten together. He was curious after he read an article in the *Atlanta Jour-*

nal-Constitution about a MacDonald's opening in Tel Aviv seeking a cheese substitute to make Big Macs. Sandy explained that the rules, which include food preparation, go all the way back to the Old Testament.

Sandy wasn't quite sure whether Cameron's parents were genuinely interested in the topic or just happy to keep the conversation going. She was about to forge ahead, telling them about the controversial dinner following the first ordination of Reform rabbis in the United States, with shrimp on the menu. Lunch arrived instead.

The conversation morphed to complimentary sound bites about their food. A few minutes later, Carlton sipped his iced tea and picked up the conversation, "Sandy, a few weeks ago, Cameron asked me what I knew about Moses Maimonides." He tried to continue tactfully, "What did you teach him?"

"I'm afraid, Mr. Stephens, Carlton, the only thing I know about Maimonides is that a hospital in Brooklyn is named after him. And the only reason I know that is my Dad went to a seminar there."

Cameron chimed in, "Dad, I heard about Maimonides at Tech."

"Oh," was all Carlton could mutter, slightly embarrassed about making a false assumption.

Sensing this, Christina shifted the conversation, "Tell me all about the Willcox and the goings on in Aiken."

Carlton settled into the Stephens' den to watch the Georgia-Tennessee game. Christina insisted Cameron join him as she showed Sandy around the house. They slowed in an upstairs hallway to look at a gallery of framed pictures. Christina said it had become a tradition to add one of Cameron each year.

Christina ended the tour by delivering Sandy to the guest room, encouraging her to take her time getting settled, then join her in the kitchen to help start dinner preparations.

It didn't take long for Sandy to unpack. She lingered in the hallway, enjoying the Cameron gallery. The early years were solo shots. Except for his high school graduation portrait, the other photos included other people and related to golf posing with clubs or on a course. There were probably famous people in them, but she didn't have a clue.

Before going downstairs to help Christina, she quietly entered Cameron's room. She had only caught a glimpse of it when Christina pointed it out earlier.

Sandy inhaled as she began to scan the room, not sure what to expect. There were some trophies and ribbons, confined to the corner shelves. There was a series of eight by ten landscapes of various golf holes, as best she could tell. A framed photo of Cameron and Brian, enlarged to about two by three feet, was the only large object on a wall. Taken well before the personas of Rusty and O.T. had emerged, it showed the two side-by-side, arms around each other's back, their free hands extended with red paper cups emblazoned with white block lettering, "The Varsity, The Fun Place to Eat."

"Hi," whispered Cameron.

Sandy jumped. "You scared me."

"I tried not to," nuzzling up to her back and putting his arms around her. "Everything okay?" as he moved her hair with his nose to kiss her neck.

"Fine."

"Really?"

"Really. Guessing you had twin beds in here when you grew up."

"Yep."

"Nice that your folks allowed you to have a queen. Too bad we can't use it."

"We'd have to be awfully quiet."

Sandy smiled, "The operative part being awful."

"Gee, thanks," as he moved up her neck to kiss her right ear.

"Yummy, but I gotta help your mom."

When Sandy entered the kitchen, Christina asked her if she would like some wine. Sandy agreed, provided Christina joined her. Christina poured two modest glasses of white zinfandel. As they each lifted a glass, Christina toasted, "Welcome to our home." They touched their glasses before sipping.

Light conversation continued as Sandy cut through a rainbow of green, red, yellow, and orange bell peppers. She sliced them into strips while Christina trimmed cauliflower and finished preparing the secret family recipe onion dip.

As Christina assembled the tray, adding some cherry tomatoes to the other vegetables, she encouraged Sandy to sample. Sandy tasted but didn't need to feign a positive reaction. She praised the crudités, delivered it to the den, and returned to the kitchen for her next task.

As they formed burger patties for grilling, Sandy learned about the housekeeper and cook now with weekends off. Cheryl began working for Christina and Carlton just after Cameron was born.

Sandy mused, half in jest and half seriously, *everyone's name in the house starts with a C. Should I become part of this family I might have to elongate my name to Cassandra. And then there was the other C in the house, Christ.*

78

AUGUSTA, GEORGIA, USA
EN ROUTE TO ATLANTA, GEORGIA, USA
SUNDAY, OCTOBER 13, 2002

Cameron had hoped his parents might attend Saint Paul's early morning service at 8:00 a.m. Wishful thinking that he could slip into bed with Sandy at sunrise. He scribbled a Post-it note, careful to fold over the edge, so it wouldn't stick where it shouldn't. He slid it under the door to the guest room. He was going to practice and would be back well in time to leave the house by 10:30. He signed 'CAM' replacing the A with an upside-down heart.

As decided the night before, Cameron and Sandy would pack up Cameron's car before church. They'd drive to church separately from Cameron's parents so they could head back to Atlanta immediately after lunch.

Sandy slept comfortably in panties. She roused about 8:30, got up to brush her teeth, wash her face, and get her hair sorted. She found Cameron's note and realized she would be spending more time alone with his parents. While she normally would throw on a Victoria's Secret night shirt leaving her legs exposed, she'd decided to bring pajamas, which she slipped into before venturing out for coffee.

She proceeded quietly into the kitchen.

"Mornin' darlin'. Did you rest well?"

"I did, thank you."

"Carlton went with Cameron to shag balls for him."

"Cameron left me a note that he was going to practice but I didn't know Mr. Stephens was going with him."

"I just made some coffee. Want some?"

"That'd be great." Returning to neutral, "And thank you for a wonderful day yesterday."

"Our pleasure. Today should be nice too. I understand we're going to have a guest speaker at church today."

····◆····

Cameron showered quickly. His high energy prompted Sandy to ready herself without delay. They left for the church around 10:15.

At 10:30 parishioners started to gather in the courtyard outside Saint Paul's Episcopal Church. Cameron parked the car and eased Sandy away from the burgeoning crowd to show her around the grounds.

The setting was indeed beautiful, nestled above the banks of the Savannah River, with manicured gardens and paved walkways. Sandy took Cameron's arm as they walked slowly, lingering to read some grave markers, several dating back to Revolutionary War times. Mostly, Sandy was struck by the serenity.

She stroked Cameron's arm, "This place is important to you, yes?"

"I suppose it is. But growing up I found church boring. Maybe that's typical. I made some friends here. People were nice, charitable. As I started to visit hundreds of golf courses, I began to appreciate this property more. Maybe this place is connected to golf."

"Huh?"

"I was just thinking about part of a conversation I had with Rabbi Sugarman."

"Rabbi Sugarman?"

"At The Temple in Atlanta." Cameron noticed his folks approaching. "I'll fill you in on the ride back."

Sandy quickly read the historical marker commemorating George Washington's visit following his first inauguration. Christina and Carlton arrived. Sandy spoke up, "Cameron gave me a quick tour. Beautiful."

Christina echoed, "It is."

"Time to go in?", questioned Cameron.

"We've still got a few minutes," responded Carlton.

····◆····

As the worshipers filed into church, Sandy whispered to Cameron that he should guide her into the pew first, as she would not be going forward during the service to receive Holy Communion, nor would she be kneeling. Sandy learned that kneeling was a personal choice for Episcopalians during the service. She would not stick out as she did when attending Catholic Mass with some high school friends one Christmas Eve.

Reverend Portman, in a green vestment, moved into position at the altar. He was flanked by forty choir members in white robes, seated in pews perpendicular to the congregational seating.

The trinity of stained-glass windows, on the wall behind him, were magnificent. A light beam peeked through a partly cloudy sky, further illuminating the small panel to the leader's right and the bottom half of the much larger panel in the middle.

All stood as the altar party entered and walked forward in the center aisle past the congregants and then the choir. The service started with a hymn and a few prayers, some almost word for word as the prayers Sandy had learned at religious school. Others were not. They referred to Christ and salvation for those that embraced him as the only son of God.

A lay reader recited Philippians 4:4-13, Isaiah 25:1-9, and Matthew 22:1-14. She concluded with the 23rd Psalm. The congregation joined in when they heard the familiar phrase, "The Lord is my shepherd."

Practically everyone adjourned back to the reception hall for coffee hour and the forum. Within ten minutes seats were taken with refreshments in hand.

Reverend Portman made the introduction. "We are pleased to have Rabbi David Sandmel, originally from Cincinnati and ordained there at the Hebrew Union College in 1983. Recently he served as the spiritual leader at Congregation Bet Ha'am, which I understand means 'house of the people' in Portland, Maine."

Sandy squeezed Cameron's hand. Cameron mouthed, "Do you know him?"

As the Reverend continued, Sandy jiggled her head, not a yes, and not a no.

"Rabbi Sandmel just completed his Ph.D. at the University of Pennsylvania on Judaism and Christianity in the Greco-Roman World. David, welcome."

The rabbi thanked Reverend Portman then started by asking for a show of hands for anyone that knew members of the Children of Israel. About half dozen hands went up. Making eye contact with a few congregants, he continued, "I delivered a similar talk there yesterday morning, so it might be interesting for your two congregations to compare notes."

The rabbi was thought-provoking right out of the proverbial gate. "Again, show of hands. How many of you believe my religion is older than your religion?" Almost all hands went up. "Makes sense, Judaism started before Christianity; the Hebrew Scriptures preceded the New Testament. But, if I were to ask you the question, framing it as to how we identify ourselves, would you know if my religion, Reform Judaism, is older than the Episcopal Church? No need to show hands. In the context of the last six-thousand years, it's a tie, but if you're curious, the Reform movement started about sixty years after your movement was formed in the U.S."

The rabbi talked in practical terms as he journeyed back to the time of Jesus' life. He explained that within the Roman Empire, Jewish followers of Jesus needed to create differentiation for their sect. They were so successful early Christians were perceived as a threat to Rome.

Relying on mitosis as a metaphor, Rabbi Sandmel formed circles with the fingers on each hand, overlapping them as a single Jewish cell at the time of Jesus' birth. He slowly separated the two circles, about an inch apart, which he indicated took about a hundred years, spanning the lifetimes of Jesus, John the Baptist and several apostles including Paul, Mark, Matthew, and John.

He drew a comparison to the laws of nature, explaining, "As we know, over the last two millennia, these circles split again and again into various Christian and Jewish movements. If I could somehow imitate Durga, the Hindu goddess with many arms, I could extend my visual illustration, but I think you get the idea."

Sandy observed many congregants laughing, chuckling, and smiling at this remark. However, it wasn't lost on her that there are hundreds of religions and female deities.

The rabbi brought everyone back to the mid-twentieth century with circles formed and arms extended widely. "Now imagine these are Reform Judaism and The Episcopal Church." For another few minutes, he talked about forces over recent decades that have moved the circles closer together, including women clergy, social justice, helping others, and addressing existential threats to mankind. He referenced the Guidelines for Christian-Jewish Relations, posted by the Episcopal Church following its General Convention less than fifteen years prior.

He stopped his arms when his hand circles were about a foot apart. He paused, then dropped them, "I, personally, do not believe these circles will come back together. Should they, it won't be anytime soon. But let's celebrate the strength in their diversity as we work to make the world a better place. Amen."

Following the reception, the congregation spilled into the courtyard. Cameron introduced Sandy to Reverend Portman, who was talking to rabbi Sandmel. The reverend introduced them to the rabbi. As other congregants converged on the reverend and his guest, Cameron and Sandy faded away. Cameron signaled to his folks, about ten feet away, to head to lunch.

When they arrived at Cameron's BMW, Sandy removed her blazer and placed it in the back seat.

Cameron noticed, "A good start but you might need to roll up your sleeves for lunch."

After a quick right on Reynolds and left on 7th street, they both said, "Well?" in unison.

Sandy said, "We do this a lot."

"We've got about ten minutes," as he turned right on Route 28. "Why don't we just enjoy the ride, get through lunch, then we'll have plenty of time."

"Aren't we headed towards the Country Club?"

"You have a good sense of direction. We'll also pass by Augusta National."

They parked at Rhinehart's Oyster Bar, went inside, and were seated immediately. Cameron explained that this was not the usual Stephens post church lunch spot, but it had become an Augusta favorite over the last twenty years and on their way back to Atlanta.

Sandy looked at the menu. "At least your parents won't be shocked today if I order oysters."

Cameron laughed, spotted his folks, and waved them over.

The food arrived quickly. The conversation centered on the decor and the tasty food. There wasn't much discussion about church or the guest speaker. Sandy couldn't tell if that was a good thing or a bad thing. She wondered if the two-hour drive would be enough time to debrief on the last forty-eight hours.

They got up from the table shortly before 2:00. Hugs, along with "thank you, great to meet you and hope to see you again" were dutifully exchanged as they strolled down the pebbled path towards their cars.

····◆····

As if a dam breached, the questions poured from both Cameron and Sandy as they began cruising west on I-20. Before either could react to a query, the other interrupted with another question. They laughed, realizing what was happening.

Sandy suggested they discuss the weekend in chronological order. That didn't work. It was more like ping-pong. When they started with the service at The Children of Israel, which led to comparing it with the service at Saint Paul's. They talked about lunch at the Country Club then the lunch they just finished.

Cameron wanted to know if Sandy was comfortable with his mother in one-on-one interactions. As best she could, Sandy replayed the dialog she had with Christina in the kitchen before dinner.

Cameron then asked, "Did you talk about Christ?"

"Funny you should ask." She explained the sensation that C was the key to the household, rattling off the names.

Cameron smiled. "That's some crazy coincidence."

"The good part is that I think she can see us together. But I'm pretty sure she'd think you'd be happier with a Christian, preferably a southern belle, no?"

"For sure." Cameron segued, asking Sandy her reactions to Rabbi Sandmel's remarks.

"He made me realize our religions, as they've evolved, share much more than I thought."

Cameron added, "From what I'm learning, seems that way. To start, neither of us takes the Bible literally. I'm curious and please don't take this the wrong way, have you or had you ever considered converting?"

"To Hinduism, yes, Christianity no."

"You're kidding?"

"Yes, but no, I never felt as I was missing anything. If I converted, it would be for other reasons."

"Like you'd be killed if you didn't.

"I think you've been doing some research."

"Yeah, and I've even thought I might want to convert."

"To Judaism?"

"Funny. But yes, Reform Judaism."

"For yourself?"

"If I did, it would be for me."

"Care to elaborate?"

"You know I spend most of my time outdoors."

Sandy laughed, "With a hat on. The bottom of your face is tan, and your forehead's white as a ghost."

"I'm happy there. I make my living there. It's natural."

Sandy tried to clarify. "Like communing with nature?"

"Not exactly. More about the natural world and eternity— in both directions, backwards and forward."

"That's pretty heavy. Keep going."

"I'm not sure. Hang on." Cameron braked hard, slowing for traffic as they approached the perimeter.

"Detour?" asked Sandy.

"Hopefully just Sunday traffic. Where was I?"

"Eternity."

"Right. It has something to do with how religion deals with the natural world. I know it probably sounds odd, but Reform Judaism feels like it may fit my eye better, something we say on the golf courses we like more than others."

79

MANHATTAN & RYE, NEW YORK, USA

FRIDAY, OCTOBER 18, 2002

The cab stopped behind a half-dozen vehicles on East 68th street waiting for the light at York Avenue. Beth remarked to Herman, "This reminds me of taking the girls to Disney World. We'd wait an hour for a ten-minute ride."

"At least the girls aren't standing with us in ninety-five-degree heat."

"Amen to that."

When the light changed, it took twice as long for the queue to clear as it did for the cabbie to corner and drop them off at 1275, the Memorial Sloan Kettering Cancer Center.

Beth checked in. Five minutes later she was summoned to a desk, interviewed, signed her name at least a dozen times, then affixed with a white polyester identification bracelet, complete with barcode.

Within fifteen minutes, a nurse called her in. Herman kissed her and stepped outside.

He called The Grand Hyatt on 42nd Street. The receptionist transferred him to Sally's room. A recording said the line was busy. Herman left a message at the tone.

Sally felt crappy. Although room service took less than three minutes to answer, it seemed like an eternity. She ordered a bowl of chicken soup, dry white toast, an English muffin, also dry, herbal tea with lemon, and a carafe of boiling hot water.

Herman called his office to check-in. Nothing urgent. After sending Sandy a text message that Beth was on schedule, he decided to take a short walk to find coffee, not from a national chain.

Mission accomplished in short order. Tasted good. He returned shortly before Beth exited.

"How was it sweetheart."

"As you predicted. Using the MRI from home and the x-rays from our last visit, the needle biopsy didn't take long."

"Any pain?"

"Nothing. I didn't even feel the IV or anesthetic go in. Should we go to lunch?"

"Let's just relax, maybe grab something around the hotel, rest up for tonight. Doctor's orders."

On the ride back, Herman called Sally to report and see how she was feeling. This time Sally answered on the fourth ring, half-asleep from a nap. Sally agreed with Herman, as doctor and dad, she should forgo dinner.

····◆····

Sandy munched on apple sections and carrot sticks she had prepared the night before. She skipped a lunch outing to be sure she wouldn't miss her dad's call, using the time to follow-up on a possible lead in Scotland on Brian's lineage.

Herman called her with an update on Sally and Beth. He closed by asking her to back down the dinner reservation by one. She responded that it may not be possible, but she'd try.

····◆····

Following the Buick Classic's second round at the Westchester Country Club, O.T. disposed of three spent water bottles into a recycling bin and dropped his caddie bib in the designated barrel.

Rusty made himself a chef's salad at the extensive lunch buffet in the Men's Grill. He took a seat next to David Duval to shoot the breeze for a few minutes about yellow-jacket golf.

Thirty minutes later, Rusty was back on the range. He handed his 6-iron to O.T. and reached for his four-iron. O.T. noticed Rusty's phone flashing from its perch on an inverted ball bucket. O.T. did his best to suppress the outside world during practice. However, with the pause to exchange clubs, O.T. told Rusty that Sandy sent a text message, confirming they'd both be at dinner. Cameron flashed a thumbs up. Brian sent back a smiley face emoticon.

Tamara's cell phone vibrated. She recognized the number and answered.

"Hi San."

"Hi Tam. This a good time? Sounds like traffic."

"Busy day. About to go inside and get on an elevator. I may lose you. What's up?"

"I'll make it quick. Can you go to dinner with us tonight..."

Tamara cut her off, "Yes."

"Don't you want to know the what, where and when?"

"You had me at 'us.' Text me the details."

"Tam. Tam? Can't hear you. Bye."

The aggressive cabbie accelerated, making a left onto 7th Avenue at 56th Street as the traffic signal changed from orange to red. After stopping with a jolt, Tamara paid the fare and stepped carefully, in her stilettos, onto the curb then used the handrail to climb a half dozen steps. She entered the Redeye Grill a few minutes before 8:00.

After indicating the "Cole party," a hostess led her past the pianist and bassist, up a stairway, to the Sky Room.

"Well, aren't you stylin' tonight," said Sandy as Tamara entered.

"Thanks, just trying to keep up." They hugged. "This place looks wonderful, but empty."

"It will refill, I'm sure. A bunch of people left for theater and Carnegie Hall across the street."

"Makes sense. I knew you'd be here early."

Sandy explained she wanted to make sure everything was in order and confirm that her dad's credit card would be used to settle the bill.

Their dedicated waiter introduced himself, took their drink orders, and vanished.

Tamara inquired about the last-minute invite. Sandy told her Sally wasn't feeling well, there was a minimum for the private room, and that it's time everyone meets her sister from another mother.

Ten minutes later Beth, Herman, Cameron, Brian, and the waiter entered the room within thirty seconds of one another. The waiter off-loaded two wine glasses then waited patiently as Sandy made introductions.

After the newcomer beverages were ordered, the decibel level increased with echoes of "nice to meet you, this place is gorgeous, I've heard so much about you, did you have any trouble getting here, beautiful day," and specifically to Beth, "How are you feeling?"

As a graphic artist working in media, the scene made complete sense to Tamara. Were she to give any passersby a test to pair items from two columns, she was confident everyone would match them perfectly. Blond, lean white guy in blue blazer, white shirt, and khaki slacks - Cameron. Dark man in black pants, silk t-shirt and linen jacket - Brian. Older man in a tattersall shirt, corduroy jacket - Herman. Dark haired woman, black slacks, heels, ecru cowl neck sweater - Sandy. Perfectly coiffed middle-aged woman, tailored pantsuit with stick pin in her lapel - Beth.

The waiter served drinks to the appropriate person with no need to ask, "who gets this" or "who gets that." The men and women segregated.

Herman inquired, "Rusty, I mean Cameron."

"Either's fine."

"Force of habit." He lifted his glass. "Cheers.".

"Cheers," responded Cameron and Brian.

"How did you guys manage to pull this off with all the goings on in Westchester?"

"We got lucky with tee times," replied Cameron. "A late start on Thursday, so I was early this morning. Brian kept me organized as there was no way he was going to miss this."

Brian chimed in, "You know that Sandy's helping me research my family tree."

"I did. What prompted you to investigate?"

"I was always a little curious. And to be perfectly honest," as he gently elbowed Cameron, "Some ribbing on my skin tone. Don't you think I'm the one who actually looks rusty?"

Herman smiled, "I'm not getting in the middle of this."

Cameron concluded in jest, "Smart move."

Meanwhile, the women conversed about the New York food scene. Beth lifted the menu, prepositioned on the table, as she grappled with her purse to locate her cheaters.

Sandy and Tamara continued to yak about their favorite Soho eateries. Sandy noticed Beth concentrating on the menu. She announced, "Mom's hungry."

"Oh stop, sweetheart. But yes."

No further prompts were needed. They took seats at the rectangular table, with Beth and Herman at the ends. Sandy and Cameron sat on one side with Tamara and Brian on the other.

The chef's specials were recited, and drink status checked. Conversation ramped up again, mostly about the menu, what to order and who wanted to share what.

A few minutes later, the waiter placed a Heineken to Brian's right and began taking food orders from the women. They ordered a Redeye chopped salad and rainbow roll to share, then branzino, salmon and wild mushrooms, and petit dover sole. The men ordered their own starters and beef. The waiter asked about sides.

Shoulders shrugged. Eyes looked at other eyes, then down at menus. Cameron spoke up, "How about cashew brussels?"

Nods and "sounds good" echoed around the table.

"And", continued Cameron, "Can you also bring us the mashed potatoes with gribenes?"

As Beth and Herman laughed, the waiter realized the order was concluded.

Cameron turned to Sandy, "Did I say that right?"

"Perfect."

Tamara and Brian exchanged glances. She leaned in, "What did we miss?"

Sandy explained, "Gribenes is Jewish food made with chicken fat and crispy chicken skin." She then relayed the lunch story when she met Cameron's parents and their reaction when she ordered bacon. They thought it'd be fun to return the favor to Sandy's parents.

Herman asked Brian if it was okay for Sandy to give an update on his family tree. Brian was fine with the idea, suggesting everyone else talk about their lineage first.

Beth and Herman could only trace back five generations to the Eastern European shtetls, Poland on Beth's side, Lithuania on Herman's. The family name was Cohen in the old country. Both lost relatives in the Holocaust.

Tamara could trace her ancestry back to slavery Alabama and a great grandparent from Kenya, but no further. Cameron's ancestors had come to Georgia hundreds of years ago rather than go into debtor's prison in England. Then Brian felt all eyes on him. He said, "What? Oh, my turn."

Brian lavished kudos on Sandy for discovering his great great grandfather arrived at Castle Clinton, which he hadn't known a thing about. He went on to explain that his great grandfather arrived many years later at Ellis Island. Then he turned to Sandy, "Over to you."

Wanting to manage everyone's expectations, most importantly Brian's, Sandy summarized. After sharing the discovery that Brian's grandfather's name was changed from Solless to Sills, she had been able, so far, to trace back four more generations in Great Britain to the mid-1700's.

Everyone reacted at once in a cacophony of, "Wow. How did you do that? Did anyone help you? It's incredible you got this far. Insane."

When the din settled, Tamara spoke up, "Brian, perhaps provenance is the wrong word, but you're the champ in this group."

Cameron admitted, "I kid Brian a lot about his heritage but now I have to eat some crow."

Brian quipped, "Lucky for you, it's not on the menu."

80

ATLANTA, GEORGIA, USA
WEDNESDAY, OCTOBER 30, 2002

The Tour Championship, held in the resurgent East Lake neighborhood at the course with the same name, was a Rusty favorite. Nice to sleep in one's own bed. Also high on his list were tournaments in metro Atlanta, particularly at the famed Atlanta Athletic Club, which moved its course from East Lake to the Atlanta burbs in the late sixties.

About 10:00 AM, Rusty slowed to a stop at the East Lake entrance. He grabbed his parking credentials from the passenger seat and placed them on the dash. The guard recognized him and waved him through.

He shifted the BMW into park as he continued his conversation with Sandy on his carphone. They speculated about the apparent chemistry between Tamara and Brian.

"Looks like Brian's here."

"Miss you," demurred Sandy. "Good luck today."

"Thanks, but it's only a practice round."

"Oh. Then have all your bad luck today."

"I like it. Love you."

"You too."

Rusty placed the phone in the console cradle as O.T. approached the car, shouldering Rusty's golf bag.

"Morning," said Rusty.

"Morning. I think we're good. You just need to check in. I'll go to the range and set-up."

As he approached the driving range, he looked up about ten feet to check the time on the old-fashioned Rolex clock, mounted on a wrought iron pedestal. He wondered how many times Bobby Jones did the same.

····◆····

On the 2nd hole, a par-3, O.T. positioned three balls at various points on the green in addition to the one Rusty landed there, ten feet away from the flagstick in the green's center.

While José-Maria's and Sergio's caddies placed several balls on the putting surface O.T. suggested to everyone that he place some tees in popular pin locations from prior tournaments. They agreed.

Rusty proceeded to putt each ball at least once. All the while O.T. watched carefully, making notes in his yardage book. It would be his Bible for the next four days.

Being a practice round José-Maria and Sergio walked around the green, as did Rusty, trying out various locations. It looked chaotic compared to regular play when furthest from the cup plays next, with caddies out of the way.

Sergio thanked O.T. then turned to Rusty, "Do José-Maria and I have to tip him?"

"Absolutely."

As all six walked the short distance to the 3rd tee, José-Maria handed O.T. a one cent Spanish euro coin. "This is for both of us."

A sarcastic, "Wow" from O.T. "This is twice as much as Rusty gave me in Marbella. Gracias."

Handing the coin to Sergio, "You take it. We want your advice. You almost won this thing last year."

Sergio responded, "First I want to hear about your Spanish girlfriend."

"She's not Spanish," responded Rusty in a monotone.

"You met her there, so as far as we're concerned, she's your Spanish girlfriend. Right José-Maria?"

"Si."

Sergio persisted, "Seve is expecting a report when we get back. What's going on?"

Continuing with a straight face, "Her name's Sandy."

José-Maria, "A golf name, no?"

"Actually, it's Sandra. She lives up north."

O.T. whispered something to Sergio's caddie, who immediately burst out laughing.

The golfers stopped and looked at them.

Caught in the act, O.T. said innocently, "All I said was Sandy canceled her flight when she heard the Spaniards were coming."

"Is that a joke?" inquired Sergio sternly.

O.T. twisted uncomfortably and stuttered, "Uh, err."

Sergio smiled. "I'm joking with you now."

They all laughed as the practice round continued in good humor.

On several par-4's they played impromptu "closest to the pin" contests from the fairway, making nominal bets. Their caddies tracked the results.

The conversation drifted to how much they all liked this tournament with only thirty competitors, reasonable starting times, an important venue in golf history, and a great time of year to visit Atlanta.

To a man, all six agreed the best part was no five-hour pro-am round. Instead, some seventy-five people affiliated with the sponsors attended a dinner at the Cherokee Country Club where the Payne Stewart award, for character, charity, and sportsmanship, was presented to Nick Price.

On the par-5 18th, nearly 600-yards, each golfer took a few practice shots, trying to reach the putting surface in two. While they experimented, the caddies compared notes. Finally, as they walked to the green, O.T. announced, "The final tally, José-Maria and Rusty owe Sergio fifty bucks each."

Sergio replied, "I'm forgiving the debt as long as I hear more about Sandy."

José-Maria piled on, "Thanks Sergio. Rusty, I'm counting on you."

Rusty conceded, "Okay. Okay. At dinner tonight. But before the other guys get there. Let's meet at about seven-fifteen."

····◆◆◆····

Rusty made the right from Peachtree onto Piedmont, immediately pulling up to Bones Steakhouse on his right. The parking attendant handed Rusty a ticket and wished him a nice evening. A hostess recognized him and escorted him to the Cork Room.

Five minutes later the Spaniards walked into the room.

"Rusty, before you say anything, Sergio and I want to apologize if we were too personal out there today."

Rusty assured him he wasn't concerned about their teasing. He asked them to sit down, which they did. "Did you know any Jews growing up?"

Sergio shot a glance at José-Maria, which Rusty noticed, "Am I being too personal now?"

José-Maria spoke first, "No, but an unusual question. I grew up in a small town, with fifteen thousand people. If there were any Jews, I didn't know them."

"Same here," echoed Sergio. "Only five thousand people where I grew up."

"And if you think Sergio and I are from small towns, there's Seve's hometown, hardly a thousand. Ironically, he told me his father knew a Jewish family nearby in Santander, which is a sizable city in Spain."

Sergio asked José-Maria why Seve told him this. José-Maria explained that years ago he and Seve were in a cab riding through the Diamond District in Manhattan. José-Maria commented that the men on the street, and in the storefronts, were all dressed the same. The cabbie interrupted, telling them they were Jews. Seve told him he knew some Jews in Spain and they certainly didn't look like the men on 47th street.

Rusty had looked up the Jewish population in Spain before arriving at the restaurant. With only ten-thousand Jews in Spain today, Rusty anticipated the responses by Sergio and José-Maria. However, after hearing about the drive through midtown Manhattan, he looked forward to following-up with Seve.

Before going any further, Rusty provided Sergio and José-Maria some context on Sandy and his interest in Judaism. Then he posed several questions, hoping to open them up, "Growing up, did you study the Old Testament? What were you taught about charity? Ever heard of Maimonides or Rambam, born in Spain eight hundred years ago? Did you know anything about 1492 other than Columbus' voyage?"

Their conversation meandered, with stark differences among them. One knew Jesus was Jewish, one did not. One studied the book of Job. José-Maria learned about the Spanish Inquisition of the Jews from Seve. As expected, neither had heard of Rambam.

As Rusty began to explain how he came to know Maimonides, Charles Howell joined them. The conversation with José-Maria and Sergio paused as Rusty immediately hugged Charles. Both grew up in Augusta. They probably walked over a thousand miles together, literally.

By the time Charles said hello to the Spaniards, Tiger Woods and Justin Leonard entered the room. As greetings broke out, Rusty decided not to enlarge the discussion. He was confident José-Maria and Sergio would circle back if they had more to contribute.

With all six having Thursday afternoon starting times, dinner was leisurely. Four Heineken beers were ordered along with two non-alcoholic Saint Pauli Girls. Salads and some cut of cow followed for each guy. Over coffee, two orders of Bones Mountain High Pie were placed on opposite ends of the oval table.

About 9:30, four high-energy, fit, and good looking twenty somethings, burst into the room. "Hi, I'm Aisha, we're from the Atlanta Hawks' dance team. This is Brandy, Christy and Dirk. We're fund raising for the Boys & Girls Clubs of Atlanta. There'll be a presentation at tomorrow night's home opener."

Dirk lifted his Polaroid instant camera as the three women cozied up to José-Maria, Tiger and Rusty. Aiming and snapping, "You buy the pictures back from me, so they don't get into the hands of your wives."

That generated a big laugh from all the guys. Sergio explained, "You picked three bachelors." Pointing at Charles and Justin, he added, "They're the newlyweds."

Wallets opened. The scantily clad women scooped up nine hundred dollars for a good cause. They handed the bills to their muscle-shirted compatriot as they left the room.

81

MANHATTAN, NEW YORK, USA
ATLANTA, GEORGIA, USA
THURSDAY, OCTOBER 31, 2002

At 8:30 a.m. Nessa, a professionally dressed, well-groomed woman, early twenties, let herself into the dimly lit entry area on the thirty-fourth floor of King & Spalding's offices at 1185 Avenue of the Americas. She usually arrived early to get settled and savor her first cup of coffee. The subway delay precluded that today.

Nessa switched on the lights and gave her right Reebok walker a tug, popping it off. She struggled with the left. She sat down to loosen the laces. She removed her socks and slipped both feet into the heels she toted.

Taking scissors, she cut the binding straps on small bundles of *The New York Times* and *The Wall Street Journal*. She fanned these on the coffee table across from her reception desk. She then collected loose copies of the *Atlanta Journal-Constitution*, and *The London Times*, adding them to the table.

Finally, she peeled off a copy of the London and Atlanta papers, placing them next to her, ready to hand them to the office managing partner on his arrival.

Before a two-year posting at the London office, Lawrence Simpson commuted to Manhattan by rail from his home in Greenwich. In his mid-fifties, fit and self-sufficient, he didn't see the need, at first, for the limo now provided to him as the New York practice leader. Two months into the job, he counted on it to prepare for the daily deluge of issues, large and small.

En route, he consumed the *New York Times* and *The Wall Street Journal*. He then flipped *The New York Post*. He wouldn't be caught dead with this rag under his arm, but he felt obliged to browse it. Besides, it was hard to mess up sports stats.

Regardless of the arrival time at the office building, Simpson's driver pulled over just past the corner of 47th Street. Simpson relaxed and meditated for a few minutes, sometimes silently reciting Peterson's poem, "Slow Me Down, Lord." His driver knew not to open the door until 9:00.

Except today.

At 8:50, only fifteen seconds after Nessa took her seat, Simpson blasted through the door, ripping off his olive-green Burberry trench coat without breaking stride.

"Good morning Mr. Simpson," she chirped, extending the two newspapers, which he ignored.

"Have Martin get Brent Lattimer and Lydia Huxley on the phone." He called out, "Please" as he vanished around the corner.

Nessa tapped in Martin's three-digit extension. Luckily, he picked up. She gave him the instructions with a "Heads up, I've never seen him like this."

Simpson entered his corner office, throwing his coat onto the couch. He walked briskly to his desk, picked up the handset on his phone and sat down. He calmed himself with a deep breath and pressed the button above a blinking red light.

"Brent. Lydia. I wanted to speak to both of you together. It's about Rusty. Big front-page photo in today's Post, with a, how should I say, a young lady strewn all over our client. And the headline, 'Getting the Rust out'."

"But Rusty's here in Atlanta, playing at East Lake today," protested Brent.

"I know that. The photo was taken last night in Atlanta, best I can tell. He has a girlfriend, does he not?"

Brent responded, "He does and she's in New York."

"Great," said Simpson sarcastically. "Chances are, she's seen the paper. Look everyone, I just want to get this under control. Fortunately, Rusty's single and it's *The Post* not *The Times*. I get that. But we don't want this to fester into a drawn-out exposé which could hurt Rusty's image, his relationship, or his game. I know he's playing his best golf ever."

Lydia took control, "Larry, I know there's a lot at stake on your end, with Rusty's marketing deals and the PR work with Edelman. We're on it. I'll have someone track down a copy of the paper. Brent, please report back to us within an hour."

"Will do."

When Simpson cradled his phone, Martin poked his head into the office. "Richard Edelman on line two."

····◆····

O.T. was busy assembling Rusty's kit for the day when his back pocket vibrated. He let it go to voicemail as his hands juggled water bottles and snacks. He'd listen to the voicemail later, but the message ping did not go off. Instead, he heard the text tone a minute later.

He looked at the urgent message and called Lattimer immediately. Brent updated O.T. on the morning fireworks. O.T. in turn, explained that after the practice round yesterday he and Rusty went their own ways. He knew Rusty was going out with some of the guys for dinner. When he talked to Rusty earlier in the morning, Rusty told him about the seemingly harmless fundraiser. As far as he knew, Rusty knew nothing about the sleaze reporting up North.

O.T. wondered, "How could a dinner photo end up on the front page of a New York rag the next morning? I wonder if Sandy saw it?"

"Shit," said Brent. "I know it's game day for you guys, but can you reach out to her now? Meanwhile, I'm going to track down the idiot who did this."

"Hi Brian," said a perky Sandy Cole. "I was hoping it was Cameron calling. You're calling about the paper here this morning, right?"

"I'd like to say it's about my genealogy, but yeah."

"I already saw it. I was just hoping Cameron was calling me."

"Are you okay?"

"This is going to happen from time to time, isn't it?"

"I'm afraid so."

"Maybe my skin is thickening. I won't let it bother me."

"Good. Glad I caught you first. I'm sure he'll tell you about last night's dinner and the charity stunt that put him on page one. But I don't think he knows a damn thing about the photo. There was no reason for it. Brent is trying to find out why."

"Then let me break it to him. We'll catch up later on your stuff. Good luck today. Wish I was there."

"Me too. I'm sure Cameron does too."

On tournament days, Sandy normally waited for Cameron to call her.

Cameron answered his phone, "Good morning. This is an unexpected pleasure."

"Not so sure. Your dinner last night made the front page of the paper this morning."

"From your tone, it's not good, is it?"

"A full page shot with a cheerleader all over you."

"Oh boy. I'm sorry."

"The good news..."

"Good news?"

"It's just a tabloid. So stupid, don't even worry about it. I wanted to tell you before you saw it or heard it from some crazy person out there today or even the press later."

They talked for a few more minutes. Sandy hung up, relieved.

Cameron tried to suppress his emotions. He called O.T.

"Hi boss."

"Sandy called me a few minutes ago."

"And.."

Rusty sensed the hesitancy in O.T.'s voice, "You know, don't you?"

"I do. There's lots of people scrambling around. It's bullshit. No one wants this." O.T. wanted to get his golfer settled on today's job. He continued, "I called Sandy. She already knew. How did she sound?"

"Actually, she's fine."

"You need to be fine too. I'll call Lattimer and tell him you want a full debrief later."

"Okay."

"See you in a few."

Lattimer's message came on, "Sorry, I can't take your call."

O.T. left the message, "Brent. Sandy's fine. Rusty's fine. I'm sure you'll debrief him later. This one was just a scare. Happy Halloween."

82

RANCHO MIRAGE, CALIFORNIA, USA
THURSDAY, NOVEMBER 28, 2002

Although the door to the second bedroom was closed, Tommy moved quietly, trying not to disturb his sleeping daughter. He purposefully hoisted his golf bag, which he had positioned next to the door the night before. He slipped out, closing the door gently behind him.

Tommy spotted the idling late model F-150 and walked towards it. Carlos saw him, got out, unsnapped the cargo cover, took the clubs, and loaded them into the back of the pickup truck. They got into the cab.

"Morning bro," Carlos said, lifting a 7-Eleven coffee from the console and handing it to Tommy.

"Morning, I think," taking a sip.

"Before you say anything else, they're outta Splenda so I used an Equal. There's a couple corn muffins too."

"Thanks."

"It's the least I could do, dragging you out of bed today."

"No problem. I'm committed to your method. Where are we headed?"

"Las Palmas, North Course again."

"Why?"

"Part of the method."

With sparse traffic on a hazy Thanksgiving morning, they reached the course in fifteen minutes.

Tommy smiled as Carlos strapped the golf bag onto a cart. Carlos returned the smile. "Happy Thanksgiving. You get to ride today."

Carlos then explained how they would be practicing only on the first five holes, primarily tee to green shots, with few putts, if any. He had arranged for the club pro to start any early morning holiday hackers on the back nine.

After a truncated warm-up on the driving range, they made their way to the 1st tee. Carlos went to the closest black marker on the tee box and paced off sixteen yards towards the blue tee markers. He placed two tees in the ground, telling Tommy that at this position, he was 501-yards from the center of the green, as he would be from the 10th tee at Augusta National.

Tommy's pre-shot routine now included five seconds with eyes closed, visualizing the 10th hole at Augusta. Tommy hit a respectable drive about 280-yards, coming to rest on the fairway's left side. As they walked back to the cart, Carlos said evenly, "Further right would be better at Augusta."

"Agreed."

Carlos then handed the driver back to Tommy, "Let's do it again as if you never hit the previous shot. Remember this is Augusta. No condos on the course."

Tommy hit four more drives, each time walking back to the cart, briefly analyzing with Carlos, and re-starting his pre-shot routine.

After maneuvering the cart to each ball and retrieving them in a shag tube, Carlos stopped at an area he had scouted. The goal was to simulate the second shot to the 11th green at Augusta, known as the entry point to the famous, or often infamous, Amen Corner.

On the 4th tee box, Carlos placed a bag of balls at 155-yards from the green, to replicate, to the extent possible, the 12th at Augusta. The water guarding the green was similarly intimidating to the layout at Augusta.

Tommy made twenty tee shots, consuming two minutes each. Unbeknownst to Tommy, Carlos was honing the words he was saying to Tommy. He then carefully monitored each shot's result looking for hidden correlations to his remarks.

Four hours later Tommy sat with his legs dangling from the front seat of Carlos' truck as he pulled off his golf shoes. He felt Carlos staring at him. Tommy looked up. "What?"

"We need to work on those clogs."

"Your method?" responded Tommy with a hint of sarcasm.

"You'll see. We're doing pine straw next week. The method assumes you won't be in the fairway a hundred percent of the time."

"True, but what course around here has pine straw."

"You'll see."

Carlos pulled the truck up to Tommy's condo. As Tommy yanked the door handle, Carlos said, "We'll see you at Mama and Papa's house at three-thirty. You and Sonya are not having Thanksgiving dinner by yourselves at a hotel, even at the Ritz."

"But..."

"We canceled your reservation. Sonya's on-board."

·•••◆•••·

Mama Santos answered the door. Like a reception line at a wedding, Sonya and Tommy, in turn, kissed Mama on each cheek following with a hug. Then they moved on to Papa, Carlos' daughter, his son, and finally Carlos.

Two minutes later, as salutations continued, Mama returned with a tray of neatly arranged wine glasses, precisely filled to the same level.

Everyone knew what to do. The children watched as glasses were taken and lifted. Papa elevated his glass a foot higher proclaiming, "We have all faced challenges over the last year as individuals and families. We are here and Louie is flying again. Our glasses are half full. Salud." An echo, in unison, followed.

Tommy took a sip, commenting, "Mmm, delicious."

Mama responded, "Casa Maduro."

Papa added, "Mexico's finest for your journey to Georgia next spring. And that's not all."

Tommy shot Carlos a look.

Carlos shrugged his shoulders. "I haven't been allowed in the dining room for the last week."

Mama turned to Inez and CJ. "Please seat your father and Uncle Tommy."

Inez took Carlos by the arm. CJ did the same with Tommy. They proceeded to the dining room. The table, modest but bountiful for the occasion, had a chair at each end, with three chairs on the near side as they entered the room. On the far side, facing them, a makeshift throne had been created for Tommy and Carlos, with boxes of pine-straw fashioned into seats with armrests. Each seat back had been constructed from five old clubs, woven together with yellow ribbon.

Inez and CJ were beaming with pride. Inez proclaimed, "See Uncle Tommy, pine straw."

Carlos shrugged his shoulders. "I stored it in the garage but had no idea what they were up to."

Tommy soaked it in, put his arms around the children, gently pulling them into him, fighting off tears. "Thanks. This is incredible."

Carlos echoed with, "Absolutely."

Tommy lifted his glass. "To Mama and Papa Santos, and Inez and CJ for this fine furniture."

Carlos turned to the kids and joked, "Now you have to help us spread it out on the course tomorrow."

83

ATLANTA, GEORGIA, USA
WEDNESDAY, JANUARY 1, 2003

The Saint Regis doorman lifted Herman's clubs into Carlton's Chevy Tahoe. Herman handed him a folded five. "Happy New Year."

Standing on the driver's side, Carlton pushed a breath into his cupped hands, "Good morning. A little chill but it looks like a nice day."

Herman chuckled, "Morning. I heard on TV this morning that we'll get into the mid-fifties. That's beach weather for me. Sleep well?"

The small talk continued as they turned onto East Andrews. They sipped coffee from to go cups as they waited for the signal at Piedmont and Roswell. With no other cars in sight, Carlton remarked, "Best time to drive in Atlanta."

The light changed. Five minutes later they parked on Chastain Park Avenue behind Cameron's BMW.

Brian approached the vehicle to welcome them. "Happy New Year."

Herman extended his hand, "You too. Nice to see you again O.T."

"It's Brian. You're practically family. Let me get your clubs."

"I only let O.T. get my clubs, not Brian."

Carlton chimed in, "I'll second that."

As they entered the clubhouse, Cameron turned from the counter, "We're all set. Happy New Year Brian. We missed you last night."

"Sorry. As much as I wanted to be with you guys and Dick Clark, I had a date. I wanted to start the year with some private fireworks."

Cameron turned to the dads, "What did I tell ya?"

With no driving range, they warmed up with practice swings and then hit some chips and putts on the two practice greens. Carlton asked Cameron why he chose this venue, when he had access to all the private tracks in the area.

Simple. It was close by, open on holidays, and considered a historical gem, at least by Cameron. He explained that the course held professional tournaments before the first Masters. Not a long course by today's standards, it was challenging in its time, with undisturbed land features like a links course, albeit inland. Cameron liked it from the first time he played it with his team at Tech.

Like their exhibition in Spain, Brian suggested they rotate carts every six holes so they all had an opportunity to ride with one another.

They rolled up to the first tee to survey light brown fairways, evergreens, and the morning sun reflecting from Buckhead's tall buildings.

When they stepped from their buggies, as they were called on the other side of the pond, Brian announced, "I've worked out a formula for some friendly wagering."

Carlton reacted, "Good luck organizing us this morning."

"You tell him Dad," volleyed Cameron.

Cameron and Brian hit their drives into the fairway on the 1st hole, a 400-yard par-4, from the blue and white markers on the back tee box. The dads played from the silver tees, eighty yards forward, both landing in the fairway. Such a simple game.

On the 2nd hole, a par-5, dog leg left with a large pond and a creek across the fairway, Cameron belted a 290-yard drive, effectively turning the hole into a par-4 for him. As he chauffeured Herman, he asked how Sandy got so interested in Brian's family history. Herman said she had been a curious from an early age, perhaps because she couldn't go back very far with his or Beth's ancestors.

They continued to talk about Sandy's childhood, intermittently, as the foursome moved quickly through the next three holes, which included two par-3's.

On the 6th fairway, while waiting for Carlton and Brian to tackle their challenging uphill shots following mediocre drives, Herman asked Cameron what he would be doing if golf was not in the picture.

Cameron responded without hesitation, "I'd have joined Dad's business, married a local girl and likely lived happily ever after. And here we are."

"And here we are. *Beshert.*"

"Sandy uses the same word."

"Destiny." Then joking, "Let's see what I'm supposed to have on this hole."

On the 7th tee, Brian re-jiggered the bags, pairing Cameron with his dad, and Brian with Herman. Carlton stepped onto the tee box on the Par-4, foregoing his standard practice swing. He hurried a drive into the trees to the left. He could hardly wait for Herman to tee off and the carts to separate.

As they drove down the cart path on the fairway's right, Carlton inquired about the first six holes, clearly implying the interaction with Herman rather than the shot making quality.

"C'mon Dad. Now's not the time to start beating around the bush. We never have."

"I like Sandy. I like her parents. Mom does too."

"That's good. But you can't see her as my wife?"

"Cam, I'm not sure. You two are so different."

Cameron let that hang. They played the next three holes quickly and quietly, while Brian and Herman talked benignly about Sandy's work on Brian's family tree.

They made the turn to the 10th tee, a narrow and lengthy par-5. Herman and Brian pulled their drives into the trees on the left. Cameron and Carlton pushed their shots to the right, fortunately not threatening the few cars on Powers Ferry Road.

As they waited for the other guys to hit their second shots, Cameron piped up, "You know we have a lot in common."

"You do have fifty percent of my DNA."

"True, but I meant Sandy. We aren't that different. Love of family, history, travel, helping others, secure in our own beliefs."

The three amateurs made pars on the short par-3 11th with Cameron dropping a thirty-footer for a birdie. As they approached the green on the 12th hole, Carlton felt compelled to follow-up, "Have you talked about having children."

"Briefly."

"Don't wait too long to get into that."

"I hear ya Dad."

The conversation diminished after the bags were shuffled for the last six holes. Carlton and Herman exited their cart by the edge of the creek which split the 17th fairway to look for their balls. Cameron used the slowdown and asked Brian, "Your New Year's Eve date. Anything to write home about?"

"You might say that."

"That was a question."

"You'll see for yourself. She'll be at lunch."

"It's Tamara, Tamara Wright, right?"

"Maybe."

Cameron put up his right hand for a high five. "You sly dog."

As the foursome putted out and advanced to the challenging finishing hole, Cameron announced, "Brian's been holding out on us. His date is joining us for lunch."

84

MANHATTAN, NEW YORK, USA
SAN DIEGO, CALIFORNIA, USA
THURSDAY, FEBRUARY 13, 2003

With two inches of fresh afternoon snow on the ground, Sandy tapped her boots on the small stoop before she pushed her way into her building and up the stairs.

Who would be her dinner companion tonight? Brokaw, Jennings or Rather. No question about dessert—Trebek. First, a cup of tea to take the chill off the commute. She took her time unpacking a small bag of groceries extracted from her backpack, preparing for the evening's research. She would listen, with one ear, to the silly antics of other young New Yorkers, like Monica, Ross, Will, and Grace, in their sillier apartments. She would switch to music at nine, when NBC morphed from silly antics to stupid antics.

Sandy's cell phone rang halfway through the evening news. She put her fork down when she recognized the number on the small screen.

"Hi Cam. Hang on a second." She fumbled for the remote and muted the TV. "How'd it go today?"

"Not bad. Six of us tied for second now. A few groups are still on the course. It's a little before four out here. What's happening with you? How's your mom doing? I know she's in good hands."

"She says she's fine. Dad says no change." They talked about Cameron's west coast swing and reminisced about the week they spent together a few weeks prior, at the Ritz in Kapalua, during the Mercedes Championships. They agreed that Maui was on their repeat list.

"How about coming out here for Valentine's Day? Torrey Pines is beautiful. A morning flight would get you here by noon."

"I'd love to but I'm meeting Sally at Killington for the weekend."

····◆····

As O.T. loaded up the courtesy van assigned to them, Rusty looked somewhat dejected, reporting that Sandy passed on the invitation. As he climbed into the passenger seat, Rusty mumbled something to the effect that her sister would understand if she changed her plans.

With elephant ears O.T. spoke up, "I heard that." Ever mindful of his guy's head space, he put a positive spin on the interaction, accentuating her positives—Sandy's self-assurance, making good on her commitments, analytical.

Rusty stared ahead, "I guess you're right."

"You don't sound convinced. Talk to me."

Rusty tried to express his feelings. O.T. listened patiently with well placed, "uh huhs," "yeps" and "okays" to keep him talking.

They pulled into the Fairmont Del Mar. As planned, Rusty took off to pump some iron. O.T. fussed with the cargo. With an afternoon tee time on Friday, they were in no rush to have dinner. They agreed to meet in the lobby at 8:00. As usual, O.T. would lean on the concierge for recommendations and reservations.

About to exit his room, Cameron pressed the "Do Not Disturb" button by the door. A red indicator light illuminated. A few seconds later his cell phone flashed with Sandy's number."

"Hi, pretty late over there."

"It is. I haven't even started to get ready for bed. I've been bothered by our call."

"That was hours ago"

"I know."

"Hold on for a second. I want to text Brian that I'll be late. If I lose you, I'll call you right back"

Cameron sent the message and returned to the couch in his mini suite, "I'm back."

"I lied."

"You're not going skiing with Sally?"

"That part was true."

"I'm confused."

"I used Sally as an excuse. Of all people, she'd understand if I changed my plans to see you. It wasn't fair to throw her under the bus."

"You're always direct, and I love that about you."

"I know. So here goes. I wasn't going to meet you this weekend, no matter what. If we're going to have a future together, it won't be me in drop everything mode."

An elongated, “Okay...”

“This doesn’t mean I can’t be spontaneous.”

“I love that about you too.”

“But it can’t be one way. Make sense?”

“I think so,” said Cameron slowly.

“But you’re not sure.”

“Makes sense. I just need to absorb it, if that makes sense?”

“It does. Say hi to Brian. If you’re under par tomorrow, let’s celebrate with phone sex.”

“Do you mean if I’m feeling ill or my score on the course?”

“Either or both. Sleep tight.”

85

ATLANTA, GEORGIA, USA
MONDAY, FEBRUARY 17, 2003

Despite rain showers, which always wreaked havoc on Atlanta traffic, Rusty arrived early at One Ravinia for his 4:30 meeting with Brent Lattimer.

The receptionist took Rusty's brown Andrew Marc bomber jacket and led him to a cozy conference room with a nice view of Buckhead and downtown. "Mr. Lattimer will join you shortly."

A small credenza on the right wall was neatly arranged with a drink and snack assortment. Rusty grabbed a Dasani water. It felt cold. He twisted off the top, forgoing the ice-filled glasses, and took a swig.

Four stacks of documents, had been placed on the rectangular table. Each document was offset from the one underneath it to make the upcoming process as efficient as possible.

Rusty had been through the drill before. Brent would come in, dial the New York office, and make some small talk while they waited for his associate to serve as the witness. Once assembled, Rusty would take the middle seat. From his left, Brent would hand him a document opened to the first signature page, Rusty would occasionally ask a question, sign, and pass it on. Repeat until done.

A few minutes later Brent stepped into the room, shook Rusty's hand, sat down, pulled the Polycom phone station towards him, and dialed.

"Hi everyone. Larry here."

Brent and Rusty, almost simultaneously, "Hi Larry."

"Rusty, fun watching you at Torrey. You going back to Riviera this week?"

"You bet."

"With me here in New York is Gail Owens. She's been working the details with your sponsors."

Brent chimed in, "We're on point here for your endorsements. There's a lot to cover. Hopefully, you won't have to do this in person much longer. The tech folks tell me they're trying out some new electronic signature system. I think it's called Sign It or something like that. There are nineteen contracts in all, so let's get started."

Rusty raised his right hand slightly, "Before we do that, were there any problems?"

"For the most part, no issues," said Larry.

Brent contributed, "Some sponsors were curious why you would give up performance bonuses with the way you're playing right now."

"What do you mean, 'for the most part'?"

Larry responded, "We had to shorten two contracts by a year."

Rusty concluded, "Even better."

Both Larry and Brent pressed Rusty one last time to ensure he really wanted to make the amendments. Rusty nodded vigorously as he grabbed a pen from the circular holder with his right hand and signaled with his left hand for Brent to pass him the first document.

The ritual concluded at 5:25.

Brent thanked Rusty as they walked towards reception. "I made a reservation at the Ravinia Club for you and O.T. He's meeting you, right?"

"Yep, thanks. You're welcome to join us, but it'll be quick. We need to be outta here before seven."

"Let's do something when you've got more time. You can eat and run. We've got ya covered."

····◆····

O.T. and Rusty turned their cars off Tilly Mill Road into the parking lot of the Marcus Jewish Community Center, commonly called the JCC. They parked close to the classroom building as Monday nights are quiet at the JCC. To accommodate Rusty and O.T.'s travel schedule, this quarter's "Introduction to Judaism" was moved from Thursday to Monday evenings.

Eleven others had already arrived when Rusty and O.T. entered the classroom a few minutes before 7:00. The room quieted. Even those not golf fans when they started together five weeks ago silently acknowledged Rusty's weekend results.

Rabbi Ruth Mardesten entered the room just after 7:00. Barely five feet tall, with long blond hair and piercing blue eyes, she radiated confidence as she looked around the room. "Good, looks like we have a minyan."

Her remark returned laughter. Before last week's class, several students had only heard the word used in a non-religious context, referring to having the required number of people. Now they all knew, historically, a minyan required ten men, each having had a bar mitzvah, to conduct a public worship service. Right before Rabbi Ruth adjourned the previous session, she relayed a story from one of her older congregants, who had recalled, while growing up in Poland, that his grandfather once conscripted a passerby to meet the required number.

For the first forty-five minutes, Rabbi Ruth facilitated a discussion on the homework assignment, Alan Dershowitz's book, *The Vanishing American Jew*. She primed the pump, reciting some key stats— two percent of the US population is Jewish, and fifty percent of American Jews intermarry.

As expected, and exactly as she'd hoped, many opinions were exchanged on assimilation, antisemitism, and religious extremism. Shortly before eight she distributed a handout for a follow-up discussion next week with a detailed analysis from the North American Jewish Data Bank, compiled by The Mandel Berman Institute.

After a short break, Rabbi Ruth spent the last half of the class presenting an overview of the conversion process. She listed the three major components on a flip chart— "1. Beit Din - Interview, 2. Tipat Dam - Men Only, and 3. Mikvah - Conclusion."

"We'll talk about *beit din*, then *mikvah*, and save *tipat dam* to the end. Beit din is a court of three rabbis, and historically they were all..." Rabbi Ruth motioned to the class which responded in unison, smiling at their synchronicity, "Men."

Rabbi Ruth elaborated on the tribunal court. It is more akin to a panel discussion, intended to explore the candidate's knowledge, views on Judaism, and motivation for converting. She provided some sample questions and shared some experiences participating on tribunals, pausing for comments before moving on. There were none. This seemed straightforward to the group.

The mikvah was a different story. First, she reminded everyone of the 613 commandments, mitzvot, in the Hebrew Bible which she had spoken about in a previous class. Several rules covered the use of the ritual purification bath, mikvah.

Rabbi Ruth explained, "Although there were many requirements for ancients, both men and women, to immerse, today it's used mostly as a one-time event for conversions and special occasions like weddings. More observant women visit the mikvah on a regular basis, following their periods, to purify themselves before resuming sexual relations with their spouses. However, I should note there are men who immerse weekly in preparing for Sabbath and even some daily."

After she detailed the preparation and process of mikvah, Rusty expressed interest in the differences between Reform, Conservative and Orthodox practices. O.T. jumped in, asking about religion in the home and why a bath or shower could not substitute for a mikvah.

Rabbi Ruth responded to both, talking about the personal aspects of ritual observation and the Reform movement's attempt to adapt to modern society.

A more circumspect student seated behind O.T. remarked that it sounded a lot like baptism. Rabbi Ruth responded, "That might be interesting to explore later in the course if we have more time. In short, many people assume John the Baptist originated baptism. Turns out, baptism was a biblical command to Moses. Baptism first happened in a mikvah."

"Back to the second element, *tipat dam*. Since mikvah is the conversion's culmination, *tipat dam* occurs some time before. In the United States, where most male infants are circumcised shortly after birth, a drop of blood is taken, effectively a ceremonial bris, or *brit mila*, the biblical commandment. In Reform Judaism, many consider this step optional."

O.T. couldn't resist. He leaned to Rusty, attempting to whisper, "So if a bad guy is converting, then you'd prick the prick of a prick."

Rusty tried to ignore O.T.

Rabbi Ruth interjected with humor, "I heard that. Come on. I've heard 'em all. Try to be more original. On that note, we'll end, but I'll hang around for a few minutes if any of you want to talk, one on one."

Chairs squeaked on the polished floor and papers rustled as the class broke up.

As Rusty and O.T. walked out, Rusty remarked sarcastically, "You gotta do part two. Sounds like fun."

"Hey, I'm just keeping you company."

86

SANDWICH, KENT, ENGLAND
WEDNESDAY MORNING, MARCH 19, 2003

Taking a big inhalation of cool spring air as they arrived at the 11th tee at Royal St. George's, Rusty scanned the horizon. Barely visible were the buildings of Ramsgate across the bay. They appeared to be glued atop a thin line of water bolstered by a grassy plain up to the sandy shoreline. Rusty exhaled, "Beautiful."

"No disagreement there," replied O.T. as he slipped the bag from his back next to the tee area. Both opened their respective yardage books.

The last vestiges of fog hung close to the water as the sun eased the temperature towards the forecast high of twelve degrees Celsius. O.T. made the transformation to Fahrenheit in his head. He scribbled it into his book along with wind speed, distance, and club information, 54°, help 10, 245, 3. He would combine this information to that obtained during the practice rounds for The Open in mid-July.

Rusty hit a slight draw, landing ten feet short of the green. The ball rolled sixty feet, ending pin high, thirty feet right of flagstick. Walking up to the front of the tee box, O.T. knew what to do. He handed Rusty a ball, exchanged his 3-iron with a 4, and made another notation, 54°, help 10, 230, 4. The ball didn't roll as far as the prior shot, but it was more online, coming to rest twenty feet short of the hole.

O.T. cleaned the four iron and without looking up, "Both good. Liked the first better."

"Agreed."

They replaced their knit caps with golf hats as they approached the green. Then both walked the circumference making notes which they would compare later. O.T. dropped three balls around the green so Rusty could experience various positions. They always used the first ball for scoring a simulated competitive round.

O.T. removed his own putter from the bag, dropped two more balls onto the putting surface for his own experimentation. A minute later O.T. collected the trial balls and joined Rusty. They concentrated on putting the first ball.

Over the years, O.T. had learned to offer advice on the greens only when solicited. Rusty studied the putt and turned to O.T. "What do you think?"

"Grandpa's pajamas."

"Huh?"

"One ball out," referring to the aiming point the width of one ball on the uphill side of the hole.

"Hadn't heard that one." Rusty tried to suppress a chuckle. O.T. needed no encouragement. "I'm just glad you say this stuff when no one's around."

Rusty missed the putt to the right, grazing the cup's edge as it passed by. "I hit that perfectly. My grandfather must have bigger *cajones* than yours."

"Okay, I'll be more precise next time," said O.T. smiling. "I wonder how the girls are doing?"

"Let's focus on this and we'll check when we get to the 19th hole," referring to the clubhouse. "I'm sure they're fine."

"Right, boss."

Both made final notations in their yardage books as they moved on to the 12th tee box.

·•••◆•••·

After a delicious breakfast of poached brown eggs and roasted tomatoes, Tamara and Sandy languished over coffee at the Solley Farm House. They both agreed the meal was as good as, if not better than, any breakfast they'd experienced in Manhattan.

Sandy concluded, "Everything about this place is top-notch."

"Brian was surprised too. He said he told the travel agent what we wanted, and she came back with this."

"And the owner is also a Sandy. Unbelievable."

Tamara then asked Sandy some questions about the research into Brian's lineage. Finally, Sandy stopped, "You and Brian, it's serious, isn't it?"

"It is. But just one thing is bothering me," as Tamara left Sandy hanging.

"Well..."

"I don't want to be your caddie."

They burst out laughing, scanning the room to see if they had bothered any other patrons.

Tamara then suggested they take a walk. Sandy agreed. They solicited some advice from Peter and Sandy Hobbs, the innkeepers. Both recommended the Sandwich Bay Bird Observatory.

Peter jotted some directions for a one-mile hike that would eliminate walking over two miles back through town. From the observatory, it would be a hop, skip and a jump to meet the boys for lunch at Royal St. George's. Tamara and Sandy thanked their hosts, telling them they looked forward to afternoon tea.

They agreed to reconvene in fifteen minutes, ostensibly to use the loo and grab their jackets.

Five hours forward from New York, Sandy decided to do a quick email check before the day started there.

After doing so, she picked up the phone and dialed O.

"Peter here, how may I help you?"

"Can you connect me with Tamara and Brian's room?"

"No worries. Cheers."

Tamara picked up, "Hello."

"Tam, I just received a crazy email regarding Brian's ancestors. I'm going to London now. Wanna go?"

"Absolutely!"

Within a few minutes, Peter arranged a ride with Sandwich Cars to pick them up. Twenty minutes later they were on their way.

Rusty and O.T. approached the hostess stand at the entrance to the club restaurant.

"Hello, I'm O.T. Sills. We have a lunch reservation for four."

They were shown to a table with only two place settings. Perched in the table's center was an envelope on Solley Farms stationery addressed to Mr. Stephens and Mr. Sills.

Cam, Brian,

We can't join you for lunch. We are off to Blackheath Golf Club. Very exciting. Will be back for dinner and explain.

Love,
San and Tam

87

LONDON, ENGLAND

WEDNESDAY AFTERNOON, MARCH 19, 2003

Realizing they were visiting a bastion of masculinity, Tamara and Sandy wanted to come across as serious. In tailored slacks, shirts, women's sports jackets, and satchels, they looked professional as they stepped away from the taxi. They faced the traditional red brick building. It was relatively tall for just two stories, with four white columns stretching to the roof line which framed large windows and a dark door with a white lintel across its top.

They took a quick look at each another, smiled, and exhaled. They ascended six alabaster steps to a small landing and entered. A receptionist looked up from her workstation. "May I help you?"

Sandy spoke politely, "Ms. Cole and Ms. Wright. We have a two o'clock meeting with Mr. Clarke."

"Please take a seat and I'll let Mr. Clarke know you're here."

Two minutes later, a portly man with sparse gray hair and black-rimmed glasses, old enough to be their fathers, approached.

"Hello. Fergus Clarke." He extended his hand which Sandy then Tamara accepted. "Right on time at fourteen hundred. Is Sandy going to be able to join us?"

"I'm Sandy."

"Pardon me." He stammered. "I'm terribly sorry."

"Not to worry," said Sandy. "You were likely expecting a man."

Uncomfortable a moment ago, Fergus started laughing, which turned the tables on the Americans.

"Now, I need to apologize again. That you knew I was expecting a man means you've done your research young lady. Please come in and let me give you a short tour."

Tamara, having been briefed thoroughly on the ride over, interjected, "Mr. Clarke, we know you're busy and had to fit us in. Thank you."

"No worries. I have a few minutes."

Clarke imagined they would be bored as he waxed on about the club's history. It was the oldest course in England, founded by Scots needing a venue to play in the early 1600's, and a place for royal competition.

He noticed he was holding their attention. "So how did you ladies learn so much about golf?"

Sandy responded, "We didn't know much until we started dating a couple guys who we left behind at Royal St. George's."

"I see."

Tamara couldn't hold back. "Perhaps you may have heard of them, Rusty Stephens and O.T. Sills."

"Brilliant. Absolutely brilliant. Excuse me for a moment."

Tamara and Sandy busied themselves looking at the old clubs in the showcase.

Fergus returned less than two minutes later. "I've rearranged my day. We'll discuss your inquiry over tea. I'll also have the artifacts brought downstairs so you can look at them while the service is prepared."

A young assistant, in his teens, stepped gingerly down the steps, carrying what appeared to be several ledgers. He placed them on a table.

"Thank you, Philip."

"Here are some gloves and face masks sir." He handed the two boxes to Clarke, looking silly as he awkwardly retrieved them from under each arm. He backed away and stood quietly.

Fergus pulled on disposable gloves, then added mouth and nose protection. He invited Tamara and Sandy to do the same if they wanted to handle the artifacts. They willingly complied.

"We don't put these on display. We do our best to mitigate lighting damage, but we just don't want to risk it with these books."

Fergus turned a few pages, ever so slowly. With spittle and body oils in check he encouraged them to lean over, as he proudly showed them some records of George IV's rounds on the course. There was a notation of clubs made for the King by Brendon Solless.

Fergus paused, "This is the surname that brought you here, correct?"

Sandy nodded and mumbled, "Yes," as she leaned a few inches closer, transfixed on the document.

He went to another ledger, turning a few pages to show markings of George III's play. Then back in time to George II and George I in two other books. All had similar notations attributing them to Brendon Solless.

Closing the last ledger then removing his mask and gloves, Fergus stated, "It wouldn't be unusual for a King and his son to use the same clubs. But there is a mystery. With over a hundred and fifty years between George the first's birth and George the fourth's death, it is virtually impossible one man made clubs for them all. Thank you, Philip. Ladies, let's have some tea."

Tamara interjected, "Could it be a type of club?"

"Interesting question, Miss Wright, but we're quite sure it is nothing of the sort. Indeed, there was a man named Solless."

Sandy could hardly get to the table fast enough. She grabbed Tamara's hand hard to settle herself.

Fergus noticed, "Are you feeling all right, Miss Cole?" as he poured for the ladies, encouraging them to sip and settle. Tamara was seated close enough to Sandy to place her hand softly on her knee.

Sandy sipped the Darjeeling tea. "Perhaps Brendon Solless had a son and named him the same. And he in turn had a son with the same name and so on."

"That would be a bit far-fetched," concluded Fergus. "We at least number our royals. I know some Scandinavians use first names to compose a last name for their offspring, but who would use the identical first name for generations?"

"Sephardim," piped up Sandy, authoritatively.

"I beg your pardon," said Fergus, crinkling his eyebrows.

"Sorry. Spanish and Portuguese Jews."

"Well," said Fergus dismissively, "The roots of this club are entirely Scottish."

Worried they had insulted him, Tamara interjected, "Well I suppose that doesn't make sense."

Sandy continued, "Would a Brendon Solless have come here from Scotland?"

"We are quite sure he did but likely changed his surname."

Sandy took a cue from Tamara. She tried to enjoy the ambiance, slowly consuming a small watercress sandwich, crusts trimmed.

Following a pause as they began to eat, Fergus turned to Tamara inquiring, "Miss Wright, do you share a passion for genealogy along with Miss Cole?"

"I became interested because O.T.'s interested. My family can't go back very far in the United States, for obvious reasons."

"Yes, I assumed so. But did you know that George the Third's wife, Charlotte, descended from a black branch of the Portuguese royal house?"

"Really!" responded Tamara.

"Many historians believe Charlotte and George's daughter, Princess Sophia, had an illegitimate daughter. Some speculate she was married off to a Solless."

"About when would that have happened?" asked Tamara.

Fergus responded, "I'm thinking early eighteen-hundreds, if at all."

They turned suddenly towards Sandy as she coughed loudly, aspirating some scone crumbs.

Gasping, she managed to say, "I'm terribly sorry." Sandy settled down gulping her tea. "My throat is sore and I'm not feeling a hundred percent. We should probably leave soon."

Fergus concluded, "No worries. I will get your cab sorted so you can head back. I hope your visit was productive. Please tell Rusty I'm a big fan."

Wanting to keep the door open for any follow-up, Tamara responded, "Would you like me to have O.T. send you an autographed photo of Rusty?"

"That would be delightful."

The women hustled back into the cab. Once the doors closed, Tamara said, "Holy Shit," immediately apologizing to their driver for the profanity.

Sandy said, "I know. Tam, I wasn't acting. He really made me choke. And thank you for keeping me from going too crazy in there."

Tamara put her arm around Sandy and brought them shoulder to shoulder, saying, "Could this have something to do with Brian's skin tone?"

"There's no doubt in my mind now. I mean there have been so many generations in between that one ancestor wouldn't have a big impact. But it's another piece to the puzzle. Cameron has some idea of what I've found out, but Brian's going to flip out."

88

SANDWICH, KENT, ENGLAND
WEDNESDAY EVENING, MARCH 19, 2002

Fighting London rush hour traffic delayed the return to the Solley Farm House. When Sandy and Tamara arrived at 5:30 Peter Hobbs handed them an envelope. It was their turn to receive a note from the guys. They were to meet at The George & Dragon, in town, when ready.

The cab dropped the women off at 6:30. When they entered, Tamara spotted Cameron and Brian standing at the small bar. She hugged Cameron and kissed Brian while Sandy did the opposite.

Tamara saw the beers next to them—a pale ale for Cameron and a dark bitter for Brian. "Look San, they ordered according to their skin tone."

Cameron and Brian looked at each other as it seemed like an odd remark.

Sandy noticed them. "Inside joke from the cab ride back from London. How was the golf?"

"You guys are fired up, said Cameron. "Golf was good."

Brian countered, "As usual, he's modest. It was very good, but I wanna hear what you guys have been up to."

Sandy suggested they get settled at their table first. There was much to talk about. The barkeeper told the guys he would add their drinks to the food bill.

As the hostess took them to their table, Tamara asked how they picked this place. Brian wanted somewhere historical as they were confident the girlfriends were off investigating his lineage.

Tamara said, "You can't get much older than this, at least according to our cab driver. He told us this place is well over five hundred years old."

Sandy thought *this all fits into the day's activities.*

The hostess offered to take drink orders. Both women chose cider. The hostess had barely turned away when Brian said, "Spill. The suspense is killing me."

"Me too," said Cameron.

Sandy set the stage. She reminded Brian that his great great grandfather, Edward Solless, arrived in New York City, in the late 1800's, at Castle Clinton; that she had traced Edward's relatives to London from census data; and she ultimately found Edward's great grandfather, Brendon Solless. "Here's what I didn't tell you, the census listed his occupation as club maker."

Brian let out an elongated, "Amazing."

"You got that right," replied Sandy.

"Looks like golf's in my blood."

"I wanted to be sure it meant golf clubs and not weapons. To be spot on, as they say here, I sent out a bunch of emails. When someone from Blackheath responded...well...to say I was excited would be a huge understatement."

A hovering waitress prompted them to study the menu. They bypassed starters and selected mains, agreeing to leave room for the sticky toffee pudding and the chocolate truffle torte with salted caramel profiteroles.

The last to order, Tamara turned to Sandy and said, "Keep going, the suspense is killing me now and I was there."

Sandy explained that she didn't think they were going to make much headway with the stuffy historian, Fergus Clarke. He was expecting a Scotsman named Sandy rather than young women, particularly a Jewish American and an African American. When Tamara dropped Rusty's name, all doors were opened.

Sandy went on to detail their examination of the ledgers for the four King Georges, each noting clubs made by Brendon Solless.

She digressed for a few minutes by talking about challenges in going back so many years. Fortunately, there was good record-keeping on royalty, religion and often money. In this case Brian's ancestors were associated with royalty.

As if working on a jigsaw puzzle, with bad eyesight and several pieces hiding in deep shag carpet, the chances of constructing a complete picture were marginal at best.

Sandy continued, "Sometimes duplicate names can lead to confusion with more paths to nowhere. In this case, the same names may have helped. I have a theory. Brendon Solless made clubs for George I. George's heir was George II. Brendon's apprentice was Brendon. There may have been at least four Brendons aligned with Georges. There's one more thing."

Tamara interjected, "She's saving the best for last."

Sandy said, "Tam, I want you to tell this part. But before she does, you guys can't have anything in your mouths. I speak from experience."

Like a game of bury the hatchet, Tamara took over. She talked about Fergus Clarke's insistence on tea. Between teacakes he mentioned that Princess Sophia, George III's daughter, had an illegitimate child.

"From what Sandy told me, it was not unusual for male royalty to have children with their mistresses, but it's unheard of for women. There's a belief that Brendon Solless married Sophia's illegitimate daughter."

"Interesting," said Cameron.

"Here's the real interesting part," Tamara continued. "Princess Sophia's mother was part African."

"That's insane," said Cameron, shaking his head in disbelief.

"Unbelievable," shouted Brian. "Do you think this has something to do with my color?"

"Maybe," interjected Sandy, tempering his expectations as well as her optimism from earlier in the day. "Remember, this ancestor was only partially black, and you probably had over a hundred people contributing to your DNA from that point. But one thing this afternoon proves, at least to me, Brendon Solless or these Brendons are your relatives."

Cameron turned to Brian, "Can you make me some new clubs?"

"No, but we could order some champagne to celebrate. What a day. I can't thank you guys enough."

Sandy responded, "Now I've got Tam into it, just don't complain when we take you around Edinburgh tomorrow."

"Deal!" said Brian. "I still can't believe it."

89

EDINBURGH, SCOTLAND
MARCH 20, 2003

The foursome stirred from semi-sleep when the British Airways commuter jet thumped onto Edinburgh's westerly runway just after 10:00 a.m. Despite the short flight, they all caught a few extra winks. Sandy needed it the most as the prior day's revelations continued to course adrenaline through her well past 2:00 in the morning.

"I know this is a silly question," said Cameron, as the plane taxied to the terminal, "We're just relaxing today, aren't we?"

"Depends what you call relaxing," replied Sandy with a sinister smile on her face. "My deal is with Brian. You don't have to go with us."

"Something tells me I should."

"It should be an interesting afternoon. I hired a genealogist, slash, local historian, a few weeks ago to do some research and take us around. Tamara mentioned a ghost tour, and Edinburgh is known for them, but that would be on my expendable list. We're going to St Andrews Friday, which should be relaxing."

Sandy immediately made a beeline to the concierge desk while the others checked into The Balmoral. With no queue she anticipated a quick stop. She secured a map and directions for the short walk to meet the local genealogist she had engaged. As she folded the map, Sandy inquired as to what Edinburgh natives are called. The concierge said Edinburgher is used most often, then began elaborating on other names including Edinburgenians, Edinburgundians, and Gits.

Cameron didn't realize he was her rescuer. As he approached, she pictured him in a tartan kilt like the male staff who welcomed them. She laughed out loud, thinking *no need to file that image*.

"Hey," said Cameron. "Tam and Brian are famished. I am too. How much time do we have?"

"We should be okay. Just a ten-minute walk to meet our guide at two. It's almost twelve. If we drop off our stuff in the rooms, we should have more than enough time for lunch."

He leaned in, hugged her, grinding into her ever so slightly, and whispered. "Sounds like a plan. You know I like your plans."

She pulled back, giving him a quick smack on the lips.

A few minutes before 2:00, the foursome made a left from North Bridge onto High Street. Five minutes later, they crossed St Mary's Street, continuing straight on Canongate. Less than a minute later they arrived at The Royal Mile Gallery.

A woman hovered outside the door. Sandy was reasonably certain she was the person she retained.

"Are you Cairstine Black?"

"Indeed," extending her hand.

Sandy took it, "I'm Sandy Cole. Thanks for meeting us. Let me introduce you to Cameron, Tamara, and Brian. This is Cairstine, did I say that right?"

"You did. Nice to meet everyone. Welcome to Edinburgh. Let's step inside and start here. This lovely shop is run by the Auld-Smith family. They have curated an extensive print collection which includes golf scenes. Turning to Tamara, Cameron, and Brian, she politely requested, "Would you mind browsing around for a few minutes while I review the plans with Sandy?"

Cairstine spoke quietly to Sandy. "First thing this morning, I read the email you sent late last night. Amazing, and I think you and Brian will be even more amazed at my findings. Are Cameron and Tamara interested in Brian's history?"

"Absolutely."

"Then I know exactly what we'll do. We will…"

Sandy jumped in as Cairstine hesitated slightly. "Whatever, as long as we experience it together."

"Brilliant."

Cairstine led the group downhill from the Royal Mile Gallery to Canongate. She pointed out two sixteenth century structures, the Huntly House and the Canongate Tolbooth. After her brief explanations, they did an about face, trudging back uphill.

Next on the itinerary, the Moubray House and the John Knox House, both built in the fifteenth century. Cairstine apologized for the backtracking on the steep streets, but she was deliberately taking them back in time. On to the Trinity Apse, the semi-circular remnant of the church built to honor James II.

From the Apse, they made their way up High Street. Cairstine slowed the pace pointing into several narrow streets, marked as courts. She mentioned that 500 years ago there were bowyers and bow makers, who moonlighted making golf clubs.

Within ten minutes they arrived at St Giles' Cathedral. Cairstine gave them an overview of the structure and its evolution dating back to the twelfth century. She ushered them into a pew in the North Chapel.

Quietly she said, "A few days ago, I planned to end with a full tour of Edinburgh Castle. With the sunshine today and some inspiration from Sandy, I suggest a brief tour of the castle then walk-through Holyrood Park, which is not only beautiful but packed with history. It's at least two hours, including stops once we leave the castle grounds. All in, it's about three miles with some severe elevation changes, depending on which path we take. We'll end up at a restaurant where I'll update you on my research."

Brian turned to Tamara. "I walk miles carrying Cam's clubs. It's a no-brainer for me."

"I'm good. Got my Big Apple sneakers on."

"Let's go," said Cameron.

Knowing ultimately what was in store for them, Cairstine continued back in time on the abbreviated tour of the castle. She ended it at the Mons Meg, one of the largest cannons ever built, weighing close to eight tons. She summarized the theories as to how it came to James II in 1454.

They started their trek to the park with a cool breeze counterbalancing a warming sun.

Cairstine challenged them to imagine monarchs hunting on the grounds. As they crested Salisbury Crags near the highest point in Edinburgh, Arthur's Seat, she suggested that King David I may have stood in the same place almost nine hundred years ago.

Looking down on two lochs, Cairstine was confident that Mary, Queen of Scots, had fished in them. Then passing a large field dotted with gorse, she told the group that Mary's father, James V, turned the area into a park in the mid-sixteenth century.

When they entered the Sheep Heid, they were immediately seated at a round table in the front corner, set with five positions.

Brian noticed, “Looks like they were expecting us.”

Cairstine smiled, bordering on a smirk, saying, “So it seems.”

Without prompting, a server placed five ciders on the table. Brian, turned to Cairstine, “And you ordered these too?”

“Indeed. I’d like to toast you with something which may have been served here five-hundred years ago.” She raised her mug, “Thank you Sandy for contacting me. This has been some of the most exciting work I have ever done. *Slanj-a-va.*”

They met her mug with theirs and echoed, “*Slanj-a-va.*”

Cairstine sipped, “Delightful, isn’t it?”

The foursome responded politely, clearly on the edges of their seats.

Cairstine continued, “As you’d expect, I used wills, testaments and records of births, marriages, and burials. There was also a hearth tax centuries ago. I researched those too.”

She took a deep breath, “Brian, your ancestors more than likely lived in this area and walked these very grounds. They probably ate and drank in this establishment.”

Motionless, waiting for Cairstine to continue, Brian’s eyes watered.

“This morning, when I opened the email Sandy sent me last night, all the pieces fell into place. Brendon Solley changed his surname to Solless when he emigrated to London in 1687.”

Raising her hand to high-five Brian, Sandy grunted a loud, “Yes.”

Brian met Sandy’s hand, “You didn’t know this?”

“Tam and I told you guys everything we knew last night. I sent Cairstine the email last night, right before I crashed. And of all the places to stay in Sandwich, we ended up at the Solley Farm House. I mean, c’mon.”

Cairstine said, “That’s very odd.” Then she continued, “I researched a club maker from the early sixteen-hundreds, William Mayne. His grandfather, John Mayne, a bowyer, made clubs for King James the Fourth. And his grandson, Graeme, was a club maker. Brendon Solley’s father, Michael, was an apprentice to Graeme Mayne.”

Cairstine let that all sink in, causing a cacophony of “Wow!” “Unbelievable!” “No shit!” “How is this possible?!” “Insane!” “Crazy! “Who woulda thought?!”

Then Cairstine raised her hand a few inches from the table, palms out, to quiet them, “There’s more. So, we know there were at least six generations of Maynes who made golf clubs. And they all had apprentices. Now the astonishing part. Michael Solley descended from a line of apprentices or assistants aligned with each Mayne generation.”

She turned to Brian, "Along with the information Sandy provided me, I am fairly certain that one of your forebearers was Benno Solley. He worked for John Mayne and most likely helped construct clubs, or at least bows and spears, for James the fourth. His father, Ben, lived in St Andrews."

Cameron, now fascinated, asked "How did you connect all of the apprentices over so many generations?"

"That mystified me," said Cairstine. "There were only two first names, Michael, and Benjamin. They alternated across generations, so Michael's father was Benjamin. His father was Michael. His father Benjamin and so forth. Other than royalty this is highly unusual."

Sandy shook her head, "Go ahead, Tam."

Tamara continued, "Not unusual if they were Sephardic Jews."

Cairstine looked quizzically.

Sandy continued, "Sephardic Jews typically name their children in honor of living people. Ashkenazi Jews, like me, name their children in memory of deceased relatives."

Cairstine stiffened. "Interesting. The first recorded Jew here in Edinburgh was David Brown, who applied to reside and trade here in 1691. It's both strange and interesting, given what you ladies learned yesterday in London."

"And that was.?" queried Cameron.

"There has been speculation, by scholars from time to time, that Scottish merchants, in the 15th and 16th centuries, dealt with Jewish traders in the Baltic ports and what many called Holland or the low countries of Belgium, Luxembourg and The Netherlands."

Sandy nodded. *Holland made perfect sense.*

Back at the Balmoral, Sandy buried herself in her laptop while Cameron showered. He leaned out the bathroom, bath sheet around his torso, drying his hair with a hand towel. "Everything okay?"

"There's one more thing I'd like to chase down for Brian."

He smiled. "I suspected as much."

"Can we wire two thousand dollars to a genealogist in The Netherlands?"

Cameron laughed, "Why not. We've come this far. It's minus five hours in Atlanta. I'll take care of it after I get dressed. I don't want you to be agitated at dinner."

Sandy closed her laptop and followed him back into the bathroom, squeezing his butt. "Love you."

90

St Andrews, Scotland
Friday, March 21, 2003

Pulling his wool cap over his ears, Hamish Dingwell met his group on the walkway behind the starter's tent for the 10:00 a.m. Old Course tour. Dingwell was assigned a private tour of four people. After decades as a guide, Dingwell now preferred smaller groups. Today would be even more interesting as he was granted an exception to walk on the course, normally only a Sunday privilege to those not golfing.

Tamara and Sandy introduced themselves, followed by Cameron and Rusty. When Cameron received a tentative handshake, he sensed something was off. He tried to put Dingwell at ease. "Please call me Rusty."

Dingwell did his best to carry-on nonchalantly. "Nice to see you again," referring to the Open Championship of 2000. "I think it's fair to say you know the course better than I."

"Perhaps. But O.T. and I were focused on trying to catch Tiger. We didn't have a chance to soak up any history. Think of me as just another tourist today."

"That will be rather difficult, but I'll give 'er a go."

Starting behind the 18th green, he set the stage. "Let's work backward in time. Mr. Stephens already mentioned Mr. Woods. Your Mr. Nicklaus won his first Open on this green over thirty years ago, in 1970, by making a birdie on the last hole of an eighteen-hole playoff. He won just over five thousand pounds. Please follow-me."

"That would hardly cover our airfares," quipped O.T.

Dingwell continued, "The ladies may not know Mr. Sam Snead. He won The Open in 1946. His winner's share of a hundred and fifty pounds surely didn't cover his expenses. Thank you for reminding me of that Mr. Sills."

Rusty was fully expecting O.T. to say *so much for calling us by our first names.*

They stopped halfway towards the 1st green, standing patiently as a golfer finished hitting his approach shot. With the ocean breeze picking up its intensity, Dingwell made sure his audience was downwind when he spoke.

"Over the centuries, the course has been played the same way. You go out to the end. End is the name of the 9th hole. Practical, don't you think? Then you come in. Five of the holes going out have names that are similar, if not identical to those coming in. The 1st hole is called Burn, what you may call a stream. That's to your left. The shortest hole is Short, the longest, Long. Eighteen is Tom Morris and ten is Bobby Jones."

Rusty remarked, "Speaking of Bobby Jones, it sounds a lot easier than remembering eighteen different flowers for each hole at Augusta."

"Ah, not so easy, Mr. Stephens. We've named our bunkers."

As they walked to the 1st green, Sandy asked Rusty, "Are you bored without a club in your hand?"

"God no. The scenery is beautiful." He took her hand, squeezing it lightly. "You're beautiful. And I think your history bug has bitten me."

When the golfers cleared the 1st green, Dingwell resumed his patter. "The Old Course has only eleven putting greens. Seven have two cups with flag sticks, a white flag for the hole going out and a red flag coming in. The 1st hole and the 17th hole shared the same green until Old Tom Morris separated them about 1870."

Sandy said to Rusty, "Now I understand what my father was talking about."

"How so?"

"Years ago, we went to a resort called Samoset, not too far away from us at home. I remember Dad saying he played eighteen holes, but the course had only seventeen greens."

"I'm surprised you didn't ask."

"Wasn't interested in golf back then."

Rusty laughed. "You wouldn't let that slip by now."

Dingwell led them to the left of the second tee, halfway to the 2nd hole, and turned left between the 18th tee and the 17th green. As they started walking on the road, Dingwell mentioned that the hole is named Road. He recited some dates. The Society of St Andrews golfers was founded in 1754. And in 1552, the Archbishop of St Andrews gave permission for the townspeople to play golf. Dingwell was quick to editorialize that was a formality.

They arrived at the 2nd green with two sticks planted in it. "As the white flag is for two going out and the red flag is for sixteen coming in, do you notice any parallel between this green and the combination undone by Old Tom Morris?"

Tamara jumped on it, "They add up to eighteen."

"Well done, madam. Hole three shares with fifteen, four with fourteen and so it goes. Makes as much sense as anything in this game. If you haven't seen the Robin Williams stand-up on golf which came out last year, I highly recommend it. It's brilliant. And we are known to enjoy a dram or two of Scotch on the links. But I hope you'll agree we're well organized."

It was hard to tell who was enjoying the tour more, Dingwell or his foursome. He extended the tour over its two-hour allotment, trekking to the 14th teeing area and crossing back to the shoreline to head in. Dingwell continued to recite facts and figures he hoped would be unknown to Rusty or O.T.

They stopped for a few minutes near the 3rd tee. Nearby, the grounds crew was gently moving dirt with their shovels around a man-made stub protruding from the ground. Dingwell called out, "Anything interesting?"

"Not sure yet Hamish."

"Luck to ya."

Dingwell turned back to the group, explaining that the eighteen-hole format emerged as a standard within the last hundred years or so. The Old Course had twenty-two holes at one point.

Sandy jumped in, "Mr. Dingwell. Does anyone know why golf ended up at eighteen?"

"No one's really sure. Perhaps just how it all worked out."

Coming in on the same line they started out on, Dingwell was about to render his boilerplate finale. But today he improvised. "Normally, I hand out souvenir scorecards for visitors to take away. May I be so bold as to have all four of you sign one for me? It's been a pleasure to host you."

"The pleasure is ours," said Cameron.

"Thank you. Let's finish by standing on the Swilcan Bridge. As you know, it's been the backdrop for many iconic photos, including several of Mr. Stephens. It's been in use by golfers, shepherds, and sheep for over seven hundred years."

PART III

"Anticipate charity by preventing poverty."

Moses Maimonides
(1138 - 1204)

91

St Andrews, Scotland
Sixteen Years Later - Saturday, July 9, 1513

By the time Ben arrived at the golf fields in mid-morning, the fog had lifted. Puffy clouds moved slowly across a bright blue canvas, casting shadows on a calm St Andrews Bay. It would be a warm summer day, reminiscent of Spain in the springtime. Ben could hardly believe he left Gibraltar over twenty years ago, about the same age Benno is now.

With Artair's flock grazing calmly on both sides of the burn, Ben figured he was already at work on the new link. He walked outward for ten minutes. "Morning."

Artair looked up from the hole he was digging. "Did you see the wee sheep?"

"I believe I saw a few Cheviot ewes with triplets. That is good, aye?"

"It is."

"And a few Blackface mixed in. Do they get along?"

"Mostly."

"I heard some are trying dogs. Maybe you should try one," jested Ben.

"Are you saying my golf is not good enough after all the help you've given me over the years?"

Ben laughed, extending him a bladder, "Here. Take some water. I can see you have made good progress this morning. Can we have it ready for tomorrow? With a fourth out and in, we'd have eight links."

"Perhaps. Let's bring the sheep up here to graze."

As they started back in, they spotted a man on horseback in the distance. He was on the opposite side of the burn, waiting for some ewes and their lambs to clear the stone footbridge.

Ben strained to look closer as he approached. "Looks like Alexander Stewart."

"Town is a short walk. Why would he ride?"

"He must be in a hurry or on his way somewhere. With his eyesight, he is much safer walking."

"I'm not sure I agree. He has some excellent mounts."

"I can't argue that. Why don't you look after the sheep? I'll see what he wants."

"I will."

"Thank you Artair."

"Greetings, archbishop. What brings you to the links today? I hardly think you want to learn golf."

"Hardly. I have orders from my brother."

"Fair enough. I was expecting to see him here after your service tomorrow morning."

"I wish that were so. Tensions are rising on the border. James requires your service at Stirling Castle."

"Not for golf, I presume."

"Cannon firing drills."

"When am I needed?"

"Tuesday morning. Arrive on Monday."

"I will do my best."

"Make sure you're there on time. I can provide you with a mount, if necessary."

"Thank you. That would be most appreciated."

Ben updated Artair on the situation. They renewed their work with purpose, to complete the new link even if Ben could not be there for its opening. By mid-afternoon they accomplished their objective. At that point, Artair retrieved his golf stick to herd his flock.

By late afternoon, Ben had guided Davis and his two mates on the new link. It provided a welcome addition, expanding the layout closer to the water. His stomach growled. He hoped Evi and their two daughters would arrive shortly, with something to eat.

Thirty minutes later, no Evi, no daughters. In their place, a lanky young man put down the basket he had carried and embraced Ben.

"Benno, it's so great to see you son. This is a nice turn of events."

"Great to see you too father."

They pulled back, looked at each other, then hugged again.

Ben looked him over, "You look well. The Maynes are feeding you I see. I didn't expect you back so soon. How long has it been?"

"I think we were all together on my sixteenth birthday." Without hesitation Benno continued, "That was forty-seven days ago."

"I've taught you well. Are your mother and sisters coming?"

"I spent the afternoon with them. Mother said we should have some time to visit by ourselves."

"Well, let's eat then. I'm starving."

After a few bites, Benno thanked his father again for arranging the apprenticeship with John Mayne. Benno got on well with John's eldest son, George, who was also learning the craft of golf stick construction.

While that pleased Ben, he was anxious, given the orders delivered by the archbishop and Benno's unexpected return home.

Benno sensed this. "Two royal messengers arrived at the shop in Edinburgh this past Thursday. One read a declaration from the King ordering a cessation of any work related to golf. The other gave Mr. Mayne a quota for making bows and arrows. I do hope to go back soon."

Ben updated Benno on the morning's events with the archbishop. Border skirmishes were nothing new. But this seemed like a serious escalation.

Benno let out a long exhalation.

"What is it son?"

"I now realize Mr. Mayne was protecting me from harm."

"He's a good man. Maybe he knew I would need you to work here while I'm gone."

They enjoyed their repast, reminiscing about their journey to Amsterdam three years earlier, when Benno turned thirteen. Spending time with Aunt Becca, Uncle Johan, and their children was great fun. He was enthralled exploring the city, so different from St Andrews. And much to Ben's amazement, Benno was fascinated by the way in which his Jewish roots sprouted into his Catholic upbringing in Scotland.

Breaking the silence as they finished eating, Benno said, "I keep thinking about why your life turned out the way it did. Why have I been given so many gifts when so many have suffered?"

"It's an impossible question to answer. One thing is certain. We never would have survived if it hadn't been for the help we received, often from people we don't even know. Do you remember what Aunt Becca taught you about Moses Maimonides?"

"I do. I understand how people have given to us from the highest rung on Rambam's ladder. And I understand the King has helped us in a way others would never. But why you, why us?"

"I wish I knew son. We can only lead our lives to inspire others to climb his ladder. How about we take a look at the new link?"

They walked slowly, waving at two golfers. Enjoying the summer breeze, they spotted the pole. As they got closer, Benno commented, "It fits right, like it's been here all along."

"I will pass along your praise to Artair. He did most of the work."

They walked in, their shadows lengthening from the setting sun. As they approached the stone bridge Benno speculated, "I wonder how many links we should have ultimately?"

"I've contemplated it from time to time. In these pastures, we could have a few or many, depending on the average length of a link. Maybe at some point, eighteen."

Benno looked at him quizzically, "Why eighteen?"

Ben hesitated.

Benno continued, "I'm guessing it has something to do with math or numbers."

Ben smiled, "Son, you know me too well." Placing his arm around his son's waist as they walked. He spoke slowly, "Back in Spain, eighteen was a mystical or lucky number, called Chai. It's composed with two Hebrew letters. They are part of an ancient alphanumeric code. The code was called Gematria and..."

Benno interjected, "Father. Are you going to tell me what it means, or do I have to write to Aunt Becca?"

Ben laughed, "Sorry for being so long winded. Chai means life."

92

BANNOCKBURN, SCOTLAND
STIRLING, SCOTLAND
TUESDAY, JULY 18, 1513

The temperate weather countered the long ride from St Andrews. The pony provisioned by Stewart performed as promised. Ben needed more rest stops than the animal on the fifty-mile journey.

About two miles from the castle Ben dismounted. He wanted to rest before arriving. Then he'd walk the remainder to give his aching buttocks some relief.

He stretched, downed some beer, sat down, and closed his eyes. His head flopped forward. He awakened when he felt the earth rumble. He opened his eyes on an approaching entourage, nearly upon him, with eight pairs of oxen, a cannon in tow, four drivers, and twenty men attending to carts of materials, tools, and round shot.

Ben righted himself and waited another minute for the party to reach him. He introduced himself and asked the apparent leader if he could join them on the final leg to Stirling Castle.

"Aye. You are more than welcome. I'm Alexander Lauder. Master Solley, how is it you know our destination?"

"I have been summoned to assist with cannon practice."

"Practice is our goal. First, we must test it. This weapon is new and has not been fired yet."

When Lauder noticed the King's coat of arms on Ben's mount, he expounded on his orders.

"This ordnance was produced in the hellish bowels of Edinburgh castle. Robert Borthwick, the King's Foundry Master, cast this one in a single piece of bronze. He and his men are working feverishly to produce many more. The King wants there to be no question that Scotland is viewed as a world power. And he must have the upper hand over England, should we need to come to the aid of France."

Ben was curious, "Why must the cannon be transported to Stirling for testing and practice?"

"A number of reasons, I believe. If there are injuries, like the mishap that killed the king's grandfather, he does not want a public spectacle. And since we built cannons in Stirling not too long ago, we have tools to make needed adjustments. Also important, he wants to test the transport. This culverin is a far cry from the Mons but she still carries over four thousand pounds of weight with her."

"Good logic. I suspect you know the King well. He's placed much trust in you."

"Have you met His Grace?" queried Lauder.

"I have."

"In what way?"

"In sport."

"Ahh. Same for me. That is, if you agree card play is sport."

"We share a predicament, as one may or may not agree that golf is sport."

Lauder laughed, while patting Ben on the back, "I trust he doesn't wager as much with you."

"I only advise him so he can become better at it."

"And he wagers with others?"

"Sometimes."

"Do others let him win?"

"He wouldn't stand for that. He is an honorable man, at least in golf."

Emerging from the woods, they saw the lavish landscape rise to meet the blue sky. The horizon split as the castle's grayness emerged.

With a quarter mile remaining, Lauder raised his right hand. The men and animals halted. All conversation ceased. They gazed upon the impressive fortifications perched atop the crag, some 350 feet above them.

Not long after they restarted, four men on horseback approached. Lauder stopped his party again.

With little enthusiasm the rider facing them spoke, "Good to see you, Alexander." Turning to the three behind him, "Take the cannon to the firing grounds with the men." Giving Ben a good up and down, noticing his dark black hair and skin, darkened from the sun, "Who is this odd-looking man?"

Ben uttered, "Sir..."

He was interrupted by the horseman, "I wasn't addressing you."

Rather than speak further, Ben bowed his head.

Lauder answered, "He is here to assist with cannon trials."

"We'll see about that. Mount up." Pointing to Ben, "Go with my men. Come Alexander, I shall fetch you mead and victuals."

Ben subtly grabbed Lauder's arm to truncate his protest.

As they prepared to mount their ponies, Lauder whispered, "That's Robert Herwort, the royal gunner. He trained under the infamous Hans many years ago. He believes he knows all there is to know about firing cannons. Be careful."

Ben nodded, "Thank you."

Lauder and Herwort sipped from their tankards. A gregarious James entered the room. "Greetings Alexander. How was the trip over?"

"Long. Four days, as expected. It is not the size of the cannon sire; it is the limitations of the oxen. We may have traversed in three days, but I recommend four days when planning to engage the enemy."

"Agreed. Glad Edinburgh can do without you for a few days."

James turned to Herwort. "It seems we are on schedule. I want us to set sail on the Michael within a week."

"Very well, Your Grace."

"Did either of you encounter Ben Solley today? He should be here shortly, if not already."

Lauder, trying to head off any embarrassment to Herwort, "He may be with the cannon brigade."

James called out, "Colban, please fetch Ben Solley and return him here. Ask the men who delivered the cannon today."

"Aye, Your Grace."

Colban had hardly ushered Ben into the room when James turned, placing his hands on Ben's shoulders.

"Good to see you, Ben."

"You as well, Your Grace."

James shifted to Spanish for a few seconds to talk about golf. Then he brought Ben in for a quick hug. Ben reciprocated, while Lauder and

Herwort looked on in amazement.

Disengaging from their embrace, James said, “How is your family?”

“Very well, thank you.”

James proclaimed to Herwort, “Robert. This man is a genius. Use him wisely. You are my master gunner. Ben can make you even better. I will leave you now. Margaret thinks I can control James now that he’s walking, but the bairn laddie has a mind of his own.”

The three visitors stood.

James concluded, “See you tomorrow.”

93

Stirling, Scotland
Wednesday, July 19, 1513

Herwort insisted on an early start. Lauder complied, joining him to rouse the men at dawn. With pay at twelve pence per day, the men responded with haste. They would eat later.

After maneuvering the carts and animals onto the field, Lauder's men moved them to Herwort's designated location. Less than an hour after sunrise the gunnery crew was ready. In anticipation, Lauder leaned forward in his saddle, stroking his horse. Ben did the same.

With the cannon level set at 0°, straight ahead, the first test firing was executed successfully. The explosion and air compression in the immediate area startled the unprepared. After reloading the cannon with a twenty-pound ball and gunpowder, a second firing occurred within ten minutes. Realizing James was observing from the castle grounds, Herwort was eager to fire down range.

However, Lauder hoisted a large red flag, signaling not to fire. Ben dismounted. He measured the distance from the muzzle to the ground, then paced the distance from the muzzle to the first depression of both projectiles, and then to where they came to rest. He paced the distance between the two balls and began recording his measurements. A frustrated Herwort yelled at Ben, "Quickly."

Ben finished and ran back to his mount. He and Lauder moved to the side. Herwort, had already ordered the cannon raised to five degrees and readied. As soon as Ben raised a white flag, the next firing occurred with two more in rapid succession. Ben was pleased to have three measurement points, again recording each shot's first depression and end point.

This pattern continued— add five degrees, fire three times, red flag up, measure, move away from landing area, and white flag up. As the launch angle increased the shots traveled further with more dispersion in their landing spots.

Lauder and Ben continued to move downrange, nearly a mile, for the launches at forty-five degrees. Lauder galloped a quarter mile back to ensure he was in view, now actively waving the red flag.

When it was clear no more shots would be forthcoming, Lauder and Ben walked with their ponies in tow. Ben wanted to have a feel for the entire set of results. Besides, they were in no hurry.

Lauder said, "I am beginning to understand why James relishes your company."

"How so?"

"You seem to have much in common even though it may not appear obvious. You both speak several languages. He is a man of science, and you are a man of mathematics. Math and science are a good marriage."

"That may be true, Alexander. But he is a man of power."

Lauder patted him on the back as they continued walking. "Aye, his power emanates from his ability to harness the people that govern the military, the church, the cities, the land, the surgeons, and barbers."

"I agree."

"Ben, it takes a clever mind to do what he has done. And you both share that."

"This clever mind is likely to irritate Herwort, if I haven't done so already. Herwort needs to fire from different directions."

"He wouldn't object, as best I can tell."

"Aye, but we should do this today."

"The men are tired. After resting and eating, they would need to reposition the equipment. Should you make notations again, we will be on the field past sunset. Is tomorrow not adequate?"

"If Herwort is amenable, we can make half as many launches."

"Why the haste?"

"First, did you notice that the further Herwort fired, the more dispersed the landings became?"

"I did."

"Would you agree then, based on what you observed, that this cannon could hardly be effective at distances over, say, six hundred paces?"

"I would," answered Lauder. He grinned. "I suspect you can do something about that."

"Let me ask you this, Alexander. Do you think Herwort considers the wind, the heat and moisture in the air, the height of the land on which he is standing, and the level he is firing upon?"

Lauder considered the question, "Aye, from his experience."

"I agree. However, with mathematics, I think I can add much more precision to his aim. This afternoon will be hotter, with more moisture in the air, and a different direction of wind. All of these put together will make a difference, I assure you."

"Ben, I will do my best to support you."

····◆◆◆····

James joined the three men for a midday dinner. Parched and hungry from the morning's work, they eagerly consumed brown bread, cheeses, chicken, dried beans, and ale, without much conversation.

After the short lull, James cast a look at Herwort, an obvious cue for him to report on the results. Herwort complimented the weapon's construction, its firing action, and the ability of the men to manage the weapon.

James listened. "Robert, I'm pleased to hear those words. However, can you eliminate English border flies with weapons like these?"

"Without a doubt, Your Grace."

"Good, that is all that matters. Ben, what advice can you give?"

Herwort tightened his face.

Ben chose his words carefully, deftly avoiding criticizing the man. "The team did well and the results at short-range were excellent. I do think we can improve accuracy at longer ranges. I'd like to continue this afternoon."

"Impossible," Herwort fired back. "The men are exhausted. They need to rest for practice tomorrow."

Ben let that settle. "This morning we fired twenty-seven rounds after the two test firings. Can you manage one-third as much, nine tests, this afternoon?"

James allowed the verbal conflict to take form, gazing up to the tall ceiling, to avoid the non-verbal appeal he expected from Herwort. Steadfast, Herwort dug in. "I need to rest the men."

Lauder tried to help his new friend, "Robert, I will labor for you. I can do the labor of two men. I can pay other men additional wages to volunteer."

James turned to Ben. "Is this all you need?"

"Aye, Your Grace. I will take measurements after all of the firings are completed. The men will not have to wait. That will conclude my work, so practice should also be much faster tomorrow."

James concluded, "I will be at this afternoon's firings." Rhetorically,

"Shall we commence in two hours?" He stood up and left the room.

Lauder pressed down on Ben's knee, hard, to allow Herwort to exit first and stifle any further conversation.

····◆····

After seven shots at various launch angles, James stepped forward, "Let's make a wager. Robert, you take a shot and then Ben takes one. I will give twenty shillings for the closest."

James ordered some timbers to be dragged into the field to fashion a target about 400 paces from the cannon. "Ben, please turn away, so you cannot observe Robert's preparation."

Herwort went into action. He ordered the firing angle at thirty-one degrees and the weapon adjusted slightly to the right to improve its aim. The cannon fired. The projectile landed thirty paces short and rolled past the target five paces to the right. Herwort tugged at his vest in a show of accomplishment and superiority.

Ben prepared for his try. He stood next to the cannon, facing the target. To gauge the wind, he turned ninety-degrees, and paused; another ninety, pause; ninety more, a final pause; return to the starting position. He dropped to his knees with his arm angled outward. The men instinctively knew what to do. They matched the cannon to Ben's angle and direction. Ben stepped away.

The cannon blasted. Perfect strike. There may have been cheers or yelling in battle, but everyone who observed this launch was stunned in silence, except James.

He reached out to shake hands with Herwort. James didn't let go. "Ben come here." He reached out his left hand. Ben reciprocated. The three formed a lattice. James said, "England is no match for us."

"Robert, you win the twenty shillings. It was unfair of me to put you in this position."

"Your Grace," said Herwort, suppressing his resentment of Ben as Lauder led those assembled in applause.

94

ST ANDREWS, SCOTLAND

FRIDAY, SEPTEMBER 2, 1513

As he generally did when the family shared a meal together, Benno took the seat across from his younger sisters, Alana, fourteen, and Blair, twelve. When Evi and Ben took their seats on the ends, Ben asked Blair to say grace, the only grace they had ever recited. As usual, Ben had challenged the children to translate it into other languages.

Blair clasped her hands, elbows on the table, reciting in perfect English, "Some have meat but cannot eat, some have none that want it, but we have meat, and we can eat, so let the Lord be thanked."

All five said, "Amen," in unison.

The pleasant aroma of simmering vegetables and haddock wafted through the room. Evi proudly announced to the men that the meal was prepared entirely by Alana and Blair.

As Evi began serving, Ben said, "It is plain to see there are no more wee lassies at our table." Evi and the girls acknowledged with a smile.

They started to eat. Ben continued, "Scotland has some serious matters before her. And you may have heard some talk around town." Ben tried his best to simplify the situation while providing some context. He explained that going back over 200 years, Scotland made an alliance with France, as both countries feared England. He knew the children had heard stories, in recent years, about skirmishes with England on the border, not too far away from where they sat.

He summarized, "Scotland and France are friends; England has attacked France; King James wants to help his friend."

It didn't take a second for Alana to interrupt. "Isn't Queen Margaret the sister of King Henry? Why would King James attack his brother-in-law?"

Ben and Evi stole a glance, as if to say, "We have a smart daughter and which one of us is going to respond."

Evi spoke up, "That is an excellent question, *bhobain*." My darling.

Benno added, "And didn't he sign a peace treaty when he married Margaret?

"This is a contradiction the King must face. There is no logic," Evi replied.

The three children laughed.

"What did I say that was so humorous?"

"Nothing," said Benno. "You just sounded exactly like Father."

Ben shifted, "I'm sure you recall, upon my return from Stirling, I spoke about the fine gentleman I met, Alexander Lauder, the provost of Edinburgh. He visited me at the golf fields this morning and brought much news."

For the next five minutes Ben held everyone's attention. He talked about Scottish raids across the border eight days after he returned from Stirling. Exactly one week later, the English retaliated, killing many Scotsmen. A few days after that, England attacked France near the border with the lowlands. Then two weeks ago the Scots gathered twenty cannons in Edinburgh and moved southward. Since then King James' forces have captured Norham Castle, Etal Castle, and Ford Castle, all of which are across River Tweed in England.

Ben stopped to collect his thoughts, remembering his father speaking at Shabbat dinner on that fateful day in Gibraltar almost two decades prior.

Evi wanted to say the next part and blurted out, "Your father has to leave tomorrow to help the King."

Ben explained that he must assist the King, as his friend, patron, and Scotland's ruler. He assured the children he would be safe. He would ride with the King's son, the archbishop, to join Lauder in Edinburgh. Fifty bowmen would chaperon them to the cannon brigade in Northumberland.

Blair left her seat to hug her mother as Benno and Alana bombarded their father with question after question. Will he have to fight? When will he be back? Won't there be much killing? What if he dies? Why can't Christians get along with one another? Can he change James' mind?

Again, Ben assured the children that James was a very smart man. The Scottish army numbered well over forty thousand men, at least ten thousand more than the English. Most important, the cannons were situated away from fighting men.

As the broad narratives did not fully mollify the children, Ben tried to relieve their concerns. "Artair and Davis are also going. We will look after one another. I should be back within a fortnight. Benno, you are now responsible for the golf fields."

95

Flodden & Branxton, Northumberland, England
Friday, September 9, 1513

On the heights of Flodden Edge, James and his commanders slept fitfully. Over the last five days their position had been fortified. Despite thousands of men coming down with sickness along with some desertions, James maintained a 7,000-troop advantage.

Following a cold and soggy night daylight couldn't come soon enough for James' army of 33,000 souls. Shortly after first light two scouts were escorted to his command tent. While he chewed on a hunk of brown bread James signaled them to speak. The scouts reported that the English army had mobilized before dawn, moving northward, east of the River Till.

James knew that Thomas Howard, the Earl of Surrey, now age seventy and the trusted commander, first of Henry VII then Henry VIII, was highly intelligent. James fully expected Howard to refuse an assault on Flodden from the south.

James questioned each scout separately to validate troop strength. Over 20,000 were advancing to the north. Even if they divided to cross the River Till in multiple locations, it would still take most the day for Howard to ford the river, march west, and mount an attack.

James dismissed the scouts. He lifted his tankard to sip, thinking *alea iacta est*. The die is cast.

He then summoned his noblemen, Lord Home and the earls of Argyll, Bothwell, Lennox and Montrose. He informed them of Surrey's movement. James posited that they should break camp immediately, reassembling two miles north on Branxton Hill. They agreed. At the meeting's he ordered Home to organize the burning of brush and rubbish to disguise their troop movements.

····◆····

By early afternoon, James was ready to confront Surrey's westward movement towards his position at Branxton. He reviewed the cannon placements. Then he requested his commanders to join him with the cannon brigade leaders, Robert Borthwick, Robert Herwort, and Patrick Paniter. He requested Lauder attend and bring Solley with him.

With two Roberts at the table, James wanted to ensure he was unambiguous. "Herwort, are you ready with the large cannons?"

"We are, Your Grace."

"And Borthwick, are you and Patrick ready with the remainder?"

"We are, Your Grace."

James nodded, "Good. Ben, your advice."

"There is much moisture in the air. There is also a steady wind behind us. Finally, there is our height to consider. Not only will you be firing downward, but we are twice the distance above the level of the sea as we were at Stirling."

Herwort fidgeted with his right hand, making a fist, twisting it, then extending his fingers.

"Mr. Herwort, are we boring you?" challenged James.

"No. Apologies, Your Grace," nodding. "We need to get back to our men."

James turned, with a look that encouraged Ben to continue.

"Your Grace." Turning slightly to address Patrick and the Roberts, "All of the factors I spoke of, when considered together, will cause your ordnance, at the maximum launch angle, to travel an additional forty paces for each one thousand paces of distance."

Paniter, the least experienced, was more concerned with survival than fine tuning his trajectories.

James concluded, "Mr. Solley will stay here. If you need his assistance, send one of your men to fetch him. Alexander," pointing out Lauder, "will bring Solley to your station." Turning to the commanders, he continued, "Our cannons will give your pikemen and archers the best advantage. I expect we will engage the enemy a few hours before sundown. Godspeed to you and your men."

····◆····

Ben continued to review his calculations, more to pass the time. He knew they were correct. Lauder checked on Ben from time to time as the afternoon seemed to crawl along.

As James predicted Ben heard the first explosion in mid-afternoon. Both sides began to exchange fire. The sound was thunderous and continuous. Ben exited the tent to view the action.

Not much later, Lauder jumped off his mount and ran to Ben, panting and short of breath. "A round, twice your fist, ripped right through Herwort's gut. He's dead. Paniter is in a panic. You must come with me now."

They cut through the smoky exhaust, inhaling the pungent black gunpowder odor. Ben met Herwort's empty stare. Ben looked away, unintentionally casting his eyes on intestines snaking from his body. No time to let nausea and chaos best him.

Ben saw the cannon barrel set at seventy-five-degrees. He screamed to be heard above the din, "Mr. Paniter, increase your distance. Lower the cannon barrel."

"Do no such thing," yelled Borthwick, as he strode over from his position at the big guns. "I am in command now. Home's pikemen are engaging. Cease fire."

Ben pleaded to Lauder, "We need to find James immediately. There will be no victor, just death, if the cannons sit idle."

Lauder countered, "He's arrogant, aye. But he made these armaments and should know what to do."

Ben spoke quickly, "Alexander, I am not a soldier. But you know I can see the soil, the men moving on it, and the flight of arrows and cannonballs."

"I suppose you're right. Let's find my mount."

As Lauder led the way, Ben reached out, tugging hard on Lauder's vest, "Stop. Look down."

They could see the English coming off Piper's Hill, meeting the Scots in Home's division at the bottom of Branxton Hill. The marshy bottom, now filled with several days of rain, swallowed them all.

Lauder confirmed, "We have to speak to James." Now totally convinced, Lauder ran full speed to his mount with Ben in tow.

With Ben riding double, gripping Lauder around the waist, they searched for James. No sign of him with the Argyll division, nor the Lennox division. As they worked their way back towards Home's division, they heard men cheering as James marched down the hill to lead his men.

Lauder and Ben had no time to decide what to do next. English longbowmen had punctured the lines. The first wave of arrows fell short. Lauder whipped his mount. They could hear the whistle from hundreds of incoming arrows. The horse accelerated into a gallop as the ordnance reigned down.

Ben felt a sharp pain. He winced as he looked down. An arrow lodged in his calf, trickling blood staining his legging. Lauder also received an arrow to his thigh but was too distracted with their escape to pay heed.

They forded River Tweed near Coldstream, dismounted, took to the ground. They both passed out.

96

EDINBURGH, SCOTLAND
SUNDAY, SEPTEMBER 11, 1513

There was much tumult as Davis escorted Evi into the The Sheep Heid. It was evident the Inn had been converted into a makeshift infirmary. They stood just inside the door, inhaling bodily smells and watching people buzzing around like nesting bees.

On a table to their right were medical supplies. Placed neatly were six bottles of white wine, two jars of honey, squares of clean linen, and one-foot sticks. A man worked behind the table, fashioning probes from linen squares and the smooth wooden sticks. He looked up from his work, "I'm Robert Kynnaird. I was King James' surgeon."

Davis reacted, "Was?"

He stopped his assembly, "I regret to inform you that His Grace has passed."

Evi felt her knees buckle. Davis caught her by the left arm, preventing her from collapsing on the floor. Kynnaird grabbed her right arm. Davis and Kynnaird eased Evi into a chair.

Davis spoke up, "This is Ben Solley's wife."

"Solley?" questioned Kynnaird.

Davis responded with a description, "He has darker skin than most. Brown eyes and hair as dark as coal."

"Aye. The King's barber, John Murray, is attending to him at the minute. Stay seated."

Kynnaird explained Ben's condition and answered Evi's questions, as best he could. Afterward, while she sipped some ale, Davis pulled Kynnaird aside to ask about casualties.

They talked for a few minutes, interrupted when Murray approached. Davis introduced him to Evi, who immediately asked, "How is he?"

"Your husband has been asleep since he was brought here late Friday night. We had to remove the arrowhead from the lower part of his right leg. He has been groaning from time to time. That is a good sign."

Evi raised her hands, lowering her head into them.

Murray continued, making small circles with his right index finger. "The arrows turn as they enter the flesh. With the barbed tip, your husband is fortunate. He may be able to keep his leg. We will show you how to care for his wound. It will take some time to heal."

"May I see him?"

Murray pointed to the steps, "Up, last room."

"Thank you," said Evi, rising from the chair.

Davis nodded in appreciation to Murray and Kynnaird as he helped Evi get back into motion.

Every thirty minutes or so Davis looked in to see Evi, seated stoically at Ben's bedside, her hands enveloping Ben's left hand. As if they were posing for a portrait, neither moved. Davis brought her cured meat and beer. They went untouched.

As dusk approached, before he had to rely on candlelight, Murray entered to tend the wound and instruct Evi at the same time. He undressed it, used some wine to clean it and then re-packed it with clean linen, placing slightly less material in than he removed. Evi paid close attention as she would need to do this morning, mid-day and evening, each time reducing the amount of linen packing.

Not an hour after Murray departed, Davis heard Evi call out loudly. He ran up the steps. Ben had opened his eyes, clearly agitated. Evi squeezed his hand. "Try not to move, my darling. Davis, please fetch him some water."

Evi propped up Ben's head, allowing him to receive the water. Ben tried to speak. Evi gently placed her finger on his lips. "Don't try to say too much right now. You must save your strength and let the learned men save your leg. Do you understand?"

Ben nodded, then whispered, "Lauder saved me."

"We know my love. Davis found you with him and brought you here. Then he came to get me. Benno is looking after the girls. They are safe but worried sick about you."

Ben whispered again, "Lauder?"

Davis turned his head dejectedly from side to side. Ben's eyes watered. Evi wiped the tears from their corners.

Davis spoke softly, "We did not prevail. Our cannons failed us."

Now Ben's head turned violently from side to side.

Evi soothed his face with a damp cloth. Davis continued, "It is no fault of yours, Ben. You know that. We suffered a catastrophic loss. At least one of every four slaughtered."

Ben forced out, "Artair?"

"I have not seen him since the battle began, nor has anyone I have asked."

Evi added, "We have to pray for him."

Ben then asked what Davis and Evi hoped he would not, "James? archbishop?"

Evi looked pleadingly at Davis. He knew Ben, even in his current condition, would know a fable if told one. Davis spoke truthfully, "The surgeon found him and his son at St Paul's in Branxton. Both passed in battle."

With tears streaming down his face, Ben grabbed Evi's hand attempting to pull himself up, trying to raise his voice with surprising volume and urgency. "Home. Now. Please."

Evi matched his tears and gently lowered her head onto his chest whispering, "As soon as we can."

97

ST ANDREWS, SCOTLAND
SUNDAY, SEPTEMBER 25, 1513

Benno walked along the golf field's coastline, leading the pony carrying Ben, whose right leg dangled with his left foot in a stirrup.

A far cry from a typical Sunday with memories of gatherings, socializing, games, and contests following Mass. The fields were deserted today.

They passed the end point, surveying land for future expansion. As they approached the Swilcan Burn, Ben called out to Benno to stop. Ben started a very slow and deliberate dismount.

"Let me help you father."

"Aye. There is a wee bit of pain when I step down with my right leg first. Throwing it over to get on her is easy."

"You are making progress every day. Soon I'll have to shorten your crutch to fashion a cane for you."

"I'll just use a golf club."

"It seems your sense of humor is returning."

"Just in time for me to leave."

Benno helped Ben sit down.

"Father, I know it is the safe action, but..."

Ben cut him off, placing his hand on Benno's shoulder. "Son, I have confidence in you. You can manage the golf fields. You are a skilled coach and a fine club maker. Most importantly, I know you can look after your mother and sisters."

Benno forced a smile. Ben continued, "Your mother is aware of what I am about to tell you. It's time you know. Over the years James helped us grow golf here. We have saved a good amount from his generosity. Your

Mother and I will show you the places we have stored the money."

They sat there for a few minutes, enjoying the intermittent sun and light breeze.

Benno broke the silence, "How long do you think you will be gone?"

"It's hard to foretell. So many of the King's court have been killed. If the infant James is anointed King, then a regent will need to be appointed until he can rule on his own. Many of the powerful people in Scotland, who didn't like the way James governed, are aware that he and I were close. To answer your question, I am hoping I will be back for the next equinox."

Benno fought back his tears and stood. "Let's get you back in the saddle. We don't want to be late for the meal Mother has prepared."

"Let me see you make a few strikes before we head home."

"A few," conceded Benno. "You name the target."

Benno and Ben entered the house. Ben noticed six places set at the table. Kissing Evi he said, "Since I'm leaving tomorrow, I was expecting just family for afternoon dinner. Maybe you are expecting the prophet, Elijah?"

Blair answered innocently, "Mother said we could invite a friend."

"Is that okay?" bellowed a familiar voice from the other room.

Artair and Ben hugged, tears soaking the scruff of their new beards.

They enjoyed a tasty meal of cheese, baked bread with honey, freshly harvested cabbage, and mutton pie. Evi carried the conversation with optimism, lest they be overwhelmed by the sorrow and misery which had swept through the country in the last ten days.

After dinner and another tankard of beer, Artair bade his goodbyes, hugging each member of the Solley family. In turn, he thanked the women for the victuals. He wished Ben safe travels and a hasty return. To Benno, he pledged support for the golf fields.

After the entire family tidied the house, Evi announced, "Your Father and I are going for a bath."

Benno and Alana smiled. Blair blushed.

98

AMSTERDAM, BISHOPRIC OF UTRECHT
THURSDAY, SEPTEMBER 29, 1513

Leaning on his cane, Ben clomped down the ship's ramp. A sailor, following Ben, carried two large sacks. When they stepped onto land, one was dropped on the ground. Ben thanked him as Johan approached.

They embraced quickly. Johan picked up Ben's bag and they moved away from the crowd.

Johan said, "We heard of the tragic events. We're glad you're alive."

"How did you know I was coming?"

"We received a shipment two days ago. One of our men saw a passenger declaration for your ship. I think it's been over five years since you were last here."

"Almost."

"And look at you. Just off the ship, walking on your own."

"It's flat here."

"Becca and the *kinderen*, they are hardly *kinderen* now, await your arrival. We have all heard so much speculation over the last few weeks, we're eager to hear what happened. I am thinking you tell the story one time. Meanwhile, I want to hear about golf."

····◆····

While unpacking, Ben was overcome with fatigue and emotion. He fell asleep. Hard to tell if minutes or hours passed when he heard a gentle tap on the wall. He stirred, inhaling the food smells as they permeated the house. For a moment he thought he was in Gibraltar.

When Ben arrived at the table, he asked Becca if he could recite the Scottish grace over the meal. She agreed and he did.

Along with Johan's parents, who had been invited for dinner, all listened intently as Ben detailed the events, starting with the King's summons to Stirling Castle in July. Every so often Becca enforced a pause so Ben could eat a few bites and sip his drink.

Of course, the adolescents wanted to hear about the fighting. Ben focused on the tactics and maneuvers, rather than the brutality and gore, finishing by observing gravely, "No person, man or woman, should ever have to see what I have seen."

As they lingered over honey cake, Ben excused himself. He returned a few minutes later, book in hand. He explained, "Your mother knows all about this book and how important it was, and is, to me, to her, to us. I gave it to Benno when he reached the age of thirteen."

Ben handed the book to Becca, "He thinks it will be safer here, at least for the time being." She opened a cupboard, placing it on a shelf reserved for books and Johan's business journals, "It will be here for Benno, whenever he wants to reclaim it."

99

AMSTERDAM, THE NETHERLANDS
MANHATTAN, NEW YORK, USA
PONTE VEDRA BEACH, FLORIDA, USA
FRIDAY, MARCH 28, 2003

Friday afternoons tended to be quiet for Rika Kleinhuis. Her infotech clients rarely submitted new requests as they powered down for the weekend. Her urgent work orders were done just after 1:00 p.m.

As much as Rika wanted to turn immediately to her true passion, genealogy, her stomach told her otherwise. She grabbed her purse, closed the office door behind, and descended four flights of steps, exiting the building onto the Leidseplein. She walked twenty meters, entered Broodje van Kootje, and signaled Audri with a hand gesture. He knew what to do.

Two minutes later, Rika exited with her regular order— a coffee and two *broodjes*, sandwiches on small soft buns, one with steak tartare and one with Gouda. She'd settle with Audri on Monday, as she had since she started moonlighting almost ten years ago. As she trudged upstairs to her office, she imagined a day when her only job would be genealogy and Friday lunches would include wine and girlfriends.

She hadn't even caught her breath when her phone rang. Still standing, she listened for a few seconds. She shuffled her desk to locate a piece of paper and a pen while saying, "*Alstublieft.*" Please.

She scribbled madly. She wedged the phone between her chin and shoulder, then sat down while fumbling with her right hand to pop the plastic top off her coffee. She continued to write with her left. The caller's monologue ended before she could complete a sip. She gasped, "Could you spell the names for me?"

Rika could hardly write with her hand shaking so much. She thanked the caller profusely, hung up, sank back in her chair, and uttered, "*Verdommer.*" Damn.

She checked her wristwatch. As much as she wanted to call Sandy, it was six hours earlier in New York. She sent a short email to call her immediately.

The waiting started. Rika would finish her lunch, try to calm herself, and organize her data, though it didn't need it. She practically inhaled the sandwiches while looking at her notepad and circling a few items. She looked at her wristwatch again.

At 1:50 Rika's phone rang.

"Sandra?"

"Hi Rika. I saw your email and thought I'd call you before I left for the office. You found something?"

"We may have found the needle in the haystack."

"Seriously?"

"Let me explain. First of all, after doing genealogy research for a decade, I thought you were crazy when you asked me to post notices in newspapers."

"I suspected as much. What did you end up doing?"

"I was able to make placements in the ten largest Dutch papers last Sunday. The message was simple, "Do you have relatives in Scotland, surname of Solley, going back hundreds of years? Call so on and so forth. I repeated on Monday."

"And?"

"Nothing, as I had expected. So, I made a placement in Thursday's *Het Parool*, which roughly translates as The Watchword. It was first published by the resistance during the war. Frankly, I'm not sure what prompted me to do that. It has a limited circulation and we already had over a million people covered in Amsterdam."

"And you're telling me this because…"

"A woman called me, not even an hour ago. She cares for her elderly father. He reads *Het Parool* first thing every morning."

Now excited, Sandy interrupted, "And they have relatives in Scotland?"

"No, but they have a book."

"A book?"

"Yes, a book. Quite astounding. During a renovation a few years ago, they found some old books in a cabinet which was plastered over, dating back who knows how long. The woman suspected the books were valuable, but her father liked reading them so much she decided to wait until he passed before investigating. The man recognized the name Solley. On the inside cover, handwritten is 'Benno Solley, St Andrews, April 23, 1509'."

"I...I don't know what to say. I'm speechless."

"Sandra. There's more. Please brace yourself."

"Okaaay."

"Below Benno Solley's inscription is written, in a similar but slightly different handwriting 'Ben Solomon, son of Benjamin Solomon, Gibraltar, November 7, 1487'."

Silence.

"Sandra?"

"I'm here," eyes watering, fighting back the tears.

"Are you okay? I assumed you'd be thrilled."

"I am."

"This appears to be authentic but before you get too excited, I'd like to check some census, birth, death and marriage records, if that's agreeable."

"Yes, good idea."

"I will call you by the end of the day, mid-day, your time."

"Thanks, Rika,"

"Goodbye then."

····◆····

After leaving an "I can't wait to see you for lunch" note under Tamara's door, Sandy stepped into a beautiful spring morning in Manhattan.

Her day would no longer be the mellow affair she had anticipated before Rika's news. Her head would be elsewhere as she cleared her final to do list at Columbia— goodbyes, pack a few personal items, attend the last research turnover meeting, close out a few emails, sit with HR for an exit interview, and finally, turn in her electronics devices and access card.

Sandy busied herself, trying to take her mind off Benno, Ben, and Benjamin. At 11:30, her phone rang. Tamara was waiting at the secured doors. The office area was eerily empty as she passed through it to let her in.

They rounded the corner to a chorus of "Surprise" led by her colleagues' co-conspirator, Tamara. They ushered Sandy into a conference room for a going away luncheon of Zabar's sandwiches, hamantaschen with a variety of fillings, popular around the Purim holiday, an assortment of Dr. Brown's drinks, and bottled water.

Sandy was appropriately roasted, from her Maine roots to her boyfriend to her newfound passion for genealogy. She was given an Emory tee-shirt and a Braves cap. As prearranged, everyone at the gathering replaced "you" with "y'all" and "all y'all" when speaking with Sandy.

With twenty people chattering and talking, Sandy didn't hear her phone ring. As people dispersed, Sandy had a moment to look down, discovering a blinking red light. She pressed the voice mail key, placing the phone to her right ear and left hand covering her left ear.

"This is Rika. I sent you an email in case this message does not come through clearly. I found a death record for Rebecca Witte, recorded in Amsterdam, in 1551, age 74. Her maiden name was Solomon. She was born in Gibraltar in 1477."

"Tam, it's my turn to surprise you today," smirked Sandy as she tapped the play button to repeat the message. She handed the phone to Tamara. Tamara listened. They hugged.

Tamara forced a breath out, "It's like you were one of millions of kids playing baseball and now you won the World Series."

"Or the Masters?" said Sandy.

"Or the Masters," repeated Tamara.

"Let me say goodbye to a few more people and we'll see what's up with the guys. They played yesterday afternoon, which means they should've played this morning."

"I'm impressed. Why don't we take your stuff home and try them from there?"

Sandy agreed.

····◆····

As they entered Sandy's apartment, Tamara asked, "Any place you want to put this?"

"Anywhere I won't trip on it. I'll be packing up everything in here soon enough. Let's put on the Golf Channel to see if they're still on the course."

"Now I'm really impressed. I'm going to put my coat in my apartment. Glass of wine?"

"Sure, we'll toast Brian."

Sandy clicked on the television and tuned to the golf coverage. She took off her shoes and pulled her legs up onto the couch. Tamara returned in a minute, two glasses of Chablis in hand. Tamara toasted, "San, what you did is incredible. Cheers."

"Cheers."

After the ads ran, Cameron appeared on screen with an announcer's voice over, "Now the shot of the day, or rather the first round, which finished this morning. Rusty Stephens, on the Par-4 15th. His approach sails over the green, spins back, drips over the lip of the cup for an eagle two."

As the crowd roared, the reply showed Brian giving the camera a thumbs up. The announcer returned, "We agree O.T."

Sandy used her cell phone to call Cameron.

"How was your surprise party?"

"You knew about it?"

"I did."

"I'm here with Tam. Let me put you on speaker. Is Brian with you?"

"Hang on." He screamed, "Yo, O.T.?"

"Where are you guys?"

"In the locker room at Sawgrass."

"You're still there. I thought you'd long gone by now."

"Actually, we got lucky. We played yesterday afternoon and didn't finish due to the crappy weather. So, we finished the first round this morning and went right back out for the second. Tomorrow we only have the third round to play, so... ...Brian's here now."

Tamara piped up, "You were on the shot of the day."

"Nice," said Cameron. "Brian figured it out. I just hit the shot."

"I can't take the credit. I saw Ernie Els do the same thing last year."

"Are you guys by yourselves?" queried Sandy.

"There's no one close by," replied Cameron.

Sandy continued, "Brian, thanks to you, Cameron and I hired a genealogist in Amsterdam just before we left Scotland. She called me early this morning. I'll cut right to the chase. You had a Jewish ancestor, a Sephardic Jew, in Amsterdam. He changed his name from Solomon to Solley in Scotland. His family came from Spain."

"Sandy, that's incredible. What can I say? Thank you."

Cameron weighed in, "Talk about a long shot. Unbelievable."

The call ended a few minutes later. Brian turned to Cameron, "Sandy's amazing."

"I know."

"And now that I know I have some Jewish blood in me, maybe I'll catch a loop with Kendall or Kaye."

"Be careful. They might be Ashkenazi."

Brian smiled. "Good one."

"Do we know our tee time for tomorrow?"

"Not yet. It will be no earlier than noon. I forgot to tell you I got a voicemail about the *beit din* on Monday."

"Who are the rabbis on the panel?"

"Mardesten and Sugarman for sure. I'm not sure about the third."

100

ATLANTA, GEORGIA, USA
WEDNESDAY, APRIL 2, 2003

On this day in years past, Rusty and O.T. participated in the practice round at the Atlanta Classic, in Duluth, Georgia. About fifty miles from his condo, it wasn't quite a home game and not quite an away game. He had always made the cut at the Classic, but never excelled on the weekends, at least to his standards.

A change of pace this year. He'd relax and practice for next week's Masters, starting tomorrow.

About 10:30 Cameron made a left off Mt. Vernon into the Congregation B'nai Torah campus. Sandy reminded him, "First right." He pulled into a small parking area, next to Brian's vehicle.

They walked up a short, inclined, sidewalk passing a small courtyard on their left. They entered the small building appended to the main complex.

Tamara, Brian, and Rabbi Mardesten awaited them. The rabbi spoke, "Good. We're all here pretty much on time. O.T. and Rusty, excuse me, Cameron and Brian, why don't you check in with the receptionist while I give Tamara and Sandy some background? I know you guys haven't forgotten anything I've taught you."

She smiled, putting everyone at ease.

There was no fee. B'nai Torah welcomed non-members to utilize its mikvah. After Cameron and Brian confirmed their donations had been received, they were directed to the changing room.

The women took a seat. The rabbi turned to Sandy. "Apologies if some of this is repetitive for you."

"I can assure you it won't be"

First, Rabbi Ruthie summarized the mikvah's key points from her introduction to Judaism class. She then explained, "A person is totally naked for immersion, free of anything including jewelry and skin care products. The body must be fully underwater, feet not touching the bottom, sort of suspended. There is always a witness, usually of the same gender, so I will listen from the outside with both of you."

The rabbi led Tamara and Sandy down a short hallway, to chairs positioned just outside the mikvah. When the men emerged in bathrobes from the changing room, Rabbi Ruthie gently herded the two couples. "Before we proceed, I'd like to recite a prayer. In ancient times, this would be said at the beginning of a journey. With the traveling y'all have done, physically and more important, spiritually, to bring this moment to fruition, it seemed apropos."

She recited the short wayfarer's prayer, *Tefilat Haderech*. Then, she turned to the men with a rhetorical, "Ready?" She opened the door for Brian and Cameron.

They entered silently, accompanied unobtrusively by a Jewish male attendant. Sunlight glistened from three small windows, located horizontally just under the ceiling line. A white and gray mosaic of tiles descended into the water. The subdued sound of water gently dripping into the pool added to the serenity. A small gallery of spectators could have fit in the mikvah, but here they were.

Brian, normally gregarious, ready with a quip at any time, stood silently. The moment's sanctity enveloped him. He slipped off his robe and handed it to Cameron. He then extended his left hand firmly gripping the railing. He slowly navigated the first two steps into the mild water. Before continuing, he recalled the rabbi's teachings—water in the mikvah is natural, collected in cisterns, as it was at Masada two thousand years before.

As Brian finished stepping in, Cameron noticed him rubbing his eyes, "Everything okay?"

Feeling the moment's full impact, Brian asked, "Cam, would it be okay with you if the others come in?"

"Absolutely, if that's what you want."

Brian just nodded. Cameron opened the door. "Brian would like all of you to witness with me."

The three women stepped inside the mikvah and acknowledged Brian. They clustered just inside the door, instinctively allowing for some level of modesty, though certainly not needed in this moment. With the entrance of required Jewish witnesses the attendant exited quietly.

Slowly and deliberately Brian fully submerged and then stood. He didn't need the printed prayers, poolside in a waterproof frame. From memory he recited the commandment to immerse, first in Hebrew then English. Taking his time, he emerged a second time, reciting the prayer of life for special occasions, the *Shehecheyanu*. Upon his third immersion, Brian recited the declaration of one God, the *Sh'ma*.

Rabbi Ruthie started with the first "*Mazel tov*." Congratulations. The rest followed. She then guided Sandy and Tamara from the room. Brian quickly toweled off and donned his robe, "Thanks bro."

"Amazing," said Cameron as they hugged.

"Sure was," said Brian. "Maybe someday I'll be your witness."

101

ATLANTA & AUGUSTA, GEORGIA, USA
SUNDAY, APRIL 6, 2003

At first light, Sandy rolled over to spoon Cameron. He murmured his approval. Half asleep, half aroused, he whispered halfheartedly, "I need to hit the weights."

"I should go for a run. What time is Brian picking you up?"

"Noon. We're playing with Dad around three."

"Then I guess we can't have a nooner."

"Is there such a thing as a ten'er?"

"If there isn't, there is now. It's a date."

Sandy pecked him on the back of the neck and popped out of bed.

Cameron pulled himself into Brian's SUV.

"Afternoon, boss. Going to be a crazy week. Did you see the dismal forecast?"

"Looks like we may get a repeat of The Players."

"Are Sandy and Tamara coming out in your car?"

"Nguyen will bring 'em over, when we have a better handle on the weather."

"Makes sense."

"It will give her some time to unpack all the stuff she brought from New York."

As they turned onto I-20 East, Cameron called his father. Cameron confirmed their meeting time. Carlton assured him that he had spoken to the starter. There would be no one behind them. This would allow them to try a variety of shots on several holes, particularly six and eight. With these greens protected by a pond and Rae's Creek, they served as a reasonable facsimile of neighboring Amen Corner.

As dusk started to descend around 6:30, they hit their last shots into the 9th green. As they walked to the green, Carlton told the guys, "Mrs. Stephens is working on a nice dinner for us, including you, Brian. But we've got time for a quick drink."

They entered the clubhouse. As they walked into the Men's Grill the few remaining members and staff hanging around this time of the week, greeted them with a low key, "Have a good week. Good luck Rusty."

They sat down at the bar, Cameron flanked by Carlton and Brian. A waiter slid bowls of pretzels and mixed nuts into range. They ordered beers, which were drawn from the tap nearby. The television behind the bar was tuned to the Golf Channel, recapping Ben Crane's first PGA tour victory at the BellSouth Classic a few minutes ago, just as bad weather moved in.

Cameron lifted his mug in a toast, "Dad, thanks for having us out."

"My pleasure. Hope it helps you play the other side of the yard," referring to the bordering Augusta National.

They clinked their mugs and sipped. Carlton continued, "I assume Sandra is coming over at some point."

"She'll come over with Tamara."

"Tamara?"

"She's my girlfriend," said Brian.

Carlton patted him on the shoulder. "Serious?"

"Yes sir."

"Well, congratulations." Carlton lifted his mug, "I'll drink to that too." He took a sip. "Do you mind if I ask you a personal question? You don't have to answer."

"Not at all, Mr. Stephens."

"Is Tamara Jewish?"

"No sir."

"I try not to talk too much about this with Cameron." He placed his hand on Cameron's knee. "But it seems obvious to me, that marrying a Jew makes life unnecessarily difficult."

"You'll have to ask Tamara."

With a blank look on Carlton's face, Cameron jumped in,

"Dad, Brian's Jewish."

"I...I...I... meant no disrespect."

102

AUGUSTA, GEORGIA, USA
MONDAY, APRIL 7, 2003

The early morning crew at The Lookaway Inn was on the ball. Coffee was staged in the lobby at 5:30. No one else was around as Tommy and Carlos prepared to-go cups.

The overnight manager emerged from behind a swinging door, bringing them two small takeout boxes packed with croissants and sweet rolls. He glanced at them then said, "I don't think they let in patrons until eight."

Tommy countered with his best poker face, "We were told if we arrived before six, we could hit a few balls before the pros show up."

An eyeroll was returned as the manager disappeared through the lobby.

Tommy and Carlos chuckled as they exited onto the covered two-story wrap-around porch, replete with ionic columns across the front and sides. They sipped, looking at the teeming rain.

Carlos remarked, "It's supposed to let up, but we can't wait." Handing Tommy his coffee, he managed to zip up his rain jacket while holding his pastries. "I'll get the van. You just make sure you hold on to the rail."

"Okay Mom."

"Just being extra careful. We haven't come this far to have your kids watch other people play."

Tommy acquiesced, returning Carlos' coffee, taking his pastry box and tucking both boxes under his left arm, transferring his own coffee to his left hand. As if seeking bathroom permission, Tommy held up his right hand, "Ready,"

"All you need is a green jacket," yelled Carlos as he bolted across the parking lot.

During the three-mile drive to the course, a gusty wind replaced the rain. The only redeeming part of the day, so far, was the temperature, which held overnight in the mid-sixties.

They weren't sure what to expect at Augusta National. It would likely be buzzing with fans and golfers trying to leverage the morning hours, assuming the weather forecast rang true.

Their goal was simple. Tee off as close to first light as possible. Then they would be deep into the front nine before fans were admitted at 8:00.

As Carlos coasted their rental down Magnolia Lane, they entered some of golf's most hallowed grounds for the first time. The limited visibility diminished the intense emotional response they anticipated.

Security was tight. Carlos dropped off Tommy and headed right to the small car park which accommodated no more than forty vehicles. He offloaded Tommy's clubs and headed into the caddie facility, a comfortable cinder block building with a fresh coat of Drylok paint, Pantone 342, otherwise known as Masters Green.

Tommy, unfamiliar to almost everyone, received a thorough screening. A few minutes after 6:00, he was formally welcomed and directed to the locker room.

He entered, stopped, and scanned the room. Without moving, he inhaled deeply, soaking up the scene with as many senses as possible. It was intimate, emotionally as well as physically, with generous dark wooden lockers, green carpet, and enough space for a few hundred members and seventy-five or so green jacket wannabees. The former champs had their own locker room.

This early in the day, there was a sole locker room attendant. He approached Tommy, "Good morning, Mr. Torres. May I show you to your locker?"

"Thank you. And you are?"

"Ted, at your service."

As Tommy followed, "Do you know all the golfers?"

"Well sir, I've had all winter to prepare. But I did see the article on you in *Sports Illustrated*. I hope you do well sir."

"I appreciate it, Ted."

Tommy got organized, put on his golf shoes, hung up his jacket, hit the men's room, then headed to the driving range. Carlos, decked out in the traditional, caddie-mandatory, white coveralls, handed Tommy a rain jacket. "You're going to need this."

Tommy stretched his legs and arms. Carlos handed him a club with a donut weight on it to continue the warm-up. Tommy was ready to hit some easy shots at first light.

Carlos was right, unfortunately. After just a handful of shots, the rain returned, light and steady. For the practice rounds, Carlos carried two umbrellas. Both were extended as they headed to the 1st tee shortly after 7:00.

For the first hour, Carlos focused Tommy on the terrain. Augusta National was surprisingly hilly. As much as they practiced over the months leading up to this week, there was no substitute for walking the course.

The steady rain gave way to intermittent sprinkles allowing them to hit several shots into the 11th green, play the 12th, and hit tee balls from the 13th.

At 10:30 the heavens opened. They took cover in the trees. Twenty minutes later, with no let up, they trudged back to the clubhouse, avoiding the ponding waters on the course.

At noon, with over an inch of rain, the temperature began to drop. As they headed back to The Lookaway, Carlos put a positive spin on the situation. Very few players had as much time on the course as Tommy did today.

103

AUGUSTA, GEORGIA, USA
TUESDAY, APRIL 8, 2003

Brian attacked his bacon and eggs. "Thanks Mrs. Stephens. Delicious."

"It's real good Mom," echoed Cameron as he buttered a piece of white toast.

"My pleasure. It's going to be cool today, so get your fill."

"Did Dad go to the office already?"

"Yes, he did."

"Pretty early, isn't it?"

"He needed to get some things done so he could get your rental house set up. He imagined you'd want to get as much practice in as you can before the next batch of rain comes in this afternoon."

"Your mom's right. We're supposed to get another inch of rain today, on top of the two yesterday. The course is soaked so I'm afraid it may be mostly range work today. Did you speak with Sandy?"

"Not yet. I'll tell her and Tam to come over tonight or tomorrow morning if they want. The par-3 tournament is likely a go for tomorrow, but it won't be much fun for the families if it's cold and rainy."

The light drizzle subsided as O.T. loaded up the SUV. At 8:15 they eased down Magnolia Lane. With a wave, the security guard approved their passage onto the grounds.

The clubhouse was busy. Rusty said hello to David Duval. While he spoke with David, he made quick hand waves to other familiar faces, including Angel Cabrera, Niclas Fasth, Retief Goosen and his childhood friend, Charles Howell.

As Rusty stepped towards the tall silver coffee urn, with a "DECAF" necklace, he overheard an unfamiliar voice say, "What else can go wrong? I can't believe your flight was canceled. Let me talk to Carlos. I'll call you back."

Rusty turned to see a man in total dejection, slumped in a chair, legs straight out, arms hanging over the side, and head bent back. Stepping towards him, he asked, "Are you Tommy Torres?"

"I am." He snapped up and extended his hand, "You're Rusty Stephens. I'm a big fan."

Rusty responded, "I am a big fan of yours. Nice to meet you. I overheard the end of your call. Anything I can do?"

"I don't think so. My daughter's flight to Atlanta was delayed. She'll miss her connecting flight. My son's coming in from Germany to Atlanta. They were supposed to meet. What a mess."

Rusty responded, "I doubt she'll find a flight, and your son won't be able to reschedule his flight. But I think I can help. My girlfriend and my caddie's girlfriend are being driven here from Atlanta. Hold on."

Rusty punched a number on his cell phone. "Hi Nguyen. Whenever you bring the women out, can you manage to pick up two more people at the airport and bring them with you?"

Rusty muzzled the phone to his chest, he asked Tommy, "Where ya'll staying?"

"At the Lookaway."

"Easy enough."

Rusty pulled the phone back to his ear. "Nguyen, that's great. I am going to give your number to Tommy Torres. He'll call you." Rusty closed his phone.

"I...I...can't thank you enough."

"No big deal." Rusty spotted a pen and scribbled Nguyen's number on a napkin. "Good luck. Hope we're both here on Saturday."

"Amen to that," said Tommy, still in a mild state of disbelief as Rusty disappeared.

104

Augusta, Georgia, USA
Wednesday, April 9, 2003

The rain ended overnight but the miserable trend continued with a steady ten mile per hour wind and a forty-nine-degree temperature reading. The forecast— afternoon showers and the thermometer struggling to break fifty.

Well before sun-up, the Augusta National ground crew mobilized. Top priority— prep the par-3 course then move on to the other 7,000 yards.

At 6:30, Tommy called Carlos' room. They agreed to meet for breakfast in a half hour. Tommy wrote notes for Sonya and Louie, "Relax, sleep in, have fun at the par-3, dress warm, meet ya' for lunch @ 2." He slipped them under their room doors on the way to the lobby.

····◆····

As Carlos prepared Tommy's bag, the Caddie Master gave him explicit instructions. Despite the excellent drainage system at Augusta, including heated pipes beneath the 12th green, the course was saturated with moisture. Carlos needed to ensure his man avoided hitting from soft spots, particularly on the lower areas of the course near the 2nd, 7th, and 11th greens.

Carlos put Tommy through his warm-up drills on the range. He didn't want Tommy to overdo it on the practice green as the greens on course would morph from Jekyll to Hyde as they dried. Even if they couldn't hit many practice shots on the course, Carlos knew they needed to walk it as much as possible.

Lightning was about the only thing that could keep families, wives, and girlfriends from attending the par-3 tournament. Gloves, knit caps and parkas were the order of the day. The players were layered in thermals and sweaters.

Trying to stay warm while waiting for the tournament to begin, Sandy and Tamara walked from the 1st tee area to the 7th green. On the way back, they spotted Sonya and Louie, exhaling into their hands, then rubbing them together.

After bonding during the ride from Atlanta yesterday, they greeted each other with a round of hugs. Two journalists wondered aloud to each other, "Who the heck are these people hugging Rusty Stephens' girlfriend?"

"Sonya and I want to thank Rusty for bringing us over."

Sandy responded, "No need for that but let me introduce you when he gets here." She spotted O.T. and waved to him.

Two minutes later Rusty arrived. For the next five minutes the six Gen X'ers talked and shared a few laughs.

Rusty said to Sonya, "I haven't seen your dad yet."

"He decided not to play in the tournament today. He's on the course prepping for tomorrow."

At 8:15 p.m. Brian's phone vibrated. He looked at the flashing number, then answered, "This is O.T." He listened. Ten seconds later his face crinkled. "No joke?" He listened for another five seconds then clicked off and exhaled. "Holy shit." He called Cameron immediately. The way he answered Brian said, "You already know, don't you?"

At 8:45 Carlos answered his phone, "Hello." Fifteen seconds later, his eyes widened. "*En serio*?" He listened for a few more seconds then closed his phone. "*Que mierda.*" He stood there, contemplating his conversation with Tommy. Less than a minute later his phone chimed. "Hey Tommy. I heard."

With a saturated course and a forecast for rain and highs in the mid-forties, the first round on Thursday was postponed for the first time since 1939. On the plus side, the ground crew could use smelly compounds with impunity to help with water absorption.

105

AUGUSTA, GEORGIA, USA
THURSDAY, APRIL 10, 2003

Carlos tried to sleep in. No such luck. He squinted at the small alarm clock. One light segment was missing from the red numbers, but he was able to decipher a six, one, and three. He fumbled for the switch under the lamp shade and turned it clockwise. Then he propped up a couple pillows, pulled himself up, and found the remote. Ten seconds later he was watching the local CBS affiliate wrapping the hour with the miserable weather forecast.

After a nine-month buildup, Carlos was as eager as anyone to start play. He suppressed his anxiety. He had to manage his man on what would be a long, dreary, day of waiting. Pounding balls with overcast skies, and highs in the mid-forties, was not the answer.

Forty minutes later, Carlos was about to slip a note under Tommy's door. He bent over. There was enough space at the bottom to reveal lights on, so he just knocked.

Tommy opened the door, "You can't sleep either."

"True, but I've got a plan. Louie and Sonya can meet us later. I left 'em notes. Let's get some breakfast, then go to work."

Tommy looked at him quizzically.

Carlos qualified it, "Work inside, but in golf clothes. Meet in the lobby in twenty?"

"Okay, where we gonna eat?"

"Think Kevin Costner, Rene Russo, Cheech Marin."

"Waffle House, really?"

"Exactly. We don't have 'em in California! And there's one two minutes away."

•••◆•••

"Gotta admit," said Tommy between bites. "These are some damn good waffles. Must be the pecans."

Carlos sipped his coffee, edging his plate forward with the other hand, "Take a bite of mine. Awesome with chocolate chips."

"I'm good. So, what's the plan."

"Patience, my man. Next stop is the...". Carlos bobbed his head and quietly sang, "Y-M-C-A."

Tommy laughed, "I guess you're the cop."

"Yep, but I'll pay."

They were out the door in ten minutes. Carlos eased the vehicle right on Georgia Avenue. Backtracking past The Lookaway, they crossed Martintown Road, pulling up to the Family Y in the North Hills strip center.

"You're serious," said Tommy. "I'm not dressed for pumping iron."

"Exactly."

They entered. Carlos identified himself. They were expected and immediately shown to a treadmill reserved for them. Carlos handed Tommy a blindfold, "You're going to walk the course, with a little help from me. Up you go. Put on the shades and hold on."

"Seriously?"

"Bro. You've got to get some exercise, or you'll never sleep tonight. More importantly, you keep telling me you don't know the course like the other guys. I'm going to prove to you that you know it better than anyone else. Augusta is the only course you've been playing, mentally, for nine months. Trust me."

"Okay officer," said Tommy getting into position.

"You're on the first tee. Talk to me."

"Trees on the left, bunker on the right. Hit a cut shot."

"Right," as Carlos started the treadmill at three-and-a-half miles-per-hour. After Tommy made about three hundred steps, he stopped the track.

Without any prompting, Tommy said, "One-fifty to the center, bunker on the left, can't go long."

"I agree," said Carlos as he might on the course. He restarted the treadmill.

Carlos was busy, starting and stopping the treadmill and cross-checking Tommy's recitations with his yardage book.

An hour later, they reached the end of the front nine. "Nice work," said Carlos. "Let's take a short break," as he twisted the top off a Poland Spring and handed it to Tommy.

"Before we start the back nine, let's review the tee shots on the front. Take your time and see the shot in your mind. Carlos started the rapid-fire dialog with, "One?"

"Cut"

"Two?"

"Draw"

"Three?"

"Cut."

"Four?"

"Depends on the pin."

"Five?"

"Straight."

"Six?"

"Straight."

"Seven?"

"Straight"

"Eight?"

"Draw."

"Nine?"

"Draw."

Carlos tweaked the treadmill settings after the simulated 11th hole. As the final seven holes were mostly uphill, he angled the ramp up three degrees and reduced the speed slightly.

An hour later, Carlos had Tommy summarize the back nine tee shots. Again, Carlos started, "Ten?"

"Draw."

"Eleven?"

"Cut."

"Twelve?"

"Hit the ribbon."

"Thirteen?"

"Draw. Amen."

"Amen. Fourteen?"

"Draw."

"Fifteen?"

"Cut."

"Sixteen?"

"Draw."

"Seventeen?"

"Draw around Ike's tree."

"Eighteen?"

"Cut."

"Good. Take off the blinders." Carlos put up his hand for a high five. Tommy removed his blindfold and returned the five. Carlos offered a confidence booster in good humor, "Impressive. At this rate, Sonya or Louie could carry your bag tomorrow."

····◆····

Louie held the door for Sonya as they entered the Sports Center Restaurant on Broad Street. Hardly 11:30, two alchies had already taken perches at the bar, beers in hand, with crumpled bills next to their thin cardboard coasters.

Louie and Sonya immediately noticed the collage of bumper stickers below the large television screen, not yet switched on for the day.

"We're not in Kansas anymore." whispered Sonya. "How did we get here?"

"Carlos talked to a few caddies. Supposed to have the best burgers in town. Look," said Louie, pointing out a US Air Force decal next to the stars and bars. "Quite the pairing."

The bartender appeared and told them to sit wherever they wanted. They took the first high-top, just past the bar area, marked by the floor's transition from brown to white linoleum. The bartender took Sonya's tea and Louie's Coke orders, at which point Louie requested, "Can you turn on the TV to the USA Network? My Dad's playing in The Masters tomorrow."

"No shit?"

"We're saving a spot for him and his caddie."

"Cool."

An hour later, Tommy and Carlos entered. Louie waved them over.

Buffalo wings, chili cheese fries, and four drafts were followed by burgers, onion rings and another round of beers.

They were still nursing their second round at 2:00 p.m. when the Masters logo flashed on the screen. The bartender turned up the volume.

"This is Bill Macatee coming to you from Butler Cabin, at the famed Augusta National Golf Club."

An eruption of hoots and bar banging gave way to quiet.

"Normally, our coverage would start at four, eastern time. With the heavy rains all week, no golf will be played today. We're happy to be with you earlier in the day. Right now, it's cold and dank here in Augusta. However, the forecast for tomorrow and the weekend is picture-perfect. The tournament should be back on schedule Saturday for its normal Sunday conclusion. Later in the program we'll bring you some live interviews. This year's tournament has several interesting angles. For that, let's bring in Armen Keteyian, from our Masters broadcast partners at CBS News in New York. Welcome Armen."

"Good afternoon, Bill. Nice to be with you."

"I understand you and your talented producer, Charlie Bloom, have put together a special piece for us."

"We have. As any serious golf fan knows, more often than not, the Masters comes down to the back nine on Sunday. But odds are, given this year's cast, they'll be no shortage of drama before we get there."

For the next three minutes, Armen's steady voiceover played, while stills and video clips dissolved into one another. He teased the audience with the plots and subplots which would resolve over the next three days.

"The incomparable Tiger Woods will be attempting to win for the third year in a row, a feat, like the man himself, that would be unmatched.

Two lefties, Mike Weir and Phil Mickelson, both vying to be the first southpaw to win at Augusta and claim their first major in the process. If Mike were to break through, he'd be the first Canadian to slip on the green jacket. For Phil, it's his forty-third start in a major and still looking for the elusive first one.

Then there are the hometown boys— Larry Mize, with his improbable chip-in to win on the second playoff hole against Greg Norman six years ago; and the emerging superstars, one-time tour winner, Charles Howell the third, and his childhood friend, Rusty Stephens, a multiple winner having already notched a major.

Of the five amateurs in the field, Ricky Barnes and Hunter Mahan are expected to turn pro this year with Ryan Moore not far behind. We should see a lot of all three in the years ahead.

Finally. Tommy Torres. He received a special invitation to play in this year's tournament. We didn't know much about his journey until we read Hank Hersch's insightful article in *Sports Illustrated* last fall."

As a Magnolia Lane photo closed the segment, Macatee picked up the conversation, "Armen, I know you took an interest in Torres' story."

"I did Bill. I faced some adversity early in my career. While not nearly the depth of challenges Tommy encountered, I can relate to his drive and persistence."

"Great work, Armen. Thank you."

Armen's final response was drowned by the bartender yelling, "Tommy's right there everyone." He pointed at Tommy, walking from behind the bar to his table. "Let's give him a proper sendoff."

The patrons raised their beers and cheered.

106

AUGUSTA, GEORGIA, USA
FRIDAY, APRIL 11, 2003

The tournament organizers had an ambitious objective— complete the first round in time to start the second round at 2:00. Rather than twosomes, all starting on the 1st tee, the golfers were grouped in threes, starting at 7:00 a.m. half from the 10th tee.

The driving range was crowded by sunrise. All slots were occupied. A few players and caddies in the queue sipped coffee while they waited. Everyone looked forward to the sun warming the 45° air.

By 8:45, a crowd had gathered to watch the warm-ups of the final two threesomes— David Duval and Davis Love III to play with Rusty; and Tiger, the defending champ, to play with Ricky Barnes, the US Amateur champ, and Ernie Els.

An hour later, after chipping, sand shots, and putting warm-ups, Tiger's group headed to the 1st tee and Rusty's to the 10th. Rusty remarked to O.T., "Looks like I'm Switzerland today."

"What do you mean?"

"Davis and David."

"So..."

"Big-time Republican and a Democrat, which is pretty rare out here."

"Maybe they know how good you are with your family and Sandy's."

"I hate to think that's a possibility, but stranger things have happened."

"No doubt."

As they stepped onto the 10th tee box, the three golfers and their caddies exchanged handshakes and customary "good luck" greetings. They viewed the steep downhill terrain for their starting hole.

With Eurorail precision, the first group on the course, Tommy Torres, Alexandro Larrazabal, and George Zahringer, finished putting on the 9th hole, and moved to an on-deck position behind Rusty, David, and Davis, waiting for them to hit their opening tee shots.

Rusty hit last. While O.T. replaced the head cover on his driver, he noticed Carlos and Tommy approaching. O.T. flashed a wave to them. Rusty noticed and did the same.

Tommy reciprocated. Carlos responded with a thumbs up.

Duval's caddie looked over. "I don't know any of those guys or their caddies."

"Probably why they got the tee time at seven."

"Who were you waving to?"

"Tommy Torres and his caddie, Carlos. Super nice guys."

"Is that the guy I read about in SI?"

"Yep. Quite a story."

"I can't imagine what he's gone through."

"Me neither. But he's here."

Tamara and Sandy, standing just outside the ropes, saw the non-verbal interaction. They looked back to see Louie and Sonya and waited for them to come over.

Sandy inquired, "How's it going?"

"So far so good. Dad's one over par," said Louie.

"That's great," said Sandy, knowing from her research that any score close to par was an achievement at The Masters.

"Fingers crossed," added Tamara.

Sonya responded, "Thanks. This place is gorgeous but it's hard to enjoy when you're agonizing over every shot."

Sandy said, "It's not easy to get used to. Good luck. We'll see you later." She squeezed Sonya's hand before she and Tamara descended along the edge of the 10th fairway.

Rusty's tee shot on the long, Par-4 10th did not draw as he had rehearsed. His ball rolled into the rough with two-hundred remaining to the pin. His approach shot missed the green.

"Good miss," said O.T.

Love's and Duval's shots came to rest on the putting surface. Rusty's chip stopped inches from the hole. He tapped in for a par. He picked his ball from the cup and walked to the green's perimeter. Curious, he looked back to see where Torres' drive came to rest.

From the 11th fairway, the entrance to Amen Corner, Love hit a perfect draw, leaving him a short putt. Duval found the water guarding the green. Rusty bailed out to the right in an abundance of caution. Love birdied, Duval bogeyed, and Rusty was able to get up and down for a par. As they walked the short distance back to the 12th tee, Rusty turned to watch Torres' approach the 11th.

Then Rusty missed the green, this time slightly to the left. The par-3 12th has ruined many great rounds, so again, a good miss. After Rusty's chip, he was able to make his third consecutive one-putt.

Rusty tried to sneak a peek at Torres' putt on the 11th green. O.T. stopped, letting Love, Duval, and their caddies lead the way to the 13th tee.

As if caught with his hand in the proverbial cookie jar, Rusty turned to O.T., "What?"

"Three missed greens."

"Three pars."

"You can scramble for a few holes but not eighteen. I know you want Tommy to do well. So do I. Make you a deal. Focus on your game and I'll get you a full update at the turn."

"Deal."

Rusty played the next six holes more routinely, albeit with a three-putt, two drives in the rough, a recovery shot from the pine straw, and a one-putt. Along the way O.T. walked over to the gallery and asked Tamara to get an update from Carlos.

Rusty made the turn to his 10th hole, the 1st hole on the course, at one under par. O.T. was pleased to tell his man that Torres completed his first round at two over par. Rusty remarked, "Now the tough part. Waiting around."

Following the typical tournament format, early starters in round one played later in round two, and those out later in round one, played earlier in round two. Late then early, Rusty and O.T. would have a short wait while Tommy and Carlos would have several hours between rounds, likely not finishing before darkness stops play.

Back on the course, into his second round, Rusty sank his putt on the tenth. Sandy suggested to Tamara, "Why don't we get something to eat and find a spot to hang where we can watch Amen Corner?"

"Sounds good."

"You sure I can't convince you to try the pimento cheese sandwich? I did some research."

"No doubt," said a smiling Tamara. "And I suppose you have to tell me all about it."

"Only because Cameron and I had some when we visited Aiken last fall. During breakfast at the hotel, the maître d' brought a curmudgeon by the table. It was Nick Rangos, who's been making his secret Masters concoction for years. Frankly, it's better on crackers than white bread."

"I'm sticking with a ham sandwich."

They approached the concession stand, hidden in woods between the 11th, 13th, and 14th fairways.

Tamara plunked down three singles for the two sandwiches. She opened her sandwich and pumped the one-gallon French's mustard tub twice.

They headed downhill. A patron on the end of the second row, in the bleachers behind the 12th, recognized Sandy. He scooted over enough to allow the women to wedge in.

With the pin slightly right of center on the 12th green, O.T. said to Rusty, "Fifty-one to cover." This told Rusty he needed 151-yards to carry the trap guarding the front of the putting surface. With a slightly helping wind, he handed Rusty his pitching wedge. Then he touched his right index finger to his thumb, fashioning a "P" and placed it behind his back for media consumption.

As Rusty's shot arched skyward, the patrons had a better view than he and O.T. The gallery confirmed its accuracy, erupting in cheers. The decibel level rose as the shot descended, landed on the green and headed directly at the hole. Then a collective moan. O.T. gave him a high five, "You can kick that one in. Nice shot."

Rusty took the momentum forward, hitting the 13th in two, then two-putting for a birdie. After a routine par on the 14th, Rusty's next tee shot found the rough. O.T. did not have to convince him to layup on the par-5 15th. He parred in, finishing the day, and thirty-six holes at even par, tied for fifth.

Rusty wasted no time shaking hands with Duval, Love, and the caddies. Usually chill after a good day, O.T. noticed Rusty moving to the scoring area with purpose, stopping only a moment to squeeze Tamara's arm and hug Sandy.

O.T. came over and said to the girls, "Everything okay?"

"Seems okay. Why?" asked Sandy.

"I usually ask him if he wants to putt a few or hit the range, but he just took off."

·••◆••·

O.T. found Rusty seated, glued to the broadcast. "How's he doing?" meaning Tommy Torres.

Cameron didn't turn his head, "Four over."

"Where's the cut?"

"Going to be four or five over."

Sandy approached and placed her hand on his shoulder. "Cam, we all feel for Tommy and what he's been through. And we're all rooting for him, but we may not know until tomorrow morning. Nguyen picked up Italian from Luigi's. Your mom says you love it."

Cameron tilted his head up. "Luvya. Be there in a minute," as he turned back to the telecast for a last look.

107

AUGUSTA, GEORGIA, USA

SATURDAY, APRIL 12, 2003

A few minutes before 9:00 a.m. the sixteen golfers forced off the course by darkness the night before, including Torres, resumed their second round. Tommy located his ball marker on the 17th green and proceeded to hole a long birdie putt.

Carlos quipped, "Nice to think about a putt for twelve hours and then watch it drain."

"I aim to please."

"Keep doin' it."

And he did, finishing strong with another birdie on the 18th.

The cut was official at 11:00. The pin placements were then updated for the next round. At noon, moving day was ready to start in earnest with fifty-one players qualified at five over par or better. Since the normal start time, 10:00 a.m., had long passed, the tees would be split with some golfers, including Tiger, starting on the back nine.

At two shots over par, Tommy Torres was right in the middle of the pack. Carlos rationalized *less pressure than top or bottom*. However, today the press would be making up for lost time with the emerging Cinderella story of Tommy Torres.

The CBS production crew prepared for a busy day. The Masters was unlike any other tournament in pressure and pacing, with few commercial interruptions. This year there would be no ads due to Martha Burk, a women's rights activist, protesting the lack of female membership.

A star-studded CBS announcing team led by Jim Nance, the network's anchor since 1989, prepared for the weekend coverage. Nance was supported with familiar names like Clampett, Enberg, Feherty, Kostis, Lunquist, Oosterhuis, and Wadkins.

As always, the course was perfected for television and those fortunate enough to witness in person. The gardeners had outdone themselves, manicuring the flowers around each green. Additional white quartz topped off the bunkers, raked smooth and pebble-free. Organic color was added to the ponds. The grounds crew walked around, armed with cans of green, Krylon spray paint, ready to cover any offensive spots.

The order of play for Saturday was established from worst scores to lowest scores based on the preceding thirty-six holes. Tommy, at two over, was slotted at 1:30 with Jeff Maggert, who finished third at The PGA Championship in 2002.

Twenty minutes later Rusty would share the 1st tee with Paul Lawrie, from Scotland, perhaps best known for winning The Open Championship in 1999 by sneaking into a playoff with Jean van de Velde, who squandered a three-stroke lead on the 18th hole.

Following them would be Ricky Barnes and Phil Michelson, then Brad Faxon and José-Maria Olazábal, and the final pairing of Mike Weir and Darren Clarke.

The broadcast crew, under the steady hand of coordinating producer Lance Barrow, worked feverishly to further flesh out the stories Keteyian reported during the rain-out on Thursday.

Barrow ensured his team was ready should life imitate art, specifically the 1996 box office hit, *Tin Cup*, starring Kevin Costner as the fictional golfer, and improbable hero, Roy McAvoy. Barrow had more than a passing interest, having played the lead producer role in the film.

····◆····

The checkout line moved quickly in the merchandise tent. As they waited to buy hats, Sandy and Tamara watched the broadcast, reading the closed captioning on the monitors dangling above the cash registers.

...TO RECAP. IDEAL WEATHER. CLEAR SKIES. EXCELLENT FORECAST. THE TEMPERATURE TOPPED 70 THIS MORNING FOR THE FIRST TIME ALL WEEK. NICE FOR THE NEXT 2 GUYS ON THE TEE, JEFF MAGGERT, RAISED IN TEXAS & TOMMY TORRES, FROM SOUTHERN CALIFORNIA. THEY ARE JUST ABOUT READY TO START THEIR ROUNDS. MAGGERT IS A 2 TIME WINNER ON THE PGA TOUR. OVER THE LAST 15 YEARS, HE'S ALSO WON IN ASIA AND THE HOGAN TOUR. TORRES IS LOOKING FOR HIS 1ST

WIN. HIS LAST START IN A PGA EVENT WAS OVER A DECADE AGO. IF THIS IMPROBABLE RUN PROPELS HIM TO VICTORY, HE WOULD BE THE SECOND OLDEST TO WIN THE GREEN JACKET AFTER JACK NICKLAUS. IT LOOKS LIKE JEFF HAS THE HONORS...

Neither Maggert nor Torres seemed to be bothered by first-shot jitters, sending their drives down the fairway's left side.

As they walked off the tee, Carlos covered the driver, replacing it in Tommy's bag. "Good start. Enjoy it buddy."

Tamara and Sandy wore their purchases. When they exited the tent, they helped each other thread their ponytails through the back of their hats. Sunglasses completed their girl-next-door appeal.

"You're ready," said Tamara.

"Thanks. You too. I think Tommy's two groups ahead. We'll look for Sonya and Louie at the left corner of the grandstand on twelve."

"Sounds good." They headed to the 1st tee. As much as they tried to blend in, several patrons recognized Rusty's girlfriend, and then wondered, stereotypically, if Tamara was in Tiger's entourage. As they approached the tee area, they ran into Carlton and Christina Stephens, also recognizable, having been photographed with Rusty from time to time.

While waiting for Rusty and Paul Lawrie to arrive at the 1st tee, Christina touched Sandy sympathetically on the arm, "How's your mom doing?"

"Okay. Thanks for asking. They should be here tomorrow."

"That would be lovely," replied Christina.

Carlton offered, "If there's anything I can do, let me know."

"Thanks, I will."

Rusty and O.T. arrived at the 1st tee box ignoring nearby family and friends, as they should.

Watching Rusty and O.T. tackle the first two holes informed Sandy just how different today would be. It wasn't the obvious...the drying course, the warmer air, half the golfers eliminated, and playing only eighteen holes. Sandy could only relate to her teenage years alpine ski racing at Sugarloaf. Friday felt like she was watching a long, methodical, relatively safe, slalom. Today felt like a downhill, where intensity, aggression, and patience had to be precisely mixed at high speed.

Rusty played methodically. He and O.T. started every shot with the acceptable target area. That guided their analysis of wind strength and direction, turf condition, club selection, shot shape, and flight distance. Only then would Rusty initiate his pre-shot routine. While this was their standard operating procedure, Augusta National required heightened attention. The greens are small and fast with subtle breaks. And the fairways undulate with significant elevation changes.

When Rusty and Paul walked to their drives on eleven, Sandy and Tamara kept on walking towards Amen Corner. Fifty paces later, they spotted Louie. His dad and Maggert had already hit their tee shots on twelve.

Tamara asked, "How's he doing?"

"Rock solid, knock-on wood," as he tapped on the bleachers. "They seem to be feeding off each another. Dad's three under for the day so far, and Jeff's two under.

"That's fantastic," continued Sandy. "Where's Sonya?"

"Went to get something to hold us over 'til dinner. How's Rusty doing?"

Tamara offered, "Pretty good. I don't know who's more nervous, Sandy or me."

"Tell me about it," said Louie.

Sonya returned quietly, almost tiptoeing as Ernie Els and Hunter Mahan were now on the 12th tee about to hit.

Meanwhile, Barrow's entire broadcast team flexed. It always did, seamlessly to the public, as moving day evolved. The interview and spot checklist for post-round interviews now included Maggert, Stephens, Torres, Weir, and as always, Woods and Mickelson.

At 6:15, Torres drained his birdie putt on the 18th. Maggert followed suit. They shook hands. "Jeff. Nice meeting you. Great finish."

"You too Tommy. A real pleasure."

"Thanks."

"Let's get the cards in. I'm starved."

"Me too."

Tommy gave Sonya and Louie a quick hug, then proceeded to the scoring tent with Maggert. They reviewed each other's cards, then checked their own scores carefully, tallying them three different ways. They signed.

Carlos found the kids and worked on dinner plans as he knew Tommy would be snared by the press.

"Great play today, Tommy. When you received the invitation to play here, could you ever imagine you would be in the clubhouse tied for the lead with Jeff at five under?"

"I've always been confident that I had a chance to make the weekend, but this is unreal."

"By now, most people know you haven't played much competitive golf in recent years. To what do you attribute your performance?"

"I have to thank my caddie and my kids. Well, they're not really kids anymore. They kept me focused. This may sound strange, but this is the only course I've thought about over the last nine months."

"You had to finish your second round this morning. Are you exhausted?"

"Finishing with two birdies early this morning got me going. But yes, I'm tired."

"Good luck tomorrow. Try to get some rest."

Tommy went back to find Sonya and Louie, who were now clustered with Sandy and Tamara around the 18th green to watch Lawrie and Stephens finish.

At 6:40, Paul lagged a thirty-foot putt which eased by the rim of the cup. Rusty had a similar line, ten feet closer, and found the bottom of the cup for a birdie and the solo lead. He smiled at Paul. "Thanks for the teach."

"Great round Rusty. Good luck tomorrow."

After Paul and Rusty signed their cards, Lawrie was pulled aside by the BBC and Rusty was asked a few questions by the CBS team.

"Excellent play today, Rusty. How does it feel to be in the lead right now?"

"I had a good day, no doubt. But there are great golfers still on the course and then there's tomorrow. The course gets harder every day."

"You're known as a long hitter. Does that help or hurt you here?"

"It's all about placement and accuracy. Tiger is long and when he's accurate, he's tough to beat. But look at Mike and Jeff and Tommy. They aren't the longest off the tee but they're making shots."

"What's it going to take to win your first Green Jacket tomorrow?"

At 8:30, Sonya's cell phone rang. She quickly put down the chicken leg on her plate, licked her fingers, and answered, "This is Sonya."

"Hi. It's Sandy." She heard the chewing, "Sorry, Am I interrupting your dinner?"

"No problem. Did Rusty end up in the lead?"

"He did. Can I ask you a quick question?"

"Sure."

"Who holed out first on eighteen, your dad or Jeff Maggert?"

"Dad."

"Cool. He's playing in the last group with Rusty tomorrow."

108

AUGUSTA, GEORGIA, USA
SUNDAY, APRIL 13, 2003

Carlos pulled himself up in bed, picked up the phone, tapped the 'O' key, and asked to be connected to Tommy's room.

A groggy Tommy answered, "What time is it?"

"8:00, I woke you," said an apologetic Carlos.

"No problem. I didn't set an alarm."

"How the hell did you sleep?"

"Everyone says you can't sleep on a lead. I'm one back, so I slept."

"You're a better man than I. Meet for breakfast at 9:00?"

"Yep."

Louie waited until 8:30, using his foot to knock on Sonya's door.

"Come in."

He stacked the two cups, secured them with his chin, and entered. "I brought you some coffee. Looks like you're way ahead of me."

"No. Yes. Good. I need another. Thanks." She peeled back the plastic tab and sipped. "I forgot to ask you where you got the chicken yesterday? It was fantastic."

"I'm glad you didn't ask me last night. I didn't want to take a chance on upsetting you or Papi."

"Really? Tell me."

"A place called Wifesaver."

Her eyes moistened. "Maybe Mom's with us."

····◆····

Herman asked Beth, "How are you feeling?"

"Maybe Sally and you should meet Sandy, and I'll come over later."

"Too long a day for you?"

"I don't want to be a bother."

"It's no bother. I don't need to walk around a lot. We can park ourselves by the 18th and have a nice day."

Beth's face showed doubt.

Herman speculated, "It's your cane, isn't it?"

"Well..."

"That's why Sally brought a ski pole for you. The course is hillier than it looks on TV. There'll be plenty of people with walking sticks."

Beth acquiesced. "Well, okay."

····◆····

As she dug her spoon's edge into a cantaloupe wedge, Christina broke the silence with Carlton, "Pretty big day for our son."

"Magnified because he grew up here. Don't worry. He's in good hands."

"Brian?"

"He's excellent. They make as good a team as any out there. Why are you asking about this?"

"I don't know. Maybe because he's playing with Tommy Torres."

Carlton let that hang for a second. "So?"

"I like it when Rusty's the underdog."

"These days, he's only the underdog if he's playing Tiger."

"I suppose you're right."

····◆····

"Did Cameron sleep?" asked Tamara, as Sandy entered the kitchen to help herself to coffee.

"I made sure he did," answered Sandy trying to conceal the grin on her face. "Did Brian sleep?"

Tamara repeated with a hint of sarcasm, "I made sure he did," then added, "What time do you want to head over?"

"I told Nguyen about noon, but he has to shuttle Carlton and Christina, and my family, so we'll play it by ear. The guys don't tee off until 2:40, so we're in good shape. We'll take Sally with us."

····◆····

The precision telecast began on cue with Tiger's opening shot. Then Nance continued, as expected, with another chapter in the Woods saga. "Tiger made an eight-foot putt Saturday morning on the last hole of his second round to make the cut. He then lived up to moving day, passing thirty-five players to begin the last round only a few shots back."

For the next minute, clips of the leaders were accompanied by a cut from Bryan Adams' song, "Here I Am." Nance's voiceovers resumed with ten-second vignettes on the top six leaders. This was followed by the instrumental version of Dave Loggins' Master's theme. The tournament logo dissolved into a sun-drenched shot of the 13th green, with pink and white azaleas in full display, on the aptly named hole, Azalea.

Barrow's team had successfully amped up millions of golf fans around the world.

There was a sizable crowd surrounding the 1st tee, as security guards escorted Rusty and Tommy into the arena.

"Good luck Tommy."

"You too Rusty."

They shook hands. "One of us is going to walk off wearing a green jacket."

"Agreed."

Rusty centered his ball midway between the six-inch hickory tee-markers. Soaking up the moment, Carlos glanced at Tommy, as they listened to the announcement, "Fore please, Rusty Stephens on the tee."

Carlos noticed Tommy's face drain with an unnatural grimace. Something was off. Carlos quickly moved the towel from his shoulder draping it across the top of the upright golf bag, pushing it down, making a depression, in case Tommy vomited. As he wretched, Carlos whispered urgently, "Lean over and let it out man. Hey O.T., little bit a help?"

O.T., only two steps away from Carlos, turned to them and stepped in to add cover. Rusty noticed and re-teed to distract the crowd. Fifteen seconds later, Carlos gave Louie and Sonya a thumbs up.

Rusty's tee ball drew just enough to skirt the fairway bunker on the right. Tommy was forty yards shorter, in good position on the left. The crowd dispersed. In all the excitement, no one noticed the towel Carlos left behind with Tommy's lunch.

Rusty and Tommy walked off the tee together, with caddies, cameramen, and scorers in their wake.

"Excellent timing," said Rusty.

"Yeh, right."

"Seriously, been there, done that. Much better before you start playing."

"Thanks," and upping his volume, turning slightly, "Thanks O.T."

The 1st green was indicative of the challenge ahead. Short approaches roll back off the surface. If you're long, your putt accelerates downhill over a ledge. They were both happy to walk off with pars.

Rusty bombed a drive on two, managed to get on the green in two but had to settle for a three-putt par. Tommy laid up to a good distance for his third shot, a wedge. He just missed his birdie putt.

Carlos and O.T. knew anything could happen on this course and it was happening all around them. Mickelson had to take a penalty drop on the 2nd hole, hit his third shot barely making the green and dropped a seventy-footer for a birdie. Meanwhile, Tiger took a double-bogey on the drivable par-4 3rd. A few minutes after that, Maggert's fairway bunker shot hit the lip and rebounded into him for a two-shot penalty. Both caddies also knew better than convey too much about the competitors' travails. Keep their guys focused on business.

Tommy and Rusty both managed pars on the par-4 3rd, and the par-3 4th. Rusty scrambled for a par at the 5th, a 500-yard par-4. Tommy could not get up and down for his par and had to settle for a two-putt bogey.

On the par-3 6th, Rusty fired his ball past the hole with enough backspin to bring it within two feet of the cup. "Nice," said Tommy.

With his 5-iron Tommy launched on the same trajectory as Rusty. The decibel level rose as the ball hit the green and gently released dripping into the cup without touching the flagstick. Tommy recorded the first hole-in-one on the 6th in over thirty years. The roar could be heard over the entire property.

Sonya and Louie held each other, jumping up and down. Tamara and Sandy joined in. The golfers walked off the green, smiling, with high fives all around. Rusty moved to seven under par with his birdie and Tommy gained two shots with his ace.

Tommy's nausea was a distant memory. Waiting a moment for the group in front, Tommy soaked up the sunshine and the warmth, with the temperature closing in on eighty. Carlos leaned over, "You enjoyed it. Now forget it. What's the most important shot in golf?"

"The next one. Say no more."

Tommy and Rusty were tied at seven under par as they climbed to the 12th tee box.

Carlos had been informed of Maggert's eight on the 12th. He'd happily take a bogey from Tommy rather than anything higher on what many call the greatest par-3 in golf.

Tommy did give up a shot with a three putt, recovering nicely with a birdie on the par-5 13th. Rusty had to settle for a par on thirteen after his drive was stymied by a tree in the pine straw.

It was Herman's turn to leave Beth at the 18th green while he used the facilities and grabbed a drink. He stopped to read the closed captioning on the monitor in the concession area.

IT CERTAINLY LOOKS LIKE THE TOURNAMENT ORGANIZERS WILL NEED THEIR TAILOR TO CRAFT A NEW GREEN JACKET. TIGER WILL BE SLIPPING IT ON A NEW CHAMPION. WILL IT BE LEN MATTIACE IN HIS FIRST MASTERS APPEARANCE AS A PRO? OR MIKE WEIR, THE PRIDE OF CANADA? OR RUSTY STEPHENS, A MAJOR WINNER TRYING TO GET IT DONE IN HIS OWN BACKYARD? OR COULD IT BE TOMMY TORRES, WHO'S PERSEVERED THROUGH SO MANY PERSONAL CHALLENGES?

Rusty and Tommy couldn't help but view the scoreboard after they both scrambled for par. Len Mattiace, finished at seven under par.

Rusty bombed a drive down the fairway on the par-5 15th. No doubt he would try for the green on his second shot. Tommy landed in the rough, so he would lay up to tackle the water fronting the green with his third shot. They waited and watched Mike Weir birdied the hole, creating a four-way tie for the lead.

Rusty cleared the pond, landing his second shot safely near the back of the green. Tommy pitched on fifteen feet from the pin. Rusty lagged his putt close to the hole. Tommy drained his putt. There were no easy putts at Augusta, but Rusty made his three-footer look routine. They walked off the green tied at eight under.

They watched Weir miss his birdie putt on the par-3 16th. Rusty repeated his performance from the 6th hole, hitting his drive perfectly, allowing the ball to trickle downhill towards the hole. Tommy followed suit. As his ball began its slow shimmy towards the hole, the patrons screamed. Would they witness a player making two aces in the same round at Augusta? Almost.

Rusty missed his birdie putt. Tommy made his, earning the honors as he moved to seventeen in sole possession of the lead.

Tommy then made his worst swing of the day. His drive hit a branch on the Eisenhower tree and dropped straight down. Rusty powered a draw up the right side into perfect position.

Tommy chipped back into the fairway, coming to rest ten yards behind

Rusty's drive. Tommy landed his third shot on the green, Rusty his second. They both holed in two putts, leaving them tied for the lead at eight under par.

The honors reverted to Rusty for the 18th. His drive leaked slightly to the right, just in the rough, leaving him a challenging approach shot to the green. Tommy conquered his nerves and hit a solid shot, landing about 200-yards from the pin.

They waited for Maggert and Weir to finish and clear the green. Weir finished in a tie with Mattiace at seven under par.

Given his lie, Rusty hit a solid shot onto the green, leaving him a forty-foot putt up a ridge running across the green. Tommy's shot came to rest about twenty feet left of the hole.

The patrons were on their feet, clapping. The guys strode up the fairway side by side, putters in their left hands, lightly pinching the brims of their hats with their right thumbs and index fingers. As the clapping morphed into cheering, louder and louder, they took off their hats, and waved them at the crowd.

At the front of the gallery stood Sandy, with Sally and Tamara by her side. Herman and Beth stood behind them with Carlton and Christina. Next to them stood Louie and Sonya. Between the nerves and rapidly cooling temperatures, they all struggled to remain still.

The savvy golf crowd did not need the volunteer workers to quiet them. The ear-piercing din gave way to dead silence.

Rusty studied his putt, calling in O.T. to take a look. He picked up his coin from behind his ball and didn't take long to stroke it. It crested the ridge but ran out of steam five and half feet from the hole.

Tommy, now furthest away from the hole, tried to calm his nerves while he and Carlos surveyed a putt to win the tournament. They talked for a few seconds before Tommy replaced the ball and picked up his mark and took one last look at the line. He pulled the putter back and released it smoothly. The putt started on the target line but just missed the cup, coming to rest inches away. The patrons moaned, as Tommy tapped in to complete his par.

Rusty took more time than usual, studying his short putt on the same line as Tommy's prior attempt. He needed to drain it to force a playoff. Finally, he settled over it. He made a beautiful stroke, but it too just missed on the high side. He quickly tapped in.

Carlos hugged Tommy, "You did it."

"We did it," said a raspy Tommy, gasping for air.

Rusty and O.T. separated from their embrace at which point the caddies hugged and patted each other on the back.

Rusty and Tommy embraced. Tears dripped from both of their faces. Tommy spoke first into Rusty's ear, "You'll be with me at the Champion's dinner someday."

"I know. Congrats man. You deserve it."

"So do you."

They eased back from one another to see the hugging among Rusty's parents, Sandy's sister and parents, the Torres children and Tamara. A target rich environment for the media.

Balanced on the top of a stepladder within the roped off walkway, Jim Drake aimed his Canon and captured Tommy and Rusty in the same frame, both waving their hats at the gallery. The clapping continued non-stop as they headed off the green taking turns patting each other on the back.

Cameras surrounded Sonya and Louie, clicking as they embraced their father, faces already sopping wet.

Several photographers turned towards Sandy and Rusty. Following a brief kiss, they hugged. Sandy whispered, "Should I be sorry, or did you miss the putt on purpose?"

Cameron pulled back slightly, looking her in the eyes intently. Then he broke into a smile. "I love you."

"I love you too Cameron, Cam, Rusty, or maybe I should just call you Maimonides or Rambam."

EPILOGUE

ATLANTA, GEORGIA, USA
EIGHT AND A HALF YEARS LATER
SATURDAY DECEMBER 24, 2011

The Sills house was quiet as 2:00 p.m. approached. Tamara and Sandy steered clear of the two installers working quietly, now checking the humidity controls and closures on the Plexiglas case. Sandy retrieved three small containers of hand-wipes, drying cloths, and thin white cotton gloves from the Staples bag. She would stash them on the shelf underneath the case.

Tamara asked, "Did you have any problems getting everyone to vanish for the afternoon?"

"None whatsoever. Who doesn't like pizza?"

"As they say, 'Everybody loves Everybody's'. The Morehouse guys used to take us over there once in a while."

"Sounds sacrilegious, taking a Spelman girl to an Emory hangout," jabbed Sandy.

"Speaking of Emory, Lars and the team at the Museum were incredibly helpful. Thanks for the referral, San."

"Glad it worked out. What time is Garda getting here?"

"Actually, they're coming twice. Someone should be here any minute to test the monitoring. Then an armored vehicle will make the delivery about three."

"Perfect. What about Lloyd?"

"Lloyd?"

"Lloyd's of London."

"Ha Ha," said Tamara, playing along. "He got me the insurance."

When the installers started packing their tools, Tamara asked them if they could slide the Christmas Tree a few feet over to mask the case. They willingly obliged, after which Sandy handed them a generous tip. She saw the expression on Tamara's face. "Just part of Cam's gift to Brian."

About ten minutes later, the Garda consultant arrived in nondescript slacks and a corporate shirt, neutralizing the redhead's thirty-something femininity. She looked at the configuration then sent a message on the pager she had detached from her belt. She then made a call to confirm the delivery was on its way.

Two uniformed armed guards, complete with black striping on gray pants, arrived a few minutes later. A burly man carried the delicate package. His slim colleague followed, her sidearm at the ready.

····◆····

A second after the tumblers clicked, the Sills' and Stephens' seven-year-olds pushed through the front door and darted across the foyer.

Tamara called out, "Benny, slow down."

Sandy echoed, "You too Beth."

Benny yelped, "Mom, Uncle Cam bought me a monkey at the zoo."

"And I got a tiger," added Beth, shaking her stuffed creature at Sandy.

When Beth heard Jingle Bell Rock on the living room speakers she said to her mother, "Can you ask Aunt Tam to play Alvin and the Chipmunks?"

"In a minute," said Sandy. "She's getting your dad and Uncle Brian something to drink." The kids took off for Benny's room. Alvin was a fleeting thought. Video games were far more important.

Tamara entered the den, cups in hand. "Looks like a good time was had by all. You guys must be exhausted. Ready for some eggnog?"

"Thanks sweetheart," said Brian.

Cameron took a sip, "Delicious, thanks Tam."

"You're welcome. By the way, Carlos called to wish us a Happy Holiday. Said he'll call back later when he gets his crew over to the Torres' for Christmas dinner."

Brian and Cameron settled onto the den couch. Brian picked up the remote, "49ers-Seahawks or Eagles-Cowboys?"

Cameron answered, "Let's start with Eagles and Cowboys. I met Jeff Lurie a few years ago in Maine. He's trying. Maybe it's the Eagles' year."

At halftime, Sandy and Tamara came into the den.

"Nice Christmas Tree, Tam," said Sandy in an exaggerated tone.

Responding even louder Tamara replied, "Even nicer after this afternoon, thanks to you and Cam."

Cameron played along, “The difference between the time I saw it earlier today and now is astounding.”

“But it’s not really the tree, is it Cam?” said Tamara.

Finally, Brian said, “What the F are you guys talking about?”

Cameron stood up, “Ladies. Shall we?” They stood. “You didn’t notice anything suspicious near the tree. Check it out.”

Brian stood up and followed them behind the tree to the den’s corner. Cameron nudged the tree towards the center, revealing the high-end display case.

“What the...?,”exclaimed Brian. He could see the book, obviously of another era.

Cameron turned to Sandy. “You wanna start?”

“Do you remember when Tam and I first called you and Cam a week after we got back from Scotland back in 2003?”

“Who could forget.”

“And we told you about your Jewish relatives that had lived in Amsterdam?”

“Of course.”

Sandy continued, “We only found out because of a book that we located. It was given to your ancestor, Benno by his father, Ben. Ben’s father, Benjamin, gave it to Ben when they lived in Spain. I tracked it for years. When it came up for auction last month, we had Tamara go to New York and get it.”

“Happy Hanukkah buddy,” said Cameron.

Brian stared into the case for what seemed like an eternity.

Cameron continued, “I think he’s speechless.”

Tamara chimed in, “Now that’s a first.”

Brian uttered, “Oh my God. This is beyond anything.” With watery eyes and his head shaking, he turned, and they hugged, “Cam, thanks bro. How did you ever get this?”

“It was a team effort.”

They spent the next half hour carefully inspecting the book. Still trying to process everything. Brian learned how Sandy kept tabs on the book, eventually found out the book was for sale, and then Tamara’s adventure at Sotheby’s.

Brian yelled, “Hey kids, come in here, I want to show you something.”

When they wandered in, Brian tried to make it simple. Placing his hand on his son’s shoulder, he said, “This book belonged to another Ben, who lived over five-hundred years ago.”

Benny looked for a second. “Cool.”

Beth echoed, “Yeh, cool.”

Off they went, as Tamara laughed and said, "Give 'em a few years." Then she called out, "Kids, we're having dinner soon. Finish your game and wash your hands."

Shortly after 6:30, they summoned the children and started to huddle near the dinner table. Brian made a request. "Beth, can you please help me light the Hanukkah candles tonight? It's the fifth night. Aunt Tam has the candles."

Beth placed five short tapers in the menorah and held the shamash candle, which would in turn light the others. Brian lit it, then prompted Beth with the beginning of the prayer in Hebrew, reciting "*Baruch atta*." That was all Beth needed, finishing the prayer as Sandy looked on proudly.

Sandy helped Tamara bring ham and turkey to the table, joining the other dishes they had placed there a few minutes before. At the table's far side sat Beth between Sandy and Cameron. Benny sat between Tamara and Brian on the opposite side.

When everyone settled, Brian raised his wine glass. "It's wonderful that we can be here together. Turning to each person deliberately, "Merry Christmas Cam. Happy Hanukkah San, Beth. Merry Christmas sweetheart, Benny."

Cameron added, "And Happy Hanukkah to you, Brian."

"Thanks. Cheers everyone."

As they sipped, Cameron spoke again, "I know y'all want to eat but I have a request. I have a few months to make a decision, but I need everyone's help to figure out my menu for next April's Champions Dinner at Augusta."

Beth jumped at it, "Dad, barbecue."

Benny echoed, "Yeah, barbecue, Uncle Cameron."

"That could be crazy interesting," added Sandy.

"Crazy interesting?" quizzed Cameron.

Sandy smiled, "Burnt ends, you know, Holes one and nine at St Andrews, Burn and End."

"Love it," said Tamara.

ACKNOWLEDGMENTS

I am blessed with a remarkable network of people that assisted me in countless ways, often extending their networks for me.

It is hard to imagine this manuscript without the touch of Reverend Frank Strasburger. Our friendship spans five decades. Thank you for your religious perspectives, your command of language, and your insights on the work's authenticity.

My deep appreciation to Don Clark. We first met in the mid-sixties at summer camp in Maine. Thank you for guiding me through the wilderness, helping me avoid word weasels and other traps along the journey. I would not have seen them without you.

My gratitude to Rhonda Cohen, who I've had the pleasure of knowing for over thirty years. Thank you for your candor and attention to each word, phrase, sentence, and chapter.

I am indebted to Mike Preston, a business colleague in three different ventures over a ten-year period. Now a burgeoning author, thank you for bolstering the structural foundations of the manuscript.

For reviewing the work's first draft, thank you Russ Broomell, my sisters, Lynn Mayfield and Susie Moss, and my partner, best friend and wife, Abby Rosenberg.

For reviewing manuscript drafts, thank Andy Aitkenhead, Alan Beck, Cathy Cruzan, Ben Fand, Jonathan Katz, Chris Kogler, Robert Stone, and Rabbi Danny Young.

To the memories of those who helped inspire this project, thank you Rabbi Sigma Coran, Robin Fand, Ed Fitzkee, Bruce Fleisher, Rabbi Robert Katz, Rabbi David Packman, Ben Spalding, and Thelma Wolf.

For sharing their personal and professional experiences, thank you John Brady, Bruce Fleisher, Andy Kolesar, Paul McOsker, and Dr. Michael Osit.

For their guidance on religious issues, thank you Rabbi Howard Jaffe, Rabbi Jonathan Katz, Rabbi Loren Lapidus, Reverend Robert Laws, Rabbi Randi Musnitsky, Rabbi David Sandmel, Reverend Frank Strasburger, Rabbi Alvin Sugarman, and Rabbi Danny Young.

For deepening my love of golf, thank you Ron Braund, Bruce Fleisher, Fred Glass, Beth Kaufman, Mark Kirk, Mark MacDonald, Pete Nelson, Anthony Pioppi, J. Larry Stevens, Jay Wertz, Charlie Yates, and the incredible athletes who competed at The Masters in 2003.

For their insights into journalism and broadcasting, thank you Adam Alter, Hank Hersch, Peter Kessler, Armen Keteyian, Bert Rudman, and Amy Shanler.

For guidance on writing and publishing, thank you Lauren Davis, Alice Early, Bob Fleshner, Roberta Isleib, Liz Keenan, Suanne Laqueur, Kate Lee, Nancy Roman, Katie Sadler, J. Larry Stevens, Michael Strauss, Caitlin Wahrer, and Lisa Weinert.

For adding to the joy I found when living in Amsterdam in the early 1970's, thank you Ian Wagenhuis.

For your suggestions and editing prowess in the stretch run, thank you Linda Seigelman and Ron Silversten. You are truly amazing.

For assistance with aviation, thank you Zach Rogers and Bert Rudman.

For creating impactful visuals, thank you Laura Billingham, Andrea Hurley, and Marko Marković.

For being there when I reached out, thank you Norm Agran, Karen Anolick, Joe Balsamo, Karin Bellantoni, Andy Christmann, Harold Cohn, Jamie Coleman, Miguel Cordova, Lee Croxton, Steve Doyle, Dave Fitzkee, Mike Flanter, Matt Fulton, Adam Goldstein, Gabe Grippo, John Harrington, Richard Hawkes, Flo Hoffheimer, Tom Ireland, Steve Jurista, Amy Katz, Skip Kendall, Patty Khoury, Waleed Khoury, Kate Kogler, Nancy Lee, Arne Lewertoff, John Lippman, Michael Lustig, Glen Mayfield, Peta McKellar, John Mone, Scott Morgan, Perry Moss, Alexandra Orpaz, Jim Robbins, Cathy Rolland, Dary Ruderman, Mark Ruderman, Jim Rudman, Sam Rudman, Cary Root, Nancy Rubenstein, Charissa Schultz, Steve Scully, Howard Seigelman, Louis Singer, Kim Sommer, Carrie Strasburger, Barbara Strauss, Sherry Strauss, Jacob Stricoff, Steve Turchan, Gérard Weinberg, Toby Williams, David Wise, Rita Wise, Susan Wise, Richard Wolf, Richard Young, Shelley Young.

For assistance from venerable institutions, thank you Nikki Scott at Historic Environment Scotland, Tara Valente at the United States Golf Association, the staff at the New York City Public Library, the United States National Park Service, The National Archives of the United Kingdom, St. Martin's Episcopal Church and the team at *The Connections Magazines*.

For their extraordinary works, thank you John Feinstein for *A Good Walk Spoiled*, Phillipa Gregory for *Three Sisters Three Queens*, Norman MacDougall for *James IV*, Moses Maimonides for *The Guide for the Perplexed*, John Prebble for *Scotland*, and Teofil Ruiz for *The Other 1492: Ferdinand, Isabella, and the Making of an Empire*.

ABOUT THE BOOK

The Middle Ages are widely defined as the period in Europe from about 500 to 1500 A.D. Throughout this millennium, empires, monarchs, and religious movements struggled to gain and maintain power. On the Iberian Peninsula, as throughout Europe, xenophobia of Islamic and Jewish populations played a central role in this struggle.

Moses (Biblical Hebrew as Moshe) Maimonides, also known as Moses ben Maimon and the acronym, Rambam, became one the most celebrated biblical scholars of the Middle Ages. In addition to his work as a rabbi and philosopher, he was an astronomer and physician, serving as the personal doctor to Saladin, the first Muslim sultan of Egypt and Syria. Rambam died in Egypt, near Giza, in 1204.

Following the large-scale emigrations during Maimonides' time, the Sephardic Jewish community in Spain was rebuilt in the 13th and 14th centuries to a population estimated at 300,000 - 500,000.

In 1391, a mob attacked the 7,000 Jews of Seville, killing about half and forcing the remainder to choose baptism over death. This event marks the beginning of the Spanish Inquisition.

In the ensuing 15th century, the Jewish population in Spain decreased to less than 100,000, due to conversion, intermarriage, emigration, and to a far lesser extent, executions.

On the eve of the renaissance, an inflection point occurred. The Edict of Expulsion was issued on March 31, 1492, by Isabella I of Castile and Ferdinand II of Aragon. It required all Jews to leave Spain by July 31, 1492. This period is considered the end of the Spanish Inquisition.

About 50,000 Jews exited during the four-month period. Destinations included North Africa, Christian countries in the Ottoman empire, and a large proportion to Portugal, particularly the Castilian Jews. With Portugal's King Manuel I marriage to Isabella, the daughter of Ferdinand and

Isabella, in 1497, the Jews' stay in Portugal was short-lived.

I placed the Solomon Family in Gibraltar, although the papal bull of Pope Sixtus IV, in 1478, resulted in purging most Jews from Andalusia, the group of southern Spanish kingdoms. I envisioned Gibraltar, in 1492, as an open port, similar to Hong Kong in the 20th century.

Another burgeoning commercial city, Amsterdam, became my destination for the Solomon family. A vibrant Portuguese Jewish community emerged in Amsterdam in the 17th century.

Ben Solomon settled in Scotland, also on the verge of historic changes that the Protestant reformation would bring.

There is speculation that Jewish refugees may have arrived in Scotland following anti-Jewish riots in England in the late 12th century. While Jews may have participated in continental Europe's trade with Scotland, there is no direct evidence of Jews in Scotland before David Brown, in the late 17th century.

Since their origin thousands of years ago, stick and ball games have morphed in various cultures and countries throughout the world. There is documentation, though sparse, on golf in both Scotland and Holland, on the cusp of the 16th century. With the proximity of these two locations in northwestern Europe, some believe golf equipment, knowledge, and techniques cross-pollinated.

When I first began working on this project, I assumed James IV would be one of many historical references to help frame Ben's journey. As I learned more about James IV and the plot lines emerged, it became evident he would be an important part of the story.

James IV is portrayed in numerous historical novels, short stories, and film. He was a polyglot. He played golf. He supported education. He pursued interests in the arts, medicine, and science. He built a robust navy. He picked up the pursuit of modern weaponry where his father and grandfather left off.

Before James IV married Margaret Tudor, Henry VIII's sister, he fathered five children with four women: Marion Boyd, Margaret Drummond, Janet Kennedy, and Isabel Stewart. With Margaret Tudor, he sired six children, only one of which survived infancy. James V ascended to the throne at seventeen months old, after James IV was killed in the Battle of Flodden, at age forty.

Most of the people I placed around James IV, in his role as King, were real. These included James Allardice, Robert Borthwick, John Damian, Gavin Douglas, William Dunbar, William Ephinstone, Robert Herwort, Thomas Howard, Walter Kennedy, Robert Kynnaird, John Murray, Lord Neville, William Scheves, James Stewart, John Stewart, Perkin Warbeck.

Also included are several men fatally injured at Flodden: Alexander Stewart, Archbishop of St Andrews and the illegitimate son of James IV and Marion Boyd; Alexander Lauder, the Provost of Edinburgh; and Spanish diplomat Don Pedro de Ayala.

Ben's family and golfing friends were fabricated.

The Sheep Heid Inn, in Edinburgh, is arguably the oldest commercial pub in the city if not all of Scotland. Some scholars date it back to 1360. I imagined a similar establishment, the Goat Heid Inn, in St Andrews.

There are accounting records indicating John Mayne was a bowyer, a maker of shooting bows. He also constructed spears and golf clubs for James IV. His son, George Mayne was also a bowyer. His grandson, William Mayne supplied golf clubs to James VI. I invented the other characters associated with club making, including further descendants in the Mayne family.

The standards for the number of holes on a course and the number of holes played in a match emanated from St Andrews, but not until well into the 18th century.

Historian Mario de Valdes y Cocom asserts that Charlotte Mecklenburg-Strelitz descended from a Black branch of Portuguese royalty dating back to King Alfonso III and his Moorish mistress in the 13th century. Charlotte married George III in 1761. Their fertile union produced fifteen children. Princess Sophia was the twelfth, born in 1777. She never married. There was speculation she gave birth to a child out-of-wedlock. I imagined the illegitimate child as a daughter who married an ancestor of Brian Sills.

By 2002, Spain had produced several golf superstars, including: Seve Ballesteros, taking the Masters title twice among his ninety professional wins from 1976 - 1995; José Maria Olazábal, also a two-time Masters winner; and Sergio Garcia, who had just started his career and would go on to win The Masters fifteen years later.

For convenience I placed the 2002 PGA Championship at the Baltusrol Golf Club in New Jersey, where Rusty achieved a victory. Rich Beem won that tournament, played at the Hazeltine Golf Club in Minnesota.

Larry Mize is the only Augusta native to win The Masters. Others born in Augusta, who have played in the tournament, are Charles Howell III and Vaughn Taylor. Though born and raised in Atlanta, Bobby Jones left an indelible mark as The Augusta National Golf Club's founder, course co-designer, and tournament co-founder.

Bruce Fleisher, who won a single event on the PGA tour, went on to win eighteen times on the Senior PGA Tour, which became the Champions Tour in 2002, and ultimately the PGA Tour Champions in 2015. I had the pleasure of speaking with Bruce on two occasions shortly before his death, at age 72, in September of 2021.

Peter Kessler, a golf historian and broadcast journalist, is best known for his work at the Golf Channel. He hosted three shows, *Golf Talk Live, Viewer's Forum* and *Golf Academy Live*. He interviewed hundreds of golf's most notable players and instructors.

Armen Keteyian is a television journalist and best-selling author. He was the anchor and executive producer for *The Athletic*. Over his career he worked for ABC News, CBS News, CBS Sports and HBO Sports. Keteyian is an 11-time Emmy award winner.

In 2003, Mike Weir and Len Mattiace finished The Masters Golf Tournament at seven under par. Weir bested Mattiace in a one-hole, sudden death, playoff on the 10th hole.

Ninety-three players competed during The Masters in 2003, with forty-nine making the cut after the first two rounds. I added Tommy Torres and Rusty Stephens to those numbers.

Jack Nicklaus is the oldest Masters winner with his victory in 1986 at age forty-six. At the time of this story, Ben Crenshaw was the second oldest winner in 1995 at forty-three. Tiger Woods won his fifth green jacket in 2019, also forty-three, sixteen days older than Crenshaw.

Rabbi Alvin Sugarman, Ph.D., Emeritus at The Temple in Atlanta, Georgia, played the role of Dr. Weil in *Driving Miss Daisy*, released in 1989.

Hank Hersch and Jim Drake enjoyed distinguished careers at *Sports Illustrated*. However, they did not know each other personally.

All the dialogue was conjured in my mind. When I put words in the mouths of living persons, I shared with those individuals to the extent possible. While I received questions, suggestions, and edits, no one insisted on any substantive changes. When requested, I did not use real names.

READING GROUP GUIDE

To assist discussion facilitators, the following lists the more significant characters in the novel.

In the Modern period

Fictional

Herman and Beth Cole
Sally Cole
Sandra (Sandy, San) Cole
Carlton and Christina Stephens
Cameron (Rusty, Cam) Stephens
Brian (O.T.) Sills
Tamara (Tam) Wright
Tommy Torres
Louis (Louie) Torres
Sonya Torres
Carlos Santos – Tommy's caddie
Brent Lattimer – Rusty's attorney
Rabbi Ruth Mardesten – Judaism instructor
Cairstine Black – Genealogist in Edinburgh
Rika Kleinhuis – Genealogist in Amsterdam

Historical

Rabbi Alvin Sugarman (b. 1938)
Bruce Fleisher (1948 – 2021)
Peter Kessler (b. ~1952)
Armen Keteyian (b. 1953)
Severiano (Seve) Ballesteros (1957 – 2011)
The touring pro golfers of the 2002 – 2003 season

In the Medieval period

Fictional

Benjamin and Esther Solomon

Ben Solomon (Solley) and Evina (Evi) Solley

Benno Solley

Rebecca (Becca) Solomon and Johan Witte

Roberto Méndez, Merchant in Gibraltar

Artair Spalding, Shepherd and golfer in Scotland

Historical

King James IV (1473 – 1513)

Archbishop Alexander Stewart (~1493 – 1513)

Margaret Drummond (1475 – 1501)

Don Pedro de Ayala (1475 – 1513)

Robert Herwort (not available)

Alexander Lauder (d. 1513)

STARTER QUESTIONS

Recall a few times when you have solicited others to give of their time or resources. How did they respond and where would those donations fit on Maimonides' ladder of giving?

Do you have, or could you imagine, a personal hierarchy of giving?

How did Roberto Méndez help the Solomon family? Why did he render it the way he did?

In addition to Méndez's assistance to the Solomons, identify and discuss events of charitable giving in the medieval portions of the story.

Did Rusty help Tommy win The Masters? Would that have been ethical? Would it have been a last-minute decision, or would it have been premeditated? Might Rusty have thought about it differently had he been competing against Tiger Woods or Jack Nicklaus, for example?

What factors may have contributed to Brian's conversion to Judaism? What factors may have contributed to Cameron's decision not to convert to Judaism?

What seemingly random events occurred, which allowed Sandy to connect the medieval storyline to the early 21st century storyline?

Think about some of the unusual coincidences you have experienced in your life. What conditions allowed them to happen and/or become visible to you?

MEET DAN A ROSENBERG

Born in 1952, Rosenberg was raised in the Reform Jewish community of Cincinnati, Ohio. He graduated from Walnut Hills High School. Following a bachelor's degree at Syracuse University, he began his career as a computer programmer.

His interest in writing took root shortly after earning a master's degree from Georgia State University in 1979. He joined Price Waterhouse as a management consultant, where he wrote several business articles, published in trade journals.

In 1994, he self-published a short, autobiographical book, *RANDOM DESTINY "A Collection of True Episodes"*. As stated in its preface, "I seem to be at the intersection of events that might confound statisticians. These happenings cause me to wonder about the essence of being."

Since 2009, he has written over sixty-five pieces for *The Connections Magazines.* His column, "Random Connections," is published in central New Jersey, where he resides with his wife, Abby.

This is his first novel.

Made in the USA
Columbia, SC
25 March 2023

89e39836-9bf2-4226-91e7-59d6859fbe75R01